book is to be returned on or before

The White Camellia

The Suffrage Ladies' Tearoom

Also by Juliet Greenwood and available from Honno Press

Eden's Garden
We That Are Left

The White
Camellia

The Suffrage Ladies' Tearoom

by

Juliet Greenwood

HONNO MODERN FICTION

First published by Honno

'Ailsa Craig', Heol y Cawl, Dinas Powys, Wales, CF64 4AH

1 2 3 4 5 6 7 8 9 10

paperback ISBN: 978-1-909983-50-2
ebook ISBN: 978-1-909983-51-9

Published with the financial support of the Welsh Books Council.

Cover image: © Lee Evison

Cover design: Simon Hicks
Text design: Elaine Sharples
Printed in Wales by Gomer Press

For Annette Morris.
Bookseller, dancer, and free, independent spirit.

Acknowledgements

Firstly, I would like to thank everyone at Honno Press, and in particular my inspirational editor, Janet Thomas, from whom I continue to learn more than I can ever say.

Thank you to the NW Novelistas, the most supportive group of writers, for invaluable advice and support – and cake! Thanks as well to my reading group for cheering me on, and to my fellow dog walkers for keeping me going and propelling me back towards the computer each morning.

Thank you to my family, and Fran Cox, Sally Hanson, Marian Florence Dawtrey, Beth Bithell and Claire Liversage, for dragging me out when I disappear for too long. To Liz Ashworth, and to Nadine Feldman for long distance conversations, and to my wonderful and supportive friends and neighbours, particularly Dave and Nerys Haynes, Delyth and Catrin.

Author's note

Both the tearoom The White Camellia, and the The Suffrage League of Women Artists and Journalists are fictitious. They are, however, based on the many ladies' tearooms and suffrage organisations that gave women a first taste of independence and enabled them to campaign over decades to improve women's lives, and achieve a voice, a legal existence, the right for education and professional qualifications, and the ability to earn (and keep) an income – the self-determination that we take for granted today.

There are many excellent books on the subject of the suffrage movement; the following are just a small example.

Margaret Forster   *Significant Sisters*
Lucinda Hawksley   *March Women, March*
Helen Mathers   *Patron Saint of Prostitutes: Josephine Butler and a Victorian Scandal*
Melanie Phillips   *The Ascent of Woman*

PART ONE

Chapter One

CORNWALL 1909

It had not changed.

Sybil stepped to the very edge of the cliff and gazed down at the rambling old house below her, topped with a maze of chimneys, a crumbling reminder of its Jacobean finery.

There was no finery left in Tressillion House, she thought grimly. Even from this distance, the place held an air of ruin and abandonment. No smoke rose up through the chill morning from warm fires within. No bustle of servants, no carriage waiting to take the ladies on their rounds of visits and charitable works in the neighbouring village of Porth Levant. Not even Hector, the stallion, steaming in the frosted morning, taking the master of the house on an inspection of the mine, just visible on the next headland.

This was what she had set in motion, all those years ago. The perfect revenge.

Sybil shivered. She unwound the scarf from her head and breathed in deeply the salt blowing in from the sea, her eyes following the North Cornish coast as it vanished into the distance in the crash of spray against rocks.

The wind tugged at her, loosening her curls from the silver clasp at the base of her neck, sending tendrils of brown hair in a wild dance around her face. Sybil turned back to the house below. She had dreamed of this for so long. The moment she would have Tressillion House helpless at her feet. When the Tressillions – who had once had more than they could ever need, but had not thought twice about taking the last hope from people with nothing – would be destroyed, the survivors learning what it was like to be totally dependent on others.

Was this how revenge felt? Sybil hugged herself, pulling the folds of her coat around her, bent almost double by the grief coiling deep in her belly.

'Beautiful, isn't it?'

Sybil straightened, banishing any emotion from her face. 'Indeed.' She turned to meet the square, squat little man emerging from the smart new Ford automobile, one hand struggling to keep his hat on his head.

'The best view of Tressillion House,' he remarked. 'You can see, Miss Ravensdale, just what an exceptional property this is. There's none finer this side of Truro.'

'So I see, Mr Roach,' she replied, almost managing to banish any hint of irony. On their first meeting, the solicitor had made obvious his contempt at a spinster, not in the first flush of youth, daring to invade his offices in broad daylight for all the respectable citizens of St Ives to see. He had changed his tune a little too quickly at the sight of her gleaming new Chevrolet, shipped all the way from New York, and speaking more of true wealth than any flash of diamonds.

Tressillion House had proved a more than usually difficult properly to dispose of, and there were impatient creditors snapping at Mr Roach's heels. She must have seemed like a miracle, a rich hotelier from America dreaming of owning a property in Cornwall. Who else, the gleam in Roach's eyes declared, would be fool enough to live in an isolated mansion fallen on hard times, with the rollers of the North Cornwall coast clawing at the rocks on wild nights, and ghosts creaking amongst its rafters?

Sybil replaced the scarf around her head. 'Shall we go?'

'Of course, Miss Ravensdale, of course.'

Sybil settled herself behind the wheel of the Chevrolet as Roach made his way back to his own vehicle. Officious little man. She grinned to herself. She knew his opinion of her. He wasn't the first, and he wouldn't be the last, to so blatantly assume there was a rich lover somewhere in the background, and that she could only have secured her prosperity with her skirts above her head.

'Idiot,' she snorted.

As they set off, she glanced down once more to Tressillion House. Her hands gripped the steering wheel, her knuckles white. The old hatred for the Tressillions was still there, for all her grief, as fierce now as it had burned inside her as a child. Let *them* know how it felt to be cast aside as if they were nothing. To feel the cold fear of being torn from their roots, the only protection of the poor, thrown out into a pitiless world, without even the rule of law to help them.

Not that the Tressillions would ever end up on the streets. Sybil sniffed. They would never know the fear of the workhouse, or the even greater terror of being a young girl thrown onto the mercy of strangers. They wouldn't even remember the lives they had cast to the desperate winds so long ago.

At the next bend in the lane, she hesitated. Roach was out of sight. The entrance to a field lay ahead, the space wide enough in front of the gate for her to turn round. She had seen Tressillion fallen, just as she had always promised herself she would. There was nothing more for her here.

There had been once, but not now. She could vanish. Never go near the house. She had taken the precaution of settling her bill at the hotel in St Ives. There was nothing to stop her starting the long drive back to London immediately, and booking the next passage of the *Mauretania* back to New York.

Across the fields, she could make out the chimneys, taller now she was seeing them from below, just as Leo had described them.

'They were our castles, our hiding places,' he would say, those sharp, photographer's eyes of his glowing with the memory. 'It's where we felt safe. Especially from him.'

Sybil stopped the Chevrolet at the turning place. It hadn't truly struck her before, just what a desperate kind of safety that must have been: children hiding high up on those intertwined networks of roofs, sloping and disjointed, where just one slip could lead to disaster. And the grief came, tearing at her, a physical agony impossible to ignore.

Having seen it, there was no turning back.

'Heaven help me,' muttered Sybil, squaring her shoulders as she set the Chevrolet racing to catch up with her guide.

* * *

Sybil followed Mr Roach's Ford through the twists and turns of the lane to the driveway in front of the house.

'It is an exceptional property,' Roach remarked, as they stepped out onto the gravel. 'Its history is said to go back to Tudor times, at the very least.' He took a sly glance in her direction. Sybil hid a smile. As she had hoped, he assumed she was an American who had never before stepped onto English soil, easily impressed with the glamour of the minor English aristocracy, but accustomed to things on a far larger scale.

Roach cleared his throat. 'It's too small to be a true manor house, of course. More likely a gentleman's retreat. A number of improvements were made during the last century, when the family came into some considerable wealth.' He waved his arm expansively towards the sea. 'And the grounds are, for their size, quite magnificent.'

'And in need of work,' replied Sybil, taking in the overgrown paths and the rotting roses in the flowerbeds. Leaves blackened by last night's frost hung greasily from stems that had given up the struggle to stay upright. The cupid at one side of the main path had succumbed to the winter storms and lay facedown in the mud. The Grecian temple at the far end, once a splendid viewpoint over the bay, was almost entirely overgrown with decaying bindweed, the protective shrubs grown into straggling bushes, their bleak branches, even in winter, extinguishing the view entirely.

'Of course, of course.' Roach coughed. 'And reflected in the price, naturally. There's not a property of this size for such a price in all of Cornwall. Not with these magnificent views.'

'I understood servants were hard to find, and that many houses are now falling into disrepair. We live in changing times, it seems.'

He smiled thinly. 'Shall we see inside?'

He opened the front door, leading the way into a large hallway, pulling open wooden floor-to-ceiling shutters covering sash windows, revealing dust and the mummified remains of a raven.

Sybil paused at the foot of the large wooden staircase. The interior of Tressillion was not quite as she had expected. She had always imagined it as large and airy, elegance and opulence shining from every chandelier and gilded mirror, and with diaphanous drapes at the windows, swaying in the breeze. A child's dream of a fairytale palace with every comfort anyone could need.

Instead, the wooden panelling on the walls, darkened by time and polishing, and the even darker heavy balustrade on either side of the stairs, stood heavy and oppressive, as if no sun had ever been allowed to enter. Not such a fairytale after all. She shivered once more. Leo's father had ruled his family with a rod of iron, banishing those who defied him. Even in the bustling streets of New York, Leo had never quite been able to escape his father's watchful eyes, his listening ears, his conviction that he was right, and his way the only one possible.

She could not breathe. Her heart was racing. It took all her willpower to follow Roach as he led her through the drawing rooms, with chairs swathed in dust sheets gathered around empty grates, and a grand piano, snowy with dust; a library scattered with papers, where the mice had made inroads into this unexpected feast.

The public rooms done, she followed him in silence as he led her up the stairs to the bedrooms on the first floor. Here too, the furniture had not been removed. Sheets covered the ghosts of armchairs and sprawled carelessly over tarnished metal bed frames. In the final room, overlooking the sea, a sheet had slipped, revealing the dull sheen of a mirror on a dressing table still scattered with empty scent bottles.

'Everything's here waiting as if they've just left,' she said, shuddering. She picked up a hairbrush, its back patterned with the extravagant bloom of a white camellia worked in silk.

'It can all easily be cleared away,' he reassured her. 'The furniture is being sold with the house. There are some good pieces amongst them. Most of the personal trinkets have been removed by the family, and there's a firm in Truro who will dispose of anything you do not wish to keep.'

'Yes.' She replaced the hairbrush carefully where its shape in clean mahogany stood out from the dust. 'It just seems a little forlorn, that's all.' She glanced up at the ceiling. 'The servants' quarters are above, I take it?'

'Yes. In the attics. The roof is sound. There is no sign of damp.'

'I'm sure.' Sybil hesitated. She'd no wish to see the no-doubt mean little rooms, sparse of any convenience, given to those who worked each waking day of their lives to keep the family in comfort. And there was no need. It wasn't as if she was going to stay. Roach was already moving back towards the door. Sybil glanced once more around the room.

Where the rest of the bedrooms had been crammed to the gills with furniture and heavy ornaments, following the old Victorian fashion, this last room was barely furnished at all. There was a wardrobe and a chest of drawers next to the bed, along with a dressing table and armchair. Few pictures hung on the walls. A small sketch over the bed caught her eye. Sybil moved closer. It was a rough drawing, in an amateur hand, of tables and chairs set next to a tall window.

'The White Camellia.'

Roach turned at her exclamation. 'I beg your pardon?'

'Oh, nothing.' She straightened up. 'I thought it looked familiar. But of course there are so many tearooms springing up all over the place nowadays. I must have been mistaken.'

'Yes, Miss,' said Roach, losing interest and heading to the door.

Sybil turned back to the drawing. Her friends in New York believed she had come up from nothing, making her fortune solely by hard work and determination. But of course nothing was ever that simple. They didn't know about The White Camellia, tucked away in a side street on the outskirts of London's Covent Garden, providing a safe place for women to escape their families, and for those who had nowhere else to go.

She smiled, remembering the earnest conversations of women huddled over tea and buns, revelling in their freedom from appearing meek and corseted, from never being allowed an opinion that might chase a respectable husband away. They were daring, those women, for leaving the house unchaperoned, risking being mistaken by the police for a woman of the streets. The poorer girls, eking a living as ill-paid clerks, were terrified of what the future held when they could no longer support themselves. They came for the plentiful tea and cheap buttered toast, and the hope that lay in the talk of strategy and protest, of equal pay and a vote for all, regardless of sex or birth.

The older women were as ambitious as the young. Their mothers and grandmothers had frequented the White Camellia when it had been a hotbed of agitation against the slave trade and, rather than returning to quiet domesticity following abolition, had turned their new-found political skills to other causes.

I owe them my life, thought Sybil, turning abruptly away. Her sleeve swept the small table beside the bed, sending something flying onto the Persian rug at her feet. Mr Roach had his back turned. Swiftly, Sybil plucked up the little object. It was a button, carved in ivory in the shape of a camellia. It lay in her hand, tiny and impossibly delicate.

Who had lived here? She glanced back around the room, taking in the sparse furniture, the forlorn air, the dressing table with its brush. Her eyes blurred. Who had Leo's father kept here?

There was a scratching at the window. Sybil gasped. She and Roach both swung round as the scratching turned to a gentle tapping, quiet but insistent, on the windowpane.

Roach recovered first, his pale face suffused with a mortified pink at being spooked so easily. 'The tide must be turning. The wind has changed.'

'I expect so,' said Sybil, pushing up the sash, allowing the twigs of cherry to creep in with the sea air.

She was a fool to hope, even just for one minute – but she still scanned every branch for a rustle or an unnatural stirring, as the wind died down once more.

'You'll need to have that tree chopped down,' announced Mr Roach behind her. 'I don't know what the family were thinking, allowing it to stay so long. It's far too near to the house.' He coughed, recalling his urgent need to sell this monstrosity at any cost. 'I'm sure Mr Jonathan Tressillion, the current owner, will make sure the job is done before any sale goes through.'

'There's no need,' said Sybil. She would never allow the tree to be touched, whatever it might be doing to the foundations. The house could fall down first. 'I would rather it remained.' She shook herself. What kind of fool was she being, clinging to a hope of ghosts she didn't believe in, in a house that would never be hers? A house she had once sworn she'd tear down, brick by brick. A house she had no intention of buying.

'I'd like to see the kitchens,' she said.

'Yes, indeed.' Roach sounded relieved. 'You'll find the kitchens more than adequate. A little old-fashioned, of course, but that can easily be remedied.' He gave an ingratiating smile.

Sybil was only just able to stop herself informing him that she wasn't a fool, thank you very much, and she'd already bought and restored four old wrecks in far worse a state than this, turning them into increasingly elegant and desirable hotels across New York, and making a small fortune along the way.

'Of course, you ladies are far more familiar with the conveniences of modern appliances, and the owners have looked into installing a generator to provide electricity. I'm assured the range is still in good working order, and many of the pots and pans – indeed, even the dishes and the cutlery – remain. It would take very little expense to bring the house up to an excellent standard of comfort and elegance once more.'

He was right, of course. But who would see Tressillion's potential, let alone take the chance? After the scandal, no respectable family would wish to breathe life back into these abandoned rooms. Her dream of seeing the place fall into nothing, bit by bit, might come true after all.

Sybil frowned. That was the thing about revenge. The passion came from a place and a time, and a particular wrong. Once, she had wished to obliterate all the memories here, never thinking that one day there might be some she would give her life's blood to keep alive.

'Shall we go?' said Roach, his hand on the handle of the door.

'Of course,' murmured Sybil, taking a last look around the room, slipping the white camellia button deep in her pocket as she hastened after him.

Chapter Two

Viewing the rest of the house was cursory. Roach's irritation increased as she failed to exclaim or give any sign of having fallen in love with the place. Sybil followed him out of the front door, back into the driveway, lost in her own thoughts.

'Thank you,' she said, rousing herself as he turned the key in the lock. 'That was most interesting. I would like to look around the grounds, before I make a decision.'

'Of course.' His tone was impatient, his fingers stealing to his pocket watch. 'I'm afraid I have a client waiting for me in Truro, Miss Ravensdale, I shall be late as it is. We can see the extent of the land from here. It takes several hours to walk the entire circumference, however, and it was an unusually heavy frost for this part of Cornwall last night. Perhaps you would like to make another appointment?'

'I've no wish to put you to any trouble. I shall be perfectly happy to explore on my own. Just to get a feel of the place,' she added, as he began to protest.

'I see.' He smiled, the glint of a possible sale back in his eye. 'Perhaps you would like to keep the key. You can bring it to the office on your way back.'

'No!' she exclaimed, her voice sharp. There was too much temptation as it was. Once back inside the house, who knew where her treacherous heart might lead her? Roach blinked. 'That is,' she added quickly, 'I wouldn't like to be responsible for any damage. I can easily come back to see the house another day.'

Roach clucked, civility finally expended. 'As you wish, Miss

Ravensdale,' he sighed, with the air of a man who knew she had no intention of coming near the office again. Not that she cared. Perhaps it was as well if he thought her simply one of the ghoulish and curious, after all.

'Mind the tide. It comes in fast in these parts.' He pocketed the key and made his way back to the Ford.

Sybil watched his machine lumber up the lane towards Porth Levant. When the engine faded into nothing, she turned back to the ruined gardens. She took a last glance up at the house, then walked down the steps, following the path between the overgrown lawns.

She paused next to the Grecian temple to find her bearings, then, without hesitation, pushed her way between the overgrown shrubs and birch saplings, following a gravel path. The high stone wall was overgrown with moss and ivy. An ornate metal gate, its delicate twists and spirals half rusted away, lay on one side of the opening. She stepped over it, careful not to catch the heel of her boots, and strode onto the sweep of fields that led down to the shore.

The tide was almost in. A salt wind tugged at her hair. She breathed it in deep, drawing it inside herself, eyes closed, a memory to take with her, back across the oceans. The beach was tempting, with its memories of carefree days, before Mr Tressillion came knocking on Dad's door, with his promise of salvation, knowing full well what he was about to do. But she had other, more urgent, matters at hand.

She turned to the house, to reassure herself that Mr Roach had not changed his mind and returned. No one was there. She struck off along a small path to the left, away from the beach, to a rise of cliffs on the far side.

The path led into a valley where a river rushed down to the sea. Sybil followed a rough path along the water's edge. Soon, the house was out of sight. The fall of water increased as the valley steepened, the path zigzagging up the hill. At the top, she paused to catch her breath. Around her, the remains of buildings rose up through scrub and saplings bent inland by the prevailing winds.

Certain now, her step quickening, Sybil took a wider path that branched upwards, towards a steep slope of rock. Within minutes, her boots struck a narrow strip of metal between the dead undergrowth. A few paces more and she found another, running parallel: a miniature railway line. Sheds and the remains of brick walls rose up on either side. She stepped off the track to avoid the metal containers on wheels, rusting in a line, frost glinting on the ruined metal as the sun reached them.

And there it was.

She had wondered, all the long journey from half a world away, how she would feel when she finally stood here, the cavern of the old mine opening up in the rock in front of her. Fear? Guilt? Despair at what she had done, which could never be undone? But now she was here, there was nothing. Nothing at all. The passion had been burnt out of her, leaving only emptiness.

She climbed a little higher, onto a ridge above the workings, to gaze down on the fields stretching towards the bay. Halfway down, the ruin of the cottage that had once been all the world she had known lay sprawled amongst the winter grasses, revealing a doorway and a partially collapsed window. A hawthorn, bent and twisted, grew from the centre.

She would never forgive them for that. For taking her childhood away, with any place she could call home.

'*Hiraeth*', one of the women in the White Camellia had called it, mourning her own home, lost to poverty and landlords' greed in the far away Welsh mountains. Sybil had not understood it at the time, focussed on survival and building a future that did not involve selling herself on the streets. But over the last years, the word had stolen back into her mind.

'Yes, that's exactly it,' Leo had said, setting his photographic camera on its stand to take a portrait of an elderly couple, framed by the elegant façade of her latest hotel. 'It's more than homesickness. I don't think I'll ever stop missing Cornwall, even though I know I can never go back.'

'Me neither,' she had replied, surprising herself. She'd told herself for years she hated the place. Who could ache for the soar of seagulls against a dying sun, when there were theatres and art galleries, and the bustle of a modern city?

He had smiled the wide, open smile that embraced her, neither as his employer nor a social inferior, or even as a woman, but simply as another human being adrift on this earth. 'Then it seems we share *hiraeth*,' he said.

'So we do.' She had returned the smile, for once unwarily, knowing he would not take it as an invitation or a sign of weakness. She'd fought off enough men in her time who'd viewed her as a commodity. When she'd had nothing, they'd wanted the hint of breasts beneath her ill-fitting dress. Once she clawed herself to prosperity, it had been her money, pure and simple. She hadn't fallen for one bit of it.

Over the years, Sybil knew she had gained a reputation for being a hard-nosed businesswoman, devoid of a heart or any female feeling. It hurt, but she'd seen other women fall for a charming smile and attention, until marriage gave a suitor control over their lives and their fortune. As far as she could see, that was hell on earth. She would never hand over to another the power to take all her hard work away, leaving her back on the streets. Despite the well-thumbed novels in the lending library, she wasn't the only woman who would rather make peace with her own company than face the loneliness of a life tied to someone who would never look for the living, breathing human being inside her.

Leo had taken no notice of her cold reputation. He never

wanted anything from her. And so she had smiled, the hard shell softening, allowing his warmth to creep through and touch her.

Hiraeth. Sybil gazed down at her ruined home, blinking tears away. *Hiraeth* was the impossible aching for the sound of waves surging over rock, the smell of the grass on a summer's evening. The flap of washing on the line, and her mother laughing, baby on hip, as the scent of bonfires stole into the evening air. The things that tied you to one place in this vast earth, and made it yours forever, maybe even when life itself had gone.

To have no home was true loneliness. Home was the warmth of human company, of lives intertwined, with their sorrows and joys, a place of shared memories. Home was the community that held you tight, safe against the indifference of the larger world. Being back, breathing in the familiar scents, seeing the landscape of her childhood, she ached with a deeper longing than she had ever felt before to find a home, a community to surround her. A family, in whatever form it might take.

On her thirtieth birthday, several years before, Sybil had accepted that marriage and motherhood had passed her by. Her life was as a successful businesswoman, increasing her wealth, supporting her charities, maybe one day becoming a pillar of society.

Standing on that Cornish hillside, hair blown wild in the wind, she felt her whole life flung apart, breaking into myriad pieces, to resettle again in a shape she could not recognise. She was no longer the Sybil who had been driven out of Cornwall in fury and humiliation. The Sybil who had spent years relentlessly hunting down wealth, to protect herself against the powerlessness of having nothing. The Sybil whose heart had been broken, more than once. The Sybil who had once so effectively, so carefully, plotted her revenge.

'I can't live without love, without companionship,' she admitted aloud. 'I can't pass my life afraid to stop and hear my loneliness. I need roots, and a place to call home. I need to belong.'

Slowly, with a sense of having no certainty any more, she made her way back to the mine.

As she reached the entrance, she could see someone had attempted to cover the gaping hole in the rock, but the boards had fallen to one side, revealing the cavern in the hillside. She pulled the remainder away easily and peered into the darkness.

She reached for the flashlight hidden in her pocket. The last time, it had been a lamp, and the flicker of a candle, that had led the way. The flashlight was the newest model, brought with her from America. It fitted neatly into her palm. She pressed the button, still not quite believing that the magic would happen. But it did. A stream of light, steady as her hand, reached into the cave. She stepped gingerly inside.

Air, bone-chillingly cold, drifted up to meet her. Water lay in an orange-tinted pool at her feet. From above her head, moisture oozed slowly, drop by drop. Far within, drips fell, sometimes near, sometimes so far she could barely hear them splash into pools in the depths of the mine. A breeze came from within the earth, with the scent of iron and peat. She raised the flashlight. Its advertisement had promised hours of sustained use, but then so had the one for the Chevrolet, and that had a tendency to overheat at the slightest excuse.

Having come this far, she was drawn inside by the slow drips and the blackness of the earth.

'Oi!' The shout came from nowhere, disorientating her. 'Oi! Miss! You can't go in there.'

Sybil swung round, jolted. Nobody – but nobody – 'oi-ed' her. Or handed her instructions. Hadn't done for years. She shoved the flashlight deep into her pocket. 'There's no law against looking,' she retorted.

'It's private land.' He was dressed like a fisherman, dark curls around his face.

She raised her chin. 'I came with the Tressillion's solicitor to view the house. The grounds form part of the purchase. I would be foolish not to inspect them.'

He crossed the large stepping-stones over the stream, leaping from one to the other with ease. 'Well, then he should have warned you. The mine is dangerous.'

'I'd no intention of going inside.'

'I should hope not.' He leapt the final stone onto the stony shore, and strode up to join her. 'That mine has caused ruin and heartache, and taken enough men's lives.'

Sybil scowled. 'Then I don't see what you are doing here.'

'Boarding it up again. Boys from the village can't resist going inside, and it's a maze of tunnels in there.'

'Are you a miner?'

He laughed. '*Duw*, no. I'm not that daft. I've spent my life doing my best not to follow my dad and my *taid* into the slate mines, back home in Wales. I've no intention of starting now.' He gave a glance at her face. 'There's no gold left, you know. Wrong place to look for gold, Cornwall. Devon's the place you want to go. The little that was in this one was worked out years ago.'

'Oh?' Her voice was indifferent.

'The power of dreams, eh?'

'I suppose.'

He set to, retrieving the broken boards, fishing out a hammer and nails from the knapsack flung over his shoulder, rapidly closing up the glimpse of the mine.

Sybil wandered around for a few minutes, as if idle curiosity alone was keeping her here. The crushing sheds were falling into ruins, with the other buildings not far behind. She glanced back. The newcomer was making a thorough job. Absorbed in his work, he was retrieving other boards and discarded lengths of timber from the old sheds. It looked a lengthy procedure.

There was nothing left for her. She had achieved her aim. She had seen the place, said her goodbyes. If she hurried, she could return to London in time for her appointment tomorrow, to inspect a rather rundown Mayfair hotel she was considering as the next expansion of her little empire, and her security.

Finding the path, Sybil retraced her steps, leaving the stream and the valley behind, never stopping until she reached the path above the beach. There she paused, brushing the leaves and trails of ivy from her skirts and smoothing her hair into a semblance of respectability, before turning back towards the house.

As she reached the Chevrolet, the brief day was already turning to evening. The clear light had softened, with the edges of a golden glow streaking through the clouds, sending streams of light across the sea. Sybil stopped, hand on the open door, and knew, deep in her bones, that she should have left with Mr Roach, all those hours ago. The visit to the mine had been foolish. This final glimpse of the house had been a mistake. This morning, the world had been her oyster. She could do anything, be anything she desired. Now, she could feel the stillness of Porth Levant Bay settling around her. Twisting itself around her heart. The kind of stillness that would never let her go.

She glanced up at the house. Abandoned and forlorn. But with its beauty still there, glowing in the softening light. Its tantalising promise of what might have been. And the emptiness in her heart was back, demanding to be filled.

Her eyes roamed once more over the wide sweep of the bay, across the ruined wilderness of the gardens and the richness of the fields, to the far cliffs where the decaying roofs of the mine sheds could just be glimpsed above the trees. The breeze blew in from the sea, bringing with it salt, and the hint of ice.

Why Mayfair? The thought slipped in, seductively. With the expansion of the railways, nowadays even the modestly prosperous could afford a week at a boarding house or a hotel by the seaside. Artists flocked to Lamorna Cove, the other side of

Penzance. Why not here? The light here just as exquisite, and the views were magnificent.

'It's perfect,' she said aloud. Hadn't her strength as a businesswoman always been her ability to spot the opportunities no-one else had the imagination to see? As testified by those unpromising wrecks she had battled to turn into elegant retreats, astonishing the businessmen who had nodded knowingly over her naivety.

'I don't even have to stay here,' she added, trying to convince herself. She had Miss Phipps in New York, ably taking charge while she was away. Surely she could find another Miss Phipps somewhere in England, eager to escape the stultifying boredom of running a household for an elderly relative, or whose children had flown?

And then Cornwall would be here for her, whenever she wished to visit. It had caught her by surprise, the ties that she still had here. She did not wish to live in Tressillion, but maybe there was a quiet retreat along the coast where she could begin to build a new life for herself.

'*Hiraeth*,' she said aloud, turning the Welsh word around in her mouth. Home never leaves you, she acknowledged. Into her grief and her emptiness came the ache to belong once more, even for a little while.

Climbing swiftly into her automobile, allowing no time for further thought, she roared up the hill, straight for Truro and the offices of Roach and Sons, to seal her fate.

Chapter Three

LONDON 1909

The fire was cold in the grate.

Beatrice stepped into the dark room, edged with the chill February morning, as the door was pulled shut behind her. The man behind the large mahogany desk continued reading the papers in front of him as if she was not there. Bea lifted her chin, chased the fierceness from her eyes the best she knew how, and waited.

Mr Ellis Rivers, Chief Reporter – she presumed it was Mr Rivers from the ornate gold plaque on the door – did not look up.

'And what can I do for you, Miss… '

She could see her name clearly on the letter in front of him. 'Tressillion,' she murmured, trying not to sound as if it were through gritted teeth. She wanted this. More than anything in her life, she wanted this. And if she had to seem demure and ladylike to get it, then that was what she would be. After all, her soul was her own, whatever her external appearance might be.

'Ah yes, Miss Tressillion. Of course. Do take a seat.'

As she perched on the shiny leather, hoping it would not squeak, he put down his papers and leant back in his chair, his eyes sweeping over her in languorous inspection. Her hands were hidden. So she clenched them.

He was handsome, in a square-jawed, swarthy kind of a way. His suit was expensive, exuding power and influence. His faint smile was designed to set a maidenly heart a-flutter. Beatrice

21

sighed inwardly. She'd met his kind before, many times, usually with the blandishment of an army uniform rather than a city suit, in the days when Papa had thought an officer might do, since she was so clearly unsuited to fall into the arms of an earl. She hadn't fainted yet. And as for fluttering…

'I came about my application for the post.'

'The post?'

She stared pointedly at her letter of application in front of him. 'The post of trainee reporter.'

'I see. And your qualifications?'

'I've learnt shorthand and typing. I have my certificates. And I have some experience. I worked as a volunteer reporter for the Red Cross at their summer camp two years ago.'

'Really.'

Despite her determination to keep her temper, Beatrice bristled at the tone of casual dismissal. 'I was offered a paid post. It was only family circumstances that prevented me from being able to take it up. I have the letter with me.'

'Very commendable.' If she'd thought to elicit some respect she was mistaken. Mr Rivers was at last watching her with close attention, but not that of a man considering the potential of a new employee. Beatrice felt the air close in around her. She became horribly aware of the heaviness of the door that had closed behind her, and how little sound could be heard through it.

Mr Rivers had clearly made up his mind what kind of woman she was. One of these new, modern women who had lost all sense of propriety long ago. She cursed herself. Damn her foolish pride! Why hadn't she pretended she'd remained closeted at home since the day she was born? He would have despised her no less, but he might have known better than to insult a respectable and well-connected young woman.

'As I said in my letter of application,' she hurried on, 'I thought you might welcome a woman's voice. It would offer a different viewpoint, and with so many more women working and leading independent lives, I'm sure it would add to your readership. There could be so much scope for articles. I have learnt photography too. Pictures could add additional immediacy to any story.'

He rose and moved around the desk. She had forgotten to adjust her skirt when she sat down, allowing a glimpse of her boot and a touch of pale stocking. She hastily moved the offending ankle out of sight.

'A woman's voice,' said Mr Rivers, leaning against his desk next to her. He casually flicked the curl that had escaped from beneath her hat.

'I had heard nothing, so I came to enquire if you had received my application,' she said, moving her head away from Mr River's touch. She met his eyes, silently daring him to insult her further, signalling her willingness to return with a male relative in tow, one who might have influence with Mr River's employers. He gave a slight grunt and moved back behind his desk. 'I see you have received it,' she continued, hoping he couldn't hear the thud of her heart. 'So I must assume you have no interest in hiring me. In which case, I have another appointment shortly. I must go.'

'Hmm.' Mr Rivers viewed her with detachment. 'The post has gone. Go home, Miss Tressillion. Women were not fashioned for the world of work. Their constitutions and their natures are not suited. Find yourself a husband, Miss Tressillion. That is the natural order of things.'

He turned to retrieve a file from a cabinet against the wall. She was clearly not young enough to be of any use to him. Or vulnerable enough, with her expensive coat – even if it was of the fashion of several seasons ago – and her cultured accent. Thank Heaven she still possessed the trappings of her class, if nothing else. It was a kind of protection.

'Tressillion.' Mr Rivers straightened, looking over his shoulder at her. 'Isn't there a house in Cornwall?'

'Yes.' Beatrice pulled her shoulders back, fists at her side.

'You're related to the family, then.'

'Yes,' returned Beatrice shortly.

'Really.' He smiled. Beatrice had an uncontrollable urge to throw the jug of water on his desk – and her chair – over his well-groomed head. 'Well then, my dear, I suggest you go home. I'm sure your family is in need of your soothing presence. London is no place for a well brought up lady to live by herself. Who knows what kinds of insults and misfortunes might befall her? You have a mother who needs your comfort in her hour of need, and no doubt an uncle or nephew who will look after you. Some unfortunate women, who have no family to look after them, may have to make a living of some kind. You are clearly destined for a more comfortable future.'

Beatrice gathered her dignity around her. I'll show you, she thought. One day, whatever it takes, I'll show you. 'Thank you for your time, Mr Rivers,' she said with exaggerated courtesy. She did not wait for him to open the door, but marched out, praying the handle would obey her. It did. She swept through the busy office, ignoring the young men lounging on their desks, their eyes measuring every curve of her figure, every line of her dress, until she escaped into the stairwell, her boots echoing as she shot out through the front door. She could still feel Mr Rivers' eyes burning into her shoulder blades. Head high, she walked briskly along the shabby little side street and turned the corner into the bustle of Fleet Street.

Bea moved between clerks in their dark suits dashing off towards the nearest Lyons Corner House. Two women passed her, pale, their clothes cheap and just clinging to respectability, scurrying towards a grubby-looking café. Beatrice winced. Was that what her own life was destined to be?

The day was damp and cold, with a hint of rain in the air. She passed by the Strand without feeling the streets beneath her feet. Instinct took her, as it always did, to the river. As she reached Waterloo Bridge, she slowed, safely unnoticed amongst the rattle of trams and automobiles and parties of visitors marvelling at the sight of St Paul's Cathedral on one side and Big Ben on the other. Beatrice lent against the balustrade, gazing at the familiar gothic outline of the Houses of Parliament, fighting back tears of frustration.

Mr Rivers was right. She was one of the lucky ones. She did not have to stay in the city, fighting a losing battle to pay her share of the rent and keep herself warm and fed, let alone keep enough saved each week to do the things she had once taken for granted, like parties and trips on the Thames or to Brighton to breathe in the clean air of the sea. Her respectability and her connections gave her another option, if she could bring herself to take it.

Beatrice shut her eyes. She could see the deep green of the fields surrounding Tressillion, the patchwork of corn and barley. The gentle curve of the valley leading down to the sea, and the wide sandy beach where she had spent so much of her childhood, racing with her brothers along the water's edge. Taking the small boat out beneath the steep cliffs and the wild rocky outcrops, watching the seabirds on their nests and the seals basking in the bay. She could smell the sea, sweetened by the scents of meadow flowers. Her whole body ached with longing for the time when life had been simple, and her future full of possibilities. All of it now gone, along with Tressillion. All lost forever.

'Such a magnificent view.' Beatrice opened her eyes fast. A man – she was in no mood to call him a gentleman – in a smart suit and top hat had stopped next to her. He was just past middle age, well fed jowls and buttons tight over a round belly. His smile was insidious, with no attempt to hide the wedding ring on his left hand.

'It would be better,' Beatrice retorted, 'if women were among those who chose the government, as they are in Australia and America. There might then be some fairness in the world. As it stands, that building is an anachronism and a disgrace.'

The man's eyes widened. Astonishment, tinged with disgust, spread over his face. From the corner of her eye, she could see a policeman approaching, his interest caught by such public impropriety in broad daylight and within sight of the Houses of Parliament.

She smiled sweetly. 'Now if you'll excuse me, I'm sure you have no wish to be seen in the street speaking to a lady who might possibly misinterpret your kind interest in her wellbeing.' She shot off, past the policeman and his shout for her to stop, and back into the network of streets leading to the Strand.

Once she was certain she was not being followed, Bea slowed. In her haste, she hadn't noted the names of the last couple of streets, and now found herself in an unfamiliar part of the city. She glanced back. She wasn't tempted to retrace her steps and risk being arrested for whatever immoral behaviour the man on the bridge might accuse her of. On the other hand, the short day was ending and the streets were growing dark. She needed to get her bearings before the light went, and find her way into the safety of more populated streets. She struck down a side street that, by the smell of it, would return her to the river. At least once she got to the Thames she would have some idea of where she was.

Bea trudged her way, looking neither right nor left, ignoring the people passing her on either side. She was cold and tired, and in urgent need of finding a tearoom where she could use the lavatory. She cursed herself for panicking like that. In her brief forays into the city she had always been so careful to locate each ladies' tearoom, where she could have a cup of tea in peace and where her bodily needs could be discretely taken care of. Here she was stranded.

'Price of a cup of tea, Miss?' A man lurched out of a doorway, a coat that must once have been the prized possession of a wealthy man, but was now patched and threadbare, pulled tightly around him.

'I…' Caught off guard, Bea hesitated.

He took a step closer. 'Just one cup of tea on a cold winter's night? Surely you wouldn't begrudge a fellow man a bit of warmth?'

'Yes, of course.' She scrabbled hastily in her purse for loose change, pressing all the pennies she could find into his hand.

'Thank you, Miss.' He doffed a pretend cap in a gesture of ironic deference. He was watching her, she realised, studying her features in the light from a distant lamp. The intensity of his gaze unnerved her.

'My friends are waiting,' she muttered, hurrying away as if she knew exactly where she was going. After a few paces, she heard the flop of loose shoes behind her. Bea swallowed. No doubt he knew these streets better than she ever would, and the stories you read in the newspapers… She slowed her pace a little. The shoes slowed. She speeded up. Behind her the shoes flapped a little faster. Ahead of her she could hear wheels and horses hooves. She must be near a larger street. She cut down a narrow alley, heading for the promise of a crowd. Behind her, the footsteps kept pace, not hurrying, but drawing a little closer, footstep by footstep, ragged breathing echoing from the dark walls of houses and the blankness of empty windows.

The footsteps were now right behind her, breath stirring the hairs at the back of her neck. At the next turn, the glow of street lamps appeared at the end of a small side street. Taking a deep breath, she doubled back slightly, rushing as fast as she dared towards the light. Behind her, the footsteps speeded up as they hastened after her. He broke into a run.

Throwing dignity to the winds, Bea hitched up her skirts and fled. A hand clutched at her clothing, seizing her scarf, which fell from her shoulders, sending her pursuer stumbling in surprise as it came free. She ran out into a larger thoroughfare of shops. She could hear him cursing behind her.

The street was a quiet one, mainly filled with goods wagons. There were a few office workers, each with a purposeful step as if heading to an urgent appointment. She looked back. The man had recovered his balance and was still in dogged pursuit, her scarf stuffed into his pocket, its bright colours spilling out over the filth of his greatcoat. Directly ahead of her was a respectable-looking tearoom. It was a public place. She had every right to be there. In desperation, Bea shot inside.

The small bell on the door rang as she pushed it open. Thirty or so masculine faces, dark suits and starched white collars turned as if one. Conversations stopped. Cups clattered back into saucers. A disbelieving silence fell. Before Bea could recover herself, an elderly waiter hurried towards her.

'Madam, this is not a ladies' tearoom, you cannot come inside.'

'I only wanted to ask—' began Bea.

'Any respectable woman would know *not* to ask,' said a second waiter, taking her by the elbow and steering her out. 'You are clearly mistaken as to the kind of establishment this is, Madam. Feel lucky I didn't call for the police to come and remove you.'

Bea stumbled as he gave her an unceremonious push back on to the pavement, colliding into a thick fur coat.

'Gallantry,' announced the owner of the coat loudly, steadying Bea against her. 'Isn't that just what you like to see in a man? Reminds one of King Arthur, and the knights of old.'

The waiter sniffed and swept back inside, slamming the door behind him, setting the bell ringing wildly.

'They'll be bolting the doors, closing the shutters and hanging up the garlic,' announced Bea's rescuer scornfully. 'Don't they know the Dark Ages ended some time ago?'

Despite her mortification, and her alarm at being out on the pavement again, Bea laughed. 'I should never have gone in there. You should have seen the look on their faces.'

'I have. I'm sure they were no different from the faces at my husband's club. They couldn't stop me there.'

Bea could imagine it. Her rescuer was tall and well built, with a coil of white hair beneath her extravagantly feathered hat. She was somewhere in her sixties, Bea guessed, with the imperious air of a woman who expects to be obeyed without question. Her green eyes scrutinised Bea. 'If you are looking for the White Camellia, it's in the next street.'

The White Camellia. She said it with such conviction that Bea (if not the entire world) would be familiar with its existence, that Bea felt too foolish to ask. 'Thank you,' she murmured vaguely. She turned round. The man in the greatcoat was standing in a doorway watching them, one hand on the trailing ends of Bea's scarf.

'It's only a few minutes away.' The woman began walking, her fur coat billowing out behind her like rich downy wings, with a clear assumption that Bea would follow. Bea raced after her, determined not to be left behind. Wherever they were going, it could hardly be worse than whatever fate the man with her scarf had in mind for her.

Her guide swept into the next street, then into a side turning. This time when Bea looked back, no-one was following. She took a deep breath, and was about to tell her rescuer that she had remembered an urgent appointment and ask for directions to the nearest tram or underground station, when the fur coat came to a halt.

'Here we are. Rosewater Street.' The woman nodded towards a tall white building. All its windows held bright window boxes already displaying some bold green shoots. 'There should be a few places left. Their tea loaf is excellent.'

'Thank you.'

'The Institute is the third on the left.' A gloved hand gestured to a large, red-brick building further down the street. 'I expect I shall see you there.'

'I expect so,' murmured Bea, not wishing to offend.

'Good. It looks as if it will be a particularly interesting evening. I'm quite decided on the issue, of course. But I'm willing to listen to other points of view.'

'Yes,' said Bea, who couldn't imagine her rescuer being persuaded by anything.

'Good.' With a brief nod, the kind that did not allow for any questions or disobedience, the woman strode off in the direction of the Institute. Before Bea could move, the door of the tearoom opened and two women deep in conversation emerged, along with the scent of freshly baked bread.

Bea watched them follow the owner of the fur coat towards the Institute. Her mind was telling her to find the nearest tram. The pressure on her bladder, now more urgent than ever, had other ideas. Cautiously, Bea pushed open the door of the White Camellia, and stepped inside.

Chapter Four

The White Camellia was like no other tearoom Bea had seen before. It was light and airy, with tables set in a haphazard way, unregimented. On the walls hung sepia photographic prints, interspersed with brightly-coloured paintings. A tapestry at the far end portrayed a statuesque woman with a flowing gown and Pre-Raphaelite hair, holding a cascading bouquet of red and white camellias. A scroll above her head declared 'Freedom and Equality for All', and a smaller scroll beneath her feet announced 'The Suffrage League of Women Artists and Journalists'.

The hum of women's voices had been reassuring as she came in. As she seated herself at a small table near the door, she realised that several men were among the women at the tables near her, all deep in discussion, with no sign of a chaperone, as if it were quite the usual thing.

Most of the women were dressed in brightly coloured coats and dresses that flowed loosely over their bodies, giving the impression there was not a corset to be found between them. Bea pulled a little ruefully at her tightly-fitting jacket. Mama would have been shocked at such impropriety and insist they leave at once. Mama could not understand Bea's longing to be left room to breathe, and argued constantly for the necessity of the eighteen-inch waist prized in her own girlhood.

'A pot of tea please,' Bea said to the waitress. Her stomach rumbled loudly. She hadn't eaten since breakfast, and then only a piece of toast. Quick mental arithmetic had her regretfully ignoring the delicious smells coming from the kitchens. She had

31

only just enough in her purse to cover the cost of the tram ride home. 'And a piece of buttered toast.'

'I'd go for the teacake.' The young man at the table next to her broke off his conversation with his companion and leaned towards her, a touch of conspiracy in his voice. 'For almost the same price, you get something that will set you up for the evening ahead.'

'*Duw,* don't bully the poor woman, Harri,' put in his companion, laughing. 'I'm quite sure she is capable of making up her own mind. Take no notice of him,' she added to Bea. 'He's just like any other man, even though he thinks he isn't. He's always wanting to order everyone to do just what he thinks is right.'

Harri grinned. 'Nonsense. I'm quite certain you can make up your own mind, and so can take a friendly tip — and throw it over your shoulder if you want to. You might have some deep personal objections to teacake.'

The waitress swallowed a smile. 'It is the cook's speciality, Miss.'

Bea nodded. Her head was beginning to swim. She could spare an additional penny, even if she had to walk half the way home. 'Then I think I shall have to try it.'

'You won't regret it,' said Harri. 'In fact, we'll have another slice ourselves,' he added to the waitress.

To Bea's relief, her neighbours resumed their conversation, allowing her to shrug off her damp heavy coat, and discreetly find her way to the lavatory at the back of the tearooms. This too was immaculately clean, with heaped lavender in patterned ceramic bowls to freshen the air, and several large landscapes showing a rich green valley of unfamiliar trees.

As she returned at a more leisurely pace, Bea saw that the walls of the corridors were also covered with landscapes, and faded and slightly dog-eared posters from the 1820s advertising the 'The

Anti-slavery League of Women Artists and Journalists' and meetings to call for the abolition of this vile trade in human misery. 'A hotbed of dangerous agitation from those with no understanding of economic realities,' Papa would have no doubt called it, thought Bea, with a faint grin. Mama would have turned faint at the mention of such unpleasant subjects. Leo, on the other hand, would have been in his element. She could just see him out there, waving pamphlets and making speeches, his brown eyes gleaming against all injustice.

Bea shut her eyes. She still ached with the longing to hear his voice, to be able to tell him about things like the White Camellia, if only in a letter. Leo had been the one with ideals, the only one of them not to be afraid to stand up to Papa, even in the worst of his moods. She had loved her brother's idealism, his eye for beauty in his photography and the magic he created in his darkroom in Tressillion. Even though he had been so much older, he was the only one of her brothers she had ever felt close to, his passion to live his life in more than wealthy idleness stirring her own.

Bea peered up at the posters again. Leo would have loved this place. He had burned with quiet anger at the fact that Mama's fortune, which had paid for the extensive improvements to Tressillion House, had come from sugar plantations. And that final, blazing, no-way-back row about the mine had come from his sense of injustice closer to home.

The sense of desolation was back, as strong as ever. She had always hoped Leo would find a way to see them, even if it had been in secret, something they could never mention to Papa. Now he never would. Because of her, he would never have the chance. And Mama would never see Tressillion, or her beloved first-born son again.

Bea returned to her table just as her tea arrived. The teapot and cups and saucers were decorated with a stylised pattern of red and white camellia flowers. A matching plate held a thick slice of fruit loaf, generously spread with butter. Hunger returned in an instant. The waitress and the man at the next table had been right. The teacake was delicious, heavily fruited and lightly spiced. Feeling the warmth of tea, cinnamon and ginger flood through her body, she sat for a while savouring the comfort, with a strong desire to sleep. In a few minutes she would have to force herself back out into the streets to get home. She wished she never had to move again.

'Perhaps she'll decide not to come.' Amongst the hum of conversation, her ears caught the young woman next to her, anxiety in her voice.

'I advised her not to,' replied Harri. 'But I doubt if she listened. She's determined to speak.'

'Yes. I just wish she'd take more care of herself, for her own sake. You saw the state she was in after the last time.'

Harri squeezed her hand reassuringly. 'I'm sure there will be no trouble tonight, Olwen. The police have never tried to break up one of Mrs Anselm's meetings before.'

'Not here, maybe. But they were horrible on that last march. And they'll always pick on Gwen because she's a working girl who's not rich or well connected.'

'But she has us,' said Harri, firmly.

Olwen smiled, the anxiety easing a little from her face. 'Yes. She has us.'

Bea had been watching them for too long. As if sensing her gaze, Harri looked up. He met her eyes and smiled. A quiet, friendly smile. One without judgement or expectation. Somewhere deep inside, her stomach contracted, making it hard to breathe.

'It looks as if the meeting will be crowded,' he remarked, drawing her into the conversation. 'The Camellia isn't usually so full. It is a subject that rouses considerable passion.'

'I'm sure,' said Bea.

'Ah, there she is.' Olwen rose to embrace a frail-looking young woman, who could have been no more than nineteen, dressed in a carefully mended coat and battered hat, coming in out of the rain.

'I'm so sorry I'm late,' said the newcomer, breathlessly. 'There was a breakdown on the machines so the shift was late finishing, tonight of all nights.'

'There's still plenty of time, Gwen,' said Olwen. 'There's fresh tea in the pot.'

'And Olwen ordered far too much cake, as usual,' added Harri, pushing the teacake towards the empty setting at the table.

'Don't be so cheeky,' retorted Olwen. 'Mam always said you ate like a horse.'

'Only because they half-starved us at that wretched school you insisting on sending me to,' he replied. 'I hope when you become the first female Member of Parliament you'll consider looking into the treatment of small boys.'

'You didn't do too badly out of it,' said Olwen, laughing, as she helped Gwen out of her wet coat. She caught Bea's curious gaze and smiled. 'And we've met a new friend and been terribly rude and not introduced ourselves.' She held out her hand. 'I'm Olwen Lewis, you don't need any introduction to my brother, of course, and this is our cousin, Gwen.'

'Beatrice Tressillion.' There was a flicker in Harri's eyes. It was brief, but she caught it. Then he was smiling and following his sister and cousin in shaking her hand. Her heart sank, but she tried to ignore it. After all, they were all perfect strangers, why should it matter what he thought of her?

Gwen drank her tea, munching hungrily on her slice of teacake. 'Are you a member of the SLWAJ, too?' she asked Bea.

'The what?'

'The Suffrage League of Women Artists and Journalists,' explained Olwen.

Bea shook her head. 'I went for an interview today at the *Tribune*,' she said wistfully.

Gwen snorted. 'They tell lies.'

'I didn't get the post,' said Bea with a faint smile.

'With Rivers, was it?' asked Harri. Bea nodded.

'You were brave,' said Olwen.

'Foolish, more likely. He would never have considered me. At least, not as a journalist,' she added.

Gwen nodded. 'So I've heard.'

'He didn't – he didn't try to harm you?' Olwen's eyes held concern.

'I'll live, I didn't have to fight for my honour. At least, I didn't stop to find out.'

'Good for you,' said Harri. 'It's creatures like Rivers that make me ashamed of my own sex.'

Gwen took a last swig of tea and stood up. 'I should go.'

'We'll come with you.' Olwen reached for her coat, which she had slung over the back of her chair. 'Perhaps you would like to join us, Miss Tressillion? If we get there early we'll be able to get seats near the front.'

Bea scanned their expectant faces. She should really get home. She was already late. Mama would be growing anxious, as she repeatedly checked with Mrs Horsham, who was hired in as Cook on the rare occasions when guests had been invited. Guests who must be impressed. Bea swallowed.

Mama would have laid out her best blue silk dress, the one that had been altered to resemble the latest styles. Next to it would be the one remaining string of pearls. She would be itching to get her hands on Bea's chestnut curls and twist them firmly away from her face, issuing instructions to keep her eyes on her feet and not to express any opinions or betray any symptom of intelligence.

Trussed up like a parcel, thought Bea. An offering to Cousin

Jonathan, who now owned everything, apart from the pearls that had been left to Bea in her grandmother's will. He could, if he pleased, have them thrown out of the house in Twickenham on a whim. The man she could never forgive – although she understood that he had little choice in the matter – for selling her beloved Tressillion, snatching her childhood memories away from her, when her grief was still so raw.

'Of course,' she said, rebellion going to her head. She wasn't quite sure what she was letting herself in for, but she didn't care. Anything was better than being a trussed up silk parcel.

Hastily grabbing her coat and hat, she followed her new friends out into the rain.

Chapter Five

On the day she took possession of Tressillion, Sybil clutched the large, slightly preposterous key in her hand, and set off to view her new acquisition.

'What have I done?' she muttered, as she drew the Chevrolet onto a patch of grass just outside Porth Levant, her nerve, for once in her life, failing her.

Matters had gone at a breakneck speed from the moment she had declared her intentions to an astonished Mr Roach, who had instantly turned avuncular, beaming at her like a louche uncle taking rather too close an interest in a young niece. Clearly, having thought he'd never get Tressillion off his hands, he wasn't about to let her slip through his fingers.

She'd barely had time to conclude her business in London. She'd sent a letter to Miss Phipps in New York to inform her that the hotel in Mayfair had not suited, but she had chanced upon an excellent proposition in Cornwall instead. She would be staying there until all the alterations had been made and staff hired, and, with a telephone already installed, she would be available if she was needed.

Well, it was almost true, she told herself. And Miss Phipps had worked with her for the past ten years, and could run the business with her eyes closed. She'd taken over each time Sybil had been fully engaged in expanding her little empire with a new hotel, and she was well aware that, despite the highly dubious condition of some of the buildings she had taken on, Sybil had an unsurpassed nose for what would work, and was nobody's fool.

Miss Phipps might be slightly surprised, but she would have no doubts in Sybil's acumen in this unexpected departure from her plan to situate her fifth hotel in London.

'Maybe she doesn't know me at all,' Sybil acknowledged to herself. There were so many things her American employees knew nothing about, or her friends. It always made her feel slightly set apart, however many jostled to attract her attention.

There had only been once – Sybil pushed the thought firmly from her mind. That was for the silence of Tressillion, when she was truly on her own. She couldn't afford to walk through the village with the marks of grief on her face. That would make her far too interesting to the villagers, who, she remembered well, knew everything as if by osmosis, sometimes before those involved had a hint.

She left the automobile and, slipping a shopping bag over her shoulder, made her way into the village. It had to be done, sooner or later. Know your enemy, Dad had always said. The village would either be her friend or her enemy. If it was the latter, she might as well leave now.

The village had barely changed, any more than Tressillion. A collection of white washed cottages lined narrow, twisting streets, some leading down towards the harbour, bringing the call of seagulls mingled with the rattle of masts, and a lingering smell of fish.

She bought eggs, butter and rashers of bacon from the grocer, and a few earthy-smelling vegetables from a cheerful little shop next door. In both, conversation stopped the moment she stepped inside. Eyes followed her every move. Not friendly, not hostile. Weighing up of the stranger. She had been careful to select a coat of green velvet, less ostentatious than a fur, but still exuding wealth, confidence and a touch of the bohemian. If she was going to turn Tressillion into an artists' retreat rather than a conventional hotel, she might as well give the hint from the start.

Why not let the village assume she was an artist herself – albeit a wealthy, of the playing at painting and pottery, variety. That would give them enough to gossip about to divert them from the truth.

She equally carefully kept her English accent, banishing any hint of a Cornish lilt, and adding a faint twang of American every now and again, just to make the point that she was a foreigner. A touch of the exotic to camouflage any resemblance to a girl they must presume dead, or worn to the bone with the drudgery of poverty.

She recognised one or two of the older women, gossiping as they waited to be served in the sun-streaked dust of the grocery shop, but she was fairly certain none of them recognised her. The hungry bare-footed girl with hatred in her eyes – who would associate her with this wealthy woman from distant shores?

People see what they expect to see. Dad had been quite right. She'd met many a conman – and con-woman – who'd fleeced the rich under the cover of borrowed finery and diamonds made of glass.

As she strolled back to the Chevrolet, Sybil relaxed a little, shopping bag swinging jauntily at her side. The last shop was the baker's. She halted outside its window, the enticing smell of fresh bread stealing out. Once, she had stood here and smelt it, tormented by the unreachable plenty. With a spring in her step, Sybil hurried inside, gleefully selecting a large white loaf, and the most expensive cake she could find.

'Taken over the big house then, have you, Madam?' said the woman serving her, as she wrapped the bread in paper and parcelled up the cake into its own little box.

'Yes.' Sybil saw no point in denying the fact. 'I expect I'll be camping out for a while, until I can get things a bit more organised and decide what I'm going to do with the place.'

'Hotel, wasn't it?' came a new voice from the shadows. Sybil stifled her start, as an elderly woman leant forward into the light.

'Hush, Mam,' whispered the daughter, mortified.

'Only asking. We'll know soon enough. There's nothing ever hidden in this village, Mary.' The face was lined and frail, but Sybil would have known Mrs Patterson anywhere. There were nights she still dreamt – even after all these years – of the stale buns, some not so stale, that Mrs Patterson had pressed into her hands. She had been so hungry, she hadn't dared take a morsel until she reached home, in case, having started, she might never stop.

'Yes,' replied Sybil, her enjoyment expelled out of her, as if from a punch. She pulled herself together. Might as well point the gossip in the right direction before it starts. 'That is my plan. I run a small chain of hotels in America. I've heard Cornwall is an excellent place to attract visitors. It seemed the obvious choice to expand.'

'Well, and I hope you'll be offering jobs to people from the village, not bringing them in from the likes of London or America,' said Mrs Patterson.

'Mam!' Her daughter finished parcelling up Sybil's purchases, her face pink. 'Take no notice, Madam. My mother means well.'

'No offence taken,' said Sybil.

She hadn't thought this through. That was the trouble with impulse, whether it was a purchase, or revenge: in the heat of the moment it was impossible to understand the full consequences of one's actions.

The big house might have its privileges, but it also had its expectations, one of which was to provide for the village. Old Mr Tressillion might not have cared much for his underlings, born only for his convenience, but Sybil knew she could never do the same. She had been one of those conveniences. Rage had driven her from guttersnipe to lady. And she knew too well, deep in her secret heart, that without help, she could never have escaped the hand fate – and the Tressillions – had dealt her.

Old Mr Tressillion had openly despised those who hadn't his riches, conveniently forgetting that he had come from wealth, and had married even greater wealth, circumstances that gave even the biggest dunce a head start. Sybil knew from bitter experience that you could work as long and as hard as you were able, that you could have ingenuity and skill, maybe even genius – but if you spent your days and nights scrabbling for enough to eat, there was nothing left to achieve ambition. Especially not when there were others to look after, smaller and more vulnerable. It was impossible to watch the grip of cold and starvation steal their lives away and just look after your own needs.

'I shall certainly bear that in mind,' she said politely, cursing herself. She knew she couldn't have anyone from the village in her home. She'd always have to be on her guard, even in her sleep, in case she let something slip. She couldn't live in terror of being found out. Of the world knowing what she had done.

On some dark, windswept nights, she hated herself with a passion that made her wish the dawn would never come. She couldn't bear anyone else knowing, and condemning her, telling themselves they would never have done the same. She knew the hatred and the contempt for those in the big house who thought they were above the law and could do as they pleased, no matter what misery it cost others. She couldn't bear to be thought of in that way herself.

And it was not her secret, or her safety, alone she was protecting. A sliver of terror shot through her. If she was found out, the village, and the Tressillions, could prove to the authorities what she had done. There was still evidence, deep within the mine, that she had attempted over the years to push out of her mind. The Tressillions weren't ones to drag their name through the mud, or to confess how easily they'd been fooled.

She'd only briefly met Mr Jonathan Tressillion, who had found himself so unexpectedly the heir. Their paths had crossed once, by chance, in Roach's offices. Sybil, who had learnt to sum up a businessman or woman in a moment, had taken an instant dislike to the man. Partially on principle, because he was a Tressillion. But also some instinct of self-preservation told her he was a man she had no wish to meet again. The kind of man, it struck her now, who would not take kindly to being made a fool of, and would use all his wealth and connections to ensure he not only won, but that his opponent was humiliated, obliterated, even if that meant the hangman's noose.

'I beg your pardon?' she murmured. Deep in thought, she'd missed Mrs Patterson's next words.

'It's no matter,' said Mary, hastily. 'Mam was just talking of the old tin mine on your land. But that was closed years ago.'

'Not tin, the gold mine,' put in Mrs Patterson, with an air of triumph.

'Mam, there is no gold. Everyone knows there's hardly any gold to be found in Cornwall. Hargreaves must have been mistaken.'

'Nonsense,' snorted Mrs Patterson. 'I saw it myself.' She turned back to Sybil. 'A lump of gold. A great lump of gold. I've never seen the like. Mr Hargreaves was taking it to Mr Tressillion. He always was a dreamer, was Tam Hargreaves. Thought the old man would invest in his mine and they'd be rich together.' She spat into the cup at her side. 'When we all knew Tressillion would have sold his own mother before he shared anything. Did sell her in the end, the old…'

'Mam, please! Never speak ill of the dead, and I'm sure this is the last thing, Mrs…' Having worked herself into a corner in the rush of her embarrassment, Mary came to an undignified halt.

'Miss Ravensdale,' supplied Sybil.

'I'm sure this is the last thing Miss Ravensdale needs to hear.'

'Pity,' sniffed Mrs Patterson, unabashed. 'This village could do with the employment.'

'I thought there was fishing,' said Sybil.

'Not every Cornishman is a fisherman, young woman,' said Mrs Patterson, severely. 'Nor country bumpkin, neither.'

'I never for one moment thought they were,' returned Sybil. 'I'd never think that of anybody.'

Mrs Patterson's sharp eyes softened a little. 'No, Miss Ravensdale, I don't think you would. You've a working-woman's hands.' She nodded with grudging approval. 'And the sense to see what Tressillion House could be.'

'I hope so,' said Sybil, as Mary took on the look of a woman who wished the earth – or at least the floorboards – would swallow her up. 'I shall take that as a compliment.' She hesitated. 'Is there really such high unemployment here?'

'Has been for years,' said Mrs Patterson, before her daughter could stop her. 'Hargreaves' tin mine employed a fair number, until he started searching for gold instead. Should have been seeking out more reserves of tin, if you ask me. Then at least there might have been an industry to keep the village afloat.'

'I'll bear that in mind, too,' said Sybil, gathering her purchases and escaping before this conversation could stray into even more dangerous waters.

* * *

As she reached Tressillion House, the sun came out. It held a fragile warmth, with just a faint hint of spring in the air.

Having successfully opened the front door and left her belongings in the hallway, Sybil found she had no wish to go inside and start lighting the range and sorting out her sleeping arrangements for the night. Not yet. Not until the elusive promise of long summer days to come had chilled into evening.

She still travelled light, from a time when she had no other choice, but these days with the best modern conveniences at hand. She retrieved a small army stove and a kettle, and camped out on the steps leading down to the lawn, making tea in a tiny teapot, and carving herself hunks of delicious bread and cheese, followed by rich fruitcake.

Once her stomach was comfortingly tight, she sipped her tea, her eyes scouring the gardens. She had never owned a garden as such. In the years when she had barely been able to make ends meet, she'd crammed as many herbs and vegetables as she could on her windowsills. This was a garden. Overgrown and neglected, as much as the house, but still a place that had once been loved.

Someone in the family must have loved the place for its lushness and its distant view of the sea. She took in the brambles and the leggy shrubs, the rose beds long since left to their own devices, and the strangest feeling crept into her heart.

Falling in love with a garden, as with a human being, was dangerous. Like any love, it could lead to a broken heart. And yet here, in the silence, with the distant crash of waves, and the blackbirds returning home around her, she could feel her heart begin to open up again. A rabbit loped past, unaware that its territory had been invaded. A robin pecked among the rosebushes for worms.

It would do her good, she decided, to clear the garden. She had always enjoyed physical exertion, even when it had been a necessity. Establishing the gardens to her own tastes would be an act of reclaiming, making them her own. And a garden would be a perfect place for her guests to sit with their paints and their easels when they didn't want to search for more dramatic landscapes.

She would stay until the summer. She could take her time to clear the place, seeing what was salvageable and what could be thrown away. After all, she reasoned, as if she was being utterly rational about this, part of her genius for bringing the most tumbledown and forlorn buildings back to life had been her ability to wait, to stay in a place until she knew its every crook and cranny, until she could work out what necessary changes would work in harmony with the past. Her establishments were known for their unique atmosphere, as well as their style. Her magic was to make her hotels places her guests would fall in love with, returning year after year, and sending their friends to experience their comfort and tranquillity, to indulge their nostalgia for a more gracious past.

And it would give her time to work out if there was still any danger from the mine, while it was in her power to head off trouble and do something about it, whatever it might cost.

The sun was retreating into its late-winter chill, but Sybil remained on the garden steps, lost in thought, casting morsels of bread and cake to the appreciative birds, as the light faded into nothingness.

Chapter Six

At times it felt as if the cold had got into the very bones of Tressillion and stayed there.

Over the next few weeks, Sybil shivered in the kitchens, the only place in the house with any semblance of warmth, staring out of ice-flowered windows at the silent gardens crisp with frost. Even the sea piled shards of ice one upon the other on the shore.

Such winter days were rare in Cornwall. As the frost retreated again, she could make out the first shoots of daffodils amongst the rotting stems, and soft gold primroses fluttered, slightly tattered, beneath the trees. The ice still held the deep valleys in its grip, but venturing outside was less of a torture.

Then, as abruptly as it had appeared, the frost vanished. A crisp, clear sun threw the overgrown flowerbeds, the fallen branches and huge banks of brambles into sharp relief. Sybil stood on the steps, sipping tea and contemplating the trees at the far end. She hadn't yet built up the courage to tackle the house, and was glad to turn her focus back onto the grounds. The trees and shrubs had been left to grow out of all proportion, entirely blocking the sea. Some could stay as a windbreak, if trimmed a little, but others would be more useful as firewood.

She was just about to make her way inside to find a saw, when there was a hesitant knock on the garden gate.

'Come in,' she called. It would be the boy from Edwards the Grocer, on the bicycle that had seen better days before he was born, under strict instructions to make sure her order had been fulfilled accurately this time. 'I'm not going to bite your head off, William,' she added, irritated, as no boy, or delivery, appeared.

'Excuse me, Miss.' Instead of skinny, rabbit-eyed William, doing his best to escape before she could skin him alive, a pale-faced girl of about seventeen stood at the gate, grocery basket in her hands. 'William couldn't bring them today. So I did instead.'

'Very well.'

Despite the heavy basket, the girl was hovering. William had clearly not left the country or had a fit of the vapours when her order was being made up. She knew the girl wanted something. She'd been expecting something similar, from that first trip to the bakery. After that visit to Porth Levant, she'd taken the coward's way out and put in orders for her supplies, to side-step any further discussion on opportunities for the youth of the village. All the same, the wonder was it had taken so long.

The girl put the basket down at her feet and took a deep breath. 'Thing was, Miss, I understood you were looking for someone. To help with the cleaning.'

'Did you?' said Sybil. 'Well, you didn't hear it from me.'

The girl bit her lip. Then the teeth disappeared again and the lip tightened in determination. 'But you must need somebody, Miss. With the house in such a state.'

'You seem very sure of that.'

'It was when the old lady lived here, so Heaven knows what it must be like now.'

'Old lady?'

'Old Mrs Tressillion. The one who died, just before it had to be sold. My mam used to come and clean for her. She brought me with her, once or twice.'

'Were you scared?'

'A little.' The lip was bitten again. 'At least, I *was*. I wouldn't be now.'

'Well, at least you're honest.' I was like that too, once, Sybil thought. But not so honest. Not even then.

'I'll need references,' she said.

'Of course, Miss.'

'And you have experience, I take it?'

'A little.' The girl hesitated. 'Mam wanted me to stay on at school, to train to be a teacher. But with my dad being injured and out of work this winter…'

'I see.' Sybil watched her face. It was a careful blank. Maybe not quite so honest, at least not so open, as she had first thought. A girl who used her brain and had wit enough to hide the fact.

Despite Mrs Patterson, Sybil was determined not to take on any help from the village. Maybe a woman from down the coast, every now and again. On the other hand…

'What's your name?' she asked, despite herself.

'Emily Lewis.'

'I'd expect hard work, Emily Lewis. There's a whole house to clean. I'll get a man in to do the heavy work, but I'm expecting to do much of the garden myself. Have you any objections to getting your hands dirty?'

Emily shook her head. There was something slightly forlorn about the movement, despite the determination on her face.

The house was very large and there was something about the girl…

Sybil folded her arms. 'Very well. I'm prepared to give you your chance to prove yourself. No promises. But work hard, and we'll see.' She nodded to the basket. 'How about we start now? Bring that in with you. There's nothing urgent to get back to, I take it?'

Emily shook her head.

'Very well. You can help me get the drawing room in order, and we'll see how you do.' She took a glance at the pale face. 'When did you last eat?'

Emily looked nervous.

'Not this morning, I take it?'

A slow shake of the head. 'There wasn't time,' Emily mumbled, blushing. 'But I'm perfectly strong.'

'Hrmph.' Sybil took the basket from her. 'Well, I can't judge your capabilities unless you are fed, so we'll start with breakfast. Can you cook?'

Emily swallowed. 'A little.'

'A little. In other words, not at all. Excellent.' She grinned at the astonished look on Emily's face, finding that she was enjoying this new burst of life into Tressillion's silence. 'I don't like the thought of anyone interfering in my kitchen. I once made my living as a cook. It proved to be the first step to making my fortune. If you show me you can clean, maybe one day I'll teach you.' She led the way over the rough gravel terrace and down a short flight of steps to the kitchen. 'Never turn your nose up at any skill,' she added at the lack of enthusiasm from Emily.

'Oh, it's not that, Miss. I want to learn. It's just, I want to learn other things. Things in books.'

Sybil placed the basket on the wooden table, taking out eggs and bacon. 'They have their uses. But I have always blessed my ability to make something delicious out of nothing. It gives you bargaining power.'

Emily blinked at her. 'Bargaining power?'

'Yes. If you ever find yourself in a corner…' She paused, a paper bag filled with mushrooms in her hands. 'If men find you'll cook for them, they'll leave you alone in other ways. And make sure the others do too.'

Emily was scarlet. Sybil softened a little at the sight of her embarrassment. 'But I'm quite sure you'd never be so foolish as to find yourself in such a position. But if you ever do, cooking can give you choices. A woman with a child and no means of supporting it, or herself, has no choices at all. Men in general don't consider that. It's not their problem. They'd behave very differently if it was, believe you me.' Emily had the look of one ready to run. 'But you are right. An education gives you choices too.'

Emily nodded, clearly thankful to be back on safe ground once more. 'I wanted to become a teacher. Maybe headmistress of my own school. Or I could be a clerk in an office in Truro. Or even London. At least, that's what Mam said I should do, and then I would never, ever have to go into service… ' She came to a halt, blushing to the roots once more.

'Don't worry,' said Sybil dryly. 'I've no intention of having an army of servants to wait on me hand and foot. I don't expect my staff to be invisible. If another human being is doing you the courtesy of looking after you, the least you can do is acknowledge the fact, whether or not a salary is being paid. And you'd better sit down if you are going to stay.'

Emily perched herself on a chair, with a slightly uncertain giggle, while Sybil bent back over the pan, smiling to herself as she turned mushrooms and bacon with the intent of a craftswoman, feeling the hunger in her own stomach stirring as the scent of cooking drifted into the house.

Well, Emily hadn't run, the girl had that much spirit, at least. Sybil spoke her mind, and she wasn't about to stop now, but Emily appeared to be prepared to accept this. Or was too desperate not to.

Sybil winced. She knew the hunger in Emily's glance, the one that had nothing to do with learning, or going out to see the world. The lack of sustenance that slowed the body, chilling it to the very core, and prevented the mind from holding any coherent thought. Sybil hurried her cooking along, cutting slabs of bread and placing them, with the butter dish, next to Emily, whose eyes widened.

Sybil returned to her pan, carefully failing to notice the slices Emily placed in her pocket, while pretending to nibble at them, as instructed. An older child, then, most probably the eldest, with plenty of hungry mouths to feed at home, and the responsibility of all the world on those too-thin shoulders. Sybil crisped the bacon, remembering, as she always would, the women at the White Camellia who had taught her to cook. She had started as the kitchen maid, scouring and cleaning, scrubbing pans until her hands bled, scrubbing floors until her back ached and her knees were bruised and swollen.

'Good grief, girl,' Cook had exclaimed one day, grasping her hands, raw and cracked, blood oozing where the soda had cut gashes in the skin. 'You'll have no skin left at this rate.'

Sybil had stared at her, terrified.

'Well, and there's no need to look like a rabbit,' Cook had added, softening at Sybil's distress. She winked. 'Time one of those fine lady volunteers had a taste of real work instead of all that high-faluting talk about the right to vote and drawing up pamphlets.' She'd shooed her off in the direction of a young woman with a tray of cups and saucers from the tearooms. 'Miss Evelynne will look after you, she can practice her nursing skills. Then we can find you something more suitable to employ your enthusiasm.'

Miss Evelynne was a slightly terrifying figure, risking public censure by refusing to wear any form of corset, while engaged in constant skirmishes with her mother, who threatened a nunnery if Evelynne refused to marry the son of a German second cousin she'd never even met.

'You don't have to try quite so hard, you know,' she had remarked, as she spread a vile-smelling ointment with efficient, and surprisingly gentle, hands on Sybil's wounds. 'Once the White Camellia takes you under its wing, we'll find a way to help you to support yourself. We all know it will take time.' She'd bent over Sybil's hands once more, face hidden. 'No-one hurt you, did they? I mean, in the way girls can be hurt.'

'No, of course not,' Sybil had returned, all her suppressed fury sending the blood rushing to her head, turning her dizzy.

'Because, if they had, and that's what you were running from, there are people who can help, you know. There are plenty of women in the White Camellia who have experience in such cases, and can help in so many ways.'

Sybil had shaken her head fiercely, not daring to trust her voice, not daring to speak, in case if she started she might never stop. She didn't dread the police as much as the look in the eyes of the women at the White Camellia.

'Very well,' Evelynne said. 'But you are going to have to do something with that rage, my dear, wherever it comes from. If not, it will eat you up from the inside, until there is nothing left, and that won't help you, or your little brother and sister, now, will it?'

Sybil had pretended not to listen, but Evelynne's words had stayed with her, turning her energies towards finding a way of earning a living. Not just a living. A good living. So she would never have to feel fear, or hear the weakening cries of cold and hunger again, and not be able to do anything about it.

A few days later, Evelynne had been joined by the grey-haired woman with the expensive clothes, who had first taken Sybil away from the bleak streets.

'Helen will reach you to cook,' Evelynne announced. 'Then you will be able to acquire a trade.'

'It will be a start, my dear,' Helen added to the rebellion in Sybil's eyes. 'The thing is to have a place to start.' She rolled up her sleeves, made of the finest material Sybil had ever seen, unfastening the little buttons at the cuffs in the shape of a white camellia as if they were nothing. 'If I'd ever learnt a trade, instead of my fine accomplishments, I might have found myself with a little more freedom now.'

The quiet sadness in her voice squashed Sybil's rebellion, like a blow to the stomach. If a lady with silk in her skirts, and ostrich feathers flowing from her hat, longed to earn her freedom in such a humble manner, then she wasn't about to argue. Helen was right: at least it would be a start.

Sybil set a heaped plate in front of Emily, who made an effort to eat slowly, but without much success. Sybil turned the remainder onto her own plate, as if unaware of how fast the food was disappearing.

'It's wonderful,' said Emily, at last, manners surfacing. 'Thank you, Miss. I've never tasted anything so delicious.'

'Good,' smiled Sybil. 'I shall definitely have to teach you a dish or two, so I know you can keep yourself safe.' Practicalities returned. Her voice was severe. 'No followers.'

'I wouldn't…' protested Emily.

'No, I don't expect you would. But when love comes out of the blue… Your morals are your own, young woman, but my reputation depends on both of us. So I'll thank you to remember that.'

'Yes, Miss.'

'And another thing.'

Gloom spread over Emily's face. 'Yes, Miss?'

'You should continue your education.'

Emily looked at her in despair. 'But you haven't even tried me, Miss. I promise I'll eat before I come, and I'll work as hard as I can from the moment I arrive to the moment I leave, and I'll be so quiet you won't know I'm here.'

'Oh, don't worry. Having fed you, I've every intention you should work for me. School won't be practical, but there may be other classes. Evening classes.'

'Miss?'

'You work hard for me, and don't let me down, and don't let me catch you gossiping about anything you see or hear, and I'll pay for any classes and books, and I'll give you two afternoons off each week for you to study. How will that do?'

'I'm not sure.' Emily sounded uneasy.

'I'm not going to drag you into a den of iniquity as part of the bargain, if that's what you are thinking.'

'I wasn't!' Emily was indignant. 'It's just, well, you don't know me, Miss Ravensdale, you don't know anything about me. I don't understand why you should.'

Sybil cut more bread for Emily and her pockets, and took the boiling kettle from the range, pouring water onto the tealeaves already measured out in the teapot. There had to be an answer, of course, both for the girl and her parents. And it must be the truth. Or at least a version of truth they would understand.

'Because once, long ago, someone did the same for me.' She didn't mean to go on, but she couldn't stop herself. 'I didn't understand at the time, that in doing so, they gave me my life, and the opportunities to have everything I have now. I've been a fool most of my life, and now it's too late to repay them. Maybe this is the only way.'

Chapter Seven

The Institute was already crowded by the time Bea and her new friends arrived.

Bea followed Harri and Olwen, who ushered Gwen onto to a small stage at the front, where she joined a row of speakers already assembled.

'Good, there are still spaces,' said Olwen, hurrying to secure the empty chairs at the end of the front row. Harri paused to talk to a man in a loose coat and sporting a fearsome beard, although how they could hear each other above the excited chatter she could not guess. Bea took the seat next to Olwen. An air of anticipation hung in the room.

'It can be a bit daunting at first,' said Olwen. 'Especially a big meeting like this one.'

'No, not at all,' replied Bea. Anticipation flowed through her veins. 'Nothing exciting ever happens at home. We only ever talk about the weather and family gossip. I never knew there were so many serious people in the world.'

'Not too serious, I hope,' replied Olwen, laughing. 'We do have fun too, you know. And I just love gossip, myself. Don't you find human beings can be just the strangest creatures?'

'Always.' Bea smiled.

Behind them, two women were deep in a discussion comparing the new soprano Tetrazzini with Dame Nellie Melba, and lamenting Sir Thomas Beecham's dislike of *La Bohème* and its disappearance from the repertoire at Covent Garden.

Next to them, a small group of women and men were assessing

Mrs Pankhurst's speech last Sunday, and her passionate defence of the urgent need to accord women an equal role in society.

'My life is very small and selfish,' Bea said wistfully. 'I wish I had something to believe in.'

'You really meant it, about being a journalist, then?'

Bea nodded. 'I don't know much about anything, but I can learn. I know I can. I loved the little bit I did when I volunteered for the Red Cross, finding out about things, and feeling that I could make a difference. Everything is written by men, as if they spoke for everybody. But that's not how I think, and I'm sure there are plenty of women who feel the same.'

'You could always try Mrs Anselm,' said Olwen.

'Mrs Anselm?'

'She's the President of the League. They print a small journal every month. I work the printing press for them a few days a week and I know they are always looking for good stories and fresh voices. I don't know if there are any paid positions going, they never have much money. But it might be a way to learn, if you volunteered to write stories for them for a while. She's speaking tonight, I can introduce you to her afterwards, if you like?'

Bea took a deep breath. She should politely decline. Especially if there was to be no money. She should be practical. Swallow her pride and her ambition and try again for a position as a clerk, however badly paid and with no prospects.

'Yes, I would very much like that, thank you,' she replied.

'There, you see.' Olwen nodded to the stage, where a woman had arrived and was divesting herself of a large fur coat. 'I knew she'd be here, she's the first speaker.' Mrs Anselm caught Olwen's wave and nodded in their direction. She glanced at Bea for a moment, with a small nod of approval. 'Oh. You know each other.'

'Not really. We met briefly. She showed me where the White Camellia was.'

Olwen lowered her voice. 'She can be a bit alarming, and she does like things done her own way. But she has the most amazing energy and people listen to her, and her heart's in the right place. Don't be fooled by the furs, that's to make a point. She makes no secret that she came up from nothing, so she understands exactly how things are and how difficult life can be. Half the people here would follow her to the ends of the earth.'

'Or a prison cell,' added Harri, joining them.

Mrs Anselm consulted an impressive pocket watch, before taking her place at the centre of the stage. Her fellow speakers moved to their positions and silence gradually fell in the hall, with a 'hush' where conversations ran on a little too long.

'Good evening,' said Mrs Anselm, looking around her audience with undisguised satisfaction. 'And welcome to this meeting of the Suffrage League of Women Artists and Journalists. We've much to discuss this evening, so I suggest we make a start.' She rustled a sheaf of papers in her hand, without consulting them. 'As you know, the question this evening is one of profound interest to us all: should the League continue to work alongside Mrs Fawcett, and follow the NUWSS' policy of peaceful protest and civil disobedience, or affiliate itself to Mrs Pankhurst's call for direct action?' She quelled the faint murmur with a glare. 'Everyone will get their chance, and, as you all know, our first speaker, Miss Lewis, is a passionate advocate of Mrs Pankhurst's methods.'

'It's the only way to get this government listening!' called a voice from the back. A murmur of agreement swelled, threatening to take over the hall. Mrs Anselm frowned the audience into silence.

'I know the arguments, and I'm sure you are all aware of my strong feelings in this matter. Like the NUWSS itself, we have a long, proud history of non-violent agitation in this League, from the day it was founded at the beginning of the last century to agitate against the evils of the slave trade. We were laughed at then, too, but we prevailed. It was the same with the Contagious Diseases Act.' Bea heard a sharp intake of breath around her. She glanced enquiringly at Olwen, who shook her head.

'That took years to repeal,' called a woman behind Bea. 'And caused endless suffering – and to many more than the wretched women it was supposed to be aimed at.'

'Men are prepared to use prostitutes when it pleases them, then take no responsibility,' called a voice from the back. 'And then take pleasure in punishing them. The act was a disgrace and should never have been passed.'

'It wasn't only the prostitutes,' returned the woman just behind Bea. 'They picked up a sister of one of my mother's maids just because she was walking alone in a street near to where prostitutes plied their trade. She wasn't to know, poor girl. She was just visiting her aunt. It was obscene what that doctor did to her with that speculum thing and the internal examination. She was only sixteen, and a total innocent. She never recovered from such violation from a man who was supposed to be a healer.' She patted Olwen on the shoulder. 'That's why we need more women doctors, my dear. I've never let a male doctor near me since that day, and certainly not for the birth of a single one of my four children.'

Bea felt faintly sick. She knew so little of the world. Protected far away in Tressillion, Papa had been strict about what was suitable for female ears to hear. Despite Leo's idealism, she knew nothing of the reality of slavery, or of girls being assaulted for simply walking down the wrong street. She looked back at the woman who had spoken. Her face was tight with the deep burning anger of injustice. The kind, Bea understood, that made people die for their beliefs. She turned back to Mrs Anselm, who was attempting to quell the rising tide of indignant conversation. She could feel the same anger burning up inside herself. A deeper anger than she had felt in Mr Rivers' office: this time the white-hot flame of injustice was not just about herself.

'But we persisted and the act was eventually repealed,' called Mrs Anselm as the room began to settle. 'Besides, we have the example of the non-violent action of our fellow suffragists in New Zealand and Australia, who have achieved the right to vote through peaceful means.' Her voice shook slightly with emotion. 'I had the privilege of being there when our New Zealand sisters first exercised their right to vote. And not just the European women, but the native women, too. We have always acted on the principle of universal suffrage of all men and women, whatever their race, creed or class: unless all are equal, none are equal.'

'Principles are all very well,' called one of the opera lovers behind Bea.

Mrs Anselm glared. 'It's not simply a matter of principle, as well you know, Violet. It's proving a point. The point that women are rational creatures, not the unhinged hysterics His Majesty's government and the so-called gentlemen of the press would like to believe. I understand Mrs Pankhurst's frustration, and, believe me, I share it. I fear that if we go down her route of direct action, it will be easier to portray us as irrational, and not real women at all. To dismiss us out of hand. If we keep our dignity, the police don't know how to deal with us. If we lose it, they have carte blanche to treat us with the violence they meter out to drunks and prostitutes. Believe me. More than one of us here has been beaten up by the police during a public demonstration. It's something we want to put an end to, not become targets ourselves.'

'So we do nothing,' said Violet.

'No, we continue as we are. Peaceful protest, civil disobedience, and negotiation.'

'And they just ignore us,' retorted Violet. 'Dismiss us, as if we don't matter. I was there in '84, remember, when we were so sure we had negotiated the vote, and they reneged at the last minute. Give a few more men the vote, is their attitude, and the women will just go away. That's exactly what they are doing now and will continue to do. Over thirty years I've been campaigning peacefully, and they just treat us like fools. It's time to make them sit up and take notice. I'm for following Mrs Pankhurst.'

'Exactly,' exclaimed Gwen, jumping to her feet, as if unable to contain herself any longer. 'Unless we make our voices heard, unless we show we aren't afraid of them, and we're prepared to die for what we believe in, just as men do in a war, then they will always put us off. It's a question of freedom. For all men and women, no matter what our class, race or creed. I've been in prison. It was one of the most terrifying things I've ever done, locked up with the drunks and the madwomen. Some of them had even murdered. But what I saw in each of them was a humanity that cannot be denied. I don't believe any of those women were born evil. Even those who had killed. How can you name as an inhuman beast the woman who had finally taken an axe to the husband who had beaten and violated her for years with the utmost brutality, without her having any chance of rescue or redress? I agree that all women and men should have a voice – but if even a very few women achieve a say in which party governs us, then we become a force to be reckoned with, and they will be forced to listen to our demands.'

'You are talking about a short cut,' shouted Mrs Anselm, above the applause and the shouts of agreement. 'One that may, in the end, do more harm to our cause.'

'I hate to point it out,' added Harri, rising to his feet. 'But it does also make it far more difficult to defend, from a legal point of view. Particularly when Mrs Pankhurst is attempting to insist that any suffragist arrested should be treated as a political prisoner, rather than an ordinary offender.'

'I don't want to be treated differently,' said Gwen.

'I understand and respect that,' he replied gently. 'But at the same time, I don't want the authorities to take the opportunity to treat all activists as common criminals and lunatics. What better way to dismiss them, and ensure the readers of the newspapers do not ask too closely concerning the argument? There are already many supporters of female suffrage in Parliament, and now that women can be elected to serve on local councils and school boards, the argument against giving women the vote is wearing increasingly thin. Surely it's better to shame and embarrass them into doing the right thing, rather than give those who oppose it the opportunity to argue they are being faced with irrational violence and a threat to national security?'

Bea exchanged glances with Olwen. Silence fell as Harri sat down again.

'But we have to take the risk,' replied Gwen, her mouth setting in a determined line. 'Or they might never give us the vote.' Cool air swept in as the door next to them was opened. Bea drank it deep into her lungs, feeling the smell of streets and horse dung sweet on the clamminess of her skin.

'*Arglwydd Mawr,*' muttered Olwen. Whatever she was saying, it wasn't a cry of joy.

Shouts erupted around them, followed by the rush of bodies. A policeman strode onto the stage, grabbing Gwen by the arm, followed by more uniformed men rushing in from all sides.

'Damn,' muttered Harri. He turned to Bea and Olwen. 'Come on, we'll get Gwen, then you all get out of here.'

'I'm not going without you,' said Olwen. 'You'll only get yourself arrested.'

'I'll only use legal arguments, I promise,' he returned. 'But you need to get Gwen away from here before she gets put in prison again. This is completely illegal. I'll do my best, but they don't look in the mood to see sense.'

He planted himself in front of the officer dragging Gwen off the stage, her coat ripping at the seams, her hat crumpled underfoot. 'On what grounds are you arresting this woman?' he demanded, loudly.

The officer hesitated at the tone of authority, loosening his grip just enough for Gwen to tear herself free. Olwen grabbed her, dodging through the chaos erupting around them, heading for the door.

'This is utterly outrageous,' came Mrs Anselm's voice above the mêlée. 'This is a peaceful, legally constituted meeting. If you are going to arrest the speakers, then you should arrest me.'

Bea bent beneath an arm, following Olwen, who was holding Gwen, trying to persuade her to leave. A group of police pushed purposefully towards them, their eyes focussed on Gwen.

'Leave her alone,' exclaimed Olwen. 'She hasn't done anything.'

'She's a known criminal,' replied the officer. 'And she's resisting arrest. Get yourself home, Madam, unless you wish to be arrested too.' He stepped forward to grab Gwen, who pulled herself free once more. Olwen screamed as his hand rose and struck Gwen a blow to the stomach, sending her crumpling to the floor.

The blood rushed to Bea's head. All the petty injustices of that day, and every day, rushed in with it. Grabbing an abandoned umbrella, she landed the policeman a satisfying thwack across the shoulder blades. He stumbled, crashing against the row of chairs.

Bea froze.

'Quickly.' She found Harri next to her, dashing the umbrella to the floor before the officer could recover himself. A large policeman, his face red, stepped back from his tussle with a burly, white-haired woman in a feathered hat, who was giving as good as she got, with earthy language to match, and began making his way towards her. 'No heroics. Go with Gwen and Olwen,' said Harri, propelling her towards his sister. 'You don't want to be arrested for assaulting an officer, believe me.'

Olwen grabbed Bea's arm, pulling her through the crowds, past the policemen guarding the door, who were engaged in a fierce argument with Mrs Anselm, her imperious voice and indignation keeping them at bay.

'The Prime Minister shall hear of this,' she said, as they passed. 'This is a free country, and this a legally constituted and peaceful meeting. This tyranny is a disgrace.'

'Come on.' Olwen grasped Gwen's hand, dragging her along behind them as they reached the far side of the street.

From the open door of the Institute, the officer, his helmet still missing, followed by several of his men, were shoving their way through. Gwen's hand dived into her pocket.

'Don't you dare,' hissed Olwen. 'I've no intention of spending a night in the cells and seeing the rest of you beaten up like prostitutes. Save your stones for another day, Gwen.'

Bea swallowed. 'They've seen us.'

Olwen cursed beneath her breath in Welsh. 'No point in hailing a cab, then. Come on, we'll have to run for it.' She shot down a side alley, dragging an unwilling Gwen behind her.

Chapter Eight

Bea ran as fast as she could behind Gwen and Olwen, her heartbeat competing with the rapid clatter of her companions' boots on the cobbles, and the louder squeak of the police boots behind them. The alleys grew narrower. Lights flickered from tenements high above. Women leant out of windows or yelled encouragement from doorways. Men lounging on street corner called after them, mockingly.

As they turned into an alley with scarcely a light to be seen, a man coming the other way brushed past, swaying from side to side, fumes of alcohol rising with his freezing clouds of breath.

'Not so fast,' he muttered, overbalancing, knocking Gwen, who stumbled against a wall, where she collapsed, coughing violently. Oblivious, he reached out to grab Bea. 'Have a dance, Miss.'

'Don't be daft, Bert,' came a woman's voice, high above. 'Who'd want to dance with you, the state you're in? Now shift yourself, unless you want to be dancing with the coppers.'

'Bloody hell.' Bert fumbled with the nearest door handle.

'Wrong bloody door, and all,' came the woman's voice, exasperated. 'Milly, go get yer dad.' A door opened next to them and Bert was hauled unceremoniously inside.

Boots were loud behind them, already in the next street. Gwen was still bent over, her breath shallow, rapid gasps.

'She can't go any further,' said Bea. 'I'll stay here, I'm the one who caused all this.'

'That won't make any difference. They want to make an example of us,' said Olwen, taking Gwen's arm.

65

'It might at least distract them, if I give myself up, and let you get away. You said Gwen mustn't get arrested again.'

'You don't know what they are like,' said Olwen. 'We'll stick together.'

A small head appeared round the open door. 'Mam says you can all come too, only you'll have to be fast 'cos she doesn't want no coppers rampaging through the house.'

They hesitated. A shout came from the next street. Without a word, the three of them shot inside.

'Mam says up to the attics,' said the girl, who looked no more than ten. From the far end of the street came the sound of doors being banged upon, loud demands to be let in. 'You can get along the attics, along all the houses to the river,' added the girl. 'Dad does, when he's got stuff to sell that he shouldn't.'

'That's enough, Milly,' came a voice from the top of the stairs. 'Don't be telling everyone our business, will you.'

'It's only Miss Olwen, and she won't snitch,' protested Milly.

'That's not the point, it's the principle of the thing.' The woman beckoned. 'Come on up, all of you.'

'Are you sure, Sadie?' called Olwen. 'I don't want to cause you any trouble.'

'There'll only be trouble if they catch you,' replied Sadie. 'Which they won't.'

Bea helped Olwen half drag, half carry, Gwen's light body to the top of the stairs, and up a rickety ladder into the attics.

'Stay still,' hissed Sadie. 'There's packing cases in the far corner. There's room behind them. Just don't look inside, for gawd's sake.'

The three of them huddled behind the packing cases, that clinked gently whenever they moved, sending the faint aroma of rum into the air. Silence settled around them in the darkness, broken only by Gwen's ragged breathing. Bea's heart slowly calmed. Then came banging on the front door and raised voices.

'Women? What do you think I am?' Sadie was outraged. 'Are you accusing me of running a house of ill repute? Me with three young daughters and a son in the army prepared to die for his country? You didn't see no women, did you, Milly?'

'Not for ages,' came Milly's voice, brightly. 'Not since the shift at the factory ended, and that was hours ago.'

'If we could speak to your husband…'

'No. He's only just come off his shift. Double one he did, too. He needs his sleep to operate that machinery. Three men have been injured there this month. A man was killed last week. Do you want to see me a widow, and thrown on the parish?' As if to confirm this, Bert's loud snores resounded through the walls.

The police began to search the house, opening doors and cupboards, Sadie protesting loudly that they were waking the baby and her girls were only just back from their shifts at the factory themselves. The footsteps continued upwards, from room to room, until they reached the ladder. Bea held her breath as, with a creaking and a flood of light, the door to the attic was flung open. A flashlight strafed the darkness, illuminating drifting curtains of cobwebs hanging from the rafters, sending spiders scurrying.

'I'm not in the habit of keeping strange women in my attic,' exclaimed Sadie from the bottom of the ladder. 'You're wasting your time. They'll be miles away by now. So what was it they've done?' She gave a loud guffaw. 'If you want to catch every thief passing my door, officer, you'll be here till kingdom come. You tell them shopkeepers to keep a better eye on their stock. And tell the factory owners to pay their employees right, or there wouldn't be any need for thieving in the first place. They'll be down by the river by now, safe on a barge, and laughing at you all the way to the open sea.'

'What d'you think, sarge?' The man holding the flashlight sounded dubious.

'Just mind the rats,' called Sadie. 'Big as dogs they are, up there. Keep my girls awake at night, they do. You can hear them, racing along all the attics. And amongst the privies, something dreadful. I've told the authorities. They need to do something about it. It's a disgrace. How am I supposed to keep a house fit for a working man, and my son due home on leave from the army…'

'For Heaven's sake,' muttered the constable. He grabbed the flashlight, sending a slow stream of light around the eaves. 'Well, they can't have got up here, that's for certain. Not a bunch of women, and one of them half dead. Come on. We're wasting time.'

Bea held her breath until the last boot had made its way down the stairs and the front door slammed. She became aware of Gwen crouched next to her, her breathing harsh. 'He didn't mean it.'

'I don't care if he did,' hissed Gwen.

Milly scrambled through the attic door, followed by the head and shoulders of her mother.

'Milly will show you to the end attic,' said Sadie. 'You can get down into Lombard Street. Follow the river then take the first right, and you'll be at the Church Hall.'

Olwen untangled herself and joined Milly, crouching beneath the low eaves. 'Thank you, Sadie. You and Milly.'

'That's all right,' said Sadie gruffly. 'I said I'd repay you, that time you brought Milly through the whooping cough, when I was at my wits end when Bert was thrown out of work.' She sniffed. 'Never did like coppers anyhow. And you watch, I'll be the first in the queue once we get the vote. Time they learnt to be afraid of us, for a change.'

Bea followed the others, bending beneath the sloping eaves. Milly's lamp sent shadows shooting into corners. They stepped from house to house, hearing the differing voices down below.

At last they arrived at the house of an elderly couple and their young grandson, none of whom appeared the least bit surprised by a party of fugitives climbing down the steep stairs. Within minutes they had said goodbye to Milly, who was swept into the kitchen for a slice of currant cake, while the grandson led them out through an overgrown garden into a street smelling of the river.

They passed through narrow streets, each more badly lit than the next, until Olwen finally slowed. 'They won't come here,' she said. Bea looked back dubiously. Heaven knows how she would find her way to the lit streets of trams and the underground. And after her narrow escape earlier that day, the very thought sent shivers down her spine. Mama would most likely never speak to her again.

Olwen led them through a tumbledown churchyard to a building standing on its own. Pushing through, they entered a heaving throng of bodies. A group of women were dishing out hot soup and bread on long trestle tables at one end of the room, while at the other end families crouched, huddling together for warmth. The stench of unwashed bodies was overwhelming.

'It's all right. You get used to it,' said Olwen quietly. 'I couldn't believe it, the first time I came here. Lillian is the last hope for the desperate and the homeless. There's always a hot meal and a roof over their heads, however many come.'

Bea followed, shivering slightly. However desperate her situation might have seemed earlier that day, it was nothing compared to the deprivation and disease written on the faces of the children, and the despair on the adults'. Even the mangy dog had no energy as they passed, his thin tail wagging briefly before tucking his nose tight against his belly and returning to sleep.

She might not want to marry Cousin Jonathan, for all Mama's plotting and planning, and her sacrifice of her blue dress, but at least the option was there. She had never gone actually hungry in her life, and even though they'd had to be careful with coal this winter, there had always been a store in the coalhouse and the fires had never quite gone out. They were respectable. They'd always had a roof over their heads.

'Lillian!' exclaimed Olwen, as a tall woman in her late twenties, with parchment skin and auburn hair flowing down her back, appeared from an inner room.

Olwen rushed to embrace her. 'It's good to see you again. Has Harri arrived? He said he would meet us here.'

'Not yet.' Lillian's glance took in Gwen and Bea. 'I heard there was trouble at the meeting. A journalist has already been around asking if it was a riot. I heard a policeman was grievously assaulted.'

Bea exclaimed indignantly, 'I only knocked his helmet off.'

'I'm glad to hear it.' Lillian's green eyes twinkled. 'The rumour going round is that he was beating up a woman and was beaten up himself. You are going to remain famous here for some time.'

'Oh.' Bea stared at her, aghast.

'Anonymously, of course,' added Lillian. 'And with great exaggeration. I'm sure the police won't mention the incident at all. Doesn't look good, does it, either the beating up, or the being beaten by a woman. And I'm certain they are well aware Mrs Anselm won't stand for one of her league being portrayed as a common criminal, and she's a force to be reckoned with.' She glanced at Gwen, who was shivering in her wet clothes. 'A cup of tea and the fire, is what you need. You can stay here tonight, Gwen, in case they think to try and find your lodgings. I'll find a change of clothes for you.'

The door opened, bringing with it the fishiness of the Thames, and the distant rush of water as the tide turned. Instantly, Bea was back on the beach at Tressillion. Sea lapping round her feet, laughter rising into the night air, the crackle of a driftwood bonfire with the delicious sizzle of freshly caught fish, and potatoes smoky in their skins cooking among the embers.

'I need to get home,' she said.

'It's all right,' said Olwen. 'Harri will be here soon, once he's made sure no-one at the meeting has been arrested. It'll be better if he's with us when we leave. He's got a reputation for knowing every loophole and not letting them get away with anything, so we'll be safer with him, if the police are still about.'

'Of course.' Bea smiled at her. On the far side of the room, Lillian was settling Gwen next to the fire, wrapping a blanket around her before disappearing to find a change of clothes. 'Is Gwen really ill?'

'She's not been strong for years. Her lungs were damaged in the last factory she worked in, and she gets so passionate about things she forgets to look after herself. Uncle Madoc has been up to London several times to try and persuade her to go home with him, but she always refuses. It might have been different if her mother were still alive.' Olwen pulled a face. 'Or maybe not. Gwen always needed a cause to fight for. I can't see her in a village in the middle of nowhere with nothing to occupy her mind.'

A rush of cold air brought a new group of men and women pushing past them to reach the fire next to Gwen, where they huddled, coughing and stamping their feet, steam rising from threadbare coats and hats.

'But if she's so ill…'

'She'll recover, if she keeps out of the cells. She's so determined. I don't think I could be that brave. But she'll be safe here. Lillian will look after her. And hopefully it will all die down in a few days. They are unlikely to arrest her at work, and we can make sure she gets to and from here until it all blows over.' Olwen gave a wry grin. 'Hopefully Mrs Pankhurst will have one of her marches and then they'll have far too much to think about to remember Gwen.' She sighed. 'I wish I was rich. Most of the time I don't mind. But just sometimes, when I know money could help Lillian keep this place going and take in all those who need it, and when Gwen is afraid of losing her job… That's when I wish I was rich and could help them all. I hate money. It's such a tyrant, and it has nothing to do with justice or someone's real worth at all, most of the time.'

'No,' murmured Bea. 'But it's impossible to do without it.'

'Not something you have to worry about.'

Bea glanced up. Not all the newcomers had headed straight for the fire. One had stayed behind and was watching her from under his hat, his face in shadow as he leant against the wall.

'There's soup and warmth by the fire,' said Olwen.

'I don't doubt it.' He didn't move. It was an educated voice, harsh at the edges and slightly slurred. A smell of whisky permeated the air. 'I don't doubt it at all.' He pushed himself away from the wall, the collar of his sodden greatcoat falling open to reveal the bright knitted pattern of Bea's scarf wound around his neck. 'All that gold, and all you can spare is a few coppers to keep a man from freezing to death.'

'I…' Bea stepped back. The venom in his tone was unmistakable.

'She doesn't have any gold,' said Olwen, keeping her tone deliberately light. From the look on her face, she was convinced the man had lost his mind. 'Come on, I'll take you to the fire. There was fresh bread arriving a few minutes ago.'

The man ignored her, taking a few weaving steps towards Bea. He gripped her arm like a vice, preventing her from moving. 'All that gold…'

'That will do.' He started as Lillian's hand closed over his, prising the fingers away from Bea's arm. 'Leave the young woman alone. You know the rules.'

'Rules be damned.' He spat deliberately on the collar of Bea's coat. 'I wouldn't stay under the same roof, not if you paid me.'

Lillian pushed him back towards the door with such force he stumbled. 'You don't have the choice. You know the rules, and that there are no exceptions. Come back when you've sobered up. Everyone here has enough troubles, without you causing them more.'

'Ah, *Miss Finch*.' His voice was a whine. 'You wouldn't send a man out into the rain to catch his death, would you? Especially not—'

'Try me,' retorted Lillian. 'The rules are the same here for prince or pauper. Whoever you are, the answer is the same: come back when there's some talking sense to you.'

He swayed dangerously. 'You're a heartless woman, Lillian. You don't care if I end up in the river.'

'That's entirely up to you. But I wouldn't take too long about it. There's not much soup left in the pot, as it is.'

The man drew himself up into some semblance of dignity. 'Heartless,' he muttered. He walked with exaggerated care towards the door, which had opened to allow Harri to step inside. As the tramp reached the door he turned, his gaze travelling back to Bea. 'I knew who you were, you know, first time I saw you. I'm not a beggar. I was only getting my due.' With that, he vanished into the night.

Bea found she had been holding her breath and let it out slowly. Her relief was short-lived when she found Lillian frowning accusingly at her. 'You gave him money?'

Bea blinked. 'A little,' she said, defensively. 'It was cold. Just a few pennies for a cup of tea.'

'Surely even you must know the last thing he would buy with your money was tea,' said Lillian. 'Alcohol for a man like that could be a death sentence.'

'I'm sorry,' whispered Bea, feeling as small as a child.

'There's no real harm done,' said Harri, shutting the door behind the tramp and coming to join them. 'And Miss Tressillion wasn't to know.'

Bea threw him a look of gratitude, then wished she hadn't. He was not looking in her direction, but at Lillian, his voice warm, his smile full of admiration. Lillian returned his smile, her face softening, annoyance easing.

Something clenched inside Bea. Exhaustion hit her, like a wave. There was at least one bruise forming on her shin, and every part of her ached. 'I must get home,' she muttered.

'I'll drive you.' Harri turned to her with a smile. No admiration, she couldn't help but notice, but it was still a smile. 'It took longer than I thought for us to stop those idiots from arresting the entire meeting. I've still got the use of Mrs Anselm's automobile, in case I'm needed. The least I can do is drive you home.'

'Good idea,' said Olwen. 'I'll come too. Is it far?'

'Twickenham.'

'Almost on our way home,' said Harri cheerfully. 'It won't take long, and you don't want to risk being picked up by the police.'

'No.'

He cleared his throat. 'And perhaps it might be as well, under the circumstances, if we drop you off at a discreet distance from your home?'

Bea blushed at this reading of her mind. 'Thank you. I'm afraid we've got guests tonight, and my mother was feeling anxious. Perhaps another day… '

'Of course,' put in Olwen quickly.

Bea felt her whole body burn. For the past hours there had been no distance between them. It had been as if they had known each other all their lives. And now her expensive coat, which had kept Rivers at bay, along with her name and her speech, made them both assume they would not be welcome guests. And the worst of it was that they were right. Mama would see a solicitor – particularly one who dealt with those who actually went to prison, and who had not the redemption of wealth, as beneath her notice. Even more so his unmarried sister, who was vulgar enough to earn her own living. She could feel Lillian's scorn travelling down her spine.

Bea glanced sideways at Harri. Since he appeared to know of the Tressillions, did he also know Cousin Jonathan, and the expectation that she would marry him, and regain her life of ease? Given what she had seen in the past few hours, he would despise her for even considering it. She lifted her chin. But then he did not have Mama's plaintive grief to meet every day, or the bewilderment of her little sister. Or the uncertainty that hung over them.

'We'll say goodbye to Gwen,' said Olwen.

'And do our best to make sure she stays here,' added Harri. 'I just hope that, for once, she listens.'

Bea watched as he strode after Olwen and Lillian, towards a smaller room set to one side of the main hall. Maybe for Harri it would be a relief, having an excuse not to be seen in company with a Tressillion. He would most likely warn his sister to keep her distance, too. Their paths were unlikely ever to cross by chance, and she doubted either of them would seek out her company again.

A tightness filled her chest, catching her by surprise. Lillian was right, she acknowledged. There was so little she knew of the world, having been shut away most of her life in Cornwall. But she could learn. Whatever Lillian thought of her, she could learn and she had to admit that she had never felt so alive as she had tonight. Whatever it took, she was not about to let that go.

As Harri and Olwen returned, she took a last look at the families huddled in every corner of the shelter, holding their last shreds of dignity close to them. It felt a lifetime since her interview with Mr Rivers this morning. There was so much she wanted to know, so much she wanted to understand. There were terrible things in the world, things that were hidden but that needed speaking about. Mr Rivers might think she couldn't become a journalist, but she wasn't going to let him stop her. She wasn't going to let anyone stop her. Not now she was more determined than ever.

Chapter Nine

Sleet swept across the terraces of Curzon Avenue. Number six was in darkness, apart from the edges of light escaping from the first floor drawing room curtains. Bea reached the door as Harri turned Mrs Anselm's automobile around, headlamps illuminating the deserted street.

Bea waited until the engine had faded into the distance, then let herself into the narrow hallway, shivering as she removed her dripping coat and the ruin of her hat and hung them on the stand next to the door. In the mirror, her face looked pale and drawn, damp ribbons of hair plastered against her forehead.

'Beatrice?' Her mother's voice, faint and complaining, came through from the drawing room. 'Beatrice, is that you?'

'Yes, Mama. I'll be with you in a few minutes.'

'You are so late, I was becoming frantic with worry. And Cousin Jonathan's been so looking forward to seeing you.'

'I'm sorry, the rain was terrible. I was delayed.'

'It will be worth the delay,' came Jon's voice, light and cheerful.

'I'm wet through,' called Bea. 'I must change. I'll join you in a few minutes.' She shot upstairs to the sanctuary of her bedroom. A lamp was burning low, revealing two small figures curled up together on her bed.

'Miss Bea!' The larger of the two – although not by much – unwound herself, stumbling blearily to her feet. 'Miss Ada wanted to wait up for you.' She swallowed. 'Is Mrs Horsham calling for me?'

'It's all right, Cally, it's my fault. I'll explain to Mrs Horsham,' said Bea. Cally, fourteen and lacking in experience, was – to be blunt about it – the cheapest maid Mama could find. After all these months, she still looked hopelessly undernourished as she hauled buckets of coal and water half her size up and down the narrow stairs, mortified at Bea's early attempts to help. She was a good plain cook, and over the past weeks she had allowed Bea to help her in the kitchen, and even begun to learn Mama's favourite dishes. But when Mrs Horsham appeared to cook for special events, Cally was reduced once more to the position of scullery maid.

'Thank you, Miss,' murmured Cally. She looked down at Ada, who was still fast asleep. 'I'm to help you to dress first.'

'Come on then,' said Bea, her chilled hands fumbling over her buttons. 'I need to be as fast as I can.'

'Miss, you're soaked through!' Cally clucked disapprovingly, like a woman three times her age. 'Here, I'll be faster.' She undid the sodden jacket and blouse, allowing them to drop in a heap on the floor. 'Bloody hell!'

Ada stirred slightly, muttering in her sleep.

'Sorry, Miss.' Cally's voice sank to a whisper. 'But you're black and blue.'

'Am I?' Bea peered at her arms. Even by lamplight there was no hiding the huge bruises on both forearms, with a smaller selection – at least one looking like the grip of a large hand – on her upper arms.

'Miss!' Cally looked scandalised, and slightly scared. The aunt who had accompanied her to the interview with Mama had insisted that Cally should be a live-in maid. Bea never questioned why that had been very much more important than the disgracefully low wages Mama was offering. Seeing the look on the maid's sharp little face, an inkling of understanding began to dawn. As if reading her thoughts, Cally's eyes slid away towards the floor.

'It's all right,' said Bea. 'I'm not really hurt. I was in a meeting that was broken up by the police and I was pushed about a bit, that's all. I hit a policeman over the head with an umbrella,' she added in a whisper.

Cally's eyes grew round. 'You never!'

'Only you must never tell anyone.'

'No, Miss.' Cally leant forward. 'Are you a suffragette, then, Miss?' she asked in a conspiratorial whisper.

'I'm not sure. I don't think so.' Bea considered this. 'It wasn't a suffragette meeting, so I'm not sure I've even ever met one.'

Cally breathed a sigh of relief. 'Only my Aunt Mary says they make bombs and blow things up and smash windows and want to bring down the government in any way they can and are terribly dangerous, and are a lot of old spinsters who can't bear to see anyone else happy.' Her headlong rush came to an abrupt halt. 'That is, I mean… '

Bea giggled. 'I'm not an *old* spinster yet, Cally. I didn't see anyone who wanted to make bombs, and from what I've read in the newspapers, Mrs Pankhurst and her daughters are terribly glamorous.'

'Oh.' Cally sounded unconvinced.

Bea smiled reassuringly at her. 'It was only an accident that I found myself there in the first place. Now I'd better get dressed before Mama and Mrs Horsham start shouting.'

At least Bea's underclothes were relatively dry, and there was no time to change into the bone-crushing corset Mama had selected for her. Cally brushed her damp hair, pinning it behind her head, and fastened her into the blue silk gown, as quietly as she could, so as not to wake Ada.

'There.' Bea viewed herself critically in the mirror. The blue dress didn't quite have the same effect over the more relaxed curves of her everyday corset. She was quite certain she didn't look the lady Mama envisaged she should be, but at least she didn't look like a harridan who had just escaped arrest for attacking a policeman and being spat at by a mad drunk. Heaven knows what Jonathan would think of that, if he ever found out. 'Let's hope that's good enough for Cousin Jonathan,' she said.

'The pearls!' Cally's hands flew to her mouth. 'Your mama was very particular about the pearls. She'll kill me if I forget them.' She shot off across the landing into Mrs Tressillion's bedroom.

Bea risked crushing the silk and perched gingerly on the bed. Ada lay under one of Mama's paisley shawls, brought all the way from India for her wedding, so many years ago. She was curled up, one hand beneath her rosy cheek, the picture of innocence. Bea shuddered, remembering Lillian and the wretched families in her shelter. Tonight, with Cousin Jonathan in the drawing room, and Mama so anxious to please him at any cost, the shelter did not feel so far away. Jonathan had not hesitated in selling Tressillion: what was there to stop him selling this house, too?

'And it's my fault,' she murmured. She was the one who had written to Leo, begging him to come home to reason with Papa, whose obsession with finding riches in the mine threatened to consume them all. Mama had never hidden that Leo was her favourite child. He wasn't like Oliver and Simon, who had always followed Papa's lead in everything. Leo had listened, had treated Mama and her woes seriously. He had been the one who had understood.

If only. Bea adjusted the shawl, careful not to disturb her little sister. If only she had never sent that letter. If only Leo had never come home. It wouldn't have changed what had happened, and maybe Tressillion would still have had to be sold, but at least Leo would never have left them destitute. At least he would have worked until his last breath to keep them together. Between them, they could have kept Mama and Ada safe, and given Ada – who at eleven still treated their stay in the London house as an extended holiday, with their old life all there to return to once the summer came – a chance to build a life, and one day have a family of her own.

'Here they are, Miss.' Cally returned with the precious pearls. She placed them round Bea's neck, adjusting the intricate clasp at the back. Grandmama had claimed they had belonged to an Indian princess and were worth a small fortune. Leo had remarked that Grandpappa, who was full of grand stories, had most probably found them in the local pawnshop, along with a dozen other family jewels he claimed to have brought back from Africa and China. Bea felt their coolness settle round her neck.

'Thank you,' she whispered to Cally. 'I'll come with you to explain to Mrs Horsham before I join Mama.' With a last glimpse at the still-sleeping Ada, she followed the maid downstairs.

* * *

She wasn't sure what she expected. She hadn't seen Jon since they were small children, and he had been travelling abroad, unable to be contacted in time to attend the funeral for her father and brothers. She had imagined a large man wearing his wealth, and the family dignity, on his expensive suit and bristling moustache. He did indeed tower over her, as he stood up at her entrance, but he was slightly built and wiry, his suit sitting awkwardly as if made for a larger man, his face (with no moustache or beard) deeply tanned. His embarrassment, she was relieved to see, was as deep as her own. She warmed to him.

'I hope you are well,' he muttered.

'Yes, thank you.' There was a touch of Papa in his face. The same heavy brows, the same dark eyes. Jon was a Tressillion all right.

'I can't tell you how sorry I am for your loss.'

'Thank you,' she replied mechanically, daring a slightly longer scrutiny. They might only have this evening together before she would need to make the most momentous decision of her life. One that, either way, would set the future in stone for Mama and Ada, as well as herself. The shadow of Papa had gone. His face had more mobility, his lips formed a sensuous line. Unexpectedly, Bea found herself wavering. Maybe she was being foolish, setting her heart against marrying a stranger. There were far worse fates. After all, she didn't hate him on sight.

'Tressillion is sold,' said Mama, as if to get the fact over with as quickly as possible.

Bea sat down next to her mother, carefully adjusting her dress. So it was settled. She would never see her childhood home again. Not that she had for months, but it had always been there, a part of them all, the possibility of returning. Now the door was shut.

She realised Jonathan was watching her. 'You do understand I had no choice, Beatrice? I've always been very fond of Tressillion. Under any other circumstances I would have fought to keep it. I would have loved to have made it my home. But as things stand…'

'Of course,' murmured Bea.

'Strangely enough, a woman is the purchaser,' said Jon. 'Roach was certain she would haggle, but in the end she didn't argue one penny over the price.'

'Good,' said Bea, to cover her mother's uneasy shifting in her chair at such a vulgar turn to the conversation.

'Yes, it is. She moved in within days and is already transforming the place, so Roach informs me.' He tactfully lowered his voice. 'I'm afraid, even so, once the debts have been paid…'

'Yes. Yes of course. And this house?'

'It's safe. For the moment at least. I'll do my best, Bea. I do sympathise with your predicament. Believe me, the last thing I ever wanted was to inherit. And especially not under such circumstances. I'm afraid it was always going to be impossible to keep the Tressillion estate.'

'I understand that.'

'I will do my best for you all, whatever the circumstances.'

'Thank you.' She smiled at him. They were lucky. Jon had proved himself to be a decent man. He could have chosen to have no obligations towards them, particularly since it was only trouble he had inherited, rather than the fortune he might once have expected.

Mama had not reacted well to their abrupt departure from ease and status. It was all she had ever known. Her childhood had been spent as the indulged niece of Lady Stockton of Belleview Court, full of grand dinners in the company of writers and politicians. Tressillion had been her queendom, with a house in London, however modest, to compensate for its seclusion. She was finding it difficult enough to adjust to a single maid. Heaven knew how she would react to any further reduction.

Bea swallowed. Sudden panic took her breath away. Always before, there had been a choice, or at least an illusion of a choice. She'd believed she could throw over expectations, fall in love with a paint-besmeared artist, or an exiled Russian prince, shake off her destiny and disappear into the sunset. But over the past months, her horizons had narrowed.

Is this all my life is going to be? she asked herself. Mama went in to dinner as if she had half of London society following her into a room of glittering chandeliers, with an ice sculpture gracing the centre of the table, instead of a dining room that would have found a party of six an impossible squeeze. It could be worse, she reminded herself. She could be one of the women crouched in Lillian's centre, filthy and half-starved. She could be Cally, facing a lifetime of cleaning grates until she grew too old to work, if she did not accept the first man to ask her, and risk finding herself in an even worse kind of servitude.

The loss of Tressillion and the move to London had given her this new curiosity, this burning sense of a world out there, full of endless possibilities. Where – far too shocking to whisper – there were more exciting things than love and the security of a husband, and a home and a life settled in its course forever.

'Oh, Beatrice, how exciting. How lovely.' The conversation had moved on, and she hadn't heard a word. What had her mother just agreed to? 'Of course she'll accept, Jon. That is so kind of you. Poor Bea hasn't had much fun since we came to London, this will be just the thing.'

It was only a party, not a wedding, signed sealed and the date delivered. Bea began to breathe again. 'I'm not sure, Mama. I know you don't like to be here on your own.'

'Nonsense, my dear. You know I would never stand in your way.' Her mother was looking more animated than she had for months. She was holding Jon's hand as if afraid to let go. 'And such interesting people, too. I know Mr Shaw's plays are terribly shocking, and he's a Fabian and a vegetarian, but he is terribly famous.'

Bea couldn't quite squash a smile. Across the dinner table, Jon met her eyes and grinned. Maybe she was being a fool. Maybe marriage to Jon would open up a world, instead of closing it down. A world of interesting people, of society and of travel. There was so much she wanted to do, so much she wanted to see. She had never been to Italy, or crossed the ocean in a liner to the splendours of New York. As a married woman, with Mama and Ada supported and no longer her sole responsibility, there would be nothing to stop her working as a volunteer journalist for a magazine run by a charity. Perhaps even the magazine Olwen printed for the White Camellia.

But it wouldn't be the same as being paid for her work, came the treacherous thought, as knowing it was good enough for someone to pay for it. She'd feel a fraud. And they'd probably see me as the silly wife of a rich man, interested only in hats. I don't know anything. I've never done anything. I've no skills. No interests. No passions. So they'd be right.

Mama's eyes were fixed on her.

'I would love to go, thank you,' Bea said.

'Good.' Jon was smiling, with an irrepressible pleasure written all over his face.

Perhaps he feels he can truly love me, after all, she thought. She was supposed to feel ecstatic at the possibility. Everyone told her so. Her friends in Cornwall had always envied her lack of anxiety at finding a husband. The few young women in their London circle of friends were either engaged or following a wild social round in an attempt to be.

But it was no good. Bea took her seat opposite Jon with a sense of gloom. However much she tried to convince herself, she just couldn't make her heart sing.

Chapter Ten

Light poured from every room of Lady Hanbury's house in Richmond as Bea stepped down from Jon's Rover and was swept inside. Mama had spent the last few weeks happily ensuring her daughter would make the best impression. She had remodelled two of her own ball gowns, making them into one. Bea felt squashed and unwilling to move her arms in case she tore anything, but at least she didn't look too much like a country bumpkin.

There was a faintly bohemian air to the gathering, which made Bea glad Mama had opted for folds of peach-coloured silk, set off by a covering of paler lace. It was more flowing than formal, even resisting the rib-crushing corset.

Jon squeezed her arm. 'You're not nervous, are you, Beatrice?'

'No, not at all.'

'Good. You look lovely.' He led her between groups of men and women discussing last night's performance of *King Lear* and a lecture given at the British Museum a few days ago. They all sounded frighteningly certain of their own opinions. Bea hoped there would be some dancing to lighten the evening. Not that she particularly wished to reveal her own lack of grace, from a childhood spent racing along cliffs rather than mincing through dancing lessons.

'No, I still don't hold with violent action.' Bea paused at the familiar voice. 'I can understand it, after the betrayal of '84, but I still don't consider it an answer... ' The speaker came to a halt. Lillian appeared more striking than ever, in a long, medieval-styled gown of rich lilac, her dark red hair worn loose, tumbling down her back as if she had stepped straight out of a pre-Raphaelite painting. Her gaze was cool, but not openly hostile. 'Good evening, Miss Tressillion. I heard you might be here tonight.'

'Hello.' Bea smiled shyly at the group clustered around. She glimpsed Harri, deep in conversation with a group of men at the outer reaches of Lillian's circle. He caught her eye and nodded briefly.

'You know Miss Finch?' Jon sounded faintly put out as they moved away.

'Not really. We met only briefly after a talk I attended. I never thought she might be here.'

'She's quite a catch for a hostess. Even one like Lady Hanbury.'

'Really?' Bea opened her mouth to wonder why a woman who worked amongst the filthiest and the poorest should be so much in demand, then thought better of it.

'Oh yes, she's really rather well-known, you know,' said Jon. 'She was quite a beauty in her day.'

'Her day?' Bea blinked at him. Lillian didn't appear to be much older than herself. Could her own day be over so soon?

'Yes. She could have married anybody. Despite her, ah, background and somewhat radical views. They say the Prince of Wales was sniffing around at one point…' He remembered himself and coughed. 'Now, of course, she has thrown herself into all kinds of quixotic schemes.'

'Schemes?'

'With the poor. The down and outs. The very worst kind of men and women.'

Bea frowned at him. 'Are they always the worst kind? Might they not be simply unfortunate?'

He smiled. 'That's what's always so refreshing about you, Bea. You haven't been spoil by the world.'

'I wish I'd had the chance,' retorted Bea, before she could stop herself.

Laughter erupted around her. Not hostile, she realised after a moment. One of the women next to Lillian clapped.

'Well said, Miss Tressillion,' called Harri.

'So you don't believe a woman should gain any experience, Mr Tressillion?' said Lillian, whose attention had been caught by their raised voices. There was an edge of danger to her tone, and glitter in her eyes. Even Jon, Beatrice was relieved to see, could spot a woman spoiling for a fight.

'Naturally, Miss Finch, I believe in women gaining experience. Along with education. And the vote,' he replied. 'Any man of any decency would. The government of '84 were cowardly to give the men the vote and not the women. I utterly disagree with them. But the world can be a terrible place. You must understand my desire to protect what is of importance to me.'

'Of course,' smiled Lillian. She turned towards Bea. 'But maybe it is better to arm those we love, than keep them in a state of childlike dependency.'

'This from a woman who doesn't agree with direct action,' put in Harri.

'Rubbish. Don't wilfully misunderstand me, Mr Lewis,' she returned. 'I'm sure you wouldn't wish to keep your sister in a state of ignorance.'

He gave a low chuckle. 'My dear Miss Finch, you know I wouldn't dare. Never argue with anyone who can already wield a scalpel with the best of them, and who is, at this very moment, acquiring a detailed knowledge of poisons.'

Laughter burst out again. Lillian smiled and returned to her previous conversation. Bea began to relax. Those around her were not such fearsome creatures, after all. She recognised several from the White Camellia. One or two nodded and smiled at her, as if remembering her in return.

'Have you lived in London long, Miss Tressillion?' asked an older woman, whose face was vaguely familiar, as conversations started up once more.

'Not very,' replied Bea. 'I'm just finding my way around.'

The woman nodded. 'There are so many interesting places to see. And so many interesting talks. Some,' she added dryly, 'more interesting than others. Or at least more eventful. And with the weather so changeable, it's always wise to bring an umbrella.'

Bea grinned. Of course! The last time she had seen her, the woman had been swapping blows and insults with a policeman, hat gone, white hair flying. 'Thank you, I'll remember that,' she replied demurely.

'Excuse me a moment…' Jon had clearly grown bored now Lillian was no longer a part of the conversation. He slipped away to join a smaller group next to the conservatory. Far from being offended, Bea felt her body ease as he went out of earshot. The conversation around her shifted, breaking into smaller groups.

'Not a gentleman with a love of umbrellas, then?' remarked the older woman.

'No,' replied Bea. 'My cousin doesn't know anything about the White Camellia, or the meeting. It's probably best if he doesn't.'

'Very wise. I always keep my husband in careful ignorance of my activities. It's better for both our peace of minds, we find.' She held out a hand. 'Mrs Timms. I'm pleased to meet you, Miss Tressillion. I thought I knew you from the suffrage meeting. You helped to get Gwen away, I believe.'

'Yes.'

'Good for you. The police were disgraceful. That meeting was perfectly peaceful, it's pure intimidation. They think a few beatings and the threat of prison will silence us. Well, it won't. Injustice can't just be left to breed.' Her eyes sharpened. 'Olwen mentioned you had an ambition to be a journalist.'

'If I can find a way.' Bea glanced over at Jon, who was now

deep in conversation with a slightly-built young woman whose pale gold hair was caught into a bun at the nape of her neck, and fixed with a jewelled comb in the form of a peacock.

Mrs Timms placed a business card in her hand. 'If you are serious about it, go and see Mrs Anselm. You'll find her address and her telephone number on here. You showed yourself to have considerable spirit, that night of the meeting. We could do with more intelligent, passionate young women like you in the suffrage movement. If you really wish to find a post, I'm certain Mrs Anselm will consider you, or at least point you towards other possibilities.'

'Thank you,' said Bea, tucking the card carefully inside the bodice of her dress.

Over the next twenty minutes or so, she was drawn into more conversations, and gradually found her feet, losing any shyness or awkwardness, and without missing Jon's presence at all. When she finally thought to check that he was not offended at being ignored, she saw him still in the same place, still talking with the girl with pale hair. She turned to the middle-aged woman who had just arrived.

'Do you know the young woman over there, the striking looking one?'

The woman peered. 'Oh, you must mean Cassie Lane. Such a lovely girl.'

'Yes. She's very beautiful.'

'He won't marry her, of course.'

Bea started. 'I beg your pardon?'

'The young man with her. He won't marry her. You can see from his face that he is smitten, and whenever I've seen him he's never left her side. But he has a family and obligations. He will never marry an actress, even one with fame and money.'

'But he's a man. He can earn money and do what he likes.'

'No-one can ever do exactly as they wish, my dear. He has

expectations from his family, or so I've heard. Unless he relinquishes his obligations, and lives with the knowledge of the hurt he has caused.'

'I suppose.' The air in the room had become oppressive. And yes, to her shame, she was afraid at the thought of what might happen to her, and Mama, if Jon should choose to follow his heart. Self-doubt crept back, this time touched with panic. It went without saying that women were not supposed to earn money, and those who did must expect to earn a pittance, because they, unlike a man, had no family to support. She could never earn enough to pay for their food and coal, let alone the upkeep of the house.

Jon would give them all security, but he would never love her. She watched his face, gentler and more animated than she had seen it before. Less pompous, she admitted to herself, with a wince. Miss Lane was smiling, a slightly wary smile, as if holding herself back from heartache. She wasn't beautiful in a conventional way – she had large features, huge eyes, and a figure that appeared almost gawky.

Cassie Lane. Of course. No wonder she was familiar. She'd seen that face come alight for the camera. She'd read the rags to riches story: 'The new Mary Pickford' the papers called her. Strong, but fragile. Confident, yet with a slight edge of anxiety. Miss Lane was one of those rare women who had made a fortune for herself, through looks and talent and a determination that appeared nowhere in her delicate features.

Bea could not breathe. Murmuring an excuse, she pushed her way through the crowds and out into a small garden leading down to the river.

'Are you all right?'

She turned as Harri caught up with her. 'Of course.' She frowned at him in the gloom. He had ignored her all evening. Well, she wasn't going to make small talk now.

A couple pushed passed them, giggling, heading for the darkness beyond the lamps set on either side of a gravel path.

'If you are sure. I don't want to interfere.'

'Then don't.'

'Something seemed to distress you.'

'I'm not distressed,' she retorted. 'I just needed some fresh air.'

'Of course. It can get a bit overwhelming in there.'

'Yes.' She wished he would go away and leave her alone, but instead he fell in step with her, following the path to the darkness of the river. They walked for a minute or two in silence.

'May I say something?' he asked at last.

'No.' She watched him in the flicker from the lamps. 'But I expect you will.'

'Just one word. Then I promise I won't trouble you.'

'I'm listening.'

He cleared his throat. 'Your fiancé…'

'He's not my fiancé,' she returned. Mortification shot through her from head to toe. Did everyone know? Had they all been laughing at her? Or maybe pitying Jon, being forced into marriage to please his family rather than find true love with the fascinating Miss Lane.

'I'm glad to hear it. That is,' he added with unflattering haste, 'the man's a fool and doesn't deserve you.'

'I doubt if he sees it that way.'

'I mean it.' He stopped and faced her. 'Bea, I saw you. You were like a knight in shining armour when you swung that umbrella at the Institute. And the look on your face – you were terrifying and quite magnificent. You were born to be Sir Lancelot, not shut up in some tower like the Lady of Shalott, seeing the world only through the reflection in a mirror.' She could hear a smile creep into his voice. 'Although you might not swap your skirts for steel, if you don't mind. I rather like the way you dress: severe but sensual. And tonight the severity has almost gone.'

In the cool of the air, her cheeks were burning. 'My family wouldn't agree with you. About Sir Lancelot, I mean.' Definitely not about the sensual. She tried to make out his expression. Was he mocking her?

'You are not your family, Bea.'

'In the eyes of the world I am.'

'Are you going to allow the world to define you? If I'd done that, I'd have followed my father down the mines until I was too broken to work any more. I'd have been old and bent by now, my back riddled with arthritis. Or dead, smothered in the earth. There are ways.' He grasped her hands, holding them tight. 'I worked all day and spent my evenings at the Working Men's Institute to pass my examinations. I couldn't have done it without help, but I did it. Your family might not help you, but when you helped Gwen, you made friends that night in the White Camellia. Friends who will help you.'

'I'm not sure I'm that enterprising.' Despair gripped her. 'And I can't just abandon my mother and sister, not after all the harm I've caused.'

'Rubbish.' He pulled her closer. 'Bea, you are not responsible for your family's misfortunes. You father and brothers were free men, who made their own decisions. And surely your mother isn't entirely helpless. She could marry again.'

'I'm not sure…'

'Bea, people marry for many reasons. In my work I've come to see that companionship and necessity can be kinder relationships than those forged purely in the heat of passion, without any knowledge of the creature you are tying yourself to for life.' He pulled her closer. 'If I was a free man…'

Bea started. 'Shhh.'

She pulled away. Footsteps were crunching along the gravel.

'I love my life here in London, but there are so many more opportunities in America,' came a woman's voice, wistfully.

'Then you must go where your heart takes you,' replied her companion.

'It's Jon.' Bea dragged Harri into the shrubbery, as deep as she could go, until her back came up against the cold hard bricks of the garden wall.

'And if my heart is torn?' Miss Lane said. The footsteps came to a halt outside their hiding place.

'Then it must be mended,' replied Jon softly.

'A cheap line if ever I heard one,' whispered Harri, leaning closer to Bea in the darkness, his mouth gently brushing her ear. 'And believe me, in my line of work, I've heard plenty.'

She fought down a giggle. His breath was warm on her face. He was so close, the weight of his body pressed her against the stones, sending the most delicious, if disgraceful, sensations racing through her. Maybe his description of her just now as severe, but sensual, had merely meant that he thought her to be not quite respectable. She didn't want to be respectable ever again.

'No, I must be practical, Jon,' Miss Lane was replying. 'And so must you. I know you have obligations to heal the rift in your family and to restore its good name. I have no wish to be viewed by them as the one standing in their way.'

'Cassie, you must know my feelings for you…'

'But can I trust you with my life?' said Cassie, her voice sharpening. 'You only risk the disappointment of your family. I could lose everything.'

'I'd risk anything for you.'

'Only because you'll never have to.' Miss Lane's crunching steps headed back towards the house. 'Words are easy. It's women who have to live with the reality. You might break my heart, Jon, but at least I can control my own destiny.'

Bea stayed very still, as Jon raced after the retreating Miss Lane, his voice low and soft as silk, Cassie short and sharp, having none of it.

'Wise woman,' whispered Harri, against Bea's lips.

'Very,' she replied, her breath coming short and fast, any wisdom she had ever possessed flung carelessly over the wall behind her, to land Heaven knows where, as she met his kiss.

'Bea…' he said, as he released her at last, his mouth travelling down her neck towards the lace of her dress.

'No,' she exclaimed, pushing him away. Her legs were shaking as she ducked between branches, getting back to the path before she changed her mind.

'Don't leave, Bea. I'm sorry, I'd no intention of offending you.' He stepped out onto the path behind her, sounding embarrassed.

Bea rounded on him. 'Did I seem offended?'

'No,' he admitted, the smile back in his voice.

'Well, then.'

He cleared his throat awkwardly. 'Bea, I can't…'

She raised her chin. No, of course he couldn't. 'I wouldn't want you to.'

Chatter and laughter were rapidly approaching them from the river. There was nothing more to say. They walked back to the house in silence.

'Wait.' As they reached the terrace, he smoothed her hair, brushing away the leaves.

'You seem very practiced at this,' she said, not quite able to keep the hurt from her voice.

'I have a sister, remember. I'm well trained.'

'Really.'

'Then don't believe me,' he said, irritated. His hand dropped and he stepped away from her. 'Lillian.'

Bea turned.

Lillian stood in the doorway, the light from the room inside turning her hair into a halo of fire.

'Miss Tressillion had a slight disagreement with a rhododendron.' Harri's voice was smooth. He was clearly lying about not being practiced at this, thought Bea, with an overwhelming desire to kick his shin as black and blue as her pride. 'It really is very dark out here.'

'So I see,' Lillian replied. There was a hard edge to her voice. She glanced briefly in Bea's direction, then away again, as if she could not bear her presence.

Well, she didn't care what they thought, either of them. The business card lay cool against her skin inside her dress. Miss Lane was right: at least she was still in control of her own destiny. With head held high, Bea marched back inside the ballroom, into the swirl of music and lights and animated conversation all around her.

How could she ever have thought she could settle to being the pre-ordained wife of a man she could never love? Well, now she had nothing to lose. She was on her own and she was about to take any chance she could get.

Chapter Eleven

Spring was in the air. Sybil could feel it as she cleared the flowerbeds and weeded the paths in Tressillion's gardens, while Emily cleaned the kitchens and pantry, and made the hallway spick and span, before turning her attention to the drawing rooms and the library.

Sybil drank in the birdsong, and the edge of sweetness to the chill air, as the primroses bloomed beneath the apple trees and clumps of snowdrops gathered in the most unexpected places. The earth was still cold, but she could make out life returning, with the first buds and shoots, and the catkins defying the storms blowing in from the sea. She peered at bushes and small clumps of unknown foliage, feeling the excitement of beauty returning to surprise her. To her chagrin, she had very little knowledge of ornamental plants, while Emily had even less.

'Well, even I can recognise roses,' admitted Sybil, as the two of them stood in the first warm day of sunshine, puzzling over the once carefully laid-out beds. 'But what kind, and what to do with them, I have no idea. I am going to have to find a book of instruction.'

'Mam says the rose garden was set out in all different colours,' offered Emily. 'And those are climbing roses along the wall, a mixture of pink and white. Mam said you could smell them all through the house in summer. Old Mrs Tressillion loved roses,' she added. 'She pruned them herself, after Mr Tressillion refused to pay the gardeners any more. Mam said he forbade her, but the old lady still went out and looked after them whenever he went to the mine.'

'Was she happy?'

Emily blinked at the abrupt question. 'Miss?'

'Mr Tressillion's mother. Was she happy?'

'It's a grand house,' said Emily, carefully, 'made for every comfort…' She caught Sybil's expression and came to a halt. 'No, Miss Ravensdale, I don't think she was. She didn't want to leave her life in London, you see, but Mr Tressillion owned everything, even the house she lived in, and everything in it. He wanted to sell the house, so he made her move here. And he insisted she lived in that room, not any other, when he knew how much it would hurt them all, taking away the last traces…' She trailed off, turning her attention back to the roses.

'She must have had some money of her own,' said Sybil, as if she had not heard the final sentence, let alone understood it. The last traces of Leo, that was what Emily meant. The final excuse for his father to destroy any reminder that Leo had ever slept in that room, or even ever existed. Spiteful and controlling to the end. 'I'd have found a good lawyer, sold my furs and my jewellery first, so I could rent a room, however poor, rather than be forced out of the place where I felt at home.'

'I don't think she did have anything, or at least not enough,' replied Emily. 'And Mam said she was too ill, and hadn't the heart to fight him, not her own son, and she was too proud to ask for help.' She bit her lip. 'Mrs Tressillion was kind to me, when I came with Mam. When I was little, I couldn't believe anyone who didn't have to worry about being warm and having enough food to eat could be sad.' She glanced up at the window, open, as it always was, with the branches of the cherry tree brushing its panes. 'Maybe I can understand it a bit more now.'

'So can I,' said Sybil, turning away to attack the dandelions with a vengeance.

Emily remembered the mission that had brought her outside. 'And the furniture in the drawing rooms, Miss?'

'Keep it.' Sybil untangled a thorny tea rose branch from her skirts. 'Unless there's sign of woodworm. We can make a bonfire if the rain holds off. Those chairs that have rotted in the conservatory can go, for a start. I'm not putting anything else in there until that roof has been mended.'

'Yes, Miss,' said Emily, sounding dubious. 'There are families in the village…'

'Absolutely not,' declared Sybil. 'There will be plenty of serviceable bits of furniture we won't be needing, but I'm not sending anything broken or half rotted. That's worse than nothing. I'd rather buy new and pretend they came from the house than palm anyone off in such a disgraceful manner.'

And so that evening the moth- (if not mouse-) eaten chairs and sofa and the dark blue velvet *chaise longue*, with its horsehair stuffing strewn half across the floor, were ceremoniously burnt in a bonfire, with the broken chairs from the dining room and every last piece of wood that had rotted away from the rain pouring in through the gaps in the conservatory roof.

Sybil manhandled the largest, and not-quite-at-the-end-of-its-life, armchair, which had clearly belonged to the master of the house, into the centre of the flames, and watched the sparks fly up into the chill night air, dancing into the crest of the old moon, a faint smile of satisfaction creasing her cheeks.

'Mr Tressillion's chair might have done for the servants' rooms,' protested Emily, returning with a small table that had almost completely disintegrated.

'No servant should have to do with cast offs,' said Sybil. 'Not when they give their lives to make the family comfortable. If you are doing backbreaking work, that's the least an employer can give you. No-one will ever sleep in an unsuitable bed or sit in a broken-down chair in this house.'

'Yes, Miss.'

Sybil grinned at the hint of disapproval, not quite hidden, in

Emily's voice. Emily could still not quite hide her astonishment that, with so many grand chambers at her disposal, her mistress slept in a small room at one side of the library, in a narrow canvas bed that looked as if it had been used by an army on manoeuvres. It was the warmest place, Sybil told herself, with the most efficient fire in the house.

'I think we should start on the attics tomorrow,' she announced, flinging the last of the rotting wood into the flames.

Emily blinked. 'Not the bedrooms, Miss?'

'They can wait.' She met Emily's frown in the firelight. 'I haven't yet decided how to arrange them to the best advantage. There's no point in touching them until I've made a decision. I don't want to throw out anything we might want to keep.'

'No, Miss,' said Emily.

'It's getting late.' She saw Emily's face was drawn with exhaustion. 'I'll drive you home.'

'There's no need, Miss. I can walk.'

'Nonsense. I can't be known to send you off across the country on your own at this time of night. I'd have pitchforks at my gates.'

'I don't think you would,' returned Emily, grinning, but she didn't protest any further, fetching her coat from the house with weary steps.

It was almost dark when Sybil deposited Emily outside the little cottage on the outskirts of the village, knowing better than to embarrass her, and her family, by appearing unannounced at their door. A single lamp burned in the kitchen, but despite the evening chill no smoke spiralled into the air from the chimney.

Sybil watched Emily disappear through the ill-fitting door. She had an uneasy feeling that, despite her long day, her maid's work was not yet done. Sybil had been the oldest daughter herself, and knew the expectations to help with the endless cooking and cleaning and minding the little ones, however hard her own day had been.

As she watched, another figure rounded the corner and knocked on the door. There was something familiar about him. She peered into the darkness, but the door opened and the visitor vanished. The light in the window strengthened, as if a lamp had been lit, to chase away the cold. As she turned the Chevrolet around, she heard a burst of laughter, followed by the clamour of exited children's voices. Sybil sped away, back to the silence of Tressillion.

She was glad to return. It was strange how quickly a place, even one as empty and broken as this house, could feel like home. She checked the bonfire had died down to glowing embers that wouldn't set anything else alight, even if the wind got up in the night, and, wrapping her coat around her, walked to the darkened house, deep in thought. Halfway across the lawns, the clouds cleared, setting a full moon to sail free, bathing the house and garden in a pale cold light.

A glint from the first floor caught her eye. The window next to the cherry tree was still open, as it always was during the day, the nearest branch resting against the windowsill. There was a crackling in the undergrowth behind her. Sybil started, swinging round, one hand reaching for the heavy flashlight in her pocket.

She would be found. She'd known that, the moment she had set foot back on English soil. Here, of all places, she would be found. And when she was…

Sybil breathed deep as a fox emerged from behind the thicket of rhododendron, slinking across the lawns, unaware of her, as it headed for the fields.

'I've been a fool,' she muttered, hurrying inside. She lit the lamp in the hallway, and made her way up to the first floor to close the errant window. In her weariness, Emily had forgotten to close the bedroom doors. As Sybil passed, shafts of uncertain moonlight revealed each one, untouched, a pale film of dust lying across the floorboards, dustsheets crouched like mourners at their own funeral, waiting to stir into life again.

Sybil pulled her coat even closer, holding the lamp up high to send as much light as she could into each corner. The kitchens and the downstairs rooms – even the servants' quarters under the eaves – were public places, too full of comings and goings to trap the thoughts of those who had gone. The bedrooms, with their private memories, held the emotions of all those who had retreated there in solitude, to be alone with their thoughts.

The day would soon come, of course, when she would have to face them. The rooms couldn't just be left untouched forever, as if Miss Haversham had come to stay. But she was not ready yet to disturb the dusty memories. She closed each door as she passed, until she came to the room overlooking the sea.

In this room, too, nothing had been touched. From the open window came the distant sound of waves surging against rock. The single armchair, the only nod towards comfort, was still facing the window. Sybil placed the lamp on the dressing table, shivering slightly. It was an invalid's chair, that spoke of hours gazing out into a world already far away, with little purpose or joy left, just the long, slow wait for a final release.

She removed the cover and sat down, gazing through an invalid's eyes. She could smell the outside world, hear the sounds of night creatures, and catch a glimpse of the far cliffs and the ever-changing swell of the sea. Fine ends of branches pushed through the open window. Had she known, old Mrs Tressillion? Sybil hunched, frowning, attempting to glean the answer from the air. Had Leo told her of his secret escape route, the only freedom in a house ruled by a man obsessed? A man slowly, inexorably, losing his mind?

Had she waited, with her dreams of freedom, and the warmth and companionship of the White Camellia, knowing that Leo would never leave her like this? That warm-eyed, gentle Leo, with his passionate sense of justice and desire to right every wrong, would never allow any human being to have their joy in life snuffed out, merely for spite. Maybe she had sat here, hoping that some way would be found to reach him, to beg him to come home.

Sybil sat there motionless, all through that moon-streaked night, as her lamp burned down and chill darkness settled around her, warmed only by her own deep longing. Waiting in the dark.

Chapter Twelve

'Attics,' announced Sybil, as Emily arrived the next morning, bleary-eyed and weary, her feet damp with dew.

'Yes, Miss.'

Sybil led the way to the bedrooms, and then up a smaller staircase to the two small rooms under the eaves, each with a bed and an ancient armchair.

'Well, I've seen worse.' Sybil opened the window in the nearest room, which had a tiny balcony overlooking the garden, with a clear view of the sea. 'The chimney has been cleaned, no reason why you shouldn't have a good fire up here. It would save you traipsing to and fro from the village.'

'You mean, live in?' said Emily, with an unflattering lack of enthusiasm.

'It makes sense,' said Sybil. 'I wouldn't forbid you to see your family.' She cleared her throat. 'I take it home is overcrowded, and you are expected to still do your share of chores as well as bringing in a wage?'

Emily nodded, blushing furiously.

'There's nothing to be ashamed of. I know they don't mean to harm your chances, and desperation can make even a mother's love blind. But you're a bright girl. There are classes starting at the lending library in a few weeks' time, and you'll need time and space to study, if you are prepared to take up my offer. Unless you fancy being in service all your life?'

'Definitely not!' said Emily, mortification vanishing. She inspected the little room closely. 'This would be mine? Just me?'

'Of course.' A spark of mischief made Sybil smile. 'Until I hire my three butlers and six ladies' maids, then it might get a bit crowded.'

Emily giggled. 'So you are staying, Miss?'

'So it would seem. Well? What do you say? And don't you dare put your family first. I can't bear female self-sacrifice. You are the one who's got to live your life, and being a disappointed drudge won't help anyone.'

Emily took a deep breath. 'Yes,' she said, as if getting it out before her conscience had time to strike.

'Good for you. And don't worry about your mother, you are supporting them enough as it is, they'll find a way. And don't you dare feel guilty about your younger sisters being left to deal with the bedpans, either. Consider that you are giving them an example, and their time will come.'

'Yes, Miss,' said Emily, sounding awed at such daring. She inspected the room, her eyes losing their exhaustion. 'I'd better get to cleaning, then.'

'Good,' smiled Sybil. 'I'll speak to your mother. The sooner you are here the better, it seems to me.'

* * *

Sybil listened to Emily's footsteps clattering down into the depths of the house. She had only given a cursory glance into the attics before. The view was breathtaking. Like looking out onto her own private queendom, where nobody could touch her, and where her word ruled. But Tressillion's grounds did not stretch to the horizon on all sides. She could make out the spire of the church in Porth Levant. Further along the coast, farmhouses crouched within their fields and a fishing village clung to the cliffs in the far distance. Smoke caught her eye. On the promontory beyond the mine, just outside Tressillion land, a small shack stood, with the curve of a beach at its feet.

Sybil frowned. 'I thought you would have been taken by the sea, years ago.'

A rowing boat was sweeping round from the distant fishing village, heading for the beach. Sybil waited for it to land, watching it closely until tapping on the stairs announced Emily's return.

Sybil hastily stepped back inside, inspecting the metal frame of the bed with care. 'You'll need a chest of drawers,' she said, as Emily appeared, loaded down with a broom and a bucket, and a small mountain of rags. 'There must be one in the bedrooms you can use. And a desk. We'll find you a desk. Much more the thing than a dressing table. Far better to ornament the mind than the body. Like cooking, it gives you a great deal more to bargain with.'

'Yes, Miss.'

As Emily began wiping the dust from the metal bed-frame, Sybil removed the mattress, re-opening the window to allow both the room and the mattress to air. The boat had landed and been moored next to the cottage, but its occupant had not disappeared inside. He headed with long strides towards the river, turning onto the path towards the mine.

'So what's your game, then?'

'Miss?'

'Nothing. Nothing at all. Looks like that bed will come up nicely. I'll leave you to it, then.'

* * *

The sea air was chill, and the river was high, but by the time she reached the ruined mine buildings, Sybil's cheeks were flushed with rapid exercise. She sat down on one of the stones, wishing she'd thought to bring the remains of the pie from the pantry. She did not have to wait long. The sweat was only just cooling from her back when there was a stirring at the open entrance of the mine, followed by a familiar figure holding a lamp with an almost burnt-out candle inside.

'Did you lose something?' she demanded, icily, rising to her feet.

He wore the same fisherman's jumper as the last time she had seen him here, and if he felt discomforted at being discovered he didn't show it. 'Good morning, Miss Ravensdale. I was about to pay you a visit.'

'I bet you were,' she retorted. She placed her hands on her hips, feet planted squarely. 'Turn out your pockets.'

He blinked. 'I beg your pardon?'

'You heard me. This is my land. Everything found here is my property. It's that or the police.'

He grinned, a faintly mischievous smile that irritated her even further, but he emptied each pocket methodically, placing the contents on the rock next to him. There wasn't much. A half burnt piece of wax candle, a surprisingly pristine handkerchief and a few pennies.

'Is that all?' she said.

He met her eyes, his gaze a challenge. 'Well, I expect there are one or two more places I might have secreted contraband, but I wouldn't care to offend a lady, so it's up to you whether to take my word as a gentleman, or to check.'

Her severity wavered. The twitch at the edge of her mouth was instantly banished into a scowl. 'I still might call the police.'

'So you might.'

Sybil considered him. He didn't have the air of a villain. But then she had met more than her fair share in her time, and many of the worst had appeared like angels. Curiosity got the better of her. 'So what are you doing here? Or, more to the point, what are you doing in my goldmine?'

He replaced his belongings. 'Your goldmine. Since you are so worried I might have taken some of your gold, I assume you have an interest in it.'

'Maybe. Maybe not. I certainly don't want prospectors pitching up here, taking it for their own.'

'No, indeed. There's enough of that in the world, as it is.'

Sybil glanced at him, but he was carefully folding up his handkerchief as if it was his only interest.

'It seems like such an attractive idea,' she said, removing her hands from her hips, and thrusting them into her pockets. 'Having gold beneath your feet, and riches most could barely dream of.' She snorted. 'Except that's an illusion, of course, but a seductive one. One that would bring men from all over, sniffing around, dreaming of the wealth they might have, and that I might hold. Riches don't bring happiness, as far as I can see.'

He looked up. 'But they bring freedom. Or at least the prospect of freedom. From hunger, from being cast out without a roof over your head. From fear. I can understand the attraction.' He brushed himself down. 'And I've seen the evil it can bring myself.'

'Oh?'

'I told you the truth, that last time. My dad was a miner, as were my uncles. One of my brothers is still a miner, back in Pont-y-Derwen. That's what I should have been, too. Never enough, always the fear of an accident, while the owners live in ease. I'm one of those who got away and took myself over to the goldmines of Australia.'

'So you are rich, then?'

'Not rich. No. The gold had gone a long time ago. Like so many others, I was chasing a dream. I was lucky, I made enough to pay my way back, to buy my fishing boat and rent this cottage, and to live. I consider myself lucky just to have escaped with my life.'

'I see.'

'But I know about mining. I learnt to be an engineer while I was in Melbourne, waiting for my passage home.' He looked back at the mine. 'It might be possible to open it again. Restore the buildings. It's unusual to find a seam of gold in Cornwall. I understand it was a tin mine before the Tressillions struck gold, so there's no saying how productive a seam it might be, but it might be enough. They obviously thought so. I heard they had experts to assess the mine's potential.'

'Much good it did them.'

'So I understand. But from what I've heard in the village, they had no background in mining. And they were unlucky.'

'That seems to me like an argument for leaving well alone.'

'It would provide work that is sorely needed in the village.' He picked up a small haversack from its hiding place behind a broken brick wall. 'The winter nights are long, and the gold mines left me with a horror of drinking any money I might have away. I like to be doing things, so I've been drawing up some plans.'

'Plans.' The world went very still. Sybil clenched her fists and hastily unclenched them again. 'What kind of plans?' she asked, with as much indifference as she could muster.

'For the mine and the restoration of the workings. It would take investment, of course. But if the gold really is there, it might be worth it, if you are interested. If not… ' He shrugged. 'It kept me amused through a long, dark winter. And I might just use my plans to find another mine.'

Sybil watched him closely. 'I've heard it ruined the family.'

'And I've heard it was no-one thing that ruined the Tressillions.' He coughed. 'Sometimes failure in business is less mortifying to admit to the world?'

'Yes, that's true.' She frowned at him, trying to make him out. He wasn't local, by his own account. He couldn't know anything more of the mine than the rumours the village must have told him. There was nothing to fear from him, or his plans. Except what he might, however inadvertently, set in motion. 'So is your intention to propose some kind of partnership?'

He grinned. 'I wouldn't dare. Besides, I have nothing to offer but my skills and my experience of mining. If you would care to employ me… Well, then you take all the risk, and I lose nothing but my pride and my income at the end of an agreed period.'

Sybil's eyes narrowed. 'There's many who think because I'm a woman I'm a soft touch.'

'Well, whether I'm one of the many is a chance you'll have to take.'

'Mmm.' She considered this. She could turn and walk away, and tell him she was not interested. But the fear stirring inside her told her she could not leave it alone. She had to know. 'Where are these plans?'

'At the cottage. You are welcome to them.' He smiled. 'That's *my* risk in this, Miss Ravensdale: that you take my industry and experience and then employ someone else, leaving me with nothing.'

She bristled. 'So you don't trust me.'

'More than you appear to trust me. I'll give them to you now. It's only a few yards out of your way on the way back.'

'Very well.'

'Good.' He replaced the cover over the mine and secured it, then accompanied her as she took the path beside the river, following the little valley back to the sea.

Sybil strode alongside him, keeping pace for pace. 'Since you appear to know my name, perhaps it might be as well to know yours.'

'Of course. I beg your pardon, Miss Ravensdale. Madoc Lewis.'

'Lewis?' She stopped in her tracks.

'Emily is my niece. My brother Twm's child. He left Wales,

too. And yes, before you ask, I was the one who suggested she tried you for a post.' He met her eyes. 'Twm has been laid up with a broken leg, one that's not healing as it should. I've done my best, but there's been little enough to go round with just my fishing until he can work again. And yes, I expect I did have the mine at the back of my mind.' A faint smile curved his lips. 'And let's face facts, Miss Ravensdale, that's your duty you know, when you take on a place like Tressillion, to provide employment. If it hadn't been Em, it would have been someone else.'

'Hmm.' It fell into place. The familiar figure entering the Lewis' cottage when she took Emily home must have been Madoc. She remembered the sudden laughter and the light burning in the previously darkened room. Had he brought the light, or come to use it rather than his own, knowing how little the family could afford such hospitality?

She'd met conmen in her time who'd sounded just as plausible as Madoc Lewis. Conman, rogue or honest gentleman? Well, she'd know soon enough. She walked on, without speaking, to the cottage on the seashore. And, whatever he was, at least she was forewarned that the mine would not be left in peace.

Chapter Thirteen

The cottage was tiny, bleached in and out by the salt wind coming in from the sea. A wooden veranda had been added, overlooking the beach, with a hammock strung across it, one end higher than the other to form a kind of chair that swung freely. On the wooden pillar next to it, a shelf had been fixed, holding a lamp.

'That's just what it needed!' Sybil exclaimed.

'You know the cottage, then?'

She recollected herself, regaining her severity. 'A long time ago. There were ten people living here then, and the old grandmother. I'd forgotten it was so small. I can't think how they all fitted in.' She looked round as the front door opened and a pale young woman, wrapped tightly in a shawl, emerged.

Well, she might have known there was a woman somewhere. And this one was barely more than a child, she observed, with a sniff.

'I thought I heard voices.' The girl bent her thin frame over almost double as a fit of coughing overcame her.

'You should be out of this cold wind, Gwen,' said Madoc. 'You are still not well.'

'There's nothing wrong with me.' She straightened and glanced at Sybil.

'My daughter Gwenllian,' explained Madoc. 'She's staying with me for a few weeks.'

Daughter? Sybil did her best not to show her surprise. With his talk of Australia and the isolation of his life, there had seemed no room for a wife, let alone a grown-up daughter.

112

'And this is Miss Ravensdale from Tressillion House, Gwen,' added Madoc.

'Tressillion?'

'I'm not related to the family,' said Sybil.

'Oh,' said Gwen, losing interest. 'Would you like to come inside for a cup of tea, Miss Ravensdale?'

'Thank you.' Sybil followed Gwen inside, into a kitchen that doubled as a living room, with doors leading off on either side.

'Please take a seat, Miss Ravensdale,' said Madoc. 'I'll fetch my notebook.'

As he disappeared through a side door, Sybil perched on one of the chairs by the wooden table, next to the neatly-blackened range. On the far side of the room, a fire burned in a small fireplace, near a single armchair. For all its sparsity, the room was clean and homely. An array of pans and cups hung from hooks in the ceiling, while plates and bowls were stacked on one of the shelves next to the range. Woodworking tools hung from hooks next to the fire, interspersed with a pile of books.

'It looks a comfortable house,' she remarked. She'd grown unused to making small talk. Gwen, she couldn't help but notice, was inspecting her from the corner of her eyes, no doubt spinning all kinds of fairy stories about her visitor's relationship with her father. 'Do you live nearby, Miss Lewis?'

Gwen shook her head. 'In London.' She swung the kettle over the fire in the centre of the range. 'I needed to get away for a short while, so Dad let me stay here with him.' She busied herself arranging teacups. 'I'm going back in a few days.'

'You know you are welcome to stay longer, Gwen,' said Madoc, returning with a large notebook in his hand. 'There's no need for you to go back just yet.'

'My friends are in London,' replied Gwen. 'And my work. My *real* work,' she added, as Madoc began to protest.

'Gwen is a tireless supporter of women's right to vote,' he explained.

Sybil sniffed. 'Oh, that.'

'You don't agree?' Gwen forgot the tea, turning to frown at the visitor. 'Are you one of those who follow Mrs Humphrey Ward's campaign to prevent women ever having the vote?'

'Gwen,' said Madoc, gently. 'Not everyone is obliged to agree with you.'

'I'd have thought women having the vote was a foregone conclusion,' said Sybil. 'I understood the majority of MPs already agree that it's ridiculous that women here cannot vote for their government. Not even Mr Asquith can ignore the workings of democracy forever. I saw American women going off to vote, and the world didn't fall apart there.'

'You saw women in America going to vote for their government?' Gwen was impressed. 'That must have been a wonderful sight.'

'Yes, it was,' admitted Sybil. She smiled at the memory of the excitement of her friends, dressed in their best, heading off together to cast their votes, laughing in glee at having a voice in the greater scheme of things, even if it was simply a mark on a piece of paper.

'It was only a start and there's a long way to go before women can vote in all the American states, let alone the rest of the world. But it's unstoppable, if you ask me. Don't worry, Miss Lewis, I'll be the first marching to the ballot box when the Prime Minister finally sees sense and agrees with his MPs.'

Gwen was watching her, a thoughtful expression on her face. 'I belong to a suffrage movement. Would you ever think of coming to London to speak to them about your experiences in America?'

'Gwen,' said Madoc, gently. 'Miss Ravensdale is a guest, not to be dragged into your campaign.'

'You wouldn't have to join our campaign, but sometimes our members get disheartened. They've fought for so many decades, and so many times the vote seemed in their grasp. It would be a wonderful inspiration to hear someone talk who has been in a place where women have won the right to vote.' She reached for a small stack of business cards on a shelf next to the range. 'This is where we meet. You'd be very welcome.'

'The White Camellia,' said Sybil, slowly, turning the card in her hand.

'Yes,' said Gwen, her thin face alight with enthusiasm. 'It's so strange. They say the world is a small place, and I suppose it's not *that* odd. I met Miss Tressillion at the White Camellia. Miss Beatrice Tressillion, that is,' she added. 'My cousin Harri said she was from the family who used to own Tressillion House.'

'Really.' Sybil kept her voice distant and her face calm, betraying not one iota of the blood drumming in her ears.

'Yes. I'm sure she'd love to hear you talk. And to meet you. She seemed so sad at leaving her childhood home. I'm sure she'd want to meet the person who has taken it over, and is saving it. She's so amazing. When the police came to break up the meeting…'

Madoc coughed in warning. Gwen came to an abrupt halt. 'Well, she was wonderful,' she added, defiantly.

Into the ensuing silence, the front door creaked, opening slightly to allow a one-eyed tabby to stalk in as if he owned the place. He came to a full stop on spotting Sybil, back arched, whiskers bristling in a hiss.

'Mind your manners, Glyndwr. That's no way to welcome visitors,' said Madoc. 'Particularly as you are only here on sufferance. I knew I should have thrown you back to the tide.'

'Dad, you wouldn't,' said Gwen, distracted from Beatrice Tressillion and the White Camellia at this injustice. Glyndwr, however, wove himself round Madoc's legs, purring loudly, before marching over to settle himself on the armchair with a pointed stare at the intruder.

'I don't know why he stays,' said Madoc. 'Apart from the fish. And the fine selection of mice when I took over the place. He was half the size when he appeared one night. But at least there are no more mice.' He took a chair opposite Sybil. 'This is the notebook.' He pushed it across to her, ignoring Gwen's curiosity.

'Thank you. Whatever happens, Mr Lewis, I'll return it to you.' As she took it, the pages opened. Page upon page of drawings and close lines of writing. She raised her eyebrows enquiringly.

'Oh, it's not been just the past months I've been working on it. I drew up the original plans for Mr Tressillion. Not that he took any notice. He was not a man for listening, as you might have heard from the village gossip. The eldest son might have, but he left soon after I came to live here.'

Sybil bent over the notebook, inspecting it closely, her face hidden. 'Really?'

'I suspect the villagers are right that the mine might have stood a chance, if Leonard Tressillion had been left in charge, rather than thrown out without a penny. If nothing else, he had the imagination to see what might happen to his mother and sisters, should the worst happen.'

'Oh,' said Sybil. The breath was tight in her chest. She couldn't stay here a moment longer. On the range, the kettle finally began to boil. 'I won't stop for tea. It's growing late. I must get back. Emily will be wanting to go home.' She stood up, tucking the notebook under her arm. 'I'll consider your plans, Mr Lewis, and let you know my decision within the week. Does that sound fair?'

'Very much so,' he replied.

'Good.' She shook his hand in a businesslike manner and turned to nod to Gwen. 'It was a pleasure to meet you, Miss Lewis. And good luck with your campaign. As I said, I'm confident you will prevail in the end.'

And before either of them could move, she shot out of the door and into the gathering dusk.

* * *

Sybil walked rapidly along the shore to the footpath, notebook tucked under her arm. Where the path rose up over the cliffs, she paused to look up at the shadow of her house etched against the darkening sky. A single light flickered in the servant's quarters. As she watched, it moved away from the window, the flame dancing down inside the house, a lonely wil o' the wisp on a mission of its own.

She shivered. There were ghosts in the air tonight. She could hear them in the crash of distant breakers, in the breeze rustling between the dead stalks of last year's grasses. They hovered around her in the fleeting moonlight between clouds and the distant smell of woodsmoke. Ghosts stirred by talk of the Tressillions, and threads that kept leading back to the White Camellia.

She wouldn't go there, of course. She couldn't. There were some ghosts that should never be stirred back into life.

The moon disappeared. Darkness clung to every part of her, lying heavy on her chest, each breath an effort as the night tightened around her. Was this what it was like, trapped within the darkness of the mine? Horribly injured, with no hope of rescue, every breath diminishing the air, and the lives around you fading, one by one, until there was nothing but emptiness and silence and finally extinction.

'This is not what I wanted,' she said aloud, her voice echoing into the chill vastness around her. 'This is never what I wanted.'

She strode up through the field until she reached the metal gate into Tressillion's grounds. The house was now filled with light. A lamp burnt in every room, the windows blazing, shutterless. Had Emily felt it too? Felt the ghosts creeping back, preparing to take over once more, and exact payment for the past?

In front of her, the gate creaked on its hinges and swung open of its own accord. Sybil jumped at this mockery of an invitation, the blood beating rapidly in her ears. In the undergrowth to one side, a branch cracked. The world stilled. Sybil reached for the large stick propped up amongst the ferns next to the gate, her hand clasping its smoothness, already brittle with a film of frost.

She waited. Nothing. Not a sound, not a movement. Only the distant rush of the river, flowing down from the mine to the sea. After a few minutes, she released the stick and stepped through the gate, clicking the latch firmly behind her.

Squaring her shoulders, she walked slowly and deliberately across the frosted lawn towards the house.

PART TWO

PART TWO

Chapter Fourteen

Bea stopped and read once more the business card in her hand. It was the right street, Tavistock Road, and the house in front of her had a large number 2 on its door. Yet it couldn't be.

'Excuse me.' She caught the eye of a woman at the edge of the small crowd that had gathered. 'I'm looking for Mrs Anselm. I've an appointment with her.'

The woman chuckled. 'I'd wait here, if I was you, Miss. You don't want to be caught in that lot. Not unless you want to get arrested. They look a bit twitchy to me.'

A cheer went up from the crowd as a couple of burly-looking men, surrounded by policemen, walked up to the front door.

'Shame!' roared the woman next to Bea, sounding more like a fishwife than a respectable lady.

'Shame! Disgrace!' echoed through the crowd, who were clearly enjoying the spectacle hugely. A large motorised van drew up, scattering the onlookers.

'No taxation without representation!' called a woman behind Bea.

'Hear, hear,' replied a middle-aged man in a bowler hat, waving an unfurled umbrella in the air.

The first burly man banged loudly on the front door. Several delivery lads who had stopped to watch the fun, leaning on their bicycles, front baskets still laden, whistled loudly. The crowd was growing. Banners were being unfurled – the first by the Suffrage League of Women Artists and Journalists, resplendent with a border of entwined camellias – accompanied by booing, fit for a night at the melodrama.

121

The policemen were indeed twitchy. One lashed out at a small boy who had dashed in, as if on a dare to get as close as possible. The baton clipped the boy on the side of the head, sending him flying.

'Call yourself a man?' cried one of the women at the front of the crowd. 'Very brave you are when facing women and small children.'

The policeman lunged, but the crowd moved, jostling in around her. Minutes later, she shot past Bea, pulling the injured boy behind her and disappearing into a neighbouring street.

The crowd had grown silent. A dangerous, hostile silence. Bea exchanged looks with the woman next to her.

'Better go, dearie. This could turn nasty.'

The banging resumed on the door. This time it was opened by a middle-aged woman in a maid's uniform. 'Good morning, gentlemen.' She sounded remarkably calm under the circumstances. 'Mrs Anselm is ready to receive you.'

The two men went inside, while the police remained on the doorstep, batons to the fore, as if facing an angry mob with pitchforks at the ready. But the crowd had decided that the possibility for a fight, and therefore some fun, had passed, and were already moving away, leaving a small group of men and women standing holding banners, silently, as if waiting for a funeral procession to pass.

Bea hesitated. The policemen looked large and more than likely to take prisoners, and that first meeting had made her wary. In the distance a church bell struck eleven. Whatever was happening, she wasn't about to let Mrs Anselm think she hadn't turned up. She could at least leave her card, and rearrange her interview for another day. She walked as firmly as she knew how to the gate.

'You can't go in there, Miss.'

'I have an appointment.'

'Well, you can't go in there.'

'At least let me leave my card.'

'You can't go in there.' He was nervous, and more than a little embarrassed, and looked about to lose his temper. Bea took a deep breath. But before she could argue again, the door opened, and the maid reappeared.

'Miss Tressillion?'

Bea nodded. 'Yes. I can come back another day.'

'No, no. That's quite alright.' The maid ignored the policeman. 'Come on in, Miss. Mrs Anselm is expecting you.'

Bea followed her through a hallway into a large drawing room. The two men she had seen banging on the door were inspecting items of furniture, making notes.

'I don't want to intrude…'

'Oh, it's all right, Miss. It's only the bailiffs.'

'The bailiffs?' Bea stared at her.

The maid grinned. 'Mrs Anselm is one of those refusing to pay her taxes until she is able to vote. "No taxation without representation", see. So the bailiffs are here to take things to be sold to cover the payment.'

'I want a full list and a description.' Mrs Anselm swept into the room, nodding imperiously to the bailiffs, who were both attempting to look grim-faced and implacable, but with the faint air of small boys caught stealing apples. 'And if anything is damaged you will be hearing from Mr Lewis, my solicitor.' She looked up. 'Ah, there you are, Miss Tressillion. Do come in. We won't be disturbed in the study. Thank you, Lucy. And if you could just watch over the gentlemen and make sure they don't take what they shouldn't.'

'With pleasure, Mrs Anselm,' said Lucy, leaning against the doorway and folding her arms in an uncompromising fashion.

'Lucy has been with me for nearly twenty years, and I'd trust her with my life,' announced Mrs Anselm, to somewhere just above the heads of the two men. 'You, I don't know from Adam. So don't try to pull the wool over her eyes. You will take the exact amount and no more. And I'll thank you not to take any of my glass. It's quite worthless, and two champagne glasses were cracked last time, making them quite unsalable, and rather missing the point. Come along, Miss Tressillion.'

Mrs Anselm led the way into a smaller room, piled high with books and papers. 'Do sit down. Beatrice, isn't it?'

'Yes.'

Mrs Anselm nodded. 'I thought there was something familiar, that first time we met. You take after your father.'

'Oh.' Bea felt the colour rush to her cheeks.

'I mean in looks. He was a handsome man. Not wise. Impervious to reason. But you could never fault his looks.' She scrutinised Bea. 'So the question is, do you take after him in other ways, or are you willing to learn?'

'I wish to learn.' Mrs Anselm's directness was a little unnerving. 'I want to become a journalist, but I don't care what I do. I'll do anything.'

'For payment.'

Bea blushed. 'Yes. But if I have to work without while I am learning, I'll do that and find other ways of earning my living until I'm ready. I'll do whatever it takes.'

'Mmm.' Mrs Anselm leant back in her chair. 'I have many talented young women I can call upon. You are educated, and you are well dressed, and you come from a wealthy family. Whatever your circumstances might be now,' she added, as Bea opened her mouth to protest. 'Many will question why you do not come as a volunteer, if you feel so passionately.'

Bea met her eyes. They were cool and questioning. Not exactly hostile, but inspecting her, as if she was a butterfly she was about to pin, still wriggling, to a board.

'I wish to stand on my own two feet and be beholden to no-one. I want to live my own life. Isn't that what the members of the suffrage movement believe in?'

'There are men, as well as women, in the suffrage movement. Several have even found the partner of their married life at our meetings. It's where I met my late husband, for which I bless the movement every day of my life. Our struggle is for equality for all. Many women besides myself have found a husband who shares their views, and is able support them.'

'I don't want to rely on someone else,' said Bea. 'How could I be certain I'd make a wise choice? I know very little of the world, and I know nothing of men.'

Just Harri in the dark, his breath warm on her face, her senses threatening to overwhelm her. She pulled herself together.

'I don't want to be like my mother, watching everything she knew being put in danger and powerless to help herself when my father died. When it was taken away, she had no means of helping herself. I may not know much, but I've learnt that if you have money you have power, and without it you have none. I want to be able to earn my own money and support myself.'

'Some men listen.'

'Do they?' Bea frowned at her. 'When Papa was alive, I felt I was invisible. He saw me as a young woman he could have on his arm, with accomplishments to give him credit. He never saw me. Not the real me inside, who hated being shut away. My brothers were the same, apart from Leo. They never talked to me about anything serious. Sometimes I wondered if I existed at all.' She had said too much. She must sound like a madwoman.

'Out!' Mrs Anselm pushed back her chair, arm raised, forefinger pointing like an avenging goddess. Bea practically fell off her seat. The youngest bailiff stood rooted to the spot in the doorway, mouth working like a fish.

'I gave you instructions not to go in there!' Lucy appeared, grabbed the man by the arm and propelled him back out. 'And I don't care who told you to, John Briggs. I'll be seeing your mother in church on Sunday, and I'm sure she'd like to hear how you treat defenceless women. And you, who I used to push in your perambulator when you were no more than a scrap…'

The door closed behind them, and silence returned.

'Hrmph,' said Mrs Anselm. She picked up a cup, identical to the ones in the White Camellia, her fingers tracing the delicate pattern of the flowers. 'I've been in discussions with one of the Camellia's benefactors to pay for a full-time journalist now the paper is growing in circulation. The question is, do I choose a woman from inside the movement, or would an outsider's views be of greater benefit?' Bea held her breath. Mrs Anselm traced the foliage on the matching saucer with equal care. 'Lillian Finch designed these, you know.'

'They're beautiful,' said Bea, her heart constricting. Had Lillian said something? Harri was Mrs Anselm's solicitor. Had Lillian told Mrs Anselm of finding them outside in the dark, and whatever conclusions she might have drawn?

'She has a remarkable talent as an artist, yet she chose to work instead among the poor and the needy. Passions can come in more ways than one.' Bea didn't dare move. 'The pieces you sent me show promise,' said Mrs Anselm, at last. 'Too much of the schoolgirl, of course, but there is an honesty about them that was appealing.' She looked up. 'If I am to give you this chance, I need you to first prove yourself.'

'Anything,' said Bea. 'Anything. I'll break into the Houses of Parliament, if you wish.'

Mrs Anselm snorted. 'It might yet come to that. But I was thinking of something a little less glorious. You say you wish to earn your own money. Well, there is a paid position at the White Camellia that I can offer you.' She grinned, showing her teeth. 'I trust you are not above washing up and waiting on tables.'

Bea swallowed. So much for dreams of glory. Mama would

never live it down if she ever found out. She straightened. Mama would never know. 'Of course not. I meant what I said, I'll do anything.'

'Well, good for you.' Mrs Anselm sounded faintly surprised. Bea sensed she had passed some kind of test. 'Very well, then you should present yourself at the White Camellia on Monday. They'll be expecting you. We'll see how you do.'

A loud thumping and clattering echoed through the house. Mrs Anselm pursed her lips, an ominous glint in her eye.

Bea stood up. 'Thank you, I mustn't keep you any longer.'

'No need to thank me, Miss Tressillion. You may well be cursing me by Monday noon.'

'I doubt it.'

Mrs Anselm laughed. 'We shall see.' The banging grew louder, ending in a juddering crash. 'I'm not just being perverse, sending you to the kitchens, whatever you might think,' she added, as Bea turned towards the door.

'I didn't think you were.'

'Oh?' Her eyes were grave. 'If you have an ambition to be a voice for those who do not have the means, then you must learn what their lives really are, not a lady's idea of them. Until you have done it yourself, it is impossible to understand what it is really like to work until you drop, at a thankless task that has to be done all over again the next day, without praise, or even notice, and with others lording it over you because they can. You'll mix with all kinds of people at the White Camellia, Beatrice. Learn to speak like them, think like them. Sharpen your wits. Learn when to keep silent, and when to speak. Then you will be ready to become a journalist.' She frowned. 'If Mrs Pankhurst has her way, there will be a revolution. Those who have power are never willing to lose it, and they have an army and a police force to support them. You will need to have your wits about you.'

A particularly loud crash sent Mrs Anselm shooting out

through the door into the hall, where a grandfather clock was perched precariously, as the bailiffs argued with Lucy.

'I did try to tell them, Mrs Anselm.'

'That was a wedding present from my late husband's family,' said Mrs Anselm. The bailiffs began to look sheepish again. She placed her hands on her hips, clicking her tongue. 'It never did keep the time, ugly great thing. Neither of us could stand it. We'd have got rid of it, if it hadn't been for his mother. What you do to keep the family peace. For Heaven's sake, take the thing away. I hope never to see it again.' She waved her hands towards Bea. 'Good morning, Miss Tressillion.'

'This way, Miss.' Lucy led the way through piled up ornaments and out through the front door, where the remains of the crowd were still waiting.

A cheer went up as Bea emerged, which transformed into theatrical hissing and booing as the bailiffs followed, carrying the grandfather clock between them.

'It's all right, Miss,' said Lucy, with a grin. 'You get used to it, being a spectacle, I mean. Myself, I was brought up to be barely seen and never heard. My dad used to preach hell fire and brimstone in his spare time, blaming Eve for all the troubles ever visited on creation. The day I came to work for Mrs Anselm was the best day of my life. It's the day I began to feel I had the right to be alive.'

'I'm sure,' murmured Bea.

'No taxation without representation' went up the chant from the group holding the banner of the Suffrage League of Women Artists and Journalists as she passed.

At least this was a first step, Bea told herself firmly. This was the first step to becoming a real journalist and earning her own money and taking her own place in the world. Just so long as Mama never found out. At least, not until it was too late for her to do anything about it.

Chapter Fifteen

That night, once Emily had returned home, Sybil poured over Madoc's detailed sketches and notes.

Reopening the mine had not been part of her plan. But then neither had been taking over Tressillion. Her artist guests would come for the peace and unspoilt beauty of the place, not the rumbling and crushing of a mine. She gazed at the intricate drawings in silence, realising just how much that idea of turning Tressillion into a hotel had retreated from her mind. She didn't want to share the gardens with all and sundry, she admitted to herself. She didn't want strangers gazing into the faded rooms, judging their old-fashioned look. Even in such a short time, the abandoned house, whose façade she had hated all her life, had come to demand her protection.

Madoc Lewis was a true miner all right, methodical and careful. But he was also daring. She left the notebook open at his final notes, a contingency plan, should the route the Tressillions had followed prove unfruitful. She slipped outside into the gardens, wrapping her coat around her.

Maybe she had known, long before the liner had brought her back to Cornish soil, that the village's memory of the disaster that had overcome the Tressillions would be fading, as such things do. That first day, Madoc had told her small boys were already investigating the tunnels. If the crops failed or storms prevented the fishermen from going out for months on end, who knew where desperation might lead some of the men? She could hire guards to protect the entrance, of course, but that would prove

129

her cut from the same mould as the Tressillions and breed resentment. Maybe even suspicion.

Maybe Madoc wasn't the only one to see beyond old Tressillion's pigheadedness. Maybe some had even guessed at the trick that had been played on him, ensuring he would never find the hidden riches, even if he blasted his way down to the centre of the earth itself.

She sat on the steps where she had gleefully enjoyed her picnic on that first day, huddled in her coat, listening to the sounds of distant breakers.

That had been her other skill as a businesswoman. She had been able to spot trouble before it arrived, and head it off in another direction, so that in the end there was no trouble, or she remained in control and could use it for her own ends. And, she admitted to herself, there was also the temptation. There was bound to be. She glanced back up at the house, towering silently above her, its chimneys shadowed against the stars. Yes, there was always the temptation to show old Tressillion for the fool he had been, a mad old fool, destroying so many lives.

But most of all, she was afraid. Just how long would it take for the cavern in the mine to be found? She'd been a child, and childhood is black and white, right and wrong, wanting justice, and with no understanding that secrets can rarely be kept forever. Now was the reckoning, and there was no escaping.

* * *

Sybil returned to the cottage the next morning, having not slept a wink, and before she could change her mind. She found Madoc sitting on the wooden steps leading down from the veranda, drinking his tea and watching her approach.

'Interesting plans,' she remarked. 'Very detailed.'

'Thank you, Miss Ravensdale. Enough to convince you there might be potential in reopening the mine?'

'Perhaps.' She joined him on the steps, sitting down next to him without a thought for her skirts, or her reputation. 'If I wanted to take the risk. If I were interested in riches.'

'It might not end in riches. Few seams of gold have been found in Cornwall, but if this seam is as rich as it is rumoured to be, it would make you a profit and it would benefit the village. There's little enough work to be found.'

'And why would I want to benefit the village?'

'Because being here, you are part of the community. It comes with owning the house.'

'So I hear. Are you part of the community?'

'In my own way.'

She took out his notebook from her pocket. 'So how would you suggest I should start?'

'On a small scale. Hire a few men who've had experience, preferably some who worked for Hargreaves and Tressillion, and have a systematic search. It would be a risk, but not a huge capital outlay at this point. And if sufficient gold was found, then you could restore the workings. Although I doubt anyone could grow rich enough to buy the whole of Cornwall, whatever crack-skulled belief Mr Tressillion held on to. But maybe enough to buy us all security for the rest of our days.'

'But no gold was found.'

'Not exactly. A little. A very little. Enough at first to give hope of more. But not what Tressillion was expecting.'

'Oh? And what was it he was expecting?'

'A rich seam. It was found once, I understand, when it was worked as a tin mine by a local family, before Tressillion took it over. They uncovered the entrance to an older mine, one that had been worked as a gold mine a long time ago. A seam of gold was found in one of the tunnels, but the family couldn't afford to work it. I presume the Tressillions took it over thinking they'd make a fortune. But the gold was never found.'

'I see.' Her hand was shaking. She hid it beneath the folds of her skirts. 'It seems a bit of a long shot, if you ask me.' There was no sound from the house and no-one came out to join them. 'Is your daughter still here?'

He shook his head. 'Gwen left on the train for London this morning. I tried to persuade her to stay, but it was no use.'

'I'm sorry.'

He gave a faint smile. 'I'd have stopped her if I could. But to be honest I wouldn't dare, and in truth, I don't feel I have the right. I left Gwen and her mother to fend for themselves while I went off to find my fortune in Australia. I convinced myself I was doing it for them, but I've a feeling it was more to escape the mundanity of life, and an attempt to recapture my youthful dreams, before marriage and parenthood. We've made a kind of peace these last years, Gwen and I. But I'm certain it's how she sees me. And in the meantime, she has built a life in London that I have no part in.'

'So now you are proposing to seek your fortune nearer to home?'

'I suppose I am. The truth is, Miss Ravensdale, I've lived a bit of a ramshackle life, particularly since I came back home to find my wife had died and Gwen had been taken in by my sister. Gwen and two of her cousins were already planning to find work and study in London, and fight for what they believe. So now I have no real family back in Wales. This could be my chance to establish some kind of place in the community here.' He turned his gaze out over the sea. 'I need roots, Miss Ravensdale. Riches would do nicely as a bonus, but roots and some kind of role in life are what I'm looking for. In my youthful self-absorption, I never thought of my Gwen being an adult, following her own dreams, any more than I thought of Harri and Olwen ever finding a life outside of Pont-y-Derwen. The world is changing, and there are new pioneers, more ambitious to transform all lives, not just my selfish dream of boundless riches.'

'I see.' She sat for a while without speaking. There was no going back now, she acknowledged to herself. The danger was there. She could not ignore it. Madoc didn't seem like a man to give up easily, and who knew who might back him to lease the mine from her, if she refused to reopen it herself? She took a deep breath. 'I notice you propose following the same network of tunnels that the Tressillions used.'

He shook himself, turning his attention back to the notebook, his tone business-like once more. 'There are still tunnels to be explored in that section, there's still a chance of finding the seam.'

'And on the other side?'

'The other side?'

Her fingers traced the map. 'Yes. Here. The tunnels here, the ones you are leaving until last.'

'Those tunnels have been explored already. There's nothing there. The miners I've spoken to in the village said they were even older than the tunnels the Tressillions followed, and didn't go nearly as deep into the earth. No seam of gold has been found there. There's just rubble. There may well be further tunnels behind the rock falls, but it's more likely there isn't.'

'Which is why you propose them as a contingency, if no gold should be found in the main tunnels?'

'Yes.'

'You tell me the Tressillions found nothing in the part of the mine they were searching. Unless this seam of gold is a fairytale, it has to be somewhere. And if it isn't in the part already searched, it might be worth trying the older part of the mine. At least it would eliminate it as a possibility.'

'Maybe.' He scrutinised her face, which was still bent over the notebook. She moved slightly, uneasy. 'You sound very certain, Miss Ravensdale.'

'A hunch, that's all.' She straightened up, frowning at him. 'Do you think I haven't taken risks in building my fortune? Many that only a fool would have dared, as plenty of investors have informed me. And, after all, Mr Lewis, it is my mine.'

'Indeed,' he murmured.

Sybil scowled. Madoc didn't strike her as the meek sort. If he thought he could soft-soap her and then just do as he pleased, he had another think coming. She lifted her chin. 'I worked hard enough for it, Mr Lewis. And put up with plenty of owners who thought they could override me.'

He looked up at that. 'When you say owners, do you mean mine owners?'

'Yes,' she replied, shortly, cursing her pride for betraying her like that.

'Australia?' He glanced at the fading tan of her face. 'America?'

'I didn't go to America to work in a mine,' she said. 'A chain of hotels made my fortune.'

He laughed. 'You are a canny one, Miss Ravensdale. I've heard that it wasn't the gold miners but those who supplied them with food and tools, a hotel to spend their money in, along with a little company, who made the real fortunes.'

'The ones who weren't hopeless dreamers, you mean.'

'Or rather those skilled at fleecing the proceeds of another's risk and backbreaking work.'

Serious annoyance washed over her. 'Then, if we are to work together, we shall not be over-trusting of each other which, it seems to me, is no bad thing.'

'No, indeed.'

'So. You will consider working for me, and reopening the mine?'

'Depending on the terms, yes. I've nothing to lose. I'd been thinking I'd need to return to London to find work, especially with Twm not likely to work for several more months, and the family struggling, even with Emily's wage.'

Sybil nodded, her face carefully expressionless. 'And you agree we try exploring the older part of the mine first before we continue the Tressillions' work?'

'As you wish, Miss Ravensdale.'

'Good. Come see me tomorrow and we can work out the details.' She cleaned an invisible speck of dust from her skirts. 'I take your point about the mine benefitting the community, Mr Lewis. Our first choice should be miners from the village.'

'Agreed.'

'My first hotel – or maybe it was a boarding house – might have been in a mining town, but it was always respectable. I started with nothing but the ability to produce the best-home-cooked meals you could find, however poor the ingredients. And that is all I offered. It was hard work, skill, and an ability to save and invest that built my business. My hotels have always served respectable clients, and any kind of impropriety – and I mean financial as well as moral – was never tolerated. It's the only way to do business, Mr Lewis. Believe me, I've seen many who didn't take such precautions who ended up fleeced, blackmailed or bankrupt. I'm fair, and I'll never ask anyone to worker harder than I do myself. But I am a businesswoman, not a philanthropist or a fool. I trust you'll bear that in mind, Mr Lewis.'

He watched her face, as if trying to work something out in his mind. Finally, he nodded. 'I will never take you to be a fool, Miss Ravensdale,' he replied.

'Good.' She allowed herself the faintest of smiles. 'Then I think we will get along just fine.'

Chapter Sixteen

When Sybil reached Tressillion House, Emily had not yet returned from her errand to fetch the curtains from Mrs Morgan, the village seamstress. They were to be the finishing touches to the room in the servants' quarters, all ready for Emily to take possession that night.

She began to unbutton her coat, but the air was clear and chill, making her shiver and wrap herself up even closer. The fire would still be warm in the library, which she had taken as her sitting room. But with her mind still full of the mine and what the future might hold, she felt restless.

She began to change into her gardening coat, to take out her pent-up energy on the remains of the raspberry canes, but as she did so, rain flung itself through the sunshine, scattering itself against the windows. It was too cold to get soaked to the skin, so she turned instead to the attics, racing up the stairs, two at a time. Emily, however, clearly had everything in hand. The floors were cleaned and polished, as were the new pieces of furniture, and the bed was made up. A nightdress was folded neatly on the pillow and a few battered ornaments, which looked like sentimental reminders of home, had been placed on a rough wooden shelf, next to a small row of books. Even the windows gleamed.

On her way back down again, she paused by the bedrooms. They had to be faced sometime, and now was as good as any.

The first was Mr Tressillion's room, dark and ordered. She shut the door. Emily could deal with that. She couldn't bear to touch anything so personal of his. She was tempted to burn the lot of it, even if it sent rumours flying around the village, which wouldn't do at all.

The next bedroom had been Mrs Tressillion's: the lace curtains still in place, delicate ornaments and hair combs scattered where they had been left.

She pushed the door of the next bedroom. She had taken only a cursory look with Mr Roach, and expected a child's, but found instead a young woman's. Not lace-strewn like her mother's, but plain, tasteful rather than extravagant. Books still remained on the bookshelf, with gaps where the most precious had been taken. She picked up a dusty volume of Shakespeare. 'Beatrice Tressillion' was written in flowing script on the flyleaf. Sybil shut it hastily, as if stung. The writing was not the neatness of a schoolgirl, but bold, striding across the page as if to seize life and all that was in it.

A movement from outside caught her eye. She wiped the nearest window with her sleeve. A smart new Ford had drawn up next to the front gate. The driver had stepped out and was talking to Emily, back from the village on her bicycle, the basket filled with the wrapped brown paper parcel of the curtains.

'Hell,' muttered Sybil, her heart clenching. There was a bitter taste in her mouth. She'd known he would find her eventually, but this was too soon, much too soon. And only hours after her conversation with Madoc. Sometimes, he had the instinct of the Devil himself.

The intruder bent forward towards Emily, who backed away, as far as her laden bicycle would allow her.

'Buggeration.' Abandoning Beatrice's room, Sybil sped down the stairs, racing across the gravel toward them.

'Miss.' Emily's face eased with relief as Sybil reached her. 'There's a gentleman here…'

'Thank you.' Sybil kept her voice chill and distant. Mistress talking to maid. Nothing more. Nothing personal. For Emily's sake, nothing he could use to hurt her, that might cause Emily untold harm in the process. 'You'd better take those curtains in and hang them before it grows dark. And get one of the men to help you.'

'Yes, Miss.' Emily hesitated. She had never been asked before to behave as if Tressillion House was overflowing with servants. Male servants, too: presumably of the big and burly kind, with rifles permanently at the ready to take pot shots at intruders. She looked from the visitor to her mistress. 'I'll let the other servants know you will be back soon, Miss.'

Sybil waited until the rush of Emily's wheels had faded into the distance, and out of earshot. 'Nice vehicle you have there,' she remarked.

'Thank you.'

'Stolen?'

'You know me better than that, Sybbie. It was acquired.'

Sybil sniffed. 'I'm sure its rightful owner sees things differently. So? What are you doing here?'

'I heard there was a new mistress of Tressillion.' He gave a bleak smile. 'You can't blame me for being curious.'

He was still beautiful, she noted sadly. Tall and straight, like the soldier he should have been. Only the eyes, pale and empty of any emotion, betrayed him. She lifted her chin. 'Well, now you know. Take your damned curiosity and go to Hell with it.'

'Sybil, don't be like that. I came to say I admired you. You did it. You took over Tressillion, just as you always said you would.' His eyes turned to follow Emily as she reached the house. 'But I find you buying curtains and hiring servants, rather than wiping the place from the face of the earth.'

'Yes, well.' Sybil sighed. 'Life was so simple then. I was a child. I've grown up since.'

'Simple?' he blazed. 'You call it simple?'

She took a step back. 'Go home, Alex,' she said, in a gentler tone. 'There's nothing for you here. Please go away.'

He stood watching her with his cold, expressionless eyes. 'I don't understand,' he said at last. 'You've changed, Sybbie. I don't know you any more.'

'Yes,' murmured Sybil. And if you did, you'd kill me, came the whisper, deep in her heart where no-one could hear. She pulled from her pocket a small packet she had snatched from the library on her way down, placing it in his hand.

'Sybbie, I didn't come for your money.'

'I didn't think that you did.'

We both know we are lying, she thought.

She watched as he returned to the Ford, slamming the door before the engine roared into life and he shot off, back towards Porth Levant. She didn't move until she could see him speeding along the coastal road beyond the village, heading into the distance.

'And we both know this is not the end of it,' said Sybil, turning slowly to follow Emily back to the house. 'I was right, after all. I have no choice.'

* * *

The mine was as she had left it.

Sybil wandered through the workings in the last of the evening sun. On closer inspection, she could see the remains of small fires in two of the outlying sheds. Large rocks and the remains of fallen trees had been pressed into crude seats. Already Madoc's attempts to block the entrance had been partially removed, leaving enough room for a grown man to make his way inside. A bonfire had been built against the rock face a little further along, towards the tunnels that had become Tressillion's obsession. A crude attempt to split the cliff open and find imagined treasure waiting within.

The stories don't go away. She should have known Mrs Patterson's tale of the piece of gold would remain an irresistible temptation for a village that had lost its two main sources of work in the mine and the big house. Sybil frowned at signs of illicit activity, wondering how far the treasure seekers had already penetrated the mine's defences. She looked around, shoulders prickling, feeling eyes watching her from the scrub of branches, or maybe even from within the mine itself.

Hastily, she clambered higher, up to the ridge above the trees, not stopping until she was halfway down the other side. There was no path, but she knew it so well, she picked her way between fields, finding the narrow point in the stream where she could leap across, until she reached the ruin, with its bent hawthorn at the centre.

The cottage was almost completely overgrown with brambles and small saplings. Sheep had made their way through a broken wall to find shelter in the arch of the fireplace. Nothing serviceable remained, even the range had vanished, no doubt carted away to some less abandoned cottage along the coast. Sybil stepped over the rotted remains of fallen beams, and through the opening that had once been the kitchen door, out into the small garden, still surrounded by a wall to keep out the worst of the storms. Primroses peeped from a carpet of weeds, between clumps of snowdrops. A twisted branch of lavender struggled to rise above the brambles.

'There's nothing left there, Miss.'

Sybil jumped, stumbling as she swung round, to find an elderly farmer, dog at his heel, approaching from the adjoining field.

'So I see.' She brushed down her skirts, attempting to sound mildly curious. 'It seems a pity. Someone clearly cared for the garden. It must have been a good home once.'

'It was,' he replied, reaching the garden wall, and leaning over, arms resting on the stones. Sybil shut her eyes. The echo of conversation, reassuring, familiar, surrounded her, bringing the scent of sweet peas and the richness of newly-turned earth. 'Mrs Hargreaves loved her garden, she did,' continued her visitor. 'A wonder, it was, the things she could grow in there, despite the salt and the winds. Fruits, vegetables, and all kinds of flowers. Her strawberries were the best I've tasted, she always gave some for my wife and our boys, each year. She knew my Flora loved strawberries. Place wasn't the same after Mrs Hargreaves died.'

Sybil glanced round at the ruined garden, with its outhouse and the pigsty at the far end, almost completely buried under ivy. 'Surely someone must have wanted to take it over. It seems such a waste to lose a garden like that.'

He shook his head. 'Unlucky. That's what people said. An unlucky place. And once a place is said to have bad luck in its rafters, there's no-one wants to live in its shadow.' He shot her a sharp glance. 'And you can't go back to the past and make things right, however hard you try.'

'No,' said Sybil. 'I suppose not.'

'I had a lot of time for Mrs Hargreaves. She was a good woman. She'd have done anything to protect those children of hers, poor little mites. It's a wicked world when the bad prosper and the good have to suffer, especially the children.'

'Yes, indeed,' murmured Sybil.

She watched as the farmer made his way a little stiffly across the fields, dog at his heels, heading for the smoke from a farmhouse chimney just visible in the distance.

Sybil turned back towards the mine. She should have known that, however far away she might be, she would never escape the shadow that had edged down towards this little house when it had warmth and laughter, and the cluck of chickens between the sprawl of beans and potatoes, just as it had inched towards the caged grandeur of Tressillion.

Even in the bustle of New York she could not escape its long tendrils forever, reaching across oceans, dragging her back. At least it was not too late. There was something she could do. Whatever might haunt her heart until her dying day, she could stop old wounds being reopened, and keep those she loved safe.

Chapter Seventeen

Bea arrived at the White Camellia on her first day almost an hour early. The streets were quiet, and she huddled self-consciously in the doorway. Her coat had been made for elegance rather than warmth.

'You'll freeze before they open the door,' said Olwen, arriving behind her, muffled by a thick scarf.

'I didn't want to be late, not on my first day.' And she'd needed to escape before Mama could question her. Cousin Jonathan had been invited for dinner again last week. He'd been as attentive as ever, charming them all, sympathetic to Mama's laments at how long it was since she had been to the theatre. The next morning, tickets to *La Traviata* had arrived.

'His intentions couldn't be clearer,' Mama exclaimed triumphantly.

'He is being kind,' Bea replied.

'Nonsense. No young man is simply kind, and especially not to an old woman like me.'

'You are not old, Mama.'

'I'm too old to be of interest to anyone any more.' She sighed. 'It was different when we were at Tressillion. We had a certain standing. Here in London, nobody knows us.' She returned to inspecting the tickets, as if they were a magic pathway to her previous life. The message was plain: her eldest daughter was now her only chance to recover any life worth living.

'Come on, Bea, you can help me in the printing room until they arrive.' Olwen took a key from her pocket and opened a small door to one side of the tearoom.

'I'm coming to wash dishes and mop floors,' said Bea uncertainly. She didn't want to fail her test before she had begun by getting herself into the magazine offices under false pretences.

'But there's no need to freeze while you're waiting,' replied Olwen, with a smile. 'And besides, there's no harm in you seeing. I invited you in, so it would be rude of you to refuse.'

Bea followed her inside. The tables of the White Camellia stood neat and still, strangely ghostlike without the rush of meals being served and the murmur of conversation. Olwen led her though a side door next to the kitchens, and down a small flight of steps to a room at the back. She pushed shutters from the windows, allowing light in from a small sunken courtyard, where a few pots surrounded a wrought iron table and several chairs.

The influx of light revealed a room lined with shelves, full of ordered piles of papers and printed copies of 'The Camellia', the magazine of the Suffrage League of Women Artists and Journalists. In the middle of the floor stood a large machine made up of handles and rollers, and a considerable amount of ink.

'There you are, you see. The heart of the White Camellia: the printing press.' Olwen pulled off her gloves and put a match to the fire in the grate. 'Isn't it wonderful? Mrs Anselm had it brought over from America when she was setting up the SLWAJ magazine. I never thought I'd ever be able to work such a thing, but it's possible once you know how. Mind you, we're all covered with ink by the end of the day.'

'Do you write articles as well?'

Olwen nodded. 'Sometimes. When they are desperate. With my studies, I don't have much time to do much extra. I'm grateful just to have work that I can fit in between lectures. There are only two of us working on the magazine who are paid, and there's never enough time to do everything. We write about the meetings and anything that might be of interest to our readers. And Harri sometimes lets me hear some of his cases. I can't discuss them directly, but I can write about the issues generally. It's fascinating.'

'Is that what you want to be, a journalist?'

Olwen sighed. 'I want to be a doctor.'

'A doctor?'

'I wanted to be a surgeon, but I don't think that will ever be possible.' Her mouth set in a stubborn line. 'But I'll be a doctor one day, however long it takes.' She caught the look on Bea's face. 'There are women doctors. Not many, but there are more and more. It takes money. But my work here helps, and Harri too.'

'Harri?'

'He's supporting me until I qualify. Even with this job I couldn't possibly pay rent for a room, or for the books and materials I need, let alone the tuition fees.'

'That's very good of him,' said Bea.

'It's like a miracle,' said Olwen. She bit her lip. 'I worry, sometimes, that I am preventing him doing the things he wants to do. If he wasn't helping me, he could take on far more cases that don't pay as well, which I know he'd love. And I hate the thought that one day I could stand in the way of his happiness.'

'I'm sure he wouldn't help you unless he wanted to,' said Bea. 'I'm sure he's very proud of you.'

'Yes, he is. And it's not self-sacrifice. It's what we agreed when we were children, back in Pont-y-Derwen. It was the only way either of us had a chance, you see. When we first came to London, I worked all hours so that he could train as a solicitor, and now he's helping me.' Her eyes grew distant. 'It didn't matter that we were both clever at school, see. If we'd stayed, Harri would have ended up down the mine, and I'd have married the first man who asked me.'

'You wouldn't!'

'You never saw our dad on a Friday night, after he'd been to the Berw Arms.'

Bea winced. 'I'm sorry.'

'The sad thing is, that now I'm free of my dad's fists, I can understand why he was like that. He could have been so much more, you see. He won a scholarship to grammar school, but my *taid,* my grandfather, didn't see the point, when he could be earning good money. And that wasn't to be rich, but just so they could keep a roof over their heads and the baby fed. Uncle Madoc and Uncle Twm are younger. They both got a chance to get away. I know why they stay in Cornwall, rather than going home. Dad's so bitter, thinking they've had chances he was never given, and there's nothing anyone can do about it.'

Bea swallowed. 'It must have been hard.'

'Yes. Yes, it was.' She gave a wry grin. 'Dad'd be cursing us both if he knew how much Harri earns. It isn't much, but would be enough to keep Dad in beer. If he wasn't helping me.'

Bea focussed her attention on the courtyard, with its collection of chairs turned towards each other, as if ready to resume an animated conversation. 'Not many brothers would do that for their sister.'

'I know, and I bless Harri for it every day. Some of the girls I worked with, they told me I was a fool. That once he'd got his qualifications and could work, he'd find a wife and a family, and forget all he owed me. They thought he'd climb on my shoulders and leave me behind without a second thought, because that's all women are good for, to support their menfolk.' She grimaced. 'Sometimes I wondered. There was no reason for him to repay me. And yet he has.' She bit her lip. 'I do sometimes wonder if it's unfair of me to ask, and meanwhile he is working all the hours there are, and doing the work for Lillian and the suffragists. I keep house for him, and we rub along together, but it's not like having a family of your own.'

'He must be happy with the choice he has made. And I'm sure you wouldn't want him any other way.'

'No.' Olwen smiled. 'No, I wouldn't. And I'd never have forgiven him if he'd taken all those years of my life and just trodden on them, as if I didn't matter.'

'There you are,' said Bea.

'But I worry, sometimes, that I am standing in his way. He wouldn't tell me, you see. If there was someone he wanted to marry. He'd worry that I'd throw it all up and never qualify.'

A door opened on the floor above, followed by boots and voices.

'I'd better go,' muttered Bea. 'Or they really will think I was late.'

* * *

Bea had never worked so hard in her life. She felt a fool at her clumsiness washing dishes, scrubbing them until her hands bled. She carried heavy pails of water and mopped until her arms ached and her back felt as if it might break in half. She was soon ravenously hungry. When they paused after the lunchtime rush for soup and thick slices of bread and butter, she forgot to be ladylike and devoured everything in front of her.

'I couldn't believe what hard work it was when I started, either,' said one of the volunteers, who worked alongside the paid staff. She pulled an expensive coat around her, as they sat in the little courtyard in the spring sunshine, breathing in what passed for fresh air. 'I used to half starve myself to have a smaller waist than my sisters. Now I don't care.' She grinned. 'Mama doesn't approve of my arms. They've developed so many muscles they don't fit my sleeves any more. She says I'm turning into a fishwife.'

'Nothing wrong with a fishwife, Vicky,' returned a smaller, stockier young woman. 'It was my life's ambition, once.'

Vicky grinned. 'Well, I know a few fish you can gut, Annie. Human ones, that is.' Vicky brought out a cigarette case finely decorated with mother of pearl. 'Half of them I'm related to, and half of those are heading for the Houses of Parliament because their seats have been in the family for generations. Including my own brothers.'

Annie laughed. 'Well, at least you'll never take your servants for granted.'

'We have hundreds of them,' sighed Vicky. 'I'm embarrassed to face them.' She proffered the cigarette case to Bea, who shook her head.

'At least it's employment,' added Olwen, bringing her soup over to join them.

'Yes, that's true.' Vicky lit her cigarette. 'I was wishing you'd be a smoker, Beatrice, then I wouldn't be here on my own. Don't tell me you're one of those vegetarians, too?'

'No,' replied Bea with a smile. 'At least, not yet.'

'Thank goodness for that.' Vicky drew on her cigarette. 'So it wasn't idealism that brought you here to scrub pans, Miss Tressillion?'

'I don't know.' Bea frowned at her. She met women like Vicky at social gatherings. They were the same, in Cornwall or London: accustomed to wealth and their social standing, surveying the world around them with idle curiosity, assuming their right to be told everything. 'I think so.'

'You're not from London, I take it?'

'I live here now.'

'Aha. I thought I could hear a trace of an accent. So where did you live before?'

'Vicky,' remonstrated Olwen, quietly.

'I was only asking.' Vicky met Bea's eyes. 'My brother Charlie knew a Leonard Tressillion, he brought him to one of our summer parties one year. He was amazingly handsome, and quite fearsomely clever. Papa said he was going to inherit a fortune, but he spent the whole time talking to some bluestocking who was terribly severe, who probably didn't want to get married at all.'

Bea swallowed a smile. That sounded very like Leo, who'd never had much patience with Cornwall's beauties being paraded in front of his nose.

Vicky continued. 'It can be a small world.'

'Indeed,' murmured Bea, noncommittally, thankful as their companions finished their soup and began returning to the kitchens.

'So, are you going to hear Christabel Pankhurst speak, Vicky?' put in Olwen.

'I don't know. It could be exciting. Papa would disinherit me if he ever found out.' She grinned. 'But since Charlie will get the lot anyhow, and if I make enough fuss neither of them will refuse to pay a dowry to any man who asks me, just to get me off their hands, I don't much care. If I knew how to work that camera the Fabian Society donated to the magazine, I could show what the police really get up to.'

'Then why don't you take it? Mrs Anselm is always trying to get one of us to learn how to use it. There's equipment to set up a darkroom in one of the cellars, too.'

'I'm hopeless. I don't have the patience.' She turned to Bea. 'That Leonard Tressillion was always talking about photography. That's what he and that bluestocking were discussing. A woman photographer. Julia somebody.'

'Cameron,' supplied Beatrice. 'Julia Margaret Cameron. She made portraits of Lord Tennyson when he was Poet Laureate. Leonard took me with him when he went to see some of her photographs. They were wonderful, especially to think of a woman making all those famous men sit for her and do as she told them. After that, I badgered Leo until he showed me how to use his camera, and let me work in his darkroom as well.'

'Well, well.' Vicky glanced at Olwen. 'Seems to me you'd be

far more useful joining us rather than washing up dishes, Beatrice, whatever Mrs Anselm wants to prove.'

'But it's up to Mrs Anselm to decide. I've only just arrived. I don't want to jeopardise my place here, or my chance to work on the magazine in the future.'

'Exactly,' said Olwen.

Vicky put her head to one side. 'All right, all right, I take your point. But there's no reason why you shouldn't be at the meeting. And if we happened to be there, with the camera, there's nothing to stop you volunteering to use it. No-one need ever know. Not unless you wanted them to. Unless you manage to get yourself arrested, of course.'

'I'm not sure…'

'Don't worry,' said Vicky. 'You can stick with me. If it comes to it, I'll make sure I get arrested instead. All I have to do is give them my name and they release me. My father's a Minister in the government, and my uncle is in the House of Lords. The police don't want me in their cells.' Her gaze was calculating. 'Unless you are afraid?'

'Of course not!'

'Good.' Vicky looked pleased with herself. Olwen appeared uneasy. 'Oh, come on, Olwen. What better way for Beatrice to prove herself? And don't you want to be on one of the suffragette's marches? They always sound so much more exciting than Mrs Anselm's speeches.'

'And more violent,' said Olwen.

'Any sign of trouble, and we'll leave.'

'Of course,' said Bea, with a sinking feeling that if trouble did arrive, her chances of avoiding it were around nil. But, on the other hand, the chance to use a camera and take photographs was a first step to proving herself as a reporter. She finished her tea. Vicky was staring into the far distance. Olwen had turned to reply to a question from one of the women working the printing press.

'So, does your brother still have an interest in photography, Beatrice?' asked Vicky, with exaggerated indifference, as they began to make their way back to the kitchens.

Bea shook her head. 'Leonard was killed in an accident, two years ago.'

'Oh my goodness.' Vicky turned white. 'Beatrice, I'm so sorry, I had no idea.' Her hands flew to her mouth. 'Papa did say something about a mining accident that killed four men in the Tressillion family, and how terrible it was, but I never thought it could be Leonard. Charlie had told me he'd gone to live abroad.'

'He came back,' said Bea, escaping to the refuge of the next load of washing up to be done.

* * *

Olwen was waiting for her, in the light from one of the streetlamps, as Bea stumbled out of the White Camellia that evening. 'You look as if you've been hit by a landslide.'

'One made up of cups and saucers.'

Olwen smiled. 'Come on, we'll take you home.'

'It's not necessary.'

'Yes it is. And anyhow, it was Harri's idea.' She nodded as Mrs Anselm's automobile drew up beside them. 'You can drop me off at my lecture, and then Harri can take you home. It's all right. It's perfectly respectable. It'll only take ten minutes or so. That's hardly long enough for Harri to turn into a fiend. Anyhow, we're friends, and that whole thing about chaperones is so old-fashioned.'

Bea hesitated. Harri was carefully avoiding her eyes.

'Oh, I never agree with chaperones.' Vicky was hurrying towards them, fixing her hat. 'And Harri is always fearsomely serious.'

'I'm afraid you'll find me horribly shallow, Lady Victoria,' he replied, sounding irritated.

'Vicky. Only my enemies call me by that dreadful name. It sounds so stuffy.' She gave a sharp glance at Bea, then Harri. 'Olwen tells me you're giving Beatrice a ride home. You couldn't give me a lift too, could you? Mama is insisting we go to Covent Garden tonight, for the opening night of some dreadful opera. One where the heroine sacrifices everything for her lover, and then dies. The usual thing.'

'*La Traviata*,' murmured Bea, her heart sinking. She had a feeling Lady Victoria's family would only settle for the best box, and she had no wish to spend the evening being stared at, as she perched next to Jon and prayed he had more sense than to attempt to hold her hand, leading to an undignified scuffle in the stalls.

'Is it?' Vicky still had her eyes on Harri, who was shuffling slightly in his seat, as if faced with a glided, shimmering boa constrictor. 'Yes, I expect so. It will be a terrible bore. Mama is tone deaf and talks to Aunt Eliza all the way through. She's only going because the Prince of Wales is supposed to be in the next box. She knows one of the Ladies in Waiting, so it's bound to be true.' She sighed. 'I think she's given me up as a wife, so is trying me as a mistress, in the hope he'll marry me off to an Earl afterwards.'

'As long as you can choose the Earl,' said Olwen, laughing, as she joined them.

'I mean it.' Vicky slipped neatly into the front passenger seat. 'I'm afraid this means I'm going to have to get myself arrested as a suffragette, and give them a false name, of course, so they don't just release me.'

Bea and Olwen exchanged glances. 'You wouldn't, would you?' said Olwen. 'The ones who've been in prison say it's vile.' Her voice became serious. 'Some of the things they do to the women in the name of force-feeding, Vicky, are almost unthinkable. I've treated some of them, the ones who were too ashamed to tell their husbands or their families, or even go to their own doctor. What I saw had nothing to do with saving their lives, it was more like the worst forms of torture, designed to break them. One or two died of a seizure only a few months afterwards. Believe me, nothing is worth that. There are plenty of other ways of embarrassing the government.'

Vicky waved her hand. 'They obviously hadn't got strong stomachs. It would serve Papa right if they did do horrible things to me. Can you just imagine the scandal?'

Olwen shook her head. Harri concentrated on driving, politely avoiding Vicky's attempts at conversation, until he drew up in front of a large house within a high wall and a gateway. Vicky jumped out, and strode up the driveway with a cheerful wave.

'Could she really get herself arrested and give a false name?' said Olwen.

'Probably. I doubt if she has any idea what she'd be letting herself in for, though,' replied Harri. 'But Vicky will do whatever she wants. I suspect she is not in the habit of listening to others.'

The atmosphere inside the vehicle had eased, now it was just the three of them, a return to the intimacy of that first night. There are things that bind you, thought Bea. Being attacked by the police and having to escape through the attics was one of them.

'How's Gwen?' she asked. 'One of the girls in the kitchens said she'd come back to London again.'

'And back to her old job,' Olwen confirmed. 'She's too good a worker for them to let her go.'

'And planning her next speech,' said Harri. 'She won't lie low. There's another one who won't listen.' He gave a wry grunt. 'But then most of my clients won't listen to my advice. It's what authority never understands. Put human beings with their backs against the wall, make them feel they have nothing to lose and, man or woman, they will fight to the death. No wonder the government are nervous. I'd be, if I was so foolish as to be one of them.'

'Unless you were elected to fight them,' said Olwen.

He laughed. 'A good thing I have no ambitions that way, it costs a fortune. I'll just have to remain a thorn in the side of the courts, with no hope of being invited to join any of the gentleman's clubs. My chances of being made a Lord are sinking fast.'

Bea smiled. 'Well, after washing up all day, my hopes of marrying a Lord have gone out of the window. I'm not quite sure how Cinderella managed it.'

'Don't worry, they'll put you on beating the cake mixtures next,' said Olwen. 'Cook always says that's a way to a man's heart.'

'Why is it that women think men are such shallow creatures?' grumbled Harri. The conversation turned light-hearted until Harri pulled up in front of the lecture hall, allowing Olwen to jump out and rush to join the rest of her evening class.

'Thank you,' said Bea, the awkwardness returning, as Harri set off once more.

'Not at all. You must be exhausted.'

They drove without exchanging a word the rest of the way, Harri concentrating on following the correct route as dusk fell. After all, thought Bea, what was the point of any conversation? There was nothing more to say. She couldn't even blame him for the emptiness that had opened up in her heart: he had warned her that he was not a free man. She only had herself to blame for her feelings.

She was glad when he drew up, as he had done before, just out of sight of Curzon Avenue.

'I never meant to hurt you,' he said.

'I know.'

'I don't know what came over me, that evening. It's not my usual behaviour.'

'It's quite all right,' she said, stiffly.

'I hope we are still friends.' He turned towards her. 'I can't offer you anything else, not for many years to come. Maybe never. There will be someone out there for you, Bea, I'm sure of it. I can't ask you to wait.'

'I understand,' said Bea. But you can't stop me waiting either, she thought to herself. Or stop me finding a way to help Olwen, so you can be free. She reached to open the door, not daring to say anything more.

'Wait.' Harri grabbed her hand, pulling her back towards him. 'Shhh,' he muttered in her ear as she began to protest.

Footsteps made their way along the pavement. Bea saw Jon's familiar figure stride past them, thankfully too deep in thought to take a second glance at the dark interior of a parked vehicle.

At the corner of the road he stopped, bending to light a cigarette, the flame flaring briefly into his face. It was not the expression of a man eagerly rushing to the side of the woman he loved. More like that of one facing an unwelcome chore. He remained under the lamp as he finished his cigarette with an unflattering lack of haste.

'Don't you dare marry such a graceless idiot,' whispered Harri. 'He could never in a thousand years be worthy of you.' Bea's answer, tart as it was, stilled on her lips. 'What?' he demanded when she gasped.

A man had stopped next to Jon, holding out a cigarette for a light. The overcoat had changed, but not the brightly coloured knitted scarf around his neck.

'It's the drunk who was at Lillian's refuge,' she whispered.

'It can't be. How on earth could he find his way here?'

The man bent closer, the match illuminating his face. 'There. You see? It is the same man. He's still wearing the scarf he took from me.'

'How very strange.'

The man was speaking to Jon, who listened intently.

'Let's hope he's not intent on robbery. We might have to rescue your cousin, much as it goes against the grain.'

Clear in the lamplight, Jon put his hand his inner pocket, and removed a wad of money from his wallet. The man took it, disappearing immediately into a small park on one side of the road. Jon stood for a while, before stuffing his wallet back inside his jacket, extinguishing the end of his cigarette beneath his heel and slowly making his way towards the house.

Bea and Harri sat without moving. 'Wait,' said Harri at last. 'I'll take you closer.' He drove past number six as Jon arrived at the door, pulling up at a discreet distance on the other side.

'The man could be watching,' said Bea, uneasily.

'Hopefully not.'

Bea swallowed. She couldn't wait here all night, and if the man in the greatcoat had been lying in wait for Jon, he must already know the location of the Tressillion's London house. 'Thank you,' she muttered, stepping out on to the pavement. Jon had gone in. Taking a deep breath, she hurried towards the house.

As she pushed open the door and stepped inside, she heard the roar of Harri's engine, racing away into the gathering darkness.

Chapter Eighteen

'Six months.'

Madoc looked up from mooring his boat. Sybil stood on the jetty next to the cottage, arms folded. 'Six months?'

She nodded. 'I'll employ you as Manager. I'll give you free reign to choose your assistants. Subject to my approval,' she added quickly. Madoc hid a smile. 'Along with the tools you need. And I'll give you six months. If you can prove to me that the mine will work, then I'll be prepared to invest in restoring the outbuildings and the processing plant.'

'And if not?'

'You and your men will have had guaranteed employment for that length of time.'

'I see.' He slung his catch over one shoulder and climbed the short ladder to join her. 'And you?'

'Me?' She bristled. 'I'll have lost nothing. Only my investment. And if I didn't have it to lose, I wouldn't be offering.'

Grief, she was prickly! Madoc shook his head. She was like no woman he'd ever met, not even the mams from the village back at home, sure of their matriarchal power, or the crotchety grandmothers, ruling the roost. He was not much of a one for women. His wife had been the only girl he'd ever had eyes for, from the day they had met, when they were barely more than children, and he hadn't had the heart for experimenting since. The cold wind and the harshness of the sea was his solace.

Miss Ravensdale he couldn't make out at all. He wasn't entirely sure he even trusted her. Was there a heart, he wondered, underneath that hard exterior? It had never mattered before, but if he was to entrust his life – and that of village men with wives and children depending on them – he needed to be convinced.

'I meant, if we don't find anything, I will have risked my time, and there will be nothing here for me, or the men I may recruit.'

'I'm prepared to risk my investment,' she returned. 'I made my fortune by having a good eye for business and a willingness to take risks. It's always paid off before. I've no intention of letting it fail now.'

Madoc hesitated. He had found a sense of purpose in the original plans he'd drawn up for the Tressillions in the dark winter evenings. But to find the elusive seam of gold that Mr Tressillion had spent years searching for – that most likely had never existed at all – in six months was madness. It was bound to fail. He'd made a kind of a life for himself here in the cottage by the sea. A quiet routine, working only to provide his basic needs, living simply, free of ties and the fell hand of a master ruling his life.

Seeking a seam of gold that had never been seen, in a part of the country where gold was rarely found, was to make a rod for his own back. Miss Ravensdale was definitely the last thing he needed. He had a feeling that every decision could become a battle of wills. Miss Ravensdale, with her empire of hotels, was clearly accustomed to getting her own way. If she was like any other employer he'd ever worked for, she was capable of utter ruthlessness. On the other hand…

'It would be good for the village,' he said aloud. 'The old people are always telling me how it lost heart when the Hargreaves' old tin mine closed. And then lost its spirit when the gold mine failed,' he added under his breath.

'So you agree to my proposal?'

'I'll consider it.'

'Good. Don't flatter yourself, Mr Lewis. If it's not you, I'll find someone else. It seems to me that the question of whether the mine could ever be profitable needs to be answered before I decide what to do with the house. Maybe I'll sell it and find a less industrial location for my hotel.' She looked back up to Tressillion, her coat whipping around her in the wind, hair shimmering with salt spray. 'If anyone was foolish enough to take it off my hands, that is. Maybe the house doesn't want to give up its secrets. No-one who has ever tried to make a fortune from Tressillion has succeeded, so I was told.'

'That's the story I have heard, too. But I don't believe a house can will misfortune on its occupants.'

'No, nor do I.' She wound her long scarf around her head to keep out the wind. 'But I sometimes wonder if those who have lived in a place leave more than their memories, once they have gone.'

'I hope not! I wouldn't stay another night under this roof, if I believed that.'

'Oh?'

'When I first asked about renting the cottage, and why it had been empty for years, I thought it would be rats, or the sea crumbling at the foundations. Instead I was told no-one would go near the place. The last man to live here drowned himself after the failure of the tin mine. He'd worked there all his life, I was told. But when Mr Tressillion took it over, he considered him too old to employ, despite his experience. He was too proud to beg or end his days in a workhouse. They say the spirit of a suicide never rests.'

She shuddered. 'You don't believe that, surely?'

'I've never seen a ghost, if that is what you are asking. I'm not sure I'd believe in them, even if I did.' He glanced at her sideways. 'But I can see how such stories arise. Even the short time I've been here, there are times when the wind is high and spray lashes the windows, that I can sometimes swear I hear a creak amongst the rafters.'

'Don't! A spirit coming back from the dead is nothing to joke about.'

'It's no joke. I never saw myself as a man of much imagination, until I came to live here.' He pulled a wry face. 'Or maybe it was a desperate hope, that if one ghost could rise again, maybe another could too. And for that I would have braved the Devil himself.'

'I'm sorry,' she said, slowly.

'Don't be,' he muttered, embarrassed at having let his guard down so unexpectedly. 'The loss of a loved one is an everyday story.'

'But no less painful.'

'True.'

Her face had softened, losing some of its guardedness. For an instant he glimpsed beneath the bristles. There was a faint glisten in her eyes that could have been the result of spray, but hinted at the passionate young girl she might once have been. 'I'll be at the house next Thursday,' she added briskly, turning away. 'I'll expect your answer then. And there is one condition.'

'Which is?'

'It's my investment that is at risk. So we follow my route first. If there is no way through, or no sign that it can be viable, only then do we try the other routes.'

She was stubborn. And quite certain she was right. He had very little choice, unless he walked away. His head told him it was madness, risking his life, and those of his men, almost certainly for nothing. Reason told him to refuse. To return to scraping a living from the sea, eked out by small pieces of building work now and again. Madoc dumped the fish in a bucket on the porch, sick of even the stench of them. He was not a fisherman, having only ever intended the little cottage to be a temporary home, a place to settle as he made a new life for himself. Now, he acknowledged, he longed for a more permanent way of living. Gold or no gold, this opportunity of settled employment, however short it might be, might be his means of starting again.

'I accept the condition,' he said. 'But for three months. Not the entire six. I can see the rationale behind attempting a new route. But it is a risk. This gives a chance of attempting both routes.'

She thought about it. Slowly, she nodded. 'Agreed.'

'I know of a couple of experienced miners and some lads who would be suitable to undertake the heavy work. I'll bring them to you to be interviewed.'

'Very well.' She held out her hand. For a moment he was slightly taken aback at such a business-like gesture from a woman. He wiped his fish smelling hand self-consciously on his non-too-pristine jacket before returning the handshake. She didn't appear to notice the dirt, or the roughness of his salt-chaffed hands. She was brisk, releasing her grip almost immediately, avoiding any hint of intimacy. A woman accustomed to dealing with men, used to finding her way in a man's world, and not giving an inch.

He hadn't felt curiosity in years. Perhaps his new appetite for life was stirring up questions he sensed would not be answered. He met her gaze. Her eyes were the green of the sea when sunlight first stirred its depths after a storm. Large, expressive eyes, set beneath fine arched brows.

He turned away, before his face could reveal too much. 'I'll see you on Thursday, then.'

'Yes. Good.' She hesitated briefly, as if willing to continue the conversation. He bent over the bucket of fish, his face hidden. When he looked up again she had gone.

Madoc watched her, the lone figure, striding across the fields. He left the fish to their own devices, reaching instead for the half-empty bottle of French brandy hidden beneath the porch, payment for repairing a small boat along the coast, with no questions asked. He poured a large dose into the tin mug placed over the top for convenience (and as a nominal disguise from the local constabulary, who knew better than to look too closely), knocking it back in one go, grimacing at the fire shooting down into his belly.

As he poured a second slug, he noted the tremor of his hand with detached curiosity. But not even the brandy could shake the feeling, that strange unsettling feeling, of blood returning to frozen limbs, stirred by Miss Ravensdale's storm-green eyes.

Chapter Nineteen

Despite Bea's fears, there was no embarrassing scene at *La Traviata*. She sat demurely, taking care not to look up at the boxes. And if Vicky saw her, she probably didn't recognise her, or at least did not signal that they were acquainted. Bea glimpsed her briefly during an interval, dressed in a gossamer lace gown, with diamonds at her throat and ears, making no attempt to hide her boredom as she sipped champagne with the crowd of admirers around her.

Mama was in heaven. With Jon beside her, old acquaintances greeted her as if she had never missed a season, as if her husband was at the other end of the room, deep in conversation with a lord or a duke, planning the next grouse shoot, or his own entrance to the House of Lords. 'Just as it used to be,' sighed Mama, wistfully. Just how Papa had promised it would be again, once the Tressillion mine had given up its gold.

Bea loved the music and the thrill of being taken to another world, but she understood Vicky's boredom. The truth was, the performance took second place to the ritual of seeing and being seen. The women around her compared performances and everyone's gowns in the same breath, ticking off just how many Russian princesses and minor members of the royal family were present from an invisible list.

She stood next to Jon, attempting to match small talk with the wives of his friends as they waited on the edges of their menfolk's conversation. She had no children, and no house of her own, nor a husband to quietly complain of. Their obvious curiosity about her made her glad when the evening ended. Tressillion would always make her an object of pity among those who had known Papa. Pity or resentment – in some cases even hatred – and a ghoulish hunger to be the first to know the true story behind the Dreadful Events retold with bloodthirsty enthusiasm in the newspapers.

Bea dodged Jon's attempt to linger, as he returned them to the house in Curzon Avenue, but it was clear she would not be able to keep him at bay for long. In other circumstances, she could have laughed at her anxiety at whether an eligible young man of good fortune would delay proposing or not, and the hope he might propose to another young lady instead. The trouble was, the longer she spent in Jon's company, the less she felt she knew him at all. She had watched him all evening, attempting to find some sign of worry, or even guilt, any sign of his meeting with the man with her scarf wrapped so tightly around his neck. Maybe some sign of wishing to confide in her. But there was nothing. Just as there had never been any sign of his passion for Miss Lane.

Jon was a man of secrets, just as Papa had been. She couldn't explain that to Mama. They never spoke of Papa and his obsession or his temper. As far as Mama was concerned, Papa banning Leo from Tressillion, his erasing of any sign of his son having lived there at all, had never happened. Sometimes, as she listened to Mama's gentle complaining, Bea wondered what else her mother had never spoken of. In her heart of hearts, she couldn't believe that her mother had always been immune to Papa's irrational outbursts of rage.

That night at the opera, she looked at Jon and wondered how many more secrets he kept beneath his calm exterior, just as Papa had done. To a casual observer, Papa had been the perfect gentleman, a doting husband and a loving father. She had no ambition to save Jon. From her experience of Papa, the task was a hopeless one. She realised she had no wish to discover what lay beneath his veneer of conventional respectability. She might not know much of the world, but she knew that by the time she found out if Jon shared her father's temper and implacable will to rule, it would be too late. Far, far too late.

The night of *La Traviata*, far from fulfilling Mama's hopes of bringing the two of them closer, had made Bea more determined than ever to find some way of being able to support them all. Jon's attempt to linger in corridors had only made the issue more urgent.

The evening was still in her mind as, a few days later, she collected the Box Brownie camera in its leather case from the White Camellia and went, with a tight knot in her stomach, to the rally held by Mrs Anselm, to be followed by a march through the streets. It was to be a small one, a relatively quiet affair, Olwen reassured her, and just the opportunity to practice with the camera.

'Just watch out for the police, and make sure you give them no reason to arrest you,' she warned.

'At least then Jon wouldn't still wish to marry me,' Bea replied, gloomily.

As she made her way into Hyde Park to join the rally, it struck Bea that Jon would consider any refusal an affront to his pride, even more so as she couldn't claim a previous love had prevented her from falling at his feet. The lack of any rival would make it quite bleakly clear that it was him she found wanting and, given her lack of fortune and prospects, equally clear to Jon's acquaintances too. Sympathy at his inability to follow his heart and Miss Cassie Lane due to family commitments, might well turn into laughter behind his back. If Jon was anything like Papa, he would be a proud man, jealous of his reputation, and not one to allow a woman who had made a fool of him live rent-free in his property.

It made it more urgent that ever that she found a way of supporting them all before Jon had a chance to propose. She didn't expect anyone would buy this first attempt at photojournalism. Even if no magazine or newspaper would print it, or if her photographs were not good enough to be exhibited on the walls of the White Camellia, she had to start somewhere. At least she was doing something, rather than sitting at home, trying to avoid any meaningful conversation with Mama and dreading a knock on the door.

She could hear the eager chatter of voices before she saw the hundreds of men and women gathering in the park. She could make out Vicky, in the middle of a large group of the White Camellia regulars, all deep in excited conversation as they unfurled the banner of the Suffrage League of Women Artists and Journalists.

Bea took refuge under a large tree and pulled the camera from its case. She had loaded the film in The White Camellia, so now all she needed to do was to negotiate the unfamiliar clips and buttons. Olwen had shown her how to unclip the front section, allowing a small runner to open out. The bellows attaching the camera to the lens rolled out and fixed into place.

She had worried that the donated camera would be one of those heavy, old-fashioned machines, requiring a tripod and taking only one plate at a time. She was relieved it was a folding Kodak brownie, similar to the one Leo had taught her to use, that could be hand-held and took a roll of film of eight photographs. She'd managed to keep aside a little of her earnings and had taken a deep breath before marching into the pawnbroker's a few streets away from the tearooms, where she pawned a brooch and ring she rarely wore to buy a roll of film, the chemicals to develop it, and the paper to print the photographs in the tiny darkroom Leo had set up in the basement at Curzon Avenue. Papa had destroyed Leo's darkroom in the cellars of Tressillion House, after selling every piece of carefully collected equipment, but he had been too distracted trying to find new shareholders for the mine each time they came to London, and the tiny room in the corner of the basement had survived.

Bea fiddled again with the aperture settings and the focus, trying to remember everything Leo had told her about exposure and making sure the pictures were sharp, with as little movement in them as possible. With only eight chances at the most, she was going to have to choose her shots carefully. She looked up at the crowd milling about, banners waving in the wind. It was almost impossible to focus on one section of the crowd now, and she had a feeling that once the march started, things were going to move quickly.

She peered through the viewfinder, her eyes already remembering how to judge a scene upside down and back to front, allowing her to frame the crowd. In the distance she could hear Mrs Anselm's voice. The crowd grew still as they listened, the banners held steady. She waited until she was sure she had a good shot and clicked the shutter. Then there was nothing more she could do until she got into the darkroom and could see if the picture came out or ended up a hopeless blur. She carefully wound on the film to the next frame, all ready, and scribbled a few lines in her notebook to go with the photograph if it was useable.

'You are going to have to hide that, if you are thinking of trying to photograph the march.' She turned to find Lillian standing behind her, holding a large package and watching her with a frown. 'The police don't like their actions being recorded.'

'I'll be careful,' replied Bea. There was something about Lillian that always made her feel like a small child who hadn't washed her hands and was lying about it. 'I'm really just practicing, so I don't expect I'll be trying to get any actual photographs when the march really starts. I didn't realise it was going to be so big.'

'This one is small compared to some of the suffragette marches. There were 500,000 on the one last October. The Pankhursts are charismatic speakers, and draw an audience, as well as controversy. I'm afraid Mrs Anselm and the SLWAJ can no longer compete.'

'You brought it!' A young woman rushed up to them, her face lit up with excitement. 'I knew you would, Miss Finch.'

'I only finished it last night, so I hope the ink is fully dry,' said Lillian, with a smile. 'Just pray it doesn't rain.'

'It will be wonderful. I know it will. You always design the best banners.'

'The most colourful, I hope.' Lillian handed over the package, which unfurled to reveal an eye-catching green border around large letters declaring 'Votes for Women' and 'No Taxation Without Representation'.

'Aren't you joining them?' asked Bea, as the delighted recipients rushed towards the march.

'I'm not fond of public display,' replied Lillian. She caught the look on Bea's face. 'I can make exceptions, Miss Tressillion. Lady Hanbury is one of the benefactors of the refuge. My relations with one or two of the others can be, well, shall we say… Difficult? Lady Hanbury enjoys bringing a touch of scandal to her gatherings, and it seems to me a very small price to pay for her very generous support.' She gave a wicked grin. 'You see, Miss Tressillion, I was employed as an artist's model when I was working my way through art school. The fact that I once removed my clothes for money will always make me a scandalous woman capable of anything. Even though I'm now displayed in some of the best galleries in London and Manchester.'

'I'd never be that brave,' sighed Bea.

'Brave?'

'I mean, to make myself so vulnerable.'

Lillian considered her. 'Yes, you are right. I did feel vulnerable and not in the least bit brave or shocking. Even though I only ever posed for female artists and men I knew would treat me with respect. I was very young, and determined to attend art school, and it was one of the ways to keep from starvation – until my family were in a position to support me.' The grin was back again. Bea had a feeling Lillian was trying to shock her. 'And then I was free to become wild and really scandalous.'

Bea kept her face expressionless. 'But now you run the refuge.'

'Yes. What's left of my family disapproves. I'm sure they think I'm throwing my life away after all that hard work and money and years of study. I still paint and design when I can.' She frowned at the marchers. 'But I suppose I always needed a mission in life. I've been fortunate in having help to finish my training and to set up the refuge. I can't just marry some rich man and live my life as a lady painter.' Her gaze was in the far distance. 'I can never forget what it was like to be thrown out on the streets when we could no longer pay our rent, however hard we worked.' Her eyes returned to meet Bea's. 'Have you any idea what can happen to young girls who are left destitute like that?' Bea shook her head. Lillian's eyes were sharp and hostile once more. There was a faint flick of contempt in her voice that made Bea feel very small. 'Well, just hope you never do.'

In the distance, Mrs Anselm had finished speaking and the marchers were preparing to move.

'I'd better go,' muttered Bea.

Lillian put a hand on her arm. Her voice had lost its edge. 'I meant what I said, Beatrice. Find a way of concealing that camera. Unlike a drawing, a photograph can't be argued with and the police don't like their tactics against protesters being made public.' She gave a grudging smile. 'I respect your determination, but be careful you don't make yourself a target. Some of the police are not afraid of using their fists and their boots, and worse, if they think someone is a troublemaker. Leave the heroics to Mrs Pankhurst and her followers. You'll be far more effective in achieving your aim if you try not to draw attention to yourself.'

'I'll do my best,' said Bea. She looked down at the Brownie. It might be the smallest camera she had ever used, but it was still very obvious, and definitely visible. 'It's going to be a bit tricky.'

'Here.' Lillian pulled a silk shawl from her shoulders. 'Wrap this around it. That might help a bit.'

'I can't take your shawl!'

Lillian's eyes sharpened. 'It's not a personal gift, Miss Tressillion. It's to help the cause of the suffrage movement.'

Bea swallowed. Whatever she did, she managed to offend Lillian somehow. 'Thank you,' she said. 'I'd really better go.'

Lillian's sharpness eased. She smiled a little. 'Good luck. I look forward to seeing the results.'

Bea hesitated. She didn't want to raise Lillian's hostility again, but she seemed to have raised it without trying before, and she might never have another chance. 'Can I ask you something?'

'Of course.'

'The man at the refuge.' Lillian looked blank. Bea swallowed. 'The one I gave money to.'

Lillian's eyes narrowed. 'What of him?'

'I just wondered if you knew more about him?'

'Unless they choose to volunteer information, we don't ask,' she replied, shortly, turning and walking away. After a few paces she stopped. 'What makes you have an interest in him?'

'I'd never seen him before that day, but he seemed to know me. I'm truly sorry I gave him money,' she added. 'But I was lost and alone in a strange place and afraid not to. I hoped it would make him go away.' She blushed. 'I know it was foolish, and I shouldn't have been so ignorant, but I was afraid.'

Lillian gave a low grunt. 'His manner can certainly be intimidating. Well, I suppose there was no harm done. If it hadn't been you, it would have been someone else.'

'Oh, no, you were quite right, and I should have known he would only spend it on drink. I wasn't seeking to justify myself.' She bit her lip. 'It's just, I'm sure I saw him again, near our house in Twickenham.'

There was a moment's silence. 'You must be mistaken, Miss Tressillion. There would be nothing for a man like that there.'

'But that's it. He was talking to my cousin Jonathan. The man who accompanied me to Lady Hanbury's party,' she explained. 'I don't know what was said, and Jon hasn't mentioned anything, but he isn't the kind to confide. I'm sure it was the same man.' She hesitated. Lillian was looking sceptical. It was on the tip of Bea's tongue to tell her about the scarf he had taken from her, that he still wore around his neck. As if it were a trophy, she reflected, with an inward shiver. She knew it was her scarf, but there was nothing to prove that. Lillian didn't think much of her as it was. She didn't want to look like a silly girl, who'd been shut away in safety all her life, reading cheap novels and indulging in morbid flights of fantasy. 'He seemed to have such a hatred of the Tressillions,' she added, feebly.

Lillian considered her. 'Very well. I'll keep an eye out for him at the refuge. He's one of those who only turns up now and again. He's quite capable of holding down a job when he's sober, but it never lasts for long, and when he returns to the bottle, as he always does, he eventually finds his way back to the refuge.'

'You don't think he's the sort of man who could be capable of blackmail?' Bea was still uneasy. 'The Tressillions have done things that have hurt many people. I'm sure there are still many who wish us harm.'

'So I've heard,' replied Lillian, dryly. She nodded. 'Very well, I'll keep a look out for him. Although if he has found a means of getting money out of your cousin, I doubt if we'll see him for some time.'

'Thank you.' There was so much more she wanted to ask, but Lillian had the look of one who couldn't wait to leave. 'I'd better go if I'm to catch up with the marchers.'

'Remember to stay out of notice of the police. Keep that camera well hidden and don't give them any excuse to arrest you.'

'I'll do my best,' called Bea, racing to join the ranks of the protestors.

* * *

For the most part, the march was a cheerful affair. There were calls of sympathy from the shopkeepers in their doorways, and windows thrown open to watch them pass. There were catcalls and insults too, from small crowds that gathered on the pavements, with even a few missiles to be dodged now and again.

'Just ignore them,' said Vicky, turning her glare on the men spilling out of the barber's shop to advise her to get herself a husband, if she could. In the confusion, Bea found it almost impossible to get a scene into focus long enough to take a photograph. She tried one of two women holding a banner between them, but she knew as she took it they had moved, and would be out of focus. This was proving to be impossible. Bea gritted her teeth. There had to be a way.

As the procession slowed to allow a tram to pass, she moved to one side of the crowd. A small group under a 'Votes for Women' banner stopped next to her, their faces still animated from chanting. Bea focussed, praying that the exposure was right, and pressed the shutter. Just in time, the tram passed and the group moved on again. But this time she had a good feeling about the picture. As the march wound its way through the streets, she hovered at the edges, keeping pace, looking for a group who might tell a story in pictures. She should get some of them to stop, she thought. She caught the eye of a group of shop girls, who willingly stepped out of the crowd and posed around their banner. Next she found a husband and wife with two little girls, who stood shyly, but smiling, as the crowd moved on around them.

As the march began to slow towards its end, she had only one shot left. Bea watched, waiting for the perfect picture, the one that might be considered good enough to grace the walls of the Camellia. She didn't know what she was looking for, but she was confident she would know it when she saw it.

'Bloody coppers,' muttered one of the women just behind her. 'I thought they were going to leave us alone for once. They can't resist.'

Bea turned. Three policemen were pulling a woman out of the crowd. Her hat was gone, her hair falling down around her face.

'Get your hands off me,' she yelled. 'Call this a free country? Get your hands off me!'

The marchers near her were turning to intervene, as the protester was pulled out, struggling, between two burly officers. Bea focussed as fast as she could, feeling the satisfying click of the shutter as the woman was dragged out by her hair.

'Watch it!' hissed one of the shop girls. Bea turned to find several large policemen bearing down on her. The one in the lead was red-faced and furious. The shop girls scurried to either side of their banner, opening up just enough space for her to slip through. Bea shot between them and in amongst the marchers. There was a shout behind her and yells of protest as the officers pushed their way through the crowd. Bea kept on going, moving against the crowd, focussed on the distant banner of the White Camellia.

'What is it?' demanded Vicky as Bea passed her, scurrying behind the banner.

'Police,' she replied breathlessly. 'They saw me taking photographs. I think they want to get the camera.'

'Idiots,' sniffed Vicky. The crowd slowed again. Bea took refuge behind the Camellia's banner while she hastily dismantled the camera, clipping it into place and shoving it into its leather pouch. She put the long strap round her neck and the pouch underneath her coat. 'Here,' said Vicky, grabbing Bea's hat and swapping it for her own. With her other hand, she took Lillian's silk shawl, winding it around her own shoulders. Not a moment too soon.

'No need to shove!' came a shout in front, as the policemen forced their way through. 'This is a peaceful demonstration.'

'Yes?' demanded Vicky haughtily, as they stopped next to her. 'I hope you caught that pickpocket. He tried to get my pocket watch, the wretched child. Can't you find a chimney for him to sweep?'

The officers blinked. Bea kept her head down, her hat over her face, out of sight behind Vicky and the banner.

'Beg pardon, Miss,' muttered the nearest policemen. 'Must have gone this way.' The two men shot off in hot pursuit of anything that took them from under Vicky's aristocratic nose.

'Thanks,' said Bea, returning Vicky's hat.

'Not at all.' Vicky handed back Bea's hat and Lillian's shawl. She smiled. 'That brother of yours…'

'Leo?'

Vicky gave a sentimental sigh. 'Yes. He was a good man. Far too good to be wasted on some bluestocking. I'm sorry he's dead. I was hoping that he and I would bump into each other again. I had a feeling that life would always be interesting if he was there, even if Papa disapproved.'

'You could always make your life interesting yourself,' suggested Bea.

'I suppose so.' Vicky sighed again. 'But the thing is, how?'

Bea gave up. She wasn't sure Vicky was looking for an answer anyhow. She took the opposite side of the banner from one of the tearooms' regular clientele, who looked if her arms were about to drop off with exhaustion, and joined in the march as if she had always been in that position, her folded-up camera safely hidden inside her coat.

Chapter Twenty

'Thank goodness,' said Olwen the next morning as Bea crept into the print room before the White Camellia opened for business. 'I heard there were a few arrests. I did wonder if we'd see you today.'

'Most of us had left by the time the police really moved in,' replied Bea. 'It was peaceful until near the end.' She took out the camera from its hiding place under her coat and placed it back on its shelf.

'And?'

Bea sighed in frustration. 'Most didn't come out as I wanted. It was hard to get everyone when they were moving. I nearly got one of the police, but it's far too blurred to see what they are doing. I'm going to have to find another way. At least I'll know to get more of the marchers to pose in front of their banners next time. I know it won't quite be the same as when they are marching, but at least you'll be able to see what the banners say. Some came out.' She held out a print showing the crush of bodies between the trees of Hyde Park, as far as the eye could see, and the shop girls smiling in front of their banner.

'Those are brilliant,' exclaimed Olwen. 'There's hardly any blurring at all and it gives a real feel of what it's like to be there.'

Bea frowned at them as she laid the prints out on the desk. 'They were getting better towards the end. The trouble was, I was too busy trying to get the right picture I didn't talk to any of the marchers and ask them why they were there. I need to remember to do both. I've still got a roll of film and some paper left. Some of the women were talking about a much bigger march Mrs Pankhurst is organising in a few weeks' time. I've learnt so much from this one, I'm bound to get better. I want to try and tell the stories of individual protestors, even if I don't use their names. Most of them were calm and rational, and not at all like the harridans they are seen as in the newspapers.'

'It's a good idea, Bea. There's such nonsense written about the campaigners for women's rights. I'm sure Mrs Anselm would be enthusiastic about putting the stories in the Camellia magazine, and they could put up a display of the photographs in the tearooms. They've got some of Lillian's sketches and some photographs of marches from years ago, but nothing to reflect what's happening now. We can see if we can find a way of incorporating the photograph into the next magazine. It's just the sort of thing they'll want to display in the tearooms, and then who knows what it might lead to?'

'I wish the one of the policeman was more than just a blur,' sighed Bea.

'Don't worry, it was brave of you to try and take it at all. One day you'll be in the right time and the right place, and then you'll have a picture that will cause a real stir.'

'I'd better go,' said Bea, hastily, as laughter announced the arrival of the kitchen staff. 'I'm being promoted to assisting with the cakes today. At least I won't spend all day washing up and mopping.'

Olwen laughed. 'I look forward to seeing you covered in flour. Just remember to do everything Mrs Teal says. She likes things done her way.'

'I'll remember,' said Bea, heading off into the tearooms. Oddly enough, she enjoyed her time in the kitchens, despite the heat and exhaustion, and her hands burning from the scrubbing and the washing soda. Once she'd settled in, she liked being surrounded by women laughing and chattering to ease the day's tasks. And the gossip! The talk amongst Mama's friends had always been polite and rather dull. Here the conversation was full of curiosity about the everyday triumphs and tragedies of the men and women who came regularly for tea and buns at the White Camellia, and those working in the shops and offices in the surrounding street, interspersed with the eccentricities of the artists and pickpockets of Covent Garden. Bea felt she had learnt about a whole side of life she never knew existed. There were political discussions, too. Few resulted in passionate arguments of policy or belief. After all, they had to work together. But none of the chatter could be described as idle.

Mama had never let them anywhere near the kitchens. At the White Camellia, Bea watched with astonishment as an unpromising collection of dried fruit, flour and butter were turned into delicious cakes. Mrs Teal, who had been at the tearooms for years and ran the kitchens with a rod of iron, could turn any ingredients into magical confections while shouting orders left, right and centre. Bea almost didn't mind washing the hopelessly sticky pans to watch the marvel of spun sugar.

'Plain and simple,' Mrs Anselm would remark, as she swept in and out of her domain. 'Plain and simple, Marjory. Cheap and filling is what most of our women need.'

'A little sugar never cost anyone very much,' Mrs Teal would retort. 'Besides, it cheers them up at the end of the day.' Mrs Anselm never stopped to argue. Mrs Teal, short and square, was as unmovable as a rock when she set her mind to it. It fascinated Bea that her large hands, mainly busy beating and stirring and clipping the odd hapless trainee around the ear, could be so delicate, her face lost in a fairy story of her own.

As the day wore on, Bea considered herself lucky to avoid a clip, in the confusion of weighing and measuring. She was taught to beat flour and sugar together, and a seemingly endless stream of eggs. By the afternoon, her back ached, her legs shook with tiredness, and her arms felt as if they had been beating carpets without stop.

'You'll do,' said Mrs Teal, wiping her hands on her apron. 'You do as you are told, and you stick at it. Not bad for your first day.' She grinned. 'You'll get used to it. It's quiet for a while. I suggest you go and have a cup of tea and something to eat. I can't have my staff fainting.'

Bea was about to protest she had no intention of fainting. But having stopped, her stomach rumbled loudly and she would do anything to sit down for ten minutes.

'Thank you,' she murmured, removing her apron, smoothing down her hair, and escaping into the calm of the tearooms. As she looked around for a quiet corner where no-one would notice her closing her eyes for a few minutes, and rest her aching feet, she heard her name.

'Over here!' Olwen was sitting at a table near the window, with a woman in a large hat. 'Over here, Bea. Come and join us.' Stiffly, legs aching with every step, Bea made her way over. 'You look as if you've been on a treadmill,' said Olwen.

'I feel like it.'

'You won't even notice it after a few weeks,' said the woman in the hat, turning to reveal Gwen's thin face, slightly rounder and with more colour in the cheeks. 'I thought I'd never get used to factory work, but it's surprising how the body can adapt.'

'You came back,' said Bea. 'Won't the police still be looking for you?'

'So what if they are?' Gwen demolished her slice of tea loaf. 'Harri found me a post in a shop that isn't so strenuous as the factory, and I've got new lodgings just a few minutes' walk away. So now I'll have more time to work for the union. I've already been asked to speak at the next march. They can't arrest me for speaking my mind. And anyhow, Mrs Pankhurst says that she wants to be arrested. If they do things to her in prison it will show just how vile they are.'

'Let them be martyrs,' said Olwen, anxiously. 'They've got friends in high places. You can bet they'll be even more vile to someone who isn't of the right class.'

'Well, I'm not going to sit here and do nothing.' Gwen put down her teacup. 'I saw where you once lived, Bea. My dad lives in a fisherman's cottage just below Tressillion House. I didn't know it was quite so big.'

'Oh,' said Bea.

'Maybe Bea doesn't want to hear about her old home,' said Olwen.

'I was very sad to leave it,' said Bea. 'But I'm bound to hear about it at some time. I'm sure the new owners are making great changes.'

'Hardly any at all,' replied Gwen. 'I can see why you were sad. It's very beautiful. And very grand.'

'Not as grand as it used to be,' said Bea, with a smile.

'But it could be. I met the woman who bought the estate. She came to visit Dad while I was there. They are going to reopen the gold mine.'

'They can't!' Bea was horrified. 'Don't they know that it collapsed? That men died there? I'm sure no-one from the village would want to work there, not after what happened. There were all sorts of stories going around about the mine and the house being cursed.'

'It sounded to me like Miss Ravensdale isn't opening that part, but an entrance further down. She was talking about an older side. Dad said she seemed quite convinced they'd find something. He doesn't think they will, but she's persuaded him to start on that side.'

'Really?' Bea shuddered. 'I'd have thought the last thing anyone would want to do would be to reopen the mine.'

* * *

However hard she tried, she couldn't get the thought of Tressillion out of her head that day. How could anyone in their right mind want to reopen a tin mine where gold had once been rumoured to be seen, but none had been found? It was as if Papa's madness had remained in the ground around Tressillion, only to infect its new owner. And if there should be another collapse, this time it would be Gwen, and Harri and Olwen, who could be grieving.

It was still on her mind, the old griefs and the memories of those terrible days after the accident at the mine, as fresh as if they were yesterday, as she trudged home.

Turning the corner into Curzon Avenue, she saw Jon's automobile standing in front of the house. She came to a halt, hands clenched. Jon never arrived at the house unannounced. He was always methodical in telephoning Mama to let her know what time he was arriving, with an invitation to take them out to dinner or to the theatre. Maybe it was the memories of the disaster at the mine that day, the explosion rocking the earth, shattering in a moment the life she had never thought would change. But she could not help the dread gripping at her heart as she rushed towards the front door.

Chapter Twenty-One

'Mama?' called Bea, as she let herself in.

'We're up here, my dear.' The relief was evident in Mama's voice. Bea shrugged off her coat, tucked her hair into some kind of respectability and shot up the stairs.

'Beatrice.' Jon's face was tense, despite the smile.

'I told Jonathan you'd be back soon, Beatrice, dear.' Mama's tone held a warning, and her eyes were dark with anxiety. 'I told him this was your day for helping out with that charity you are so fond of.'

'Yes, Mama,' murmured Bea. Her stomach tightened into a knot. Had Jon come to propose? If he asked her outright to marry him, she could hardly play for time. He hadn't appeared to be in any hurry the last time he had visited, only a few days ago, and she couldn't flatter herself that he had suddenly been overwhelmed by her charms. Jon had never shown any signs of being an impetuous man, and she couldn't tell herself the expression in his eyes was passionate love.

'It's good to see you again, Jon,' she said. 'I hope you had a good journey.'

'I was in town on business,' he replied shortly. 'I thought you might like to take a walk in Curzon Park.'

'Of course,' said Bea, glancing at Mama.

Jon followed her glance with irritation. 'I'm sure you don't need a chaperone. After all, it is a public space and we are related by blood.'

'Yes, of course.' His brusqueness had only served to deepen

Mama's anxiety. 'You two young people go and enjoy yourself. It's a lovely sunny evening, and it seemed such a long winter this year.'

'We'll be back before dark,' said Jon, making for the door. Bea followed him, choosing her best coat which, unlike her everyday one, could be guaranteed not to have flour or grime clinging to its hem.

They walked rapidly along the pavement without speaking. When they reached the path between flowerbeds leading to a small central pond, Jon began to slow. 'I'm glad you have found an occupation, Beatrice,' he said at last. 'My mother was always very fond of her charitable work with the poor. I believe a woman should always have something to occupy her mind.'

'Thank you,' said Bea, wondering what on earth she was going to say if he asked her about the charity she was devoting her time to. To say it was the suffrage movement was probably the surest way to deter him from proposing. Perhaps he'd throw them out on the streets that night. But luckily Jon showed no further interest. Instead they walked on until the path reached a small Chinese-style bridge over the pond.

'You haven't heard anything from Tressillion?' asked Jon, as they watched the ducks speeding towards a small girl, who had just arrived with her nanny and handfuls of bread.

'Tressillion?' Bea felt the evening air cool upon her face.

'I thought you might still have friends there.'

She glanced at him. Surely Jon must know that many of their acquaintances had been lured into investing in Papa's mine? Even Mama's friends, some she had known all her married life, had refused to attend the funeral and had not written or spoken to her since. Mama's hurt was plain to see when she caught a glimpse of them at the other side of a theatre auditorium or at social gatherings, acknowledging Jon briefly, but passing Bea and Mama by as if they didn't exist. Jon must have some inkling of this?

'I haven't heard from anyone at Tressillion for a while,' she said.
'No-one?'

'No.'

'Pity.' He sighed. 'I thought you might be able to shed some light on these rumours about the reopening of the mine.'

'So it *is* being reopened.'

He swung round, his eyes accusing. 'I thought you said you hadn't heard from anyone.'

'I haven't. It was just something that was mentioned today at the tearooms.' She stopped, but he didn't appear to notice her slip. And, after all, she could just as well be referring to a Lyons Corner House or the Criterion at Piccadilly Circus. It probably never crossed his mind that she might dare the scandal of the Gardenia in Covent Garden, or the White Camellia. 'I thought they must be mistaken, or heard incorrectly.'

'There was no gold.' Jon was talking to himself, as if to convince himself. 'All the information I was given was quite clear: your father's ideas were perfectly irrational. It was a wild goose chase, from some made-up story. There is no gold in the Tressillion mine. There's no longer any tin. It was simply a fairy story. A trick. A hoax. No man in his right mind would have taken them seriously, let alone bankrupted so many on such flimsy evidence.' He scowled at the swans, who had arrived for their share of the crumbs, scattering the rest of the wildfowl as they sailed purposefully towards the shore. 'I was so sure this new owner, Miss Ravensdale or whatever she calls herself, had no head for business, taking on Tressillion without even trying to beat down the price. Ridiculous. It was clear from the state of the place, and the circumstances of the sale, that I'd have taken less, just to get the place off my hands and the creditors from my door.' His frown deepened. 'But maybe she – or whoever was backing her – was not such a fool, after all.'

'She might have just fallen in love with Tressillion,' said Bea, uncertainly. 'The rumours might not be true, or she might just be thinking about the idea. Surely anyone who understands what happened…'

'But maybe she knows more.' He swung round to face her. 'Everyone I consulted said the same: the mine was valueless. I'd hardly have sold it with the house if there had been any possibility of it being worth anything. I'd have taken no chances in losing a fortune. Supposing this Miss Ravensdale knew what the Hargreaves had found? I won't be taken for a fool.'

'I'm sure it's just curiosity,' said Bea. 'They won't find anything and then it will be forgotten again.' There was something in his tone that she couldn't quite put her finger on. But she knew she didn't like it.

'I won't be made a fool of,' he said, without hearing her. 'And I won't lose a fortune, and especially not to some hard-faced spinster.' He took her hands. 'You must still be in touch with people in Porth Levant. If there's anyone you can think of who might be able to tell you more, could you write to them, Beatrice? You would do that for me, wouldn't you? I would look such a fool if the family thought I'd had the wool pulled over my eyes and I'd sold Tressillion without exploring the possibility that the mine could earn us a fortune after all.' He drew her closer, his voice like silk, eyes soft on her face. 'You would do that for me, wouldn't you?'

She'd throw him in the river first. Bea looked down at her boots to hide the expression of her eyes. Even Jon might notice the flames in them at the insulting assumption that she would do whatever he wanted to preserve his name. That already, without a word of affection, or even a ring to her name, he was the entire focus of her life.

She took a deep breath, quelling the impulse to stamp on his toes. The look Cassie Lane had given him shot into her mind. Cassie had been wary, as if she had known Jon would always do what suited him, without any consideration for anyone else. Bea cursed herself for not seeing it sooner. She had known Jon as a child. He had always had his own way, always been the centre of attention, doted on by his parents and looked upon by the rest of the Tressillions as their future leader, one who would achieve great things. She'd seen it with her own eyes: she'd heard it in Mama's delight, and Papa's complacency, when Jon had been singled out as their future son-in-law.

There was something cold about Jon. If he was capable of any kind of love, that love was reserved for Cassie. But maybe even that was simply an ambition to own something so many men desired. She could no longer bear his touch. There was no way on this earth she would ever consent to be his wife. No amount of material comfort could ever compensate for a life of misery.

But she still needed to play for time while she could, to allow her to find an affordable apartment for Mama and Ada. She swallowed her pride. 'Of course,' she said. 'I'll do what I can.'

Relief spread over his face. 'Dear Beatrice.'

Her stomach lurched. He was ushering towards one of the secluded arbours, no doubt to reward her for her loyalty with passion. 'Hadn't we better be getting back?' she said, disengaging herself. 'I don't want Mama to be worried.'

'Of course.' He kissed her hand gallantly. 'Your Mama knows I will always look after you.'

'So, do you know anything more about the new owner of Tressillion?' she asked, setting up a rapid pace.

'A woman of considerable wealth, so I was told. A middle-aged spinster. No doubt in need of some kind of occupation. Not a family that I know.'

'Are you staying in London long?'

She managed to keep the questions going, barely listening to his replies, until at last they reached Curzon Avenue.

'Beatrice,' he said, his voice lowering as they reached the front door.

'Mama will be waiting,' she said, pulling herself gently free. 'We can talk inside.'

'I'd rather talk to you alone.'

She glanced at his face. 'I'm never quite at ease in this street, I'm never quite sure who is listening. There can be such strange people hanging around.'

'Really?' His eyes met hers. The sentimental expression vanished in an instant. 'I always thought this a most respectable neighbourhood.' He cleared his throat. 'Perhaps we should alert the police.'

'Perhaps we should,' replied Bea. 'Although I'd rather Mama was not alarmed.'

'Of course. I'll see to it.' There was suspicion now at the back of his eyes, she could feel it, and something approaching dislike.

'We are back, Mama,' she called, racing upstairs without pausing to remove her coat. 'Shall I ring for tea? We went further than we thought and the evenings are still cool.' She smiled brightly at Jon, arriving behind her, impatience on his face. 'And I'm sure Jon would love to stay for dinner.'

'I am dining with friends,' he said, his customary courtesy slipping. 'A long-standing arrangement.' He nodded meaningfully towards Bea. 'But perhaps you would like to join me for a performance of *Hamlet* next Thursday? I've heard it is excellent. And hopefully you will have heard back from your friends, Beatrice.'

'That sounds lovely,' said Mama. She glanced from one to the other, a slight crease appearing between her brows. 'You are so kind to us all, Jon, and especially to Beatrice. I'm quite sure we don't deserve it.'

Jon left before the arrival of the tea.

'Everything is all right, isn't it, Beatrice?' asked Mama anxiously as Bea handed her a filled cup.

'Of course.'

'Between you and Jon, I mean.'

Bea looked sadly at her mother. It had never struck her before how little she had ever felt able to confide in Mama. It was one of those things she had always taken for granted: Mama had always repeated anything she said to Papa, as if it was some kind of duty. Her loyalties had been to her husband, never to her children. Not even to Leo. How else could she have ever stood by and let the only child to whom she'd displayed any love be cast out, never to return?

'Everything will be for the best, Mama. Just you see. It will all work out in the end.'

'Of course,' replied Mama, the fear easing in her eyes. 'He is such a good, kind man, and he will always look after us.'

'I'm sure,' said Bea, taking her own cup and saucer to the other side of the fire. 'How's your book?' she asked, smiling down at Ada, who was kneeling in front of the flames.

'I left it upstairs.' Ada looked at her with discontented eyes. 'Why are you never here, Bea? No-one's ever here.'

'Then perhaps you should go to school.'

'Beatrice!' Her mother frowned at her. 'You know we could never afford it. At least not until…' She left the implications hanging in the air.

'I meant a local school,' said Bea. 'Or somewhere you could learn a profession one day. You could become a teacher.' Ada looked unconvinced. 'Or a clerk. Or how about an accountant? You always enjoyed working with numbers.'

'Don't be ridiculous,' said Mama. 'What man in his right mind would ever marry an accountant?'

'A man who didn't wish to pay for one,' snapped Bea, before she could stop herself. Ada's eyes were like saucers at this unheard of rebellion.

Mama's eyes filled with tears. 'You've no right to talk to me in that way, Beatrice. No right. Have you no respect for your elders at all?'

'I'm sorry, Mama,' murmured Bea. 'I'm not myself tonight.'

Her mother's face was bent over her teacup, lost in self-absorption. Bea frowned. She would do nothing for Jon, but there was something she would do for herself. There was no point in asking Mama any questions about the mine, but Jon had given her an idea. 'Mama, do you remember Emily, the daughter of the maid who was hired to look after Grandmama when she came to live with us? Grandmama was very fond of her. I thought she and her mother might like some of Grandmama's handkerchiefs, as a keepsake. They are so delicate it's impossible to unpick the initials, but Emily might be able to make use of them. We had no chance to thank her mother, and I don't like anyone in Tressillion believing us to be ungracious.'

'That's very thoughtful of you, my dear,' replied, Mama, smiling again.

'I'll find them before dinner,' said Bea, jumping to her feet. All she wanted to do was sit in front of the fire and rest her aching feet before tomorrow's return to the kitchens at the White Camellia, but she could not bear to stay still a moment longer, listening to Mama's gentle complaints and hopes for Jon to be the answer to all their problems.

'Beatrice…'

'Come on, Ada, you can help me choose some for Emily. I'll write a note to go in with them.' She caught Ada's hand, pulling her up from the fire. 'Wouldn't you like to hear the news from Tressillion?'

'Mama?' Ada glanced anxiously at their mother, who waved them away without speaking. Ada smiled. Already her eyes had brightened at the prospect of some kind of activity. 'Grandmama and Emily tried to teach me embroidery,' she confided, placing her hand in Bea's as they left Mama by the fire. 'But I couldn't do it.'

'Did you enjoy embroidery?' asked Bea.

Ada shook her head. 'Not at all.' She frowned. 'Grandmama

was like you, Bea. She said every woman should have an occupation, and that no-one should ever be idle, and that's why she should never have left London.' She came to a halt. 'Does that mean Grandmama worked for money, just like you do?'

'I don't know. I don't think so.' Bea squeezed her hand. 'But she was right about some kind of occupation. You liked Emily, Ada, perhaps you could write to her, too?'

'But I'm not very good at writing.'

'I'm sure you are better than you think, and anyhow, I can help you.'

Ada nodded. 'Yes. Yes, I would like that.' She gave a sideways look at Bea. 'I hate being poor and never seeing anyone. Could I earn lots of money as an accountant?'

'I don't know,' replied Bea. 'But I can try to find out. And anyhow, even if it didn't make you rich, it would mean you could always earn your own money and never be completely dependent on someone else, and have to be nice to them even when you didn't want to be.'

'And I could buy things and no-one could stop me.' A thoughtful expression had come over Ada's face. 'I could buy anything I wanted.'

'Within reason,' replied Bea, with a smile.

Ada giggled. 'I wouldn't want to buy Buckingham Palace, silly. Or dresses, or necklaces. Could I get a ticket for the tram?'

'If you wanted to.'

'Or the train?'

'If you earned enough.'

Ada took a big breath. 'How much would I need for an automobile like Papa's?'

'A lot,' replied Bea. 'Only rich people can afford automobiles.' Ada looked crestfallen. 'I don't know exactly how much, but you could look at the advertisements and find out.'

'Yes, I could,' said Ada, a sense of purpose, as she raced upstairs to find the writing paper for their letters to Emily.

Chapter Twenty-Two

Within weeks, the reopening of the Tressillion mine had begun in earnest. Despite his isolated way of life, Madoc managed to employ a mix of older men with some experience of mining and younger lads, who had brawn on their side.

Sybil observed them as they settled to work, busying herself removing years of dead brambles from the mine buildings, to reveal the true extent of their decline. Madoc had already repaired the roof and replaced the door and broken windows of the smallest shed, leaving it secure enough to leave the heavier tools in overnight, and as a watertight retreat for the workers. Summer was appearing, with the last of the bluebells fading and the leaves a rich green above their heads.

The men chatted quietly among themselves as they passed her, following Madoc's instructions with dubious shakings of their heads.

'Makes no sense going a way that has been abandoned,' said one. 'Chances of finding anything will be even less. I never heard of anyone working on that side.'

'Didn't you?' One of the older men slung his backpack over his shoulders and picked up his lamp. 'My dad worked for Hargreaves when it was still a tin mine. He always swore a seam of gold was found somewhere.' He took a furtive glance towards at Sybil, who was pretending to be absorbed in a deep tangle of brambles. 'He never said exactly where. Many of the men didn't like it when Tressillion took over the mine, especially the way he did. A lot of them had plenty of time for Hargreaves, didn't like what was done to him. Not one of them would have told Tressillion where to look, even if he'd thought to ask. Dad wouldn't work for him, however hard things got. But I know Tressillion used to keep a lump in his office. I saw it with my own eyes. That was what he was seeking. Why he wouldn't give up, see.' He gave a low grunt. 'Fuelled his obsession it did, made him blind to all else.'

Sybil bent over the brambles, keeping as inconspicuous as possible, every nerve tense as she listened.

'They said he was like a gambler, those last years,' added one of the other men. 'Caring of nothing else, just the dream of finding riches, driving himself to ruin, and taking all those he'd persuaded to invest with him.' He lowered his voice. 'I've heard it's not just the house that has ghosts. Why do you think so many of the men still refuse to work here, for all they need employment?' He sniffed. 'I'm too old to fear ghosts, or to be bothered with riches or obsessions, and old Tressillion never did me any harm. We'll see…'

Sybil stood up as they vanished one by one into the darkness, their lamps flickering in the depths until their footsteps could no longer be heard.

Ted was right about the obsession. She'd seen it for herself: the madness that threw all reason to the winds, clinging to a dream of riches that would make all things right. It was the gambler's conviction that they'd gone too far to go back, and no longer had anywhere left to return.

She shivered. Streaks of sunlight escaped the racing clouds, dancing among the abandoned mine buildings then vanishing again, leaving a chill wind behind. She couldn't stay here, waiting for them to return, wondering what they might find. It would take them several weeks to shore up the tunnel before they could reach the rock fall, so there was nothing she could do for now. But she had to be there when they broke through. They could go on to find gold if they wished, but she had to be first through into the cavern, hidden deep within the mountain. If it came to it, she'd go alone, at night when the mine was deserted, and remove the stones herself. Except that might bring the whole roof down on her head.

Restlessness overcame her. She couldn't wait here, her imagination running riot. Sybil hung the sickle from a hook on the wall in the newly mended shed, and strode back to the house.

Emily was sitting in the garden, painting a small table from the servants rooms, bedding billowing from long lines strung up between the trees behind her.

'Leave that,' said Sybil, peremptorily. 'It's high time we made a start on those bedrooms.'

'Very well, Miss.' Emily hastily finished the last leg and gave the top a final brush, before following Sybil inside.

'There are still so many belongings,' said Sybil, as they entered the first room.

'They were given so little time,' sighed Emily. 'They could only take what they could carry, a few valuables and their clothes.' She looked round at the bookshelves, with the gaps of absent books, the rest falling down like the pillars of ancient temples. 'Miss Beatrice was heartbroken at having to leave her books. My mam promised her she'd try to look after them.' She bit her lip. 'But at home there's no room, and we never did quite dare to approach Miss Bea's friends, and I'm not sure they'd have wanted anything from Tressillion.' She picked up the small pile on the dressing table, which looked as if they had been left at the last minute. 'Perhaps we could get someone to take some of them to her. If you don't want them yourself, that is, Miss.'

'Miss Tressillion can have them,' said Sybil, with a dismissive sweep of her hands. 'And the clothes and the trinkets. I've no idea how to get rid of them. But I can hardly parcel them up and send them into the ether.'

'I've the address of where they are living in London,' said Emily. 'Miss Bea was kind enough to write and ask after my dad only a few days ago.' She busied herself in pulling back curtains. 'If you would like to send them a message, I still have it.'

Sybil winced. More tendrils. She might have known. 'It can wait until we've been through the rooms. Anything you think they might want can be put up into the second room in the attic, until we know if they wish to send someone to fetch them.'

'Or they might wish to come themselves,' said Emily. 'They still have friends nearby, well, at least Miss Bea must have. They can't blame her for what happened.'

'Hmm,' grunted Sybil, brushing the dust from her hands, as if sweeping the belongings away from her. 'The clothes can be packed in my trunks. That should keep the moths and the mice out for a while.' She looked round at the room. 'I shall keep this for guests, so the books and the ornaments can stay. With a bit of cleaning, they'll make the place homely. I'll see what can be kept in the rest of the rooms.'

* * *

They worked for most of the day, sorting through the rest of the bedrooms, each one more cluttered and dusty than the last. As the afternoon wore on, Sybil shooed Emily away to attend the weekly lecture at the lending library, before continuing sorting and packing until rays of evening sun slanted through the thick clouds of dust hanging in the air.

At last she placed a final pair of men's shoes on the pile destined for a local charity for the destitute, and straightened. The house had grown still around her. Just the gentle creaking of rafters now and again in gusts blowing in from the sea, and the distant tapping of a branch on glass. Sybil wiped her hands on her skirt. Slowly, she made her way down the corridor to the one room still untouched, right at the very end.

'What am I going to do with you?' she muttered. The heaviness of old Mrs Tressillion's room settled around her. The deep green curtains on either side of the bay window, and the overhanging branches of the tree outside, never seemed to allow the sunlight to enter the dark room.

She threw open the windows and pulled the drapes from the furniture, leaving it bare and exposed. As she passed the dressing table, one end of a dustsheet caught the bottles, sending them jangling. She deposited the cloth on the empty bed frame and returned to set them back in order. The hairbrush was still lying on the dressing table. Gently, Sybil brushed the dust away, tracing the delicate pattern of white camellias with her fingers.

There was a quiet brush of leaves on the windowpane. Sybil started, swinging round, half in fear, half in anticipation.

The room was empty. Just shadows racing along the floor and dustsheets falling from their pile on the bed.

Sybil glared at herself in the dressing table mirror. 'You're a fool,' she told herself. 'A stupid, utter fool.'

She could not bear to be in this room a moment longer. She couldn't bear to be within the walls of the house, or the confines of the grounds. Racing down the stairs, she grabbed her coat from the rack, and made her way back to the mine.

* * *

Men were just emerging at the end of their shift as she reached the entrance. The young men passed her shyly, head down. The older men gave her a quick glance, before nodding in recognition and setting off back to the village. Was there pity in their look? Or maybe condemnation. They all clearly thought she had caught the Tressillion madness, believing in the ancient legend of endless gold. They were probably expecting her to start raving at any moment.

Sybil gritted her teeth. She might be the employer, but Madoc would have chosen the men for a reason. His own life depended on it. She would be foolish to let pride lead her to dismiss an experienced miner out of hand.

'Well?' she demanded, as Madoc emerged behind the rest, boarding up the mine entrance behind him.

'You were right. There are signs of several tunnels being worked. Three come to a dead end and look as if they have been abandoned. We've been a little way down the other. It ends in a rock fall.' He straightened up. 'It's your decision, Miss Ravensdale: we can work the ends of the tunnels and see where they lead, or we can concentrate on the central one with the rock fall. That one will take longer, of course. We would need to sheer it up as we go. It's too risky otherwise: if one part of the roof has gone, there's no telling which part might go next.'

Sybil squared her shoulders. 'I hope you are good at sheering up, Mr Lewis.'

'Now why did I suspect you might choose that option?'

'Did you?'

'You are not one to take the easy road.'

'I'll take that as a vote of confidence, Mr Lewis. But I'm just using logic. If there is a forgotten seam, it's far more likely to be lost due to an accident, than simply disappearing entirely.'

'I agree.'

'Good.' She left him to finish closing up the mine, and followed the path along the river to the beach.

So they had found it. The rock fall was still in place, and the rest of the tunnel had not collapsed. Sybil slipped off her boots, allowing the water to flow over her toes until they were numb. She was going to have to find a way to join them. The village would be shocked at a woman joining in men's work, forgetting the coal mines where women and children worked until they dropped. Her own grandmother had helped her grandfather reopen the ancient tin mine abandoned on Hargreaves' land. Sybil stirred the water, breathing in the salt air, light glittering in bright patterns, her belly tight at the very thought of going underground, deep within the merciless earth once more.

* * *

She was still there, pacing up and down at the water's edge in her bare feet, boots in one hand, skirts held close to her knees with the other, as Madoc strolled down to the cottage.

Summer might be approaching but the evenings were still chill, and that water must be freezing. There was one troubled soul, he told himself. It takes one to know one. He hesitated and half-turned to take the path between the rocks to join her. But by the look of her pacing, she wouldn't thank him for his interference. Bite his head off, more like. And if they were to work together as employer and employee, the less personal their contact the better. It would make ending their contract – whether her risk paid off or there was no gold to be found – that much more straightforward. He settled his haversack more closely over his shoulder, and set off down the track to the fisherman's cottage.

He hadn't been underground in so long. He drew in breaths of sea air gratefully, feeling his back straighten from hours of bending and his leg muscles ease as he walked. This was how he had walked with his father and brothers, in the days when his future was mapped out, when he had expected to see his own sons join him one day. The easy camaraderie of those whose lives depended on each other, and the blissful escape from the fetid air beneath the ground. He'd no wish to return to the work, but he missed the companionship.

He left his bag under the porch, and rowed the fishing boat out into the bay, sucking the air deep into his lungs. Sybil was still there, now standing still at the water's edge, gazing over the horizon as if searching for the answer to a question that had no solution.

What on earth was she doing here on the wilderness of the Cornish coast, when she had the elegance of New York at her fingertips? The men's gossip had been reticent when he had been within earshot, maybe wondering what his exact relationship was with the lone woman, with no sign of family or friends, let alone a husband. But he'd heard their curiosity.

He could just make out the outline of the mine. The mended roof and a few broken walls were still visible between the leaves that had not yet quite unfurled. A few weeks and they would be invisible beneath the green. He let his eyes travel back to Tressillion.

No good ever came from that place, the locals had told him, even before the mad obsession of finding riches. Old Tressillion had terrorised the village and kept his family strictly under his thumb. Unhappiness clung to the walls, he'd heard the old men say in the Fossick Arms, from the moment Tressillion had claimed the failing Hargreaves tin mine stood on Tressillion land, and paid a small fortune to prove it. The Hargreaves had fought, of course, but no-one could argue with money and influence. No-one else had dared to raise their voice in protest, they admitted, as smoke rose from the fire and the men's pipes until you couldn't see from one side of the bar to the next. The village itself was on Tressillion land and every tenant and every business had known where they stood. One word, and they'd have been out, and what good would have that done anyone?

On the beach, Sybil was pulling on her boots as the wind whipped her skirts around her. Madoc shook himself. She was his employer. He had no further interest. Of course she was intriguing. Half the village were speculating on who she might be, from the secret lover of the Prince of Wales to a fugitive from justice. He grinned to himself. He could quite see Sybil's defiant scowl staring out of a 'Wanted' poster, daring anyone to bring her in.

He pulled the oars strongly, heading back to the shore. By the time he turned towards the beach, Sybil had vanished. Out of sight, out of mind. The sea was darkening, a deep crimson settling over the waters.

From the corner of his eye, he caught a movement on the cliffs. He looked again. A figure was walking across the top. Sybil must have turned back for something. But when he glanced up towards Tressillion, Sybil was striding across the fields, skirts flying, scarf a banner in the wind, already at the ornamental gate into the grounds.

The figure on the cliffs had vanished. Madoc turned the boat around, scanning both the shore and the cliffs with care. Nothing. By the time he looked back to the house, Sybil had disappeared into the gardens.

It was most likely a fisherman, settling down on the rocks to catch an evening meal for his family, he told himself. But he looked at the mine. It was a killer, villagers were not shy of telling each other. Open the Tressillion mine, and you opened a hornet's nest, he'd been informed over the past few days. And pray you don't find anything, the old men in the corner had declared, nodding wisely behind the spiralling smoke of their pipes. It wasn't only the rocks and the suffocation that could drag men to their doom: the darkness inside the Tressillion mine crept out, infecting everyone and anything nearby.

Of course, he didn't believe such superstitious nonsense. But all the same, he pulled on his oars, until he was out of sight of both the mine and the beach, heading to the cottage. The remains of the brandy stashed under the steps had never seemed so alluring.

It must be the cold, he told himself, as the sun sank slowly into the sea.

Chapter Twenty-Three

As the weeks went on, mending the mine buildings was finally completed, and as the slow, laborious clearing and shoring up of the mine continued, Sybil appeared with increasing regularity.

Each morning she left Emily methodically placing clothes into piles, cleaning and polishing the furniture, washing walls and making the bedrooms habitable once more. The gardens were strung with lines of curtains and bed linen swaying in the breeze whenever the rain held off, making bonfires impossible. The flowerbeds were rampant with colour and her carefully attended vegetable plot no longer needed her full attention, swelling with beans and pea pods.

While the men worked, repairing a rusted wagon from one of the sheds to remove debris blocking their way as they went, Sybil cleared the last of the brambles and weeds clogging the ruins. She became a familiar sight to the miners going to and from their shifts, until finally she dispensed with any pretence, swapping her skirts for the freedom of men's trousers.

'You're not superstitious, are you, Will?' she demanded of one of the young lads, the first time she ventured inside to help pull the truck carrying rock waste to the surface.

'No, Miss,' he muttered, face aflame.

'I'll stop if I'm embarrassing the men,' she announced to Madoc, who gave the rueful grin of one who knows a liar when he sees one.

'They are only concerned for your safety, Miss Ravensdale.'

'Since I can be in no more danger than they are, they needn't be.'

Within days, she was making her way down the tunnel as if she were just another of the hired hands. She was strong, too. 'Nothing like washing and cooking for a few hundred men to make you tough as old boots,' she remarked to one of the older men, as he hesitated to let her take the weight of a rock, as they carried it between them.

'And where might that be, Miss Ravensdale?'

'The goldmines in America. A place where women worked in the mines too, and then came home and cooked and cleaned. Very few women sit around looking fetching, despite what you men are led to believe. The rest of us are working like slaves. We just don't make a fuss about it, that's all.'

The man carrying the other end of the stone laughed. 'That's what my wife keeps telling me. I agree for the sake of the peace.'

Sybil smiled at him in the lamplight. 'Your wife is wise, Ted, and so are you.'

He chuckled. 'Age comes with its benefits. Not having to keep up a front is one of them.'

'Well, I never saw a front that everyone else couldn't see through,' she returned, sending him chuckling again, deep in his chest, in grudging admiration.

Sybil grinned to herself. Despite the cramped conditions and the darkness, and the creak of the roof now and again as the rock above them was shored up with timber, her fear of the darkness and the earth had eased now she was there in the mine, ready to spring into action when need be, her future back under her own control. Meanwhile, she found herself enjoying the jokes flying past her as the men grew accustomed to her presence and almost forgot she was a woman at all.

'Looks like you've got mining in the blood, Miss,' remarked Ted, as they paused to munch on the thick slices of fruitcake Sybil had brought with her.

'I suppose in a way I have.'

He scrutinised her face. 'Your family from round here, then?'

'Some. A long time ago.'

'Still alive, are they then?'

'I have no family,' she returned.

'I'm sorry, Miss. Beg your pardon.'

'Not at all.' She took a drink from her flask of cold tea. 'Sometimes no family can be a freedom. Free not to spend your life worrying about them, or to fear shaming them.'

Ted scratched his head. 'Well, and that's a novel way of seeing it. I suspect Mr Tressillion would have agreed with you.'

'Really?' her voice was sharp. 'I don't intend to get myself killed.'

'Apart from being down here,' he replied.

She grunted. 'I trust your skills. I'd never take unnecessary risks chasing a dream.' She took another slice of fruit cake. 'Did you work with him? Tressillion, I mean? People tell me very little about the previous owner of my land.'

'For a short while. I didn't like his methods. Too desperate. Too reckless. Anyone with any sense could see what was going to happen, sooner or later. That's why, in the end, no-one would work for him. He pressed his sons into helping him after the last miner left. The two younger ones who were still at home, that is. They were scared, and so they should be, but they couldn't disobey their father. They'd seen what would happen if they did, and neither of them were the kind to take the chance, if you see what I mean.' He shook his head. 'They had no experience, any of them. They should never have been down there.'

Sybil crumbled her piece of fruitcake in her hands. It was a question she had to ask and had never dared. The opening was there: it was now or never. 'What happened?'

Ted chewed for a while in silence. 'No-one can be certain. He was using explosives recklessly before I left. There was an explosion in that part of the mine he was so set on, over there, on the other side. A rock fall trapped them all, one much larger than the one we're heading towards. Some of us from the village made a rescue party, when we felt the ground shake beneath our feet and knew what had happened. Don't get me wrong, Miss, I had no for time for Tressillion. No man worthy of calling himself a man should treat his fellow creatures in that manner. But, whatever his faults, the man was still a human being, and the boys were no more than lads, poor things. But we were too late. The eldest son had arrived home just the day before. Trying to make peace with his father, they say. By the time we arrived there, he'd gone in to try and rescue them. We heard the second collapse. It was like thunder under your feet. Killed them all instantly. There was nothing we could do in the end but bring out the bodies.'

Young Will swallowed. He downed the last of his tea, folding up the rest of his food untouched.

Sybil caught her breath. 'How horrible,' she murmured, hearing the shake in her voice, and thankful it was only to be expected. She hugged her knees, folding in on herself to fight off the sensation of earth crowding in on her, stifling her breath.

'I've seen it before,' said Ted, taking a thoughtful swig of cold tea. 'I'll see it again, no doubt. A damned waste, that's what it was, so many lives lost so needlessly. He was a good man, that eldest son, too. Things would have changed if he'd been allowed to take over, instead of being sent away without a penny. Mr Leonard and Miss Beatrice weren't like the others. There was something more about them.'

'How do you mean?' asked Sybil, clawing herself back out of her thoughts, forcing her breathing to come evenly again.

'Oh, I don't know, Miss. Curiosity, I suppose. Looking out beyond themselves to see more than just the big house, if you know what I mean. I used to see Leonard with that camera of his, Beatrice following with his equipment. It wasn't just the landscapes he was interested in, but the people in the village too. They stood up for what they believed in, the two of them, whatever the old man threatened.' He grunted. 'Tressillion was a fool, as much as he was a bully. Searching for something he could never have, to make himself appear better than those around him, never looking to see what was already there. He drove Leo away, and you could see Beatrice would be the next to go, the first chance she had. He was born a fool and died a fool. My only regret is that he took so many with him. It must have broken their mother's heart.' He stirred himself. 'Which is why we are taking our time and making sure this roof is secure,' he added.

There was a general coughing and shuffling among the workers. 'We'd better get going, if we are to get this part done before we leave,' said Madoc, stamping his feet to get the circulation going again. He glanced towards Sybil, who was still sitting hunched over her uneaten cake, lost in thought. 'Will can accompany you back to the surface, Miss. You look done in.'

'There's nothing wrong with me,' she replied, stashing the fruitcake away and repacking her knapsack. 'I'm ready for anything.' Anything to wear out her body, and keep her thoughts at bay.

They worked for an hour or so at the laborious process of strengthening the ceiling and taking the excess rock back to the surface.

'This looks like the main rock fall,' said Madoc, inspecting the boulders in front of them with his lamp.

'Hadn't we better move carefully then?' muttered Will.

'Don't worry, we will,' Madoc reassured him. 'I've no more wish to remain down here for eternity than you do.'

They took the stones out, bit by bit, carefully judging each one to ensure it was not the key, methodically shoring up every piece of new ceiling that was revealed.

'This could go on for miles,' said Madoc, after they had worked solidly for several hours. The talk of rock falls had left the men silent and thoughtful. Even Sybil was subdued, lifting stones in a mechanical manner without a word. They were all tired, and the lamps were starting to burn low. They could finish a little early tonight, Madoc decided, start again tomorrow, when they were fresh. Tiredness led to clumsiness, and he didn't want any mistakes.

'We'll take this lot back, and see what we've got,' he said, putting his hand on the wagon. 'We've done enough for today.'

Behind him, there was an exclamation from Will. 'There's a gap!'

'There can't be.' Madoc turned back.

The boy lifted away a few more stones, and stuck his hand right in. 'There, see. Just empty space.'

Sybil watched as Madoc held the lamp high, inspecting the hole. Her exhaustion had fled, leaving her tense and alert. She mustn't seem too eager, but be ready to act when the time came.

'It must have been a smaller fall than it looks,' said Madoc, finishing his inspection. 'A few more minutes won't harm. But we go carefully. We don't know what's holding the rest of it up.'

The work was painfully slow. Ted made a prop to support the ceiling, and they removed the stones, one by one, until there was just enough of a gap at one side to wriggle through.

'Try this,' said Sybil, pushing through the men to join Madoc and Ted next to the gap, holding out her flashlight. Madoc took it, sending streaks of light inside.

'It opens right out. It looks like a cave in there.'

'Any gold?' asked Will, eagerly.

'It's not likely to be waiting there, like dragon's horde,' replied Ted.

Madoc swung the flashlight again. 'Looks as if it's part of an old tunnel that goes right on into the hillside.' He wriggled gingerly through, followed by Sybil and then Ted. 'It's enormous!' He swung the beam of the flashlight up into a great cavernous space.

'This feels very old,' said Ted, inspecting the sides with his fingers. 'These walls weren't made with any tool that I know of.'

Sybil peered around in the streams of light raking the walls. There was nothing obvious to be seen. The shadows disorientated her. Already the others were fanning round, inspecting every nook and cranny.

'We can look properly tomorrow,' she said quickly. 'It's too late tonight.'

'Yes, of course, Miss Ravensdale,' said Madoc, sounding uneasy. 'And we still can't be sure how secure that entrance is. This is too much of a risk, if you ask me.' He motioned with his head to Ted, who was looking ready to explore the depths further in. 'Damn!' He stumbled over something on the floor, staggering, almost dropping the flashlight as he steadied himself against the wall. 'Bones. Someone has been here before.'

'Better go, Miss,' said Ted hastily, taking Sybil by the arm and steering her back towards the waiting men.

She pulled herself free, heart thudding in her chest. 'I'm not afraid.'

Madoc crouched down over the twisted jumble of at his feet. 'It's all right.' He gave a sigh of relief. 'They're not human. They're some kind of animal.'

'You sure it's not human?' demanded Ted, sounding more than a little unnerved.

'Not unless it's a giant. With tusks.' Madoc detached an enormous curve of bone. 'A museum might be interested rather than the police. I've seen such curiosities before. They are found in many places.'

Ted peered around. 'It must have been caught behind the rock fall.'

'Yes. That must be it,' broke in Sybil. 'They'll still be here in the morning. And shouldn't we be securing the sides?'

'There's nothing to secure,' said Madoc, sending the beam of the flashlight round one more time. 'But you are right, Miss Ravensdale. It will all be here tomorrow.' He turned the flashlight back towards the hole to guide them back. 'What the Devil…?'

'Whatever it is, it can wait,' snapped Sybil.

'What is it?' demanded Ted.

'I don't know. Something glinted. Looked like it's behind the skull.' Madoc reached behind the huge bones of the head. He pulled, and a metal lamp appeared, with the oozing remains of a candle spread across its base.

'Let me see?' demanded Sybil.

He handed her the lamp. 'I think we should go now, Miss Ravensdale.'

'Yes. Yes, of course.'

It could have been worse. Sybil placed the lamp deep in her backpack, daring her hands to shake. She had caught the look between the two men, and knew that, having found the lamp, they would be taking a far closer inspection next time. Their instinct to protect her female feelings from any horror would mean they would not want her to join the search. She would have to find another way.

The lamp was undamaged. Even after all this time, there was scarcely a blemish. Which meant that the thing she dreaded, with the power to betray them all, was still there, waiting for the beam of a lamp to find it.

She hurried back to the rock fall, breathing a sigh of relief as the others followed.

* * *

Behind them, Madoc swung the flashlight around with care. Nothing. The lamp looked old, but not ancient. The atmosphere of the cave was dry, and there were no insects to eat away any human remains, yet there was no sign of clothes or tools, or even the remains of a knapsack. And no sign of a human skeleton.

He pointed the flashlight into the dark tunnel. Heaven knows what they would find tomorrow. He turned to follow Sybil and the others out of the cave.

It was growing dark as they emerged into the fresh air, slotting the covers back over the mine.

'It's all right,' Madoc remarked to Ted, who was waiting for him. 'I'll finish up here. You go with the others.' He peered towards the men walking home, lanterns bobbing in the dusk. 'Has Miss Ravensdale gone?'

'Not yet.' Ted shouldered his backpack. 'She was still in the shed, last time I looked.'

Madoc waited until Ted set off to catch up with his comrades, before making his way to the shed. The glow of a light spilled through the half-open door. He paused, one hand raised to push it fully open.

Sybil was inside, bent over the lantern. At first he thought she was examining the lamp carefully, to determine its age, or the identity of its owner. But what kept his hand paused on the rough door was the way she held the lantern loosely in her hands, and her rapt expression, as if she could not tear her eyes away.

He pushed the door open loudly, turning his face away, as if he had just arrived and did not expect to find anyone there. When he turned back, her face was expressionless as she returned the lantern to her bag.

'It's late,' he announced, stamping his feet and blowing on his hands. 'Looks like the others have gone.'

'I told them to,' she replied, her voice thin. She cleared her throat, and her voice was strong again. 'They're an hour over their time as it is. I don't want half a dozen wives and mothers cursing me.' She tied up her bag carefully. 'Or thinking the worst.'

'They all know the risks,' he said. 'As do all who go down there.'

'Yes, that's true.'

'You were right,' he remarked, as they locked the door and set off down the path, the river gleaming orange in the last of the light.

'I was?'

'About there being a tunnel behind the rock fall.'

'A lucky guess,' she murmured.

'There might yet be gold there, after all. '

'Not necessarily. There could be a dead end. Or another rock fall.'

'Of course.'

She slipped on a root and almost fell. He put out his arm to steady her, releasing her as she pulled herself free, shaking him off like a dog.

All the same, when she turned onto the path through the field to Tressillion, he did not go home, but followed at a distance, watching the bobbing of her flashlight until she was through the gate and safely into the house.

Chapter Twenty-Four

As soon as she was certain Emily was fast asleep, Sybil gathered up her flashlight and her store of candles, slipping them into her backpack. She moved silently in her bare feet until she reached the kitchen door, where her boots were waiting. Trying to make as little noise as possible, she slipped into the night.

A moon slid between the clouds every now and again to light her way. The mine was still and silent. She had watched Madoc secure the entrance often enough, and she was soon able to open up a gap just wide enough to allow her through. Dripping water echoed about her, the silence making her feel utterly alone. The deep chill of the earth settled around her, holding her in its grip. For a moment her courage failed her.

Taking a deep breath, she set off as quickly as she dared, her flashlight in one hand, the other firm against the damp walls.

With the obstacles removed, she reached the barrier of rocks faster than she had expected. Taking care not to move the smallest pebble, she wriggled her way back into the cave.

It had to be here somewhere. In the roar of the explosion, and the terror of the rocks falling around them, they had simply fled for their lives. There was no other place it could be.

The great horned bones sent strange shadows racing over the walls as she searched every corner. She did not have long. Soon the beam would die, and then there would only be the candles, making it almost impossible. She felt in every nook and cranny near where the lamp had been found. Her fingers touched dry smooth bones, sending her leaping back with an exclamation that echoed around her, whispering to torment her.

It must be here. She could sense the beam dying. She must have been down here longer than she had planned. Soon the men would be arriving for their shift, and the last thing she needed was to be found down here, searching. That would lead to all kinds of speculation, the very kind she was now risking her life to avoid. As the beam died, she swung it round one final time. Further in, just out of reach, something gleamed.

She hastily lit her first candle, and crawled towards the flash, trying to keep its location clear in her mind. Her hand touched bone. As she lifted her flickering candle, the huge eye socket of the skull opened up in front of her. Stifling a gasp, that sent whispers and hisses into the darkness, she scrabbled at the base of the skull, until her hand finally rested on metal. Holding the candle close, she could make out the knife, its wooden handle still intact.

With a sigh of relief, she placed it deep into her backpack, out of sight. Whatever happened, at least now she knew it would never be found.

Steadying her candle, and ignoring her shaking legs, Sybil hurried back to the entrance as fast as she could.

* * *

Madoc was the first to arrive. He saw the cover had already been partially removed, and the door of the shed was open. Should he follow the intruder, or to wait for reinforcements? A candle flickered in the depths, followed by the echo of footsteps.

'The propping of the roof looks stable,' said Sybil cheerfully, splashing her way through the puddles as she emerged to join him.

'You went on your own?' He didn't attempt to keep the disapproval out of his voice.

'It's my mine, I'll do as I please.'

'Tell that to the unfortunates who would risk their lives to find you, not knowing where you were, should an accident occur,' he retorted.

She flushed slightly and busied herself retying the laces of her boot. 'I didn't go far.'

He eyed her suspiciously. 'And is there gold?'

She shook her head. 'I don't know,' she said. 'I told you, I didn't get nearly that far, and besides, we'll need more props for the roof.'

'Very well,' he murmured, prevented from any more questions by the arrival of Ted and the rest of the men, stamping in the cool morning air, anticipation on their faces.

As the miners gathered the wooden props, and began their descent into the mine, Sybil escaped out of sight behind the ruined wall. No-one would dare follow her, as they'd assume she had slipped away to answer an urgent call of nature. Once certain she could not be observed, Sybil retrieved the knife, holding it gingerly in her hands. It was old, and well used, but there was no sign of rust. The wooden handle, grown smooth and shiny with use, had no sign of rot. She turned it over. On the other side of the handle the initials 'AH' had been roughly chiselled into the wood, a little worn, but still as clear as the day they had been carved.

Sybil shuddered, forcing down the urge to retch. At least it was safe. She had found it. And now no-one would ever know. Quickly, she wrapped it as tight as she could in the spare jumper she kept in the bottom of her knapsack, and shoved it down again as far as it would go. Stilling her breathing, and carefully keeping her expression as bland as possible, she went to join the others.

* * *

The cavern they had uncovered was huge. Sybil joined Madoc and the rest of the men as they explored its seemingly endless vastness. As she had suspected, they kept her away from dark corners, where the murdered remains of an army might have lain, but nothing more than a few more animal bones were found.

As they reached the far end, the men began to relax a little, focussing on their mission once more. A pile of stones had fallen where the cavern shrank into a tunnel again, blocking their way. It took most of the day to secure the first rock fall, then to begin to move the stones blocking the new tunnel, leading deeper into the mountain.

'Looks like this happened around the same time as the other one,' said Ted, viewing it with expert eyes. 'It's not so deep. I'd say it was probably caused by the vibrations of the first rock fall we found.' He looked round at the cavern. 'If the owners of the lantern were here when it happened, they were lucky to escape.'

'Very,' agreed Madoc. Sybil didn't say a word.

It was late, and the lamps were burning low, when they finally made a gap into the second tunnel. Madoc sent most of the men to the entrance to wait, with instructions to go for help if the rest were not back within the hour. Sybil, who was aching with exhaustion and would have given anything to escape into fresh air, stubbornly refused to go with them. She couldn't afford to reveal that she no longer cared what they found, or let them suspect that she knew what remained in the deeper tunnels.

Once they heard the other men safely emerge though the first rock fall, Sybil directed the beam of her flashlight into the tunnel. They made their way gingerly into the unknown.

'This is far enough for today,' said Madoc, after a while. There was no sign of gold and no sign of the tunnel ending. His foot kicked against something hard. Not a skeleton this time, but an ancient tool of some kind, made out of bone. He held it in his hands, his lamp sending shadows across its surface.

'This feels like an even older place than the cavern.' He sounded a little unnerved. Will and Ted behind him were shuffling. 'I'm not entirely sure we are welcome here.'

'Just a little bit more.' Sybil swung her flashlight beam. 'Just to the bend. We should be able to see if it goes much further.'

'The bend, then we turn back.'

'Agreed.'

They reached the bend in the tunnel in minutes. It was simply a curve in the rock, scattered with stones, threatening to turn an unwary ankle.

'Well, that's that, then.' Madoc stared gloomily at the wall of rock looming up in the distance just beyond the reach of his lamp.

'And there was me, dreaming of a dragon's cave filled with gold,' said Ted behind them, attempting to sound cheerful.

Madoc grimaced. It had been worth the risk. But it was always a disappointment when so much work came to nothing. 'Come on then,' he said to Sybil, who was standing, staring into the dark, as if in a trance. He could understand her disappointment. His pride would be hurt too, if he had gone against all advice and all reason to try the abandoned section of mine on a whim, or a dream.

'Look.' Sybil raised a flashlight, strafing the beam over the wall in front of them.

'Well, I never,' said Madoc, slowly.

In the rock face, something gleamed.

* * *

As the dusk began to gather, Sybil followed once more the path down to the sea. This time she did not take the well-worn route to the beach, but followed the line of cliffs until she reached a small promontory sticking out into the bay.

She walked to the furthest point and paused on the rocks above a boiling sea. She glanced back, reassuring herself she was out of sight of both the house and Madoc's cottage on the coast. Ted and Will and the rest of the men had been sworn to secrecy for now, but that was not going to last long. The gold was there, and a rich seam of it by the looks of things, which meant it would be claimed by someone, even if she ignored it. Even if they shut off the mine and placed boulders over the entrance, there would be no burying it this time.

She sat down amongst the rocks, greasy with spray. She took the knife from her pocket, holding it in her hand, gazing down intently in the fading light. Whatever happened from now on, at least this secret would be safe. Her fingers traced the roughly-carved initials.

Now there was no proof left of what she had done, or who had helped her.

'Only the lives my blind hatred destroyed,' she said.

She stood up abruptly, flinging the knife as far as she could, out into the sea. The last ray of sunlight caught the blade as it sunk forever beneath the waves.

Chapter Twenty-Five

Bea arrived at the White Camellia one morning to find Mrs Anselm's Ford waiting outside.

She thrust Emily's letter back in her pocket. There was nothing much that Emily could tell her, just that her new mistress was taking care of the house and redoing the gardens, and had employed Gwen's dad to explore the mines to see if the stories of gold were true. It was a phase, Emily said. It wouldn't last. Miss Ravensdale was used to working hard, that was all. She'd soon find something else to occupy her.

Bea felt sure there was more. She was certain Emily wasn't one to bad-mouth anyone, but there was a slight defensiveness in her tone. As if, even after such a short time, she felt protective towards her new employer. It made Bea feel guilty at bowing to Jon's wishes. She wouldn't tell him she had written, she decided, as she pushed through the door into the tearooms. She would tell him it was, after all, no longer anything to do with her.

As she stepped inside, she found Harri waiting. 'I've a mission for you,' he said, with a grin. 'It's all right,' he added, as Mrs Teal passed, clicking her tongue disapprovingly. 'Mrs Anselm has arranged for Vicky to replace you for today. I'm under strict orders that it has to be you. You are needed for your level head and your respectability.'

'Respectability?'

There was a gleam in his eye, but no sign that he was mocking her.

'Mrs Anselm's daughter usually does the deed, but her

youngest has a fever, and naturally she doesn't want to leave him, and there's no-one else to fill in at short notice. I'm certain Vicky would volunteer, but that might draw the attention of the press and who knows what.' He nodded towards the door of the print room. 'Come on. Olwen has your disguise all ready for you.'

Bea didn't move. Every man she knew seemed fond of handing out orders as if she had no choice in the matter. 'And why would I need a disguise?'

He laughed. 'You'll see. We're going on a rescue mission.'

Intrigued, she followed him into the print room, where Olwen was laying out a selection of coats and hats. 'Well, at least Mrs Anselm didn't sent her own coats.' She held a heavily veiled and feathered hat at arm's length. 'They'd have drowned you. Alice is a bit more your size.' She extricated a coat and the least flowered of the hats. 'There, these should do.'

Intrigued, Bea obediently removed her own coat – which had grown a little shabby – and replaced it with the luxurious one sent by Mrs Anselm's daughter. It was meant for a larger, slightly taller, woman, but the skill of the cut retained its elegance.

'Very expensive,' said Olwen, fixing the hat to Bea's head and standing back to admire the effect. 'Yes, you'll pass.'

'What am I supposed to pass for?' demanded Bea.

'We're rescuing Mrs Anselm's belongings,' said Harri.

'Rescuing?' She had a vision of breaking into a store and handing over chairs and tables to a crew of assorted ruffians.

'It's the auction today,' said Harri. 'You're going to bid for them and get them back. Oh, it's all right,' he added. 'Lucy, her maid, will guide you and make all the necessary arrangements afterwards. She and Alice usually arrange it between them, although it's always Lucy who takes charge. They pay for the ornaments, Mrs Anselm gets her belongings back, and her taxes are paid. Honour is satisfied, and the government have been made to look like fools, which they are. And there's nothing they can do about it. Mrs Anselm isn't the only one. They've been doing this for years.'

Olwen grinned. 'It's a pity you can't take the Brownie, but that might cause trouble. Go on, you'll have fun. Harri's been charged with making sure you and Lucy keep out of trouble, in case Gwen and her friends decide to storm the auction. Don't worry, they'll all be at work and in any case I've warned Gwen you'll be there and not to try anything.'

Harri grimaced. 'Now Gwen's joined Mrs Pankhurst's suffragettes, making a fool of the law no longer interests her. The talk is all of direct action and being martyrs for the cause.'

'That sounds like she's prepared to die,' said Bea, alarmed.

'Fortunately, that's not the aim.' A shadow passed over his face. 'I'm not sure the police and the prisons will see it that way.'

'Gwen's talking about embarrassing the government by showing how they make women suffer when they ask for such a simple thing as a vote,' said Olwen. 'Especially as the majority of MPs are in favour in any case, and the situation is ridiculous.'

'Well,' said Bea, 'I'd rather be a photojournalist.'

Harri said, 'I'd rather see you as a photojournalist influencing public opinion with the truth, rather than locked up in a prison.' He nodded at Bea's outfit. 'You look very lovely, Miss Tressillion. Very rich and of the highest respectability. Come on, we need to pick up Lucy. I've the use of Mrs Anselm's automobile again, but it will still take time to get across London, and we'll need to plan tactics.'

'It's more exciting than baking cakes,' smiled Olwen. 'And it's a sign that Mrs Anselm trusts you to keep your head and not make a fool of yourself. Think of it as one step nearer to being offered a post on the magazine.'

* * *

The hall was packed full as Bea followed Harri and Lucy inside.

'There she is,' whispered Lucy, indicating a sparse woman beneath an enormous hat. 'Mrs Harris would love to get her hands on Mrs Anselm's belongings. Well, she won't.'

Bea looked around at the assembled crowd. She wished she'd dared bring her camera, but instead she made pictures in her mind, trying to catch faces with a telling expression, like the group of elderly men lounging in a corner. The bored, the curious and the businesslike.

Once the bidding began, it was fast and furious. Bea had no idea how Lucy followed the nods and hand movements. One by one, Mrs Ansell's ornaments and bits of furniture appeared. Bea, following Lucy's hissed instructions, secured them all, with few bidders apart from the woman in the hat, who glared as Bea outbid her for a particularly fine vase.

'It's the grandfather clock next,' whispered Bea. Lucy nodded and leant back in her chair.

Harri, who had stayed demure throughout proceedings, raised his eyebrows. 'You're not going to let Mrs Harris win, are you?'

'Mrs Anselm would kill me if I brought that back,' said Lucy.

'No reason for it to go cheap,' replied Harri, raising his hand. Encouraged by Harri's enthusiasm, the bidding rose rapidly. The woman in the hat grew more irritated with each bid, her lips tight. This was the last of Mrs Anselm's items and she was clearly determined to trounce her at least once.

'That's enough,' hissed Bea, barely containing a laugh.

'One more,' he muttered.

'Too much,' hissed Lucy. 'She'll never fall for that one. You'll be landed with the dratted thing!'

Mrs Harris bid a few pounds more.

'Don't you dare,' said Bea, grabbing his arm, decorum or no decorum.

Harri subsided, with a defeated shake of the head. The auctioneer nodded with a knowing smile.

'He's wise, you see,' whispered Harri. 'He knows I've got my wife and mother-in-law on either side of me, who rule the roost in our household, whatever the law might say.'

'Don't be ridiculous,' she muttered, releasing his arm, her face turning scarlet. She caught a glimpse of Lucy quickly swallowing a smile.

This time there was no more bidding, leaving Mrs Harris with a mix of triumph and faint suspicion she had been made to look foolish.

'Oh, she has plenty of money. I've seen her buy far more ridiculous things,' said Harri, as they made their way in Lucy's wake, while she paid for her purchases and arranged for their transportation.

'You were enjoying that.'

'Was I?' he grinned. 'Yes, I suppose I was. It does you good to laugh now and again. So much of my work is serious and utterly hopeless. It's good to know there are still battles that can be won, however small.' He smiled as Lucy stopped haranguing the deliverymen and came over to join them. 'Now, Miss Tyler, I'm under strict instructions from Mrs Anselm to take you and Miss Tressillion out to afternoon tea. The only stipulation that it's not the White Camellia and that we make notes on their most successful buns and cakes. I was also informed it should not be the Gardenia in Covent Garden, as that is far too close, so it has to be Oxford Street.'

'I ought to get back,' said Bea. She didn't want to stay close to him any longer than necessary. Just his presence, on the other side of Lucy, was quite disturbing enough. Over the more relaxed atmosphere of a tearoom, she might turn to jelly.

'I'm afraid those are my instructions. I am then to deliver you both back to your front doors afterwards. I daren't disobey.'

'Well, you are going to have to disobey with me,' said Lucy. 'I'm meeting my sister. It's a longstanding arrangement. So you will have to excuse me.'

'Oh,' said Harri, his face falling.

'But I think you should still take Miss Tressillion. Mrs Anselm will be most displeased if you don't, and a tearoom is hardly a den of iniquity. You young people have so many more freedoms than we did in my day. Besides, keep your gloves on, Miss Tressillion, and no-one will be able to tell you're not a young married couple enjoying a day out together. It doesn't mean you have to act like one,' she added as Bea and Harri exchanged glances. 'I've found many good marriages built on friendship. You are both rational creatures. I'm quite sure you're able to act like ones. Now, if you'll excuse me…'

Bea and Harri watched her hurry away into the crowds.

'You don't think she did that deliberately, do you?' said Bea.

'Quite probably.' He coloured slightly. 'I suspect Lucy of sharing Mrs Anselm's romantic heart. I wouldn't be at all surprised if they hadn't engineered the whole thing between them.' He coughed. 'I'm afraid I don't have the skills to be quite so devious.'

'I should get back, and I'm sure you have work to do.'

'I have my instructions. I promise to be very respectable.' He grinned. 'I don't often have an afternoon when I'm ordered to be free of responsibilities, and I'm sure neither do you. I've hardly had time to see anything of the city since I've been here. It's a sunny day. What harm can it do for the two of us to be tourists for a short while? I can whole-heartedly promise not to lead you anywhere in the vicinity of any shrubbery.'

Bea laughed and suppressed a blush. She knew what he meant about being tourists: it felt as if since they had left Cornwall she had spent all her hours working or listening to Mama's gentle complaining. 'Very well,' she said. 'I shall feel safe from shrubbery in Oxford Street, and besides, if you remember, I was the one who dragged you in.'

'So you were,' he replied, sounding thoughtful.

Chapter Twenty-Six

Lucy was right. No-one looked twice at a man and woman visiting the National Gallery and admiring the Houses of Parliament. Harri was as good as his word, being an easygoing companion without any hint of the lover. After a short while, Bea relaxed and began to enjoy herself.

'Don't you ever think of becoming an MP?' she asked, as they passed by the slightly intimidating grandeur of The Criterion at Piccadilly Circus, walking instead up Regents Street to Alan's Tea Rooms on Oxford Street.

'Sometimes.' He grinned. 'But I'm not sure I'd be welcome at the Houses of Parliament. I'm from the wrong class, and went to the wrong school. I think I'll stick to serving my clients and offering support.'

Bea smiled. 'When I was home, I never had the freedom to work in a place like the White Camellia and becoming a photojournalist felt like a dream. I suppose it still does. Mama still misses Tressillion, and my sister is so sure that one day we'll get back there. Now, even if I had the chance, I don't think I would. I'll always miss it, but there are so many more things I want to do with my life that would be impossible if I was in Cornwall.'

'I know what you mean. For me and Olwen and Gwen, our lives are here now.' He glanced at her. 'Aren't you ever tempted to go back and visit? Gwen said it was a beautiful place.'

'Maybe.' She had forgotten her unease at Jon's words. Now they came creeping back. 'You were right,' she said, 'I can't possibly marry my cousin.'

He cleared his throat. 'I may be biased, but it seems to me he is not the kind of man who would ever have been able to make you happy, however financially secure you might be, and however much you pleased your family.'

Bea grimaced. 'The trouble is, I don't know what I'm going to do now. I can't just abandon Mama and Ada. I'd never be able to live with myself. Any more than you would be able to live with yourself if you abandoned Olwen.'

They were silent. A nanny in uniform pushed a perambulator past.

'We make a proper pair,' said Harri, as the wheels trundled out of earshot.

'I suppose we do.' She cursed herself for saying anything about Jon. Now there was a question in the silence between them.

'Come on, I'm lax in my orders,' said Harri cheerfully. 'I'm supposed to be taking you for tea.' He tucked her arm through his. They reached Oxford Street, making their way through the crowds towards Alan's Tea Rooms at 263.

'Can I ask you something?' she said, as they paused to look at the items displayed in a shop window.

'Of course.'

'If something is sold, the seller can't get it back again, can they?'

'Not if the sale was legal. The only way would be to try and persuade the new owner to sell it back.'

'But if they didn't want it, they wouldn't have bought it in the first place.'

'Oh, I don't know. I've known of a few cases where the original owner has changed their mind and managed to persuade the new owner that their property was not what they had wished for, after all. I've even known a couple of cases where threats were involved.' He glanced at her. 'I take it this has something to do with Tressillion?'

'In a way.' She peered closer at the display. 'And if the sale wasn't legal? I mean, if it didn't belong to the seller in the first place?'

'You'd have to prove it.'

'Could it be done?'

'If you get hold of the right documentation. I've heard of cases where it's been done. It's not easy, but it's possible.' He frowned at her. 'Do you suspect your cousin was not the rightful owner of Tressillion?'

'No, of course not.' She hesitated. 'At least, not the house or the estate.'

'The mine?'

She nodded without looking at him. 'Mama won't ever say, and I'm sure the rest of the family don't know, but that last time Leo came home, he said something. I heard him talking to Mama. About the mine and the way Papa had claimed it, as soon as there was talk of gold being found. Leo said it would never stand up in a proper court of law, and the only way to stop Papa bankrupting the family was for him to lose the mine.' She shivered. 'I think he was too late, even before the accident. Papa had gone too far. I'm certain that whatever had happened, we would still have lost everything to Papa's creditors.'

'And now it's sold, and no-one need ever know,' he said gently. 'Surely that all happened a long time ago? Has anyone tried to reclaim the mine since?' She shook her head. 'Then maybe it is best not to stir up the past again?'

'I suppose.'

'You don't sound convinced.' He turned to face her. 'Bea, what is it that's worrying you?'

'Oh, it's probably nothing. Just something that Jon let slip. I have a feeling he's regretting selling Tressillion.'

'If Miss Ravensdale strikes gold, I bet he will,' replied Harri dryly. 'But there's nothing he can do about it. I've never met Miss

Ravensdale, Bea, but I do know Uncle Madoc, and I know that he'd never work for anyone for whom he had no respect. I can ask around, and see if I can find out more, if that would put your mind at ease?'

'You've got enough to do as it is.'

'I'm not promising miracles, but I do have some contacts who might help.'

'Thank you,' she replied with a smile, slipping her arm through his, as they continued along Oxford Street. 'I'm being ungrateful, I'm just not used to anyone doing anything for me, that's all.'

His arm tightened on hers. 'Bea, you know how I feel about you.' He gave a wry smile. 'I rather think I demonstrated it beyond doubt. But I can't ask you to wait for me.'

'Why ever not?' demanded Bea.

He blinked. 'Because you are young, you have your whole life ahead of you. Because I've seen you save Gwen from the police, and dare arrest or assault on the suffrage marches. You are finding your own way in life. This is just the start. Who knows what you may become in a few years' time? You could achieve anything. I don't want to be the weight dragging you back, with obligations you may one day regret. Or to become a prison if you meet someone who is rich, and brilliant, and who could support you in achieving everything you want to be. I can't stop being who I am. I can't imagine my life without the work I do.'

'I'm not asking you to change,' said Bea.

'You have to believe me, I didn't plan this. When Olwen was supporting me, I knew I could not be distracted by any personal feelings. Or by love. I made a pact with myself then. And I won't let it distract me now it's my turn to support Olwen.'

'And when she qualifies as a doctor?'

'I'll have my work. Bea, I've seen too many men who follow their selfish passions, expecting their womenfolk to wait for them. Olwen will tell you that my work consumes me. I'm not sure I'm capable of anything else, and I hope I'm not selfish enough to wish you to be the one to find that out.'

'And I have no say in this?'

'Of course. But you've said yourself that you've only just discovered your freedom after being shut away from the world under the rule of your father. I don't want to take that freedom away from you.' His voice lowered until she could barely hear the words. 'I want to see you grow, and fly as high as you can go, not hold you back.'

'We could work together. Pool our resources. I don't want you to support me,' said Bea. 'Surely we could work it out together?'

'But that would still constrain you.' He hesitated. 'Constrain both of us.'

She scowled down at her boots. Of course. How stupid of her, how truly naïve. Harri would never say so, but he knew as well as she did that she could never match the salary he earned from his paying clients, modest though that might be. The burden would still fall on him, and that would include supporting Mama and Ada.

They walked, side by side, each lost in thought, until Harri came to a halt. 'That looks like Selfridges up ahead. We've gone too far, we must have walked straight past the tearooms.'

Bea laughed. 'Mama would have been proud of me, luring you to the hallowed ground of Selfridges. But I'm starving, I'm afraid I'd much rather find Alan's Tea Rooms.'

'We'll save the diamonds for next time, then, shall we?' returned Harri.

'Probably for the best. I'm only likely to lose them.'

The mood had lightened again. They turned back towards Oxford Circus, past the shops and the coffee houses, this time finding Alan's Tea Rooms with ease. They found a small table in one corner and settled themselves down.

'There must be plans afoot for that next march,' remarked Harri, under cover of perusing the menu. 'Mrs Pankhurst and her eldest daughter are at a table behind you. It all looks very serious.'

Bea looked over to where several tables had been pushed near to each other, surrounded by a group of well-dressed women, deep in discussion. 'I wish I could hear what they are planning,' she whispered, as she turned back.

'To cause the maximum publicity possible,' replied Harri. 'I take it you are still determined to photograph the march?'

'Yes. I have to. It might be my best chance to convince Mrs Anselm to employ me as a reporter.' She turned to the menu without seeing it. After their conversation earlier, she couldn't tell Harri that this might also be her final chance. The apartment she had seen advertised a few streets away from the White Camellia might be small, and she had no doubt that Mama would be tearful at the very thought of moving to such a neighbourhood, notorious as the haunt of suffragettes and radicals, but at least it was one they could just about afford, if she worked every hour there was. If she didn't succeed in persuading Mrs Anselm to employ her as a reporter, she would need to take the first post as a clerk she could find, on top of her hours in the kitchens of the White Camellia. She'd barely have time for sleep, let alone proving her skills as a photojournalist.

Harri was watching her anxiously. 'The Pankhursts are charismatic speakers, Bea, and feelings are running high. This won't be like the last march you photographed. This one is going to be far larger and, given the suffragettes' reputation for direct action, the police are bound to be out in force.'

'I'll take care. They've never managed to catch me yet, remember.'

'Just make sure that camera of yours is well hidden. Mrs Anselm has already made sure I'm on standby to help any who fall into the hands of the police, including Gwen.'

'You don't really think she'll be arrested, do you?'

'She's one of the speakers.' He glanced over towards Mrs Pankhurst. 'One of the suffragette tactics is to make sure they are arrested. That means being sentenced to Holloway Prison for several weeks, or a month or more, which gives them plenty of opportunity to go on hunger strike.'

'Oh.' Under the cover of the menu, Bea squeezed his hand. 'Gwen may not be arrested, and surely there are doctors who'll be able to say that she's not strong enough for something as horrible as force feeding?'

He smiled and returned the pressure of her hand. 'Let's hope so. Whatever happens, I'll do my best to make sure she never gets further than being remanded, if there is trouble. And that goes for you, too. I've fought on behalf of enough of the prisoners, Bea, to know that being in prison is best left to the imagination.' He moved his hand away as the waitress arrived to take their order.

Bea looked back to where Mrs Pankhurst was still in the midst of the intense discussion. The other women at the table hung on her every word, as if drawing inspiration from her pent-up energy.

'It's Christabel you should hear speak,' said Harri. 'She's mesmerising. She's the kind of speaker who could lead her followers to the ends of the earth.'

'You make it sound as if that's a bad thing.'

Harri frowned. 'The fight to achieve universal suffrage has been such a long one. I suppose I believe in democracy and the rule of law.'

'And when the law is unjust and democracy fails?'

He turned back towards Mrs Pankhurst. 'Then a cause can attract true idealists, who feel so passionately they are prepared to die for what they believe in. It can also attract those who are drawn to martyrdom, or feel justified in any means to gain their ends.'

'You mean, like Gwen?'

'Among others. Gwen is passionate and she has such utter faith in where Cristabel and the others are leading her. When power is challenged it can be cruel, and there are plenty who enjoy inflicting cruelty in the name of preserving the peace. I've seen it happen. I'm not sure I can bear to see it happen to those I love.'

'I'm sure Gwen will be fine.'

'Let's hope so. There's nothing anyone can do to change her mind. And to be truthful I wouldn't want to.' He smiled as the waitress arrived with their tray. 'That looks delicious. This is supposed to be a cheerful occasion. I propose we leave Mrs Pankhurst to save the world and undertake some espionage for the White Camellia.'

'So now it's espionage?'

He nodded. 'You don't think we were directed towards two of the most successful tearooms by chance, do you?' He waited until the tea and a delicious selection of cakes and buns had been placed in front of them and the waitress was safely out of earshot. 'Mrs Anselm is a romantic and an idealist, but she is also an astute businesswoman. I suspect we are expected to be taking notes on everything from the décor to the types of cake. I'm quite sure we'll be quizzed when we get back.'

Bea laughed. 'This time I shall enjoy taking notes.'

Mrs Pankhurst and her entourage swept past, still deep in conversation, out into Oxford Street. They paused for a few minutes, clutching their hats in a gust of wind, before setting off towards Hyde Park.

Excitement, with a touch of fear, went through Bea's belly, remembering the wild rush with Gwen and Olwen through the streets, and Vicky beneath the White Camellia banner at Mrs Anselm's march, pulling her to safety. The suffragette march would be far larger and attract more attention. She quashed her unease. It was merely nerves. After all, if she was ever going to be taken seriously as a photojournalist, she was going to brave strikes and disasters, maybe even wars. A suffragette march seemed the best place to begin.

Chapter Twenty-Seven

Sybil sat on the bank above the mine in the warm summer evening, wicker basket by her side, watching the men repair the sheds and the outbuildings, and the cart wheels being oiled and polished.

A burst of laughter came from the men fixing the waterwheel that would work the crushing machine. Already they had become a tight-knit group, bringing the mine back to working order to start crushing and processing the gold. This time, she had no desire to join them. She had achieved her purpose, and had no wish to return into the dark tunnels again.

She looked up as Madoc walked up the hill to join her. 'It's going well, Miss Ravensdale,' he announced. 'We should be ready to get the first load out in a few days' time. It will be small scale at first, and then we shall see.'

'Unless there's no more to the seam.'

'It'll be there,' he said cheerfully, 'I can feel it in my bones.'

Sybil smiled. Madoc had a sense of purpose she hadn't seen in him before, as if he had recovered a zest for living that had been lost for years. 'I hope you are right, for all our sakes.' From here she could just make out the weather-vane on the tower of the church. 'And for Porth Levant.'

'Ah, so you are thinking about the village?'

'I need to make good use of any profit. The house doesn't need any glorification, it's quite large enough for me and Emily as it is.'

He grinned. 'You could travel the world in luxury, or buy every kind of precious jewel.'

'I could do that already, if that's what I wanted,' she retorted. 'From what I've seen, jewels are meaningless, except to keep in a vault, or to impress those who need outward signs of wealth. They are not the kind of people I want to impress in the first place. And as for travelling...' She gave a faint smile, catching herself by surprise. 'I've found that if you are cocooned in luxury, all you see are your fellow wealthy travellers, the bored and the spoilt, who you could more easily escape in a ballroom in London. That kind of travelling is often an excuse for not living. Just filling in meaningless days admiring the work of those who spent their lives passionately painting, sculpting and creating buildings that make you catch your breath. I'd rather live myself.'

'In Tressillion.'

She started. 'I can think of worse places.' She chuckled softly. 'I can see me becoming quite the philanthropist in my old age. I never did agree with the rich keeping all the wealth to themselves. A good school would do, for a start. Educating the working classes is the best form of revolution, if you ask me. It gives them the tools to question their self-styled betters.'

'You sound like a suffragist,' he said, smiling.

'Do I? I rather thought I was a rational human being.'

'And the suffragists are not?'

She sniffed. 'I'm sure some of them are...' She came to an abrupt halt and shook herself. 'Well, I've listened to worse sense in my time than I've heard in the White Camellia. And your Gwen seems to me a very rational young woman.'

'She is. Her mother was determined she should stay on at school as long as possible and get a good education.'

'My point exactly,' she replied.

He glanced at her. 'So you know the White Camellia.'

'Do I?'

'Just an impression,' he said, evenly.

She met his eyes. Her chin jutted. 'Ladies' tearooms, like the

White Camellia and the Gardenia are, in my experience, one of the few places where a woman can hold an intelligent conversation with her friends, without a man butting in to tell her how she should think, and that her view of the world is entirely mistaken.'

Madoc laughed. 'You don't believe that, any more than I do. *Duw*, I'll grant you there's many a foolish man in the world who likes nothing better than the sound of his own opinions. But they are not all of us.'

'And I'll grant you there's many a very silly woman,' she replied. 'Who should not be used to obscure the rational majority of us.' She smiled. 'And you raised one of the rational ones.'

'I'll always be proud of Gwen, whatever she does. I never thought I'd raise a daughter to have such a passionate belief in life.'

'But you did,' replied Sybil, 'once you turned your mind to it. Well, time to inspect progress, before it gets too dark to see,' she added, jumping to her feet and practically leaping down the hillside to the mine.

* * *

By the time Sybil followed the men down the path by the stream, dusk was turning into darkness. As she turned, the bobbing lamps continued on the path to the village.

She looked towards the house. She had forgotten Emily was at her evening class tonight, and she had not thought to leave a light burning. Tressillion rose up, its windows a hard jet black, its chimneys etched against the night sky as the clouds parted.

It had almost begun to feel like home. She still avoided going into rooms after dark, unless the gas was lit. Even with Emily under the eaves, she still sat bolt upright at the slightest creak, waiting for the footsteps (ghostly or not) in the hall below. But it was easing. Taking Roach's hint, she had been reading about the practicalities of installing the new electric lights that could be turned on at the flick of a switch. She had even been planning where to put the generator. Tressillion flooded with the bright lamps, flaring out a defiant beacon on the cliffs, would be a different place.

'Besides, I'm just being foolish,' she scolded herself.

But these last weeks, even electric light had begun to fade from her mind. Thanks to Emily's touches, the bedrooms were fresh, windows opened every day, with not a speck of dust to be seen. Heaven knows what she was going to do with them all, but at least she was beginning to feel that their previous occupants had finally left, swept away by the fresh new curtains and the bowls of dried lavender. It was not just the air blowing through, but Emily, brisk and cheerful, bringing youth and optimism, treading through the old memories as if they never existed. She seemed to have set the air moving, bringing in new life.

Even the village was growing used to her. Over the past weeks, as the loneliness of Tressillion settled around her, she had taken to walking into Porth Levant to pick up her loaf from the bakers, instead of having it delivered, and choosing a selection of seeds from the hardware shop. Today she had found herself being greeted by nods and 'Good afternoon, Miss Ravensdale', instead of the usual sideways glances.

So, finally, she had ceased to be the oddity, the strange woman without a husband or family, living at the big house. Instead, she had become the employer of a son, a husband or a brother. The grocer's shop had been freshly painted and the broken handle replaced. She tried her best to block such feelings, but her pride stirred at the thought that she could influence the prosperity of the village.

'It'll be invitations to join committees and the board of the charity hospital next,' she muttered to herself. She lifted her head, with a defiant stare at the house. 'I might even accept.'

She set off once more, up through the fields until she reached the metal gate. As she pushed it open, she came to a halt, with Tressillion looming up in front of her. She might have known it would not last. That something would come, disturbing her peace, raking up the past. The house itself would not let it go. She had almost thought it had accepted her. The creaks had lessened over the past weeks, as if the house had settled, bowing to the new order, even acknowledging that it was for the best.

But tonight… She shivered slightly as the breeze caught the dried leaves around her. Tonight the house stood dark and blank, shutting her out. Reminding her that she was an interloper.

'Ridiculous,' she said aloud, hearing her voice echo in the chilling air. She was tired. And talk of Gwen, and of the White Camellia, had brought up memories. That was all. Tomorrow the sun would shine and things would be as they had been before.

Something cracked in the undergrowth, sending the leaves rustling. She turned. The field was still. The vast coastline stretched around her, with not a light to be seen. She shook herself. There was no-one there. That was the trouble with riches, they brought freedoms, but could also be a prison. She knew all too well that those who had money and possessions had something to lose.

She hastened towards the house, flashlight in her hand. Reaching the door with relief she reached in her pocket for the key, her breathing harsh in her ears. And something else. She held her breath.

'Emily?' She swung the flashlight around. Nothing. Not the gleam of cat's eyes. Not the slink of a fox.

The sound came again. This time the unmistakeable crunch of feet on gravel. Slow. Stealthy. A human stealthiness. To her relief, the key turned. She pushed open the door and shot inside, slamming it behind her.

She was too late. Before she could push the bolts home, she

was thrown back, stumbling, falling into a corner, hitting her head on the wall, her flashlight clattering over the tiles, smashing. She was plunged into darkness.

Sybil remained very still, dazed, every sense focussed on trying to make out her attacker in the faint starlight coming from the open door. A shadow crossed in front of a window, cursing as it crashed into a chair, sending it flying. She moved slowly, inching towards the door into the drawing room. The intruder came to a halt, head poised, focussed on the faint rustle of her skirts.

'You opened the mine,' he said.

Well, it could have been worse. Sybil scrambled to her feet, brushing herself down. 'It's my mine.'

'It's not what we agreed.'

'Agreed?' She paused, then felt for the matches kept next to the candles on the windowsill. 'We didn't agree to anything.'

'It was understood. It was always understood.'

She lit the candle with care, ignoring the lamps. A candle was easily blown out, and she knew the layout of the place like the back of her hand, if necessary. At least he didn't stink of alcohol. Her hand barely shook. 'Is it money you want?'

'Of course not, Sybbie. That's never what I wanted.'

'You do when you're drunk,' she retorted, unable to stop herself. 'Or when you've drunk yourself into penury.'

'I've been sober for months,' he replied, sounding hurt.

'Months? You expect me to believe that?'

He took an angry step towards her. 'She's a liar. Lillian was always a liar, trying to get me into trouble. She'll want the money for herself. She'll always want money, for that refuge of hers.'

'I haven't heard from Lillian,' Sybil replied slowly, fear tight once more inside her. 'Alex, you know we haven't spoken in years.'

'I bet you haven't.' He lent closer. He'd lied about the drink. Not so much as to reek through his pores, as when he had been drunk for weeks, but enough to remain stale on his breath. 'Not now she's oh-so-friendly with that Tressillion girl.'

'Beatrice? You must be mistaken. Lillian wouldn't exchange a single word with a Tressillion. It must have been somebody else. Young women all look alike.'

'I wouldn't miss a Tressillion.' He spat, slowly and deliberately, onto the floor. 'She works at the White Camellia. In the kitchens. Not so high and mighty now.'

'I expect she'll find it very instructive,' said Sybil. 'At least she's not moping at home waiting for her prince to come. This is nothing to do with me.'

'Don't be so certain, Miss I'm-so-clever. I've been watching her. She's been photographing those marchers who want to get women the vote.'

'Well, then good for her,' said Sybil, managing to sound disinterested.

He swayed slightly. 'She's got ambitions, see. That brother of hers taught her to use a camera, didn't he. Now she thinks she's going to be a photojournalist.'

'Oh,' said Sybil, flatly. She didn't dare trust her voice. From his tone, Alex still didn't know. It had never crossed his mind. The secret she kept deep in her heart, shutting out the world to keep it safe, was still hers. The reason that Beatrice Tressillion could still break her.

She clenched her fists. Alex must never guess any of it. Unhinged. That's what Lillian had called him, all those years ago. She hadn't believed her. But now she saw his deeply shadowed face in the light of the candle. Thin, unshaven, bloodless. The face of a man for whom sustenance of any kind, apart from the oblivion at the bottom of a bottle, had long since gone. The ruin of the handsome boy she'd fought so hard to save, and now dared not even love.

His greatcoat was the same one as on his last visit, its finery reduced to his usual sorry state. The stench of unwashed flesh and rotting material surrounded her. Revulsion, mingled with pity and despair, rolled in her stomach. The practical things she could at least do.

'Wait here,' she said firmly. In the candlelight, she opened the latest parcel of clothes waiting under the stairs to take to the charitable ladies of the village. From near the top she retrieved a man's coat. 'The wind's still cold at night. This will keep you warmer,' she said, handing it to him.

'I don't want your charity, Sybbie.'

'It's not mine,' she said dryly. 'It's Mr Tressillion's coat. It doesn't look as it's been worn,' she added, as he pushed it away with a curse. 'Come on, Alex. Isn't it a kind of revenge?'

He grunted, peeling off his sodden and rotting coat, replacing it with the new one. As she helped him retrieve his belongings from his pockets, she reached for her purse, pushing all the money she could find into the nearest pocket.

'There. That's better.' She began to breathe again. 'Come on. I haven't eaten. I'll cook us something. There's a bed down here, if you've nowhere to stay tonight.'

'I wouldn't stay here if you paid me,' he retorted, his temper stirring again.

'Then at least have something to eat,' she soothed. 'You'll feel better then, my dear.'

'She thinks she's so clever.' She had lost him. The brief moment of lucidity had gone. He was back on the old subject again.

'I've brought eggs and bacon from the village, and a fresh loaf,' she said, somewhat desperately.

But he was like a dog with a bone. 'Beatrice Tressillion. She thinks she's so clever.'

'I've no interest in Beatrice Tressillion, Alex. You, of all people, should know that. It will be warmer in the kitchen. I'll make us a cup of tea while I cook. Let's talk about something more cheerful.'

'But she doesn't know that I've been watching her. Every move she makes.' He gave a low chuckle that made the hairs on the back of Sybil's neck rise. 'She doesn't know what we've got planned for her.'

'We?'

'That cousin of hers. He soon saw sense.'

'Which cousin might that be, Alex?' she said. A little too gently.

His eyes focussed on her, narrowing. 'You opened the mine. You shouldn't have done that, Sybbie. I came down to tell you what I'm going to do. But now I won't. You'll just have to wait. You'll see. You and that Miss Beatrice Tressillion, you'll see.'

'Alex.' She reached for his arm, but he shook her off, stumbling back through the door, out into the night. Fright and temper got the better of her. She shot off after him, boots slipping on the gravel of the driveway. 'Damn you, Alexander,' she yelled into the darkness. 'Don't you dare issue threats like that to me. Don't you dare!'

Something moved in the darkness next to her, with a glint of eyes in the starlight, sending her off balance. 'Don't you touch me, you fucking little shit.'

'Are you all right?'

'Madoc.' She collapsed against the doorpost, winded with relief and fury. 'What the hell are you doing here?'

He stepped into the faint light coming from the house. 'Making sure you are safe.'

'What the hell business is that of yours?'

'It's not.' He cleared his throat. 'I thought it must have been my imagination. I once saw someone follow you back to the house. I've kept an eye out since. There's been nothing until tonight. It's what good neighbours do,' he added.

'Oh.' She scowled. Gratitude could wait. Deep fear was coursing through her veins. It would be Madoc, of all people. 'Did you hear all that?'

'A little. Not enough for it to mean anything. I was going to leave when it was clear it was someone you knew.' He hesitated. 'But then he sounded so angry, and more than a little drunk… Shouldn't you call the police?'

She shook her head. 'No. It wouldn't do any good. It would only make him believe I'd betrayed him. It would only make things worse.'

'You're a grown woman, who can take care of yourself, but Emily is my niece.'

'He won't hurt us. Not in that way, at least.'

'He sounded pretty unstable to me.'

Sybil began to shiver. 'It's not Emily he's angry at. She's the last person he'd hurt, and he'd never lay a finger on me, however much he imagines I've betrayed him. He's said his piece. I doubt whether we'll ever see him again.' She caught the expression on his face. 'He's not my husband, or a jilted lover, if that's what you're thinking.' She gave a defiant sniff. 'That's the trouble with blood, isn't it? However hard you try, you can't ever quite escape, and there is always that hope, deep in your heart. He won't harm us. He owes me everything, and he knows it, and I can still hope that, somewhere, love never really dies. He's angry, that's all. Angry and frightened that the world is not as he thinks it should be, and there's nothing he can do about it. It's all in his head.' She straightened. 'Although I might take up riding and be in need of a permanent stablehand from now on.'

'But all the same…' He sounded concerned, and not just about Emily.

Sybil tried her best to harden her heart, and failed miserably. 'Thank you, Mr Lewis. But I've lived in some pretty lawless places in my time, and I'm not entirely defenceless.' She swallowed. 'But perhaps you might find yourself passing the lending library as Emily's class finishes, and escort her home, just this once. Just for my peace of mind.'

'Of course. I wouldn't think of anything less. Goodnight, then.'

'Goodnight.' As she made her way back inside the house, she turned. 'Mr Lewis?'

'Yes, Miss Ravensdale?'

'Thank you.'

'Not at all. As I said, it's what neighbours do for each other.'

'Not all neighbours,' she replied wryly. 'And I'd rather you didn't mention this.'

'Of course not.'

'Thank you.'

Sybil watched his shadow move away in the dark, finding his way by starlight to Porth Levant. He hadn't attempted to stay or look after her. He hadn't swept in, taken charge, and found the brandy bottle to settle her nerves. He'd accepted her opinion that she was in no physical danger, and left her alone. Not a romantic hero, then. She smiled to herself as she bolted the door and checked the latch on every shutter in the house.

As she reached old Mrs Tressillion's room, she paused. The window, as ever, was open slightly, the curtains swaying in the night air. Sybil switched off her flashlight, and stood for a while in darkness, the salt breeze cool on her face. She could just make out the shape of the fisherman's hut by the shore. She strained her ears, but there was nothing but the sound of the sea and an occasional owl to be heard. In the fields below, nothing moved. It was a peaceful, reassuring scene.

Her legs were aching unbearably, shaking. She sank into the armchair set next to window.

'What did he mean?' she asked aloud. 'What on earth could he mean about Beatrice? He must be bluffing. I mean, just look at him: if he isn't killed hustling for the next drink, the drink itself could kill him. There's nothing I can do about it, even if I knew.' She put her head in her hands, feeling the creaking of the house settling around her, rocking herself to and fro in her distress.

She never asked for help. Even when she had most needed it, she had been too proud to ask, but now she ached with the need for one single word of reassurance.

'You'd know,' she whispered, to the creak of branches against the window. 'You'd be able to advise me, help me to decide what to do for the best. You'd know how to keep Bea safe.'

Around her, the house was silent.

Chapter Twenty-Eight

'Does it have to be today, Beatrice?' Mrs Tressillion's voice was plaintive.

Bea pulled on her coat, trying her best to hide her impatience. 'I'll return long before Jon arrives, Mama.'

'I don't see why you need to go at all.'

'I've promised I'll support my friends in their charitable work.' The lie came so easily nowadays, she scarcely noticed it. Mostly it was convenient, meaning that Mama didn't have to admit that her daughter was working to support them. Her excuses for disappearing on the day of Mrs Pankhurst's march felt no different. She smiled brightly. 'You wouldn't want me to let them down, would you?'

'But Jon was very particular about tonight. He asked to speak to me alone.'

'Mama…'

'You must know what that means, Beatrice,' said Mrs Tressillion. 'It's what we've been waiting for. It's such an opportunity for you.' She met Bea's eyes and flushed slightly. 'For all of us.'

'But Mama, I don't understand why Jon feels it's so important to marry me.'

'He's clearly fond of you and thinks you two are suited for each other.'

'But I don't know him. Even after all this time, I feel I know nothing about him. He's pleasant and attentive, but he is always so guarded in what he says. I don't know what he is really feeling.

Mama, how could I be happy with a man like that? How could I love him, when he seems determined not to let me close to him?'

Not to mention the exquisite, forbidden attractions of Miss Cassie Lane, who had been contracted to a movie studio in America, and was set to become one of its biggest stars. Bea shivered. Even if she had been passionately in love with Jon, she would never marry a man dreaming of another woman whose face would be constantly in front of them in the gossip columns and on the silver screen.

'You will get to know him.' Mrs Tressillion's mouth was set in a stubborn line. 'That will be your purpose, Beatrice, in your married life. Your husband will teach you of the world, and you will learn to understand him and anticipate his needs. Dreams are all very well, I had them myself once. But this is the reality of married life. When I married your papa, I had only spent minutes in his company, and never without a chaperone. You young people have so much more freedom today, but that does not change how things are. You will come to love him.'

'And if he should never seek to understand me?' retorted Bea. 'How can there be any kind of love without understanding? Or is the understanding to be all on my side, however he behaves towards me?'

'Beatrice!'

Bea's temper evaporated. Her mother looked stricken, as if she had been slapped. She had never before seen Mama, not as her mother, but as a woman who had, once long ago, made a pact with herself, to survive a life governed by a man who had only desired obedience, and a world arranged according to his wishes. Mama had had no White Camellia to support her, or to offer her another way of living. Just her family telling her, most probably in exactly the same words as she was using now, that there was only one choice, and it was up to her to make the most of it.

Looking at her mother's fragile face, she could find no trace of any dreams or desires. Just the empty shell of a human being who had hidden any inner life for so much of her life, it no longer existed.

'I'm sorry, Mama,' she said quietly, pity overcoming her. 'I was only talking about myself, truly.'

'And you will listen to Jon?' With a heavy heart, Bea saw Mama's pleading face, as if her words had already been forgotten. Her mother's every hope still rested on the offer she was so certain would be made tonight.

It was impossible to argue with her. She would never understand. More to the point, she could never afford to understand. The questions she would have to ask herself would go too deep.

'I'll be back in time,' Bea murmured, making her escape.

* * *

Harri was right. This march was like no other she had seen. There were men and women of all ages. She was certain she would never find Gwen and Olwen, but at last she spotted the familiar banner with its intertwined camellias.

'Over here!' came Olwen's voice.

Bea ducked between bodies until she reached them. 'Are all Mrs Pankhurst's marches this big?'

'I've never see so many,' called Gwen, who was holding one side of the banner. 'So many people are angry that no-one is being listened to. Well, they'll have to listen to us now.'

'I wouldn't bet on it.' Bea turned to find Lillian standing just behind Gwen.

'There won't be any trouble, surely?' said Olwen, as an elderly woman being pushed in an invalid chair passed by. 'There are too many of us. And it's out on the streets.'

'I wouldn't put it past them,' muttered Lillian.

In bright sunlight, Lillian's pale beauty had lost none of its ethereal qualities. Wrapped in an ancient coat of green velvet, that looked as if it had once been the height of fashion but was now threadbare in places, she had the air of a river spirit. Yet there was something solid, almost intimidating, about her. No wonder the police had not dared to stray near her refuge, or that she walked unafraid amongst the roughest of city's drunks and troublemakers.

'No taxation without representation!' came the booming voice of Mrs Anselm from near the front of the assembled crowd. Bea grinned. She caught Lillian's wry smile. Lillian's face softened slightly.

'I'd better go,' said Bea. 'I want to take some photographs before the march starts. It's easier when people are standing still.'

She made her way through the crowds, every last part of her attention focussed on finding the striking image that would make the photographs stand out from the rest. If she knew she had a few good pictures now, before the chaos of the march began, she could take risks to try and capture the essence of the march later.

She had just taken a picture of a smiling young woman, arm in arm with her husband, next to an elderly woman, when she felt a tap on her shoulder.

'Miss Tressillion…' It was Lillian.

Bea saw the tension in her face. 'Is anything wrong? Is it Gwen?'

Lillian shook her head. Around them, the marchers began to take up their positions, jostling them as they prepared to set off. 'I need to speak to you,' Lillian shouted above the rising noise of the crowd.

'Afterwards.' Bea tried to hide her frustration as the women around them began to surge forwards. She had not found her special image, and now it was going to be even more difficult.

'Very well.' Lillian grasped her arm. 'Come to the White Camellia once this is over. They are laying on soup there for the marchers.' Her grip tightened. 'Bea, I need to speak to you before you go home. Promise me you'll come?'

'Of course.' Bea pulled herself away. Heaven knew what Lillian was up to. Probably to give her a lecture on not embarrassing the poorer women by demanding pictures of them standing next to their better-dressed sisters, she thought bitterly. Or to inform her she was being unfair to Harri, leading him astray when he had a sister to support, and a cause to fight, one that she could not possibly understand.

Fuelled by her irritation, Bea soon lost herself walking between the crowds, running in front to photograph them as they passed. This time she remembered to speak to any marchers who would reply to her questions, jotting down a few notes, storing the rest in her memory.

As they turned the next corner, the police were waiting for them. Bea found herself jostled. Several of the banners were torn down as policemen waded in. Disorientated in the chaos, she saw Gwen, her jacket torn, her hat gone and hair half loose, being dragged to one side. As she ran towards her, she saw Harri was next to Gwen arguing with the policeman. The man hesitated, his grip slipping from Gwen's arm. Bea reached for Gwen's other hand.

'Quickly,' called Harri. 'They're going to stop the march at any cost. We need to get her away.' They pushed through, to the edge of the crowd where Lillian and Olwen were helping the elderly woman whose invalid chair had been turned over, leaving her sprawled, helpless, in the middle of the road. The crowd had joined in, with stones and shouts and insults being thrown. They had nearly reached Olwen when a new rush of police came at them with batons raised.

Bea lost sight of the others once more, swept by the crowd to one side of the melee. She still had a few frames left in her camera, which she had been saving for the march at the Houses of Parliament. Quickly, she steadied herself, her back to the nearest lamppost. She bent, peering through the viewfinder on top of the Brownie, frantically attempting to focus. Another baton charge went through the crowd in front of her. She clicked, hoping she had caught the policeman with his arm raised and her hand had been steady.

She wound it on to the next frame. She could risk one more. She waited as the crowd opened up in front of her. The struggling had eased slightly. Her stomach rolled as she caught sight of a woman lying full-length on the floor, blood oozing into a dark stain around her head. She clicked the shutter. The crowd moved again, hiding the injured protester. Bea wound on the film again. She had one more frame. She was no longer afraid. She had pushed the bodies jostling around her out of her mind. Cold, clear determination filled every part of her. She would not keep the final frame for Mrs Pankhurst in front of the Houses of Parliament, even if that was the picture a newspaper would be interested in. Her mind was focussed solely on recording the scene.

'No you don't, you little bitch.' She was shoved roughly away from the lamppost. A hand closed over the Brownie, tearing it from her, sending it crashing into the road. She saw its remains, the lens smashed, the bellows broken, sliding into the gutter.

'Leave me alone,' she yelled, as loud as she could, as the policemen grabbed her. She was dragged back towards him, knees scraping the floor as she fell.

'Get up.' A boot landed in her back, nearly winding her. 'Get up.' She was pulled roughly to her feet, and marched to a motorised police van. As they drew nearer, other police joined in, as if containing some dangerous animal. She was punched, her skirts torn, hands grabbed at her breasts, until she was thrown inside the Black Maria, which was filled with women. A woman was pushed in behind her, the door slammed, and the vehicle roared off at speed.

For a few minutes there was a shocked silence. The woman who had been shoved in behind Bea began to cry. 'I've got my boys at home. They're only little, what are they going to do?'

'Who's looking after them now?' asked an older woman.

'My sister, until my husband gets home.'

'I'm sure she'll be able to look after them a bit longer,' said the older woman. 'They just want to frighten and shame us. They might just keep us on remand for tonight and let us go.'

'Or they could charge us and send us to prison,' remarked a voice further back. 'That's what they did to me last time. A whole month I got in Holloway. You're not allowed letters or to speak to any of your family for the first month. Horrible.'

'Shhh,' hissed the older woman, as the mother began to sob in earnest. 'Are you hurt?' she whispered to Bea.

'I don't think so.' She felt slightly sick from a blow to her head, and every part of her felt scraped raw and bruised.

'I saw you taking photographs of what they were doing. That was very brave of you.'

'My camera was destroyed,' replied Bea gloomily.

'But some of your pictures might have survived. I saw a woman pick it up and hide it under her coat. Let's hope she managed to escape being arrested.'

'I hope so,' Bea said, bracing herself as the Black Maria drew up at the police station.

Chapter Twenty-Nine

Her first night in Holloway prison was the loneliest Bea had ever spent.

'How can anyone be sent to prison for a month for peacefully protesting?' she whispered to Gwen, after they were sentenced, following the briefest of court appearances, and taken in a Black Maria to begin their sentences.

'It's to make us feel dirty and ashamed and keep us quiet,' replied Gwen. 'Well, it won't work.' A look of determination came over her thin face. 'It won't.'

'You're not planning to go on hunger strike, are you?' whispered Tilly, a pale girl of nineteen. Bea shook her head. 'Me neither.' She shuddered.

'Have you been to prison before?'

'Just once.' She glanced at Gwen. 'Don't give them any excuse. Just keep your head down and serve your time. Some of the warders are all right. Others love hurting you and making you look small. And the others who don't, they still have to carry on and do things, they'd lose their jobs otherwise, see. It's all very well, but who's going to give up a job when they won't get a reference to get another and they've a family to feed? Make their life easy, and most of them won't pick you out.'

'No, of course,' said Bea. Like with the violence of the march, she must keep on making notes, mental notes of anything she could use afterwards. She had no way of knowing if the film in her camera would ever find its way back to the White Camellia, but she could still paint a picture with words, like the best

251

journalists. She scanned the faces of the women in the back of the Maria. Some, like Gwen, held a steely determination, huddled together with comradeship and purpose. Others were closed in on themselves, with a look of dread. One or two, first time prisoners like herself, she suspected, held expressions of suppressed terror.

'Will we all be kept together?' she asked Tilly, feeling panic rising despite of herself.

'Probably.' She gave a wry grin. 'Well, the ones they think are ladies.' She bit her lip. 'But they won't allow us to talk to each other at meal times. Not for the first month. And there's no visitors until the end of the first month.' She lowered her voice even further. 'That's why you need to keep quiet and not cause trouble, see. You're completely in their power. They can do anything, and there's nothing you can do about it.'

* * *

As soon as they arrived, there was no more talking. They were put in reception cells to be processed in turn. Bea was commanded to undress, before being examined by a doctor and led to wash herself in a bath. She had never felt so exposed and vulnerable without her clothes protecting her. No-one had seen her undressed since she was a child. Even the bath, grateful as she was for the feeling of water on her bruised and filthy body, was a hasty affair, behind a screen so low she was easily watched.

She was instructed to take a dress of green serge from a pile on the floor, that scratched and fitted loosely over her frame, accompanied by a white cap and an apron. The shoes were ill-fitting (although she was later to learn she was lucky to have ones that were almost a pair) and the stockings refused to stay up, with no garter to hold them. She was given sheets and a toothbrush, a bible and a few other worthy-looking books, and led to her cell, which was tiny and narrow. There she was given a yellow badge with the number of the cell and the letter of the block. That was how she would be known from now on.

She had never been in so bleak a place. The electric light, which was controlled from outside, left no shadows, making it bleaker than ever. She curled up in a corner, hugging her knees against her chest, the sounds and smell of the prison overwhelming her. It was a hot night and her cell was airless. As the light was switched off, she felt the walls close in around her. She couldn't imagine an entire month of being stuck in this place, without a name, subject to a faceless authority.

'Bea?' The whisper was quiet, but clear. 'Bea, is that you?'

The voice was on the other side of the wall she was leaning against. 'Tilly?'

'Yes. Don't give in. Don't let them break you.'

'Nor you,' replied Bea.

She tried to settle herself down on the narrow bed, finding a position that eased the worst of her bruises. At least Olwen had not been arrested, nor Lillian, as far as she knew. She thought of Mama and Ada, settling down at home in Curzon Avenue and ached to be back with them, to feel the familiar worn furniture, and the smell of polish and lily of the valley. Along the corridor a woman screamed. Shouts erupted, followed by shouts and hammering on cell doors. Boots raced along the corridors, with raised voices and the jangling of keys.

'It's all right,' whispered Tilly, as the commotion began to subside. 'Just someone panicking. They'll get used to it. It's when you hear them doing the force feeding, that's when it's really vile.'

'No surrender,' came a voice from the other side of Tilly's cell.

Bea shivered. She knew it couldn't be Gwen. She'd seen her being taken towards another block. She might not even be able to see her while they were there. After seeing the determination on Gwen's face, she could only dread what she was planning to do.

* * *

The next morning she was woken early by a bell. Breakfast was
a pint of sweet tea, a small brown loaf and a small amount of
butter, given to her in her cell.

'Don't eat it all at once,' said the warder, who was brisk, but
not unkind. 'That's all you'll get apart from lunch.' Her eyes
sharpened, as Bea stared down at the unappealing loaf. 'And make
sure you eat it.' Her voice lowered. 'Or give it to someone who
will. There are some here who just love doing the force feeding.
Don't give them the excuse.'

After the first few days, Bea began to adjust to the routine.
Each morning there was slopping out. Lunch was held in silence,
and there was very little else to do.

At the beginning of the second week, a young girl of around
seventeen, a brown dress hanging from a wasted frame, appeared
in her cell.

'I'm to clean your cell, Miss,' she murmured under her breath,
eyes on the floor.

Bea looked at her in horror. 'I'm a prisoner, just as much as
you are. I don't want anyone to act as my servant.'

'Please, Miss,' she whispered. 'I've been told.'

Bea gritted her teeth. Even in this she had no say. 'Of course,'
she replied. She crouched on her bed as the girl set to work,
scrubbing and cleaning with an energy she would not have
thought possible.

'What's your name?' she asked at last. 'Your real name,' she
added, as the girl glanced at the number on her badge.

'Eva. Eva Wilks.' She relaxed a little. 'Are you a suffragette,
Miss?'

'I didn't think I was,' replied Bea. 'But I suppose I am. I
thought I was just protesting and it was a free country. So now I
know I'm wrong.'

Eva grinned slightly as she resumed scrubbing the floor. Bea took a deep breath. The division of the prison was as rigid as the society outside. She had seen the third division prisoners, but there had never been an opportunity to speak to one. 'What are you here for?' she asked tentatively.

'I tried to throw myself in the river,' came the reply.

Bea stared at her. 'And they put you in here?'

'Yes, Miss.'

'And what will you do when you get out?'

Eva paused. 'I don't know.' She looked up, her pale eyes filled with tears. 'I can't go home. Mam says I'm lying, and Dad wouldn't. But he won't stop, and now there are other men, ones who pay him. And I won't.' She bent her head so that it was resting on one arm. 'I won't.'

'Don't you have any friends, anywhere you can go?'

Eva shook her head. 'My aunt got me a position as a maid, but Dad found me and took me back, without me giving notice, and now I can't get a reference. I won't be one of those women who sell themselves, I'll only get killed or get one of them horrible diseases, and I've seen what happens when they have babies.' Her voice was empty of any emotion. 'I've thought it through, Miss. I'm going to get killed anyhow, I'd rather it was the river now, before I've got babies to take with me.'

Bea shuffled off the bed, crouching next to her. 'Listen, Eva, there is a place that I know will take you in.' She hesitated. She had nothing to write with, and in any case she couldn't embarrass Eva by asking if she could read. 'You need to find a Miss Finch.' Eva had begun scouring the floor again, but Bea could feel she was listening. 'Like the bird.'

'Like the bird.' She looked up. 'I don't want charity.'

'It's not charity, Eva. It's a place where you can stay for a while, and get help to find work. If you help out in return for a bed, they'll be able to give you a reference, and give you training so you can find other kind of work, too.' Heavy footsteps were making their way towards the cell. Bea hastily gave Eva directions to find Lillian's refuge before the wardress arrived.

At least I can still be a journalist, she thought to herself, when Eva had gone. It didn't ease the tedium of the regime, or the lack of any meaningful occupation, or any human contact apart from a few snatched whispered conversations, but at least it gave her some purpose in the long empty hours. She had little opportunity to speak to the women of the third division, but she could observe them, and find out a little of their stories, parcelling away the information into her mind, ready for when she would be free to act on it. Harri would be able to help her to find out more, and maybe even Lillian, who surely wanted the wretched circumstances of those who went to her for help to be publicised. Eva did not come to her cell again, but when she caught a glimpse of her, Eva gave something approaching a smile. 'Finch', she mouthed silently across the room. Bea nodded, smiling as broadly as she dared.

At least she had begun to sleep. It was a sleep haunted by the shrieks and bangs of the prison, but sometimes, just sometimes, she escaped to a place far away. But with sleep came dreams, and the dream that came back night after night was the old one that had never quite gone away.

She was back in the fields below Tressillion, on a still spring day, the sea a shimmering turquoise, the air perfumed with the bluebells she was gathering for Grandmama. She was happy, a brief, stolen happiness, away from Papa's grim mood and the worry in Mama's eyes. She felt the first heat of a long, hot summer on her face, and knew that everything was going to be all right, now that Leo was home, tanned, with contentment glowing through every pore. She was going to meet him at the Fossick Arms.

He had something for her, he'd said. He wouldn't say any more within the grounds of Tressillion, where Papa or one of the servants might hear. But she knew from his expression that it meant freedom. Leo was prosperous, making his name as a photographer. Wherever he had found his home, he was happy. And even if Papa refused to speak to him, she knew he would take her back with him, to a place where she could live her own life and be free.

She turned towards the path leading up to the village. In the far distance, just below the village, she could make out Leo, walking to meet her. Then came the rumble, the shaking of the earth beneath her feet. Leo paused, turning as she did, to the mine. Then she was running, as fast as she could, across the fields towards him. But Leo had already vanished. And she was flung to the ground as the earth shook again. She clambered to her feet, scrambling up beside the stream to the mine, dread freezing every part of her, knowing what she would find.

Chapter Thirty

A few days later, she was released.

Bea stepped outside the prison gates, bewildered by the clamminess of her own clothes, the cool air on her bare head, to find Jonathan waiting for her.

'I've come to take you home.'

'Why am I being released? What about my friends?'

He didn't meet her eyes. 'Your Mama is beside herself with worry.'

A woman rushed past them. 'Mr Lewis.' Bea was shocked to see Harri standing a short distance away. 'Thank you, Mr Lewis. I knew it was you.' It was the woman she had travelled with in the back of the Black Maria, who had been so tearful about her children. She grasped Harri's hands. 'I can't ever thank you enough, Mr Lewis, I can't ever.'

Harri smiled. 'It was my pleasure, Mrs Saunders.' He met Bea's eyes as Mrs Saunders ran towards a man with two small boys.

'Just one moment.' As Mrs Saunders was gathered up by her family, Bea walked over to Harri. 'How's Gwen?' she asked.

'I haven't been able to see her. I'll do my best to get her out as quickly as I can.'

Bea nodded. She could hear Jon's footsteps behind her. 'Thank you, Mr Lewis.'

'Not at all,' he replied.

'We are grateful for your assistance, Lewis,' said Jon stiffly. 'You know where to send your bill.'

'Indeed,' replied, Harri, equally formal. 'Goodbye, Miss Tressillion. I hope you can now get some rest.'

She turned back briefly as she was led away, but he had already disappeared.

* * *

Jon drove her home without a word.

Bea leant against the back of the passenger seat, eyes closed, pretending to be asleep. She stole a quick glance at his face. It was set and expressionless, mortification in every sinew. She shut her eyes again, preventing any conversation.

As they drew up in front of the house, Jon cleared his throat. 'I thought we might move.'

'Move?' Bea blinked at him. She was completely disorientated, and a little dizzy, from being out in the sunlight. A couple walked past on the pavement, making her nervous. Already, in that short time, she had forgotten how to act, how to make her own decisions. She fought down a rising sense of panic. It was a natural reaction to being in such a dull, remorseless routine, she told herself. Her old self was still there, waiting to come back.

'I was thinking America. We could make a fresh start. I have business interests out there.' He shuffled on his seat. 'A group of us are considering investing in films.'

The fogginess in her brain began to lift. 'Films?'

'Yes. It's an excellent business opportunity. It's quite the new thing, you know. They are looking for backers for a huge production of *Cleopatra*. They haven't chosen the actress yet.' His gaze was distant, as if he was talking to himself. 'It would be a great thing to be a part of such an enterprise. To ensure it was all done for the best.'

You can't buy love, she thought, staring at her hands, squeezed together in her lap. She could see the elegant figure of Cassie Lane, swathed in diaphanous gauze, eyes heavily lined beneath an exotic headdress, ordering her troops, and dying for her beloved Anthony.

And no prizes for guessing who'd be in the role of Octavia, Anthony's reassuringly plain wife, safely left at home with nowhere to run, thought Bea. She had never been so thankful to see Mama, who had, for once, left dignity behind and rushed out into the street to greet her.

'Beatrice.' She hugged her tightly. 'Darling girl. I was so worried. I was convinced that I had lost you too. And then that dreadful message from that solicitor, Lewis, or somebody, to say where you were, and that he was going to get you out. Heaven knows how much money he'll want for his pains.'

'Mama, I'm sure payment was the last thing on Mr Lewis' mind.' She could feel Jon listening and rushed on. 'I've heard he gets people out of prison all the time after these marches. There were several other women released at the same time as me.'

'Awful.' Mama placed her hands over her ears, as if to shut the words out. 'Truly, truly awful. How could you let yourself get mixed up with such people, Beatrice? I haven't slept a wink. Thank you, Jon, for bringing her back to me.'

'I'll leave you,' he muttered.

'But you will come back soon?' Mrs Tressillion put an anxious hand on his arm. 'I'm sure Beatrice has learnt her lesson, and will never do anything so foolish ever again. You will come back and visit us, Jon?'

There was a moment's silence. 'Yes. Yes, of course,' he replied. With a brief nod at Bea, he returned to the driver's seat and set off at a rapid pace.

'Well, what are you waiting for?' snapped Mama, as the engine roared into the distance. 'Don't just stand there, Cally. Miss Beatrice needs a bath immediately and new clothes.' Her nose wrinkled. 'These can be burned.'

'They can be washed and mended, Mama,' said Bea, as they reached the front door. 'And what am I to do without a coat?'

'You are best without a coat, if you ask me,' said Mrs

Tressillion, sharply. 'You won't be tempted into getting into more trouble.' She clapped her hands. 'Come on, Cally.'

'Yes, Mrs Tressillion.' Cally shot off in the direction of the kitchens.

'How could you?' As soon as the door was shut, for the first time in her life, Bea found herself being violently shaken by her mother. 'How could you do such a thing, Beatrice? Our future was secure. He was going to propose. He asked for my permission while we were waiting for you to arrive home that dreadful night, before Mr Lewis' telephone call. Of course I gave it to him. I told him it was the happiest day of my life, and soon it would be yours, too. Heaven knows what will happen now. How could you?'

Bea stumbled, her head swimming. 'Mama, I'm very tired.'

'Oh my dear.' Her mother's eyes grew large, as she took in the pallor of Bea's face, the bruising on her neck and cheek. She caught her arm. 'Did those wretched policemen hurt you?' She hesitated. 'Did anything…?'

'No', replied Bea gently. 'Nothing like that, Mama. They were a bit rough, that's all. I'm just tired and in need of a wash.'

'Of course.' Mrs Tressillion gave an anxious smile. 'And he did promise to come back. He knows you didn't mean this to happen, and that it was just an accident, and it was these new friends of yours who dragged you into it, and that soon it will be all forgotten and it will never be mentioned again.' She kissed Bea's cheek. 'At least that solicitor…'

'Mr Lewis?'

'Yes, Mr Lewis. He must be a clever man. At least he made sure you were released and your name didn't get in the papers.' She smiled. 'I'm glad at least some of your friends have sense enough to employ him.'

'Yes, Mama,' said Bea. Trying to explain about Harri would only make things worse. She escaped upstairs before her mother could question her further. She sat down on the bed, her eyes closing.

'Miss?' There was a gentle knocking on the door.

'I don't need any help, Cally. You've enough to do.'

'I've brought you some hot water and a cup of tea.'

Bea stumbled to her feet. Just the few minutes of resting her body had stiffened her limbs, and she felt she would never remove the stench of the prison clinging to her clothes.

'Thank you.'

Cally handed her the largest and least dainty teacup in the house, and placed a jug of hot water on the washstand. 'Miss Ada's helping me make you up a bath.'

'You shouldn't have gone to all that trouble, Cally, you've enough to do. Now I've caused you more work.'

'I wanted to. And anyhow, Miss Ada's doing most of it. Just don't tell your Mama. Was it very horrible?' She lowered her voice. 'The prison, I mean.'

Bea nodded silently. 'They were horrible to all of us. I can't believe that could happen. Not in a civilised country.'

'The coppers are vile, if you get on the wrong side of them. My friends who were on the march said they were grabbing them.' Her voice lowered to a whisper. 'In places. You know, private places. Like they were girls from the streets, selling themselves. They tore nearly all the clothes off one of my friends. And they were laughing, she said, and the crowd who were watching were cheering and joining in. They did it to the old ladies too. Respectable ones. My cousin's a policeman. A good policeman,' she added hastily. 'There are some. He said they were told to do it, to hurt the women in that way. They were trying to make them ashamed. Scare them, so they'd never dare raise their voices in public again. Making them feel dirty and disgusting, that's even worse than hitting them.' She sniffed loudly. 'That won't stop anyone, if you ask me. I'll be going on one myself next time, just you see.'

Bea covered her face with her hands. She could feel herself beginning to shake.

'It's all right, Miss.' She was gently helped out of her blouse. 'Bloody hell! Oh, I'm sorry, Miss. But them bruises…' Cally turned pale. 'Are you sure you're all right? You must have been black and blue, they still look bad now.'

'I'm all right.' She caught Cally's hand. 'Some of the women had much worse beatings. The doctor at the prison said there was nothing broken. I might have had a cracked rib, but that doesn't even hurt any more. Please don't say anything to Mama, she's upset enough as it is. And you'd better keep Ada away until I'm dressed again.'

'Do you want me to stay?'

Bea shook her head. 'I'll call you if I need you. I'll be able to manage myself now.'

The water was hot as she stepped into the bath Cally and Ada had prepared. She eased in slowly, feeling her limbs relax. For a while she lay, luxuriating in the peace and the privacy, without having to scrub hastily, being watched at every moment, one in a line of many. As the water cooled, she scrubbed herself clean, every single part of her, trying to rub away the smell and the vileness and the screams.

When she had dried herself and eased herself into her oldest, most loose dress, she wrapped herself into a quilt and sat by the dying embers of the fire. The normal sounds of the household settled around her. Mama's voice giving instructions to Cally drifted up from below. Through the window came the clip of horse's hooves and the turn of wheels on the road outside.

She hugged herself, arms round her knees, trying to regain the sense of herself. No policeman with his boots and his grasping hands could ever take that away from her, nor the prison warders with their rules and their faceless regimes. Deep inside, the anger was still there, for the women who had been assaulted and imprisoned for simply asking to have their opinions heard. For Eva, and the poor wretched women of the Third Division, who had no voice at all. She thought of the men and women in Lillian's shelter, and understood Lillian's determination to never give up, whatever happened.

Lillian. She had forgotten about Lillian and her urgent need to speak to her. She sat up straight. As far as she knew, Lillian had not been one of those arrested. She pulled the quilt closer about her, shivering despite the warmth of the fire. She had to speak to Lillian, as soon as she could, and she had to return to the White Camellia. She had already lost two weeks' wages, and the apartment near the tearooms must surely have been taken. She had to speak to Mrs Anselm and tell her what had happened to the camera, and then she had to find a new apartment, and the first clerical job she could secure. Now she not only had to find a way of supporting Mama and Ada, but to replace the camera donated to the White Camellia. And she had to do both fast.

* * *

For the next two days, Bea remained at home, regaining her strength and adjusting to the strange sensation of freedom. She ventured out for walks in the little park, sitting in the evening sun watching families pass by, breathing in the wonderful ordinariness of everyday life. Mama looked out for Jon to arrive, fussing over the state of Bea's hair and laying out the last of the dresses she had managed to create for Bea for the invitation to dinner or the theatre that would surely come.

On the third day, Bea could stand it no longer. Her legs still felt slightly wobbly, but she was growing used to wide open spaces again, and besides, she had no time to waste. She slipped downstairs early, collected her newly cleaned and mended coat and her hat, left a note for Mama, and shot out into the summer morning.

Chapter Thirty-One

'Ah, there you are,' said Mrs Teal, as Bea made her way down to the kitchens, just as the work of the day began.

'I'm sorry…'

'I heard what happened,' replied Mrs Teal. She clicked her tongue. 'Nasty business. Call this a free country, beating women and throwing them into prison just for asking for their rights.' She took a quick look at Bea's face, still pale, with the remains of a bruise visible on one cheek. 'We've plenty of work for you to do. You can start by helping me weighing out for these scones.'

'Was it very awful?' whispered Vicky, who was scouring pans in a slightly slapdash fashion, while managing to regularly pass Bea.

'Horrible.'

'I tried to stay. I told them my name was Anne Smith and I was a seamstress, but they didn't believe me.'

Bea hid a grin. When she'd glimpsed Vicky on the march she had been dressed in a coat she had clearly felt to be plain, but was obviously of the most expensive material, and even more expensive cut. The buttons alone probably cost more than a seamstress earned in a week. 'And then of course Papa sent my brother to fetch me.' She sighed with irritation. 'You should have seen them, they really grovelled then, when Charles appeared and they realised who I was. I wanted to be heroic, and go on hunger strike like Gwen and the others. Then when they'd found out who I was, that would really cause a fuss.'

'You don't want to do that,' said one of the older women,

pausing in beating eggs for a cake. 'My sister's been on hunger strike three times. The way they treat them, it's like torture. More than once the tube went into her lungs and she nearly choked, and then ended up with pneumonia. She was lucky to survive. The doctors have told her, her heart has been weakened. She'll never regain her strength. And it's not just through the nose that they insert those feeding tubes, if you get my meaning.'

'But where else…?' Vicky came to a halt. 'You couldn't possibly mean… They couldn't!'

'What's to stop them? If you really are poor and powerless, they can do what they want.' She caught the look on Bea's face. 'Don't worry, Mr Lewis and Mrs Anselm are making sure Gwen and the others are not forgotten. Let's just hope they get them out soon.'

* * *

Bea worked hard, glad to be back in the warm, slightly chaotic atmosphere of the White Camellia, with laughter and banter flying across the kitchen whenever Mrs Teal's back was turned, reassured to be able to earn her living once more. However tired she became, she was determined to visit Lillian before she returned home. A battle was brewing with Mama, and she needed to know what Lillian was so anxious to tell her.

She was just collecting her hat and coat, when a familiar figure appeared at the entrance. He peered around the half deserted tearoom, clearly looking for someone.

'Jon!'

He nodded to her tightly. 'Beatrice. I came to give you a lift home.'

'I'm just finishing, but I…' The chatter from those left in the tearoom had grown noticeably quieter. It was hardly the place to argue. 'Of course,' she murmured. Thankfully, he immediately turned on his heel. She followed him outside, buttoning up her coat as she went.

His automobile was waiting a short distance away. Bea came to a halt.

'I can't go with you,' she said. 'I have arranged to visit a friend. I'm going home straight afterwards. I'll meet you there.'

Jon turned. There was thin line of temper in his lips, and his hand on her arm was less than gentle. 'You'll come home now.'

'Don't be ridiculous.' She could feel her own temper rising, as hot as his was cool. 'You can't order me. You are not my father. Or my husband. And you can't possibly want to marry me now.'

'Didn't your mother speak to you?'

'Yes. But that was before I was arrested. You've made it quite clear since you met me outside Holloway that you don't care for me. I'm not sure you even like me. You don't think me suitable to be your wife. Surely there's no more to say?'

His grip tightened. 'It was agreed that we would marry. It is what our family wants. What I want. '

'But I don't love you, and you certainly don't love me.'

'This is marriage, Beatrice. It's a matter of practicalities, not some silly schoolgirl's romantic dream.' He pulled her closer, his voice lowering. 'It's the best solution for both of us, Bea. It's not lost. We can still get it back. But only if we work together.'

Bea stared at him, a myriad of questions rushing through her brain. 'I don't understand. What am I supposed to…?'

He raised his voice again. 'So you will come with me, and we'll talk to your mother?'

There was something wrong. She took in the strain on his face, the air of carefully preserved dignity. Even his cavalier order wasn't the Jon she knew. It wasn't the way he behaved at home with Mama, or with his friends at the theatre or opera. This tone of authority had only appeared outside the prison, when he had been horribly aware of Harri and the guards, and the need to maintain his position as a man in firm masculine charge of his womenfolk.

'Of course,' she said, slowly. His grip lessened, relief eased his face. His dignity had been preserved. But for whom? It had to be for an audience. Certainly not for her. It was someone he wanted to impress. Someone he was slightly in awe of. Or maybe feared. Someone who was close enough to them to hear every word. She remembered the expression she had seen in the flicker of a match of the man in the greatcoat, with her scarf around his neck as he bent to speak to Jon.

'My hat!' She clapped her free hand to her head. 'I've left it in the tearoom. I can't go home without it. Wait for me here.' Pulling herself free, she hurried back to the White Camellia. She didn't dare run, and she was certain Jon would follow, but she had managed to give herself a precious few seconds. She slipped through the door, praying everyone left was too engrossed in their own conversations to notice her, and rushed down to the kitchens.

'Good Heavens!' Mrs Teal looked up from her pastry. 'What on earth has got into you, young lady, bursting in like this?' She glanced at Bea's face. 'Is it the police?'

Bea shook her head. 'Worse,' she mouthed. Above, loud footsteps strode across the wooden floors, and she could hear Jon demanding to know the whereabouts of Miss Tressillion.

'This way.' Mrs Teal opened the door to the larder. 'There's a space behind the sacks of flour at the end. Wait there and don't move. I'll have no abductions in my kitchen.'

Mrs Teal grabbed a jar of blackcurrant jam from a shelf and disappeared back into the kitchen. 'Yes?' she demanded, as she pulled the door closed behind her. 'What is the meaning for this intrusion, young man? I run a respectable kitchen here. No followers. Of any kind.'

'I'm looking for Miss Tressillion,' came Jon's voice, loud and irritated. 'I was told she came down here. It's her mother's birthday, I need to get her home on time.'

'Oh?' replied Mrs Teal, blandly. 'First I've heard about it. I shall be having words with Miss Tressillion tomorrow morning, just you see. She asked to leave early today, all right, but I understood she had an appointment. In Maida Street, as far as I can understand. Number 32. If you go now you'll soon catch up with her. She left through the back door just a few minutes ago. It's the tradesman's entrance, but you are welcome to use it. Well go on, young man, if you want to catch up with her. Turn right at the end of the street and then the first left. She can't have gone far…'

Bea crept from her hiding place as Mrs Teal's voice faded into the distance. She heard a door being closed and bolts pushed into place. Cautiously, she opened the larder door, ready to run.

'That should keep him for a while. It isn't easy finding your way back to the main road from behind the Camellia if you don't have a map in your head.' Mrs Teal placed a bowl over her pastry and grabbed her own coat and hat. 'It will give us time to make a sharp exit. You don't think I'm leaving you, do you?' she added, as Bea began to protest.

Bea followed the cook up to the tearooms, retrieving her own hat on the way. They then followed a group of customers walking out onto the street, staying close until they reached the end of the road.

'Thank you,' said Bea.

'You'll be safe getting home?' said Mrs Teal.

Bea shook her head. 'I can't go home. He's going to be there, and Mama won't listen to me. I'm not sure what I'm going to do.'

'Hmm.' Mrs Teal thought for a moment. 'Then there's only one thing you can do, my dear. We need to get you to Mrs Anselm. She's the best person to sort this out.'

'We?'

'My dear, you don't think I'm going to leave you to be caught by that young man, do you? He had an eye like a fish, and not a drop of blood in him. They're the dangerous sort. The planning, calculating kind. Give me a crime of passion any day. Not that I'd want to experience it personally, you understand.'

* * *

Bea was ushered along narrow streets, twisting and winding to avoid the main thoroughfares, until they arrived at Mrs Anselm's front door.

'We're on a rescue mission, Lucy,' said Mrs Teal, in tones of huge enjoyment, as she pushed Bea inside, eyes scanning the respectable street as if it was the depths of the jungle. 'Miss Tressillion is in danger of being kidnapped by unsuitable young men.'

'One unsuitable young man,' said Bea, hastily. 'And not exactly kidnapped.'

'Kidnapped,' asserted Mrs Teal in tones of an argument won.

'Very well,' replied Lucy, who was a woman to take everything the world could throw at her in her stride. 'You'd both better come this way.'

'My dear,' exclaimed Mrs Anselm, as they were shown into the drawing room. 'Is everything all right, Mrs Teal?'

'Fine and shipshape at the White Camellia,' replied Mrs Teal. 'But Beatrice here needs rescuing.'

'From unsuitable young men,' added Lucy, with a smile at Beatrice.

'Well, yes, of course. Good Heavens.' Mrs Anselm frowned at her. 'You haven't been followed again, have you, Miss Tressillion?'

'Followed?' For a moment Bea's mind went blank, but then the vision of landing into the softness of Mrs Anselm's fur came into her mind. She shuddered slightly. 'Not exactly followed. Only by my cousin Jonathan.'

'Oh, a cousin.' Mrs Anselm raised her eyebrows. 'I thought you quite able to deal yourself with unwanted suitors, Miss Tressillion.'

Bea flushed. Now Mrs Anselm believed she was a weak-headed fool. Perhaps she was right. There had been no reason to be frightened, or to feel there was someone else watching. It could be all her imagination. What kind of weakling couldn't tell a man to his face, once and for all, that she would never marry him, and use the heel of her boots to good effect if he tried to change her mind?

'I'm sure it was nothing,' she murmured.

'Well, it didn't look like nothing to me,' said Mrs Teal, who wasn't about to let go of this drama, almost as good as the moving pictures and with a real-life Mary Pickford safely under her wing. 'You looked proper scared, young lady.'

'I'm sorry,' said Mrs Anselm, looking mildly irritated. 'But you must excuse me. You can both stay here for as long as you wish, and there's a bed for you if you feel you can't go home tonight, Miss Tressillion. Just make sure you send a message to your mother to let her know you are safe. Lucy will look after you. I'm due to see Gwen off on the train.'

'She's out of prison?' said Bea. 'Harri managed to get her out?'

'Not before time,' said Mrs Anselm, grimly. 'We are getting her away tonight before they can change their mind, and before Gwen can do anything to give them the excuse to make an example of her again.' As she reached the door, she halted. 'Tressillion,' she said, with a frown on her face. 'Jonathan Tressillion. Is that who you were running from? The dealer in gold bullion?'

'Gold!' Bea stared at her.

'Precious stones, too. But however he dresses it up as fine jewellery, that's what his business is. Surely you knew?'

'We never discussed business,' said Bea. 'Mama never said. It seemed rude to ask where his money came from.'

Mrs Anselm folded her arms over her chest. 'The first thing you should always ask, young lady, if only of yourself. Particularly of a man who is proposing to marry you. Men of business rarely marry for love, in my experience. My husband, I might add, was one of the rare ones. But then his ambition was to be comfortable, not an obsession with becoming rich. From what I know of Mr Jonathan Tressillion, he wants to be immensely rich.' She snorted. 'I bet he was sore at having to sell that gold mine of yours, especially now the new owner is making a nice profit from it.'

'She is?' Bea stared at her. 'Jon said something I didn't understand. About the two of us working together. About something not being lost. That we could still get it back. He couldn't mean the mine, surely?' She stopped. 'Whatever Jon is planning, I'm not going to be part of it. The Tressillions have caused enough heartache as it is. Miss Ravensdale bought the mine in good faith. I don't care if Jon thinks he's lost a fortune and wants to get it back and thinks he can, and she doesn't matter just because she's a woman. I'm not going to be a part of it.'

There was a loud knocking at the door. Mrs Anselm frowned at her. 'That sounds like my cab arriving. You had better come with me, Miss Tressillion, to see Gwen and Olwen get on the train. You can stay with me until we can get to the bottom of this. We can get a message to your mother when we get back.'

* * *

By the time the cab arrived at the station, Harri was already there, helping Olwen ease Gwen out of the passenger seat of Mrs Anselm's Ford, while Lillian placed several small suitcases on the ground next to them.

'Thank goodness,' said Mrs Anselm. 'So they did release her. Thank you, Mr Lewis. I knew you'd make them see sense.'

'They couldn't wait to get rid of us,' said Harri.

'So I see,' said Mrs Anselm. Curious glances rested on Bea. 'Miss Tressillion has come to help make sure you all get on the train,' she added, with a no-questions-asked finality.

Bea helped Lillian carry the suitcases onto the platform, as Mrs Anselm berated the ticket office.

'You are going to Cornwall, then?' said Bea, as Mrs Anselm's voice spread across the platform.

'Yes,' said Harri, joining her and Lillian, slightly out of earshot of the others. 'I'm taking Gwen to stay with her father. Olwen is going to stay for a few weeks to look after her. Gwen's very weak. We need to get her away.'

'To Porth Levant.'

'Yes.' He hesitated, with a glance at Lillian.

'My sister lives nearby,' said Lillian, slightly stiffly. 'She's not the easiest of women, but I'm hoping to persuade her to allow Gwen to stay with her.'

'She might find Gwen employment down there, and maybe a way of pursuing her campaign without the constant arrests,' said Harri.

'She will kill herself if she doesn't,' added Lillian. 'I've seen it with other women who've been on hunger strike, particularly when they've been rough and the tube has gone into the lungs. I don't believe Gwen has a death wish, but that's what it will be if she continues this way.'

'Yes,' said Bea. She hesitated. More people were arriving, and the train was drawing into the platform. She took a deep breath. 'Harri, you remember I was asking you about if something was sold, it couldn't be claimed back?'

He blinked. 'Yes of course.' The train had come to a halt beside them.

'You couldn't ask for me? Try and find out. Make sure it's all right?'

'Yes.' There was no more time for explanation, or questions. Bea helped them put their luggage into their compartment, to stash them away on the luggage rack above the seats. She kissed Gwen, who was huddled in a corner, enveloped in a large shawl, leaning against the window pane with her eyes closed, as if barely conscious.

Olwen followed her back out into the corridor. 'It will be up to you to finish the edition of the magazine,' she said, with an attempt at cheerfulness.

'But you will be back? You can't leave your studies?'

'Of course not.' Olwen kissed her. 'It's just a few weeks, until Gwen is settled.' She made a wry face. 'Besides, I have a feeling I'll be practicing my nursing skills, if not my skills as a doctor, as well.'

'I'd better go.' On the platform outside, Mrs Anselm was gesturing, as the train prepared to leave. 'I hope Gwen gets well soon.' She hugged Olwen tight, and made her way to the nearest door.

'Bea!'

As she took the first step down towards the platform, there was a rush of footsteps behind her. Along the platform the guard was closing doors, flag at the ready. 'You need to leave the train now, Miss, she's ready to go,' he called.

'One moment…' She turned as the footsteps reached her.

'Why did you ask Harri those things?' demanded Lillian.

'It was nothing.'

'The train cannot be delayed, Miss.' The guard was growing impatient.

'It wasn't nothing. I saw the passion on your face. It was Tressillion, wasn't it?'

Bea blinked. Behind her, she could feel the guard itching to drag her bodily onto the platform. 'Not the house,' she muttered.

'The mine.' Lillian drew in her breath. 'I knew it. I knew he wouldn't leave it alone. It had to be the mine.'

'Miss…' A firm hand was placed on Bea's arm.

'No.' Lillian pushed the guard away. 'You're wrong. I'm the one leaving the train.' She drew a ticket from her pocket, placing into Bea's hand.

'I can't!' Bea stared at her. 'What about your sister?'

'Oh, don't worry.' Lillian jumped down onto the platform, closing the door, forcing Bea back inside. 'I'd have only made things worse,' she added through the open window. 'We always end up arguing like furies. I'll speak to her by telephone. You're the one she needs to speak to.'

'Me?' With a jerk and a crunch of metal, the train began its journey. 'But I don't know her! I don't even know her name or where she lives.'

'Oh you will,' called Lillian, over the hiss of steam. 'Don't worry, Bea. You will.'

PART THREE

Chapter Thirty-Two

Madoc was sitting on the wooden steps that evening, warming his face in the last of the sun, a tin mug between his hands.

The work at the mine was going well. By the looks of things, the seam they had uncovered was a rich one, enough to make Miss Ravensdale a wealthy woman, even without her existing business interests, and to keep them all employed for years to come. He finished the last of his tea, and smiled. For all his ambitions to escape the mines, he never thought he would find contentment in managing the most unlikely of goldmines, in the middle of nowhere.

Sybil could be infuriating at times. Always questioning and wanting to know, controlling her mining interests as no doubt she remained in charge of her hotels. The old library in Tressillion House had been turned into her office, the shelves filled with carefully arranged files from floor to ceiling. At the same time, he appreciated the way she never questioned his judgement in front of the men, and she respected his point of view, even if she disagreed with him.

Once or twice in her office, when she had been bent over a map or a set of figures, he had inspected the rows of files, with names like 'The Clarion' and 'The Endymion', and understood her trust in Miss Phipps, her manager. Sybil Ravensdale was one of those rare employers who could inspire respect and fierce loyalty from her employees. He could see it already in the gruff men of Porth Levant, who didn't usually have a good word to say about a boss between them, but rarely grumbled at the uncompromising woman who now paid their wages. Perhaps it was her willingness to work just as hard, and to share the danger. A sense that she would never ask anyone to do anything she would not do herself.

Whatever it was, when Davy Adams, who everyone knew was a lazy so-and-so only kept on the straight and narrow by his long-suffering wife, passed a remark in the Fossick Arms about not being seen dead working for some bony female no man had ever looked at twice, the silence had been deathly. Madoc – who was careful not to jump to Sybil's defence because she could more than look after herself, and it wouldn't help anyone if he was suspected of harbouring feelings for her – had noted in surprise the closed faces, as the smoke curled up towards the beams in the unexpected stillness. Conversation started up again almost instantly, but Davy, possibly remembering that his only attraction as a farm labourer was that he came cheap, had been careful not to repeat his opinions.

Madoc grinned to himself, and reached under the steps for the brandy bottle, splashing a small amount into his empty mug. Funny how life turned out. Funny how contentment came in the most unexpected of places. Funny how….

'Well I never.' He placed his mug untouched on the weathered boards of the porch. Out of the dusk, a small group of people were walking towards him. He had eyes only for the slight figure at the centre, heavy supported on either side. His contentment vanished. 'Gwen.' How could he have been so thoughtless, focussed only on his own affairs? Manon would never have forgiven him. Gwen might be living her own life, but she was still his child. Yet again he had abandoned her. He raced towards the shore.

'She's all right,' said Harri, as he reached them. 'She just needs rest and time to heal. Olwen has come to look after her.'

'Gwen.'

Her face was pale in the dusk, her eyes half-closed. He could feel the unnatural heat from her body, and his stomach was gripped by fear at the sharp smell of fever sweat. Her eyes opened briefly but rested unseeing on his face.

'We didn't know where else to go,' said Olwen.

'No, of course. This is the right place. This is Gwen's home.' He lifted up his daughter's light body and carried her inside.

* * *

The next morning was bright and clear. Bea was awake as soon as the first light crept in through the window. After a restless night, Gwen had at last settled into sleep. Bea slipped from the mattress next to the bed, arranging the covers over Olwen, who had fallen asleep without even crawling under the blankets.

The cottage was quiet apart from the soft pull of waves on the pebbles. It was such a familiar sound. The sound of her childhood. Even the smell of salt, edged with seaweed and sun on sand was the same. Last night, she had been too exhausted to do more than stumble after Harri and Olwen in a haze. Lights had burned, she remembered, high above the cliffs. The windows of Tressillion, still warm and welcoming, but never to welcome her home again.

She pulled herself to her feet. None of them had had the energy to undress last night, only to fall into the best sleeping places Gwen's father could arrange. Collecting her boots and her coat, she crept outside.

The sea was still, gentle rollers snaking across the turquoise expanse, before buffeting the dark rocks on the far side of the bay. She sat on the wooden steps to pull on her boots, breathing in the clear air. From here, she could just glimpse the roofs of her old home, the large windows of one of the bedrooms, and the smaller panes of the servants' quarters beneath the eaves. It was still a knot in her heart, seeing the familiar shape of the house.

The view was clearer than she remembered it, the trees in the garden less enveloping. A sign that Tressillion was no longer anything to do with her. There was no-one to remember her childhood games, now her brothers had gone. Ada was too young, and any visiting children had only been invited to their safer games. The wilder adventures, chasing wolves amongst the undergrowth and pirates along the cliffs, had gone forever. This place had moved on beyond her, as if she, and all her memories, had never existed.

There was a coughing and a stirring inside the cottage. Guests or no guests, Gwen's father had work to go to. She could make out the roofs of the mine buildings through the trees. Even the mine had changed, the roofs clearly repaired, and the surrounding trees thinned.

An inner door opened. She wasn't ready to face anyone. She'd seen the startled look on Madoc's face when she had been introduced. Had she imagined his suspicion? She wasn't ready to speak to him, or anyone from Porth Levant. She didn't want to have to explain herself. Not until she had got her bearings. Shrugging herself into her coat, she slipped away down to the beach.

She walked along the water's edge, unable to stop herself from looking up to the house now and again. She had nearly reached the far end, where a path wound up a short cliff face to join the wider path through the fields, when a figure came walking down from the house. For a moment she hesitated. Just a few steps to the side and she would be hidden under the cliffs.

She pulled back her shoulders. Whoever it was up there had most probably already seen her. She was a Tressillion. Her family might not own it any more, but this was still the land of her childhood, and she wasn't about to be caught skulking in corners as if she was an intruder.

She continued walking towards the path, watching the

approaching figure from the corner of her eye, pretending she wasn't looking at all.

'Bea!' A voice called through the clear air.

Relief flooded through her. She didn't have to face anyone from the village, or the new owner of Tressillion. She waited as Harri raced down the path.

'Hello,' she said, feeling suddenly shy.

'Bea.' He caught her in his arms and held her tight. 'Dearest, bravest, foolhardy Bea.'

'Is that how you always greet a jailbird?' she replied with a smile.

'Don't even say the word.' He held her tighter, a sheen of tears in his eyes. 'I know what goes on in those places.' He clasped her face between his hands, meeting her eyes. 'They didn't harm you?'

'I got roughed up a little when I was arrested, but that's all.'

'More than a little,' he replied. 'Mrs Frobisher, who rescued your camera, saw what happened.'

'Did the film survive?'

He laughed. 'Trust you to think of your photographs.' He kissed her. 'Yes. Mrs Anselm has a friend with a darkroom. She developed the film and printed the photographs. I'm seen them. Even if I didn't love you, I'd still have to admit they are brilliant. Mrs Anselm is arranging for the prints to take their place on the walls of the White Camellia.' He kissed her again. 'You are fearless.'

'No, I'm not. I was terrified.'

'But you kept your head and took the photographs. Not many people could do that.'

'Maybe.' She smiled. 'Are they really going to be displayed at the White Camellia?'

'You'll be able to see them for yourself when we get back. I'm sure Mrs Anselm will want them up as soon as they are all printed as large as they will go.'

'I can't wait to see them, they'll make all the bruises and being in prison worth it.' They began to walk back towards the fisherman's hut.

'So this is where you used to live,' he said.

'Yes.' She glanced at him. 'You went up to the house?'

'Just to the entrance of the grounds.' He gave a faint smile. 'It's grander than I imagined.'

'But I'm not,' she retorted. 'I'm the one who washes dishes in the White Camellia for a living, remember? Not to mention having been in prison.'

He was still observing the house. 'I can see you living here.'

'Well, I can't. Not any more. So much has changed since I left. I've changed. I'm not sure I could even live in a place like this now, however beautiful it might be.' She scowled. 'And if you think that's an excuse for not loving me, I'll never speak to you again.'

'Bea, you didn't see where Gwen and I grew up.' He winced. 'You'd have been the lady bringing us poor peasants a charity basket, if we'd ever met at all.'

'I've never taken a charity basket anywhere,' she snapped. 'That was never my idea of charity work, invading people's homes.' She grabbed his hands, pulling him into the shelter of the rocks, out of sight of anyone on the land or the beach. 'Don't you dare turn honourable and cowardly on me now, Harri Lewis. If there's one thing that vile prison taught me, it was not to be afraid. We're both healthy. We can both work. I don't want you to support me. If I can persuade Mrs Anselm to employ me as a photojournalist, couldn't we pool our resources? Surely we could find a way so that you can still support Olwen and I can support Mama and Ada? I don't care if I still have to work in the kitchen as well, where we live, or how, just so long as I never lose you.'

He hesitated. 'But Bea, when children arrive…'

'There are ways and means.' He started. 'Now I've shocked you.'

'No, of course not,' he said, colouring slightly. 'You just caught me by surprise, that's all.'

'Because I've thought about it? I'm immodest enough to have investigated the subject? Because I want to keep control over my life and when and where I have my children?' She took a step back. 'Because I've thought about putting my desire to work and having a meaningful purpose to my life before I'm a mother?'

'No, of course not.' He grinned. 'I do have a sister training to be a doctor, and I've never argued she should avoid her course in anatomy to protect her modesty, or against her decision to remain single until she has achieved her goal.' He drew her back towards him. 'I don't want to lose you, Bea. I'd rather be surprised by you for the rest of my life than live a calm and decorous existence with anyone else.'

'I'd have to persuade Mama that I'm not going to abandon her.'

'And I'll need to reassure Olwen that we both want to support her, and that she shouldn't feel guilty and want to give up her career.' His eyes searched her face. 'Bea, are you sure about this?'

'More than ever,' said Bea. 'I'd rather die than marry a man like Jon, and live my mother's life.' She gripped the lapels of his jacket, holding him tight. 'I can't abandon her, but I'm not going to put her wishes in front of mine. I'm going to live my own life.' She practically shook him in her fierceness. 'Whether you want to marry me or not.'

He kissed her. 'Of course I want to marry you, you goose.' His kiss was longer, more insistent, sending her legs to jelly as she leant against the warmth of the rocks. After a while he released her. The mischief was back in his eyes again. 'I'm not very practised at this, but I have a feeling I'm supposed to fall to one knee at this point, and protest my undying devotion while presenting you with my grandmother's diamond ring, if she had ever possessed such a thing.'

Bea giggled. 'Don't you dare. Since this might be our only opportunity to be alone, I'd far rather have a rational conversation about our choices. And it doesn't mean,' she added, between kisses, 'that I feel any less passionately.'

Voices made them jump apart.

'It's all right,' said Harri. 'They're a distance away. It must be the men on their way to the mine.' He kissed her wistfully. 'Madoc must have gone too. We should be getting back before we are missed.' He hesitated. 'Do you mind if we keep this to ourselves, until we are certain Gwen will recover?'

'I agree.' She kissed him. 'We both need time to talk to Olwen. And I'd rather start my new life, even just talking about it, without any taint of the old. If that makes sense?'

'Perfectly.' He considered her. 'I take it you are planning to go up to the house?'

'I need to speak to Miss Ravensdale, if she'll listen, that is.'

'Because of what your cousin said about the mine?'

She nodded.

'Would you like me to come with you?'

Bea shook her head. 'Not this time. If I can make her listen to me, and if there is something that is worrying her that you can help with, maybe.' She kissed him again. 'You need to be with Gwen and Olwen. This is a journey I need to make on my own.'

'Very well,' he said. 'Bea, I solemnly promise that I will never stand in your way, whatever danger you want to throw yourself into in the cause of photojournalism, but, this once, if you are not safely back in a few hours, I'll be coming to find you.'

Bea watched him as he walked back across the sands to the cottage, where she could make out Olwen, standing on the wooden veranda, looking out for their return. She waited until Harri joined her and disappeared inside. Then she turned her face towards the path through the fields, towards Tressillion.

Chapter Thirty-Three

Bea walked up the familiar path, as she had once done every day of her life. In the distance, she could hear the conversation of the men crossing the river to the mine. It was so still, she could barely hear the crash of breakers, just a gentle sighing every now and again above the call of gulls.

The metal gate was not bolted, and there was barely a squeak as she pushed it open. The overhanging branches and overgrown shrubs had been cleared to make a path through to the house. It looked well-used, the grass short and flat where feet had trodden over the months.

Bea stood in the protective shadow of the trees, looking up at the house. The chimneys stood stark against the sky, windows glinting in the early light. The gardens had been tidied and new planting done. There was order, instead of the wilderness she'd seen when she had taken a final walk around the gardens on the day they left.

She shivered a little as she saw it was as she remembered, from when she was a child. Papa had always had a passion for order. She could see him inspecting the trimming of the hedges, and the edging of the beds, in the days when there had been three or four gardeners coming in on a daily basis from cottages on the edge of the village. She and the boys had never been allowed to play on the finely manicured grass, or go near the roses waiting to drop their petals at the slightest excuse.

Strange, she had forgotten the order of the gardens. The regimented paths and lawns, the rows of flowers for cutting, the more exotic blooms in the greenhouses. The sense of everything having its place.

She looked once more at the house. It was a huge monstrosity, far too large for one family, despite the employment they had given to the villagers. So much space, so much grandeur. Papa had been obsessed with changing this feature and that, to put his stamp on every brick. He had never been satisfied. There was always something to be done. He must have spent a small fortune over the years, she thought, looking back with her adult eyes at the decorating. Changing the second drawing room into a library. Building the conservatory with its matching turrets.

And each time a change was completed, there had been a dinner held for any notable in Cornwall who could be persuaded to attend. Mama – who had constantly bemoaned the lack of London society – had prepared for them anxiously, sending out the invitations on Papa's list, and ticking off the acceptances as they came. Over time, Mama had grown increasingly nervous about the lack of acceptances, watching for the post each day, jumping at the sound of the telephone. But the large dining table, beautifully laid out with silver and exotic blooms, a model of Tressillion made in ice at the centre, had grown emptier over the years. She remembered the silences, the awkward, painful conversations, Mama watching each face, as if dreading what might be said once the wine began to flow.

She had been here, returning from a rare escape to the beach, the morning of Papa's dreadful argument with Leo. She had hesitated at just this spot, hidden by the trees, frozen by the raised voices coming from the library.

'I will not be ruled by your guilt,' she had heard Leo shout. 'What you did is on your head. Not on mine. I will never be a part of it.' She had heard the door bang, followed by bicycle wheels as he pedalled furiously towards Porth Levant.

He had only returned after dark. She had waited for him,

curled on the armchair next to the fire in his room. The rest of
the household had gone to bed, apart from Papa, who was still
in the library. She hadn't dared move, knowing any creak of the
floorboards would betray her, bringing Papa up, reproaching her
for siding with her brother when her loyalty – her utter and total
loyalty – should be to him.

When Leo had finally returned, he did as he had always done
when the front door was locked, or he wished to avoid Papa,
climbing the tree next to the house, swinging himself in through
the open window.

'Thanks, Bea. I knew you'd wait for me,' he'd said.

'I was worried Papa might find me, lock me in my room and
bolt the window.'

'Then I'd have broken the glass,' he'd replied.

His face was set. Leo, who was the least like Papa, at that
moment looked just like him. That's when she had known that
this wasn't the same as the other times, when she would go down
next morning to a silent breakfast, with Papa and Leo ignoring
each other, Simon and Oliver bracing themselves for an outburst,
and Mama close to tears. Then by dinner Leo, who could not
bear to see Mama's distress, would be his usual cheerful self,
burying deep whatever hurt lay between him and Papa.

Not this time. She'd known from his face that there was no
going back.

Papa must have heard them. The library door opened.

'You'd better go,' said Leo. 'You don't want to give him proof
you opened the window. I'll speak to him.'

She'd stopped to argue, but there were footsteps on the stairs,
the slow, heavy steps of Papa when he had been drinking. When
Mama kept her room firmly locked and they all remained as
quiet as mice, not wanting to draw his attention. So she had fled
to her room before he reached the bend in the stairs. She had sat
on the floor, braced against the door, listening for the argument

to rekindle. For the sound of blows. But there was nothing. Just Leo's voice, quiet, not fighting. Judging by his tone, agreeing to everything Papa said, until Papa left. She had not dared to make her way down the corridor again.

In the morning Leo had gone. He had taken a few belongings, climbed out of the window and caught the train to London. He'd sent a letter to Mama, when he was boarding ship to America. Nothing to the rest of them, knowing that Mama could not keep such news to herself, and to write to anyone else would be a sign of conspiracy in Papa's eyes. A letter would have marked any one of them out as a traitor, to take Leo's place as the scapegoat for Papa's temper.

Leo had written again to Mama, Bea was sure. There were times when Mama would smile, however dark Papa's mood. Once she filled the house with flowers. Bea didn't dare ask why, but she had caught a glimpse of a letter addressed to a Reverend White on Mama's dressing table, for her maid to take to the post office, the only way of avoiding Papa's eagle eyes.

If only. If only she hadn't gone into Mama's room that morning. If only Mary had taken the letter earlier, or the envelope had been placed face down, so she had not been able to copy the address. If only she had never known where to reach Leo. If only.

'Are you expected at the house?'

Bea jumped. Lost in thought, she had not heard anyone approach across the lawn.

Sybil searched the intruder's face, still not quite able to believe who she had seen standing on the lawn. The fear was back. Had Beatrice been sent by that damned cousin of hers, full of who-knows-what accusations? She could already feel the life she had built here beginning to slip from her grasp.

Bea shook her head. 'No.' She swallowed. 'I beg your pardon. I didn't mean to arrive unannounced.'

'Miss Tressillion, isn't it?'

Bea started. 'Yes.'

'Beatrice Tressillion.'

'Yes.' Bea's courage failed her. What had she been thinking of, turning up in the grounds of her old home, as if she still owned the place? Miss Ravensdale, with her sharp eyes and her uncompromising expression, would never listen to her fears now. She would see this as some kind of trick, or at the very least impertinence.

'I thought it must be.' Sybil's voice was dry. 'It was either that or a ghost gazing so intently at the house. I've no wish for any kind of ghostly visitations. Especially not in broad daylight.'

'I'm not a ghost.'

'No. So I see.' Sybil scrutinised Bea's face. Her presence was unsettling, especially hot on the heels of a vile letter from a fancy solicitor in London, with its veiled threats. Built on the assumption she was some silly-headed woman who didn't know how the world worked. Beatrice might have been sent to report back on her reaction to the suggestion that the land on which the mine stood was not legally hers. Her eyes narrowed. 'Are you visiting friends in the village?'

'No. Yes. In a way.' Bea found a tide of scarlet rising from her boots to her hairline. She nodded in what she hoped was a vague direction. 'I'm staying in a cottage on the coast.'

'With Mr Lewis?' Sybil's voice sharpened.

'He didn't know we were arriving,' said Bea. This was going from bad to worse. She had forgotten Miss Ravensdale was Madoc's employer. The last thing she wanted was to cause trouble for their host. Miss Ravensdale held all the cards. Bea knew all too well that she could forbid Madoc to have any guest in his house, ensure he lost his home and his income if he disobeyed. 'We are only staying for a few days. His daughter is ill. We brought her here.'

'We?'

'Gwen's cousins.'

'Oh.' Sybil frowned. 'The brother and sister who live in London?'

'Harri and Olwen. Yes.'

'I see. Is Mr Lewis' daughter very ill?'

'I think so. She has an infection in her lungs.' Bea bit her lip. She knew nothing about Miss Ravensdale's political opinions, but she was clearly rich and successful and hardly likely to have much sympathy for the working classes. Heaven knows what might happen if Madoc's employer found out his daughter was considered a dangerous agitator. She might be the cause of Harri and Olwen's uncle losing everything. Miss Ravensdale did not look like a woman who was worried about anything. She had the air of one who could handle whatever life might throw at her.

Bea cursed her stupidity. She'd been a fool to think she could just burst into her old home and announce that her cousin, and a man whose name she didn't even know, might try to take Tressillion away from her. Or ask if she was Lillian's sister in Cornwall – she must be imagining that. Lillian must have meant someone else. Miss Ravensdale would laugh in her face. 'I must go,' she muttered, mortified. 'They'll be worried, wondering where I am. I'm sorry for disturbing you.'

'Of course,' said Sibyl. She watched Bea hurry away as if a dozen wolfhounds were at her heels. She couldn't resist following her to the gate to stand in the shadow of the arch, watching her until she vanished.

Sybil turned back towards the house, puzzlement mixing with unease. Beatrice didn't seem a woman on a mission to find out her reaction to threats. She hadn't even attempted to draw her into conversation. She had been embarrassed at being surprised like that. And, Sybil admitted grudgingly to herself, those brown eyes were clear, and devoid of subterfuge. It must be a coincidence. If there was such a thing as coincidence.

She paused to deadhead the roses at one side of the steps. The sudden apparition had unnerved her, more than she liked to admit. Neither Emily nor Madoc had mentioned Gwen's illness, or this visit, so it could not have been planned. Beatrice was not likely to confess she had been up to the house, Sybil reasoned, and the arrivals at Madoc's cottage were none of her business. She needed to carry on as if nothing had changed, and nothing would change. They would not stay long, by Beatrice's own admission, and there must be barely room for them to sleep, crammed together in that small space.

It was nothing to do with her, she told herself, as she returned inside. It would pass. All she had to do was to wait inside the grounds until the visitors had left. Maybe Madoc's daughter would stay and recuperate. As for the rest, they would be gone in a few days. She would never see them, never know of them. And they would never be mentioned again.

'Oh, hell and high water,' she exclaimed as she reached the hallway.

'Miss?' Emily paused on the stairs, open-mouthed, her arms full of freshly laundered curtains.

'You be my witness,' said Sybil, grimly. 'I'm going to regret this.'

Chapter Thirty-Four

Bea managed to cook for them all on the tiny range in the cottage that evening, using every trick the White Camellia's kitchen's had taught her. Harri sat at the small wooden table, sleeves rolled up, chopping vegetables.

'What?' He looked up and caught her smiling.

'I wish I still had that Box Brownie.'

He grinned, his face losing its anxiety. 'What's left of my career in the law will vanish if anyone should see me in such an unmanly task.'

'I'm sure soldiers chop vegetables,' said Bea. 'And they are considered manly.'

'Do I look like a soldier? The army was one option many of my friends took. At least there you are out in the sun and there are regular meals. I couldn't do it. I'd be an ambulance driver or a stretcher bearer, but not a soldier.'

'I hope you never have to make the choice,' she replied, at his sudden seriousness.

He smiled. 'There's quite enough of a battle here, if you ask me, without worrying about another war in Africa.' A fit of coughing came from the bedroom, leaving them both silent.

'Olwen will make a wonderful doctor,' said Bea. She'd watched in admiration as Olwen had treated Gwen with the little there was, watching Gwen's face, always knowing what to do next. 'If I was ill, I'd want her to treat me.'

'She will,' said Harri. He sighed. 'I wish I didn't have to return to London…'

He came to a halt, his eyes resting on the door, which had been left slightly ajar to dispel the steam of the cooking. He rose abruptly to his feet. 'Good evening.'

'Good evening,' said Sybil, stepping inside. She had nearly turned and run at the intimacy of their conversation, half heard through the open door. It had taken all her determination to push the door open, and to nod calmly at the two of them caught in, to Sybil, a painfully domestic scene. 'Miss Tressillion. And you must be Mr Lewis's nephew.'

'Good evening, Miss Ravensdale,' said Bea, trying to conceal her mortification.

'Pleased to meet you, Miss Ravensdale.' Harri sounded wary. 'Do you wish to speak to my uncle?'

'Yes. No.' Sybil came to a halt. But there was no going back. She twitched her shoulders and planted both feet firmly, as if preparing for a boxing match. 'I came to see how the patient is faring.'

'She is recovering, thank you,' said Harri.

'Have you called a doctor?'

'My sister is a doctor, Miss Ravensdale. At least, training to be one. She is very experienced.'

'Good for her.' Sybil's eyes ran around the little room. It had seemed small with just her and Madoc standing there. Now she could see boots next to the door, coats hanging up. Even the steam from the pan spoke of a space too crowded. She focussed on Madoc, emerging from the bedroom, followed by Olwen. There was scarcely room for them all to stand.

'Miss Ravensdale,' exclaimed Madoc in surprise. 'Good evening. No problem at the mine, is there?'

'It's not the mine I'm concerned with,' said Sybil. 'You can't all stay here.'

'We have no choice,' said Olwen. 'Gwen is too ill to be moved.'

Sybil scowled.

'Harri is going back to London in a few days. I can find a guesthouse,' said Bea. 'It will only be for a week or so. Until Gwen is better. Then we can find somewhere else.'

'They are all welcome here,' said Madoc, gruffly.

Sybil squared her shoulders. 'It makes no sense you all being crammed in here, with the sea wind rattling through the walls. Let alone what the gossips in the village might make of it. You shall come to Tressillion.'

'No!' exclaimed Bea.

'Yes,' said Olwen, almost drowning her out. 'Yes, please. If you are certain, Miss Ravensdale.'

'Not in the least,' said Sybil grimly. 'But I'm certain it's the right thing to do.' She met Madoc's eyes briefly. 'Besides, I could do with the company. That should fox anyone who might entertain themselves by haunting the house.'

'Haunting?' Olwen looked uncertainly at Bea.

'Not that kind of haunting.' Sybil frowned. 'Well, I hope not. Or Miss Tressillion could stir up all kinds of spirits better left alone.' She grinned. 'In which case, I shall leave them for you to deal with, Miss Beatrice.'

Bea blinked. There was something in the way she said her name. The slight flick of malice. Maybe there was a resemblance to Lillian, after all.

'I'd rather risk the spirits,' said Olwen firmly. 'Gwen needs more than is here,' she added, as Madoc began to protest. 'Really she should be in a rest home, or a hospital. She is going to need help and comfort, and warmth, if she is to get well. It could take some time,' she added to Sybil. 'But once we can get her over the worst, she can be moved back here.'

'I'm not in habit of throwing my guests out on a whim,' returned Sybil. She gave a low chuckle. 'But then I haven't had any guests since I moved to England.' She cleared her throat. 'I can read the papers and I have friends in London. I heard about the violent disbandment of the suffrage protest, and the imprisoning of so many. I can put two and two together. I've little time for the police. I shall enjoy undoing their handiwork and returning a thorn to their side. I can run this place, run a business, and yet I can't vote for who governs me, while most of those I employ can. If the Houses of Parliament don't follow the example of New Zealand and American states soon, I rather suspect I might end up throwing stones with the best of them. You are welcome to stay for as long as you need.'

As she turned to go, she paused, hand on the door handle. 'And you too, Miss Tressillion. I insist. I can hardly leave you unchaperoned for all the village to gossip at.' Her voice was wry. 'It seems being lady of the manor has its responsibilities and its obligations.' Her voice softened slightly. 'You will all be very welcome.'

Madoc followed her out into the encroaching night. 'Are you sure about this? I've no wish to impose on you.'

'Don't talk nonsense, Madoc. You're my employee. I have responsibilities towards you. I shall tell the neighbourhood Gwen is suffering from a lung disease caused by the factory she works in and has come here to recuperate. They might not believe me, but they'd expect nothing less, and that should be the end of the matter.'

'Thank you.'

'Besides,' she said, with a sniff. 'I can't have you at home fussing like a nursemaid when you should be keeping your mind on bringing me out riches beyond dreams.'

He blinked. Then he grinned. 'You are just saying that to shock. Why can't you admit when you are being kind?'

'I'm not in the least kind,' she returned, as if profoundly insulted. 'This is purely my self-interest. As you said, I shouldn't be alone in the house.'

'So you think your visitor might return, after all.'

'Of course not.' She came to a halt. 'Perhaps. In daylight I can be rational. But when there is darkness, and particularly after…'

She cleared her throat. She'd no wish to discuss with Madoc the recent attempt at intimidation. That would be opening a can of worms. 'So you see, kindness has nothing to do with it.'

'Kindness is seen by some as vulnerability.'

Sybil's strung nerves descended into irritability before she could stop them. 'What's that got to do with the price of fish?'

'I just wondered what happened to make you so determined never to reveal any emotion.'

'That, Mr Lewis, assumes you know me.'

'Don't I?'

She kicked a stone from the path. 'Nobody knows me.'

'Only because your guard is so impenetrable.'

'So you suggest I become a soft-headed weakling and give in to the first person who tries to bully me, then have half the village overrunning the house and helping themselves from the mine?'

'That's not what I meant, Sybil, and you know it.'

He sounded annoyed. Sybil found she didn't like his annoyance directed quite so sharply towards her. She softened. 'You are right, Madoc. Too many ghosts. They make me crotchety.'

He tried to catch her expression in the dusk. 'I'll walk you home.'

'There's no need.'

'I can walk with you, or follow on behind. You might not care who could be waiting in the shadows, but I might have to live with the consequences. I've no intention of losing my position at the mine because you've been found dead in a ditch. How can I know what the next owner might do?'

Sybil suppressed a laugh, her temper easing at his plain speaking, which more than matched her own.

'Well, if you put it that way, we'd better go then,' she said.

They walked on for a while in silence. 'I'm sorry about your daughter,' she said at last. 'I've heard what the prison warders are capable of, particularly to the men and women of the suffrage movement. I hope she can recover her strength while she is here.'

'To go straight back.'

'You don't know that.'

'It has never stopped her before. It's her passion. I know she would rather die than stop fighting for her beliefs. Heaven knows, I have no power to stop her.'

'Because you created her.' She faced him. 'Madoc, you brought her up with your belief in justice. Surely it is better to have something to die for than to have no purpose in life at all?'

'Yes. I suppose it is. And I admire her courage and the strength of her conviction. I'm not sure I could do the same.' His voice shook. 'And I'm not sure I could bear to lose her.'

'If you locked her in a room and forbade her to leave, you would lose her even more profoundly,' said Sybil. 'You have given Gwen her life. The freedom to live as she chooses. None of us know when life might be snatched away, or how. Surely the only way is to live to the full the life we have, however long or short that might be?'

'Yes. You are right.' He set off again. 'I know all that in my head, but my heart is still torn to see her in pain.'

'I wouldn't argue with your heart,' replied Sybil, quietly.

They walked as darkness fell, until they reached the gravel in front of Tressillion, where they paused. One light peered between the blinds in an upstairs room.

'Tomorrow it will be filled with light,' said Sybil. 'And with life. You might not like it, you old monstrosity of a folly, but it will do you good.' She turned to Madoc. 'Thank you, Mr Lewis, for your self-interest in ensuring I should not have my throat slit

by some random villain. And for your company. You will, of
course, be welcome to visit at any time.'

'To a house of women? That will set the village gossips to work.'

'Then we'll have to find you some male protection, since we
are so violent and out of control and might get up to anything
with any male so foolish as to venture near.'

'I was trying to guard your reputation,' he retorted.

'I don't have a reputation,' she returned. 'No single woman –
and particularly a single woman with money and no father or
husband to control her – has any reputation at all. And I'm not
sure I want one. I would most certainly not be walking home
with a man alone in the dark, if I did.'

'Sybil…'

'That was not an invitation,' she said sharply, stepping away
from him as if she had been stung.

'I didn't take it as such. I value you too much as a friend and
neighbour.'

'And as an employer who pays you well,' she snapped. He
didn't reply. 'Now you are offended.'

'I had better go.'

'I'm sorry, that was unfair of me. I must be more shaken up
than I thought.'

'I'd be shaken up if I had someone haunting my footsteps,' he
said awkwardly. 'I hope your guests will finally send them away.'

Sybil unlocked the door. Light spilled out onto the gravel.
'One day I'll tell you about my ghosts, Mr Lewis,' she said, her
voice so low he could barely hear the words. 'But there are some
barriers that once broken can never be rebuilt. Some knowledge,
once known, can never be taken back. And now is not the time.
Not for either of us.' She raised her voice slightly, as if aimed at
any shadow lurking in the garden. 'You are welcome to visit, Mr
Lewis, with, or without, a chaperone. No-one can make a scandal
out of a father doing the best that he can for his daughter.'

She went inside before he could answer, calling in her usual imperious manner for Emily as she locked the door behind her.

Chapter Thirty-Five

She had never thought she would be here again.

Bea stepped into Tressillion, and wished she had never come. They had left so fast, so shockingly, so unexpectedly, there had been no time to say goodbye. Life since had been a blur of new friends and new experiences in London, with no space to deal with her grief.

But there was no time for sentimentality. 'You'll be more comfortable here,' she said to Gwen, who looked worn out. They'd carried her across the field to a wider track where Sybil could bring her Chevrolet, to drive them up to the house.

'It's dark,' whispered Gwen, shivering slightly, as, supported between Bea and Olwen, she began to climb the wooden staircase, one step at a time, pausing to catch her breath.

'It's only because of the panelling down here,' Bea reassured her. 'The bedrooms are much lighter and they all have beautiful views.'

'There, you see,' said Olwen. 'Once you get a bit stronger, you'll be able to sit by the window and watch the world go by.'

'I'm not very good at sitting still,' said Gwen, pausing yet again, her breath coming shallow and fast.

'Don't worry,' remarked Sybil, who was leading the way. 'There's a fine selection of books here. I suggest you embark on a course of study while you get your strength back. The fact they have given a working woman the opportunity to study is the best revenge, if you ask me.'

'I don't know…'

'You could start with the law,' added Bea.

'Or accountancy,' said Olwen. 'You've always said you wanted to teach yourself a trade, then you wouldn't be so tired at the end of each day.'

'That sounds an excellent idea to me,' said Sybil. 'My maid is learning all kinds of things in her evening classes. I don't expect she'll be mopping floors for much longer. I'm sure she'll help you.'

'I suppose…' Gwen still sounded uncertain, but for the first time since they had left London, Bea could see a gleam in her eye.

'I've put Gwen in here,' said Sybil, motioning to a door halfway down the corridor. She glanced at Olwen. 'We've put up an additional bed in there, but there's an interconnecting room next door, with a private sitting room between. I thought this might suit.'

'It was my mother's room,' whispered Bea. 'You'll love it, Gwen. There's a view of the gardens.'

'Thank you,' said Olwen, guiding Gwen inside. The little sitting room was cheerful, with a fire in the grate.

'And this is for you, Miss Tressillion.'

Bea hesitated. 'It's my old bedroom.'

'Oh?' said Sybil, with careful indifference. 'There is a smaller one, if you would prefer.'

'No, not at all. This is perfect. You mustn't think me ungrateful. I was surprised, that's all.' She stepped in. The walls had been freshly painted and the dressing table polished. The bed was the same, and so were the pictures. 'You kept my books, even after I told Emily I had no room for them in London.'

'It would have been a waste to burn them,' Sybil muttered. She coughed. 'I, ah, understand you left London in something of a haste, Miss Tressillion, with no time to pack.'

'Well, yes.' Bea turned to her curiously. 'How did you know that?'

'Someone must have told me. We've got rid of much of the

clothing, I'm afraid, but Emily managed to retrieve some of your clothes and shoes. You'll find them ready for you in the wardrobe. They might smell a little musty, but they are clean. Emily has washed several of the skirts and blouses, and other things you will need. They should be dry by tomorrow morning.'

'Thank you.' Bea felt her eyes prick with tears at this unexpected thoughtfulness.

'I'll leave you to arrange things as you wish. You'll find there are nightdresses in the drawers.'

Bea sat down on the bed as Sybil closed the door behind her. It was strange to be back. All her childhood dreams and wishes had once been held in this room. Coming back, it appeared smaller than she remembered it. Narrow, and, despite the fresh wallpaper, dark and a little dingy. So much had happened over the past months. A widening out of life. She was no longer the girl who had left here with a broken heart and no future at all.

The air felt close. She crossed the room to open the window. With her hand on the latch, she looked over towards the sea, where Harri was making his way back across the fields to Madoc's cottage. Tomorrow he would be catching the first train back to London. Already he felt far away. She could not bear to watch him vanish. She tore her eyes away, to focus on the grounds. Despite the felled trees and the newly-planted beds, it was still the view of her childhood.

Something moved. Bea stepped back. Perhaps it was her imagination. The shadows of those who had once strode the grounds with Papa, the men she had seen daily about their work. Cautiously, she looked down again. The figure looking up at her had gone.

She crouched down to mend the fire, warming her hands against its glow. Floorboards creaked. Footsteps ran past, followed by Emily in conversation with Miss Ravensdale on the landing outside.

'William has promised the supplies will be here by noon, Miss Ravensdale, but I'm not sure I know how to cook for so many.'

'I'll cook,' came Miss Ravensdale's gruff tones. 'Well now, off you go, Emily. That tea won't make itself.'

Feet clattered down the stairs, echoing as they reached the tiles of the hallway. The house settled again.

Bea shivered. She couldn't quite bear to look at her old clothes, but she found a shawl in one of the drawers and walked down the corridor to her mother's rooms. Like her own, the walls were freshly painted and the curtains clean, but much of the furniture was the same, making the room appear less cluttered, and a great deal lighter. She wasn't sure Mama would approve of the absence of lace and china ornaments, but it must make for far less dusting. Gwen was dozing in the chair by the fire. Olwen was next to her, a medical textbook on her knee that had not been opened, as she watched Gwen's face as she slept. She smiled as Bea entered, indicating the seat next to her.

'I can't believe you lived here,' she whispered. 'Harri was right, it's very grand.'

'Although not always happy,' replied Bea. 'But I'm glad to be here with you and Gwen,' she added, squeezing Olwen's hand.

A short while later, Emily arrived with a tray of tea and a large, slightly lopsided fruitcake. 'It's not very elegant,' she remarked, viewing her handiwork dubiously. 'It was my first attempt, but at least the fruit didn't sink to the bottom and it didn't burn, and Miss Ravensdale thought you might all need building up.' She grinned. 'And my mam always said you liked fruitcake, Miss Bea.'

'I still do,' said Bea, grateful that at least one member of the village didn't loath and despise a Tressillion returning to the scene of the crime. 'It's nice to see you again, Emily.'

'And you, Miss Beatrice.' Emily's eyes filled with tears. 'I wish it wasn't just you, and I wish it wasn't like this.' Putting the tray on a small table, she fled.

'Not always happy, you see,' said Bea, biting back her own tears and turning to make the tea as Gwen began to stir.

* * *

A short while later, when Gwen sank back into a doze, and Olwen nodded over her textbook in front of the fire, Bea took the tray, with the remains of its demolished cake, back down to the kitchens. Instead of Emily, she found Sybil, swathed in an apron, chopping vegetables.

'Can I help you?' Bea hesitated at the door of the kitchens. She had never been permitted in here. Cook had ruled her domain with a rod of iron and Papa had possessed a sixth sense when it came to his children sneaking off where they should not.

Sybil was making short work of the carrots. 'It's not necessary.'

'I'd like to help. Gwen has Olwen to look after her, and I can't stand idle.'

Sybil wiped her hands on her apron.

'I've worked in a kitchen,' said Bea to her sceptical look. 'In a ladies' tearoom. So I'm accustomed to cooking for large numbers.'

Sybil nodded slightly, handing her a small knife and pushing a bunch of carrots towards her. 'Is that what your aim is to be? A cook?'

'No. I mean, I enjoy cooking. I don't have some silly idea that it's beneath me. But I really want to be a photojournalist.'

Sybil grunted. 'I'm sure you'll find plenty of interesting subjects at the White Camellia.'

Bea glanced at her sideways. 'Do you know the tearooms?'

'Not exactly.' Sybil turned to stir the pot on the stove. 'I know it has been a centre for the suffrage movement, but now Mrs Pankhurst is convinced working class women aren't up to leading the protest. So now it's the genteel.'

'Like me.'

'Yes, I suppose.' They worked for a short while in silence. Sybil's face was a careful blank, bending over the pot on the stove, adding the prepared vegetables to the meat as if there was nothing so fascinating in all the world.

The lack of welcome was distinct. Bea began to feel that coming down here had been a mistake.

'Gwen seems much better already,' she ventured at last.

'Good.'

It was as if there was a wall, keeping her out. And yet Bea could sense Sybil watching her every move from the corner of her eye, aware of her very breathing. 'But it's still an imposition on you.'

'Is it?' Sybil looked up with a frown. 'I've no objections to visitors. This place can be rather too silent at times.'

'It always was,' said Bea, with a shudder. 'Either that or the sound of conflict. Tressillion was never a happy house, for as long as I can remember. I'd do anything to change the reason we had to leave, but I'd never want to return here.'

'Well, at least you are honest.' Sybil was standing at the table, knife in hand. Bea took a step back. 'That makes a difference in a Tressillion.'

'You sound as if you hated us.'

Sybil's eyes narrowed. 'I've hated the Tressillions for as long as I can remember. I'm hardly likely to stop now.' There was a moment's silence.

Bea swallowed. 'I know Papa harmed so many people in his obsession with the mine. I'm sorry if you were one of them.'

'You don't know the half of it.' Sybil glared at Bea, face white, hands in fists, as if she had indeed seen a ghost. 'Don't worry, Beatrice. I've never yet finished off my guests in their beds.' She threw the knife onto the table. 'And I doubt if I'm about to start now.'

Before Bea could move, Sybil swept out of the room, racing up the steps into the hallway, and then out into the gardens.

'Now where did Miss Ravensdale go to?' said Emily, appearing from the side door with a bucket of coal. 'The wind's getting up, and it's pouring with rain out there.'

'I'm sure it's nothing,' said Bea, taking the coal from her. Emily took off her coat and shook the rain from her hair. 'I expect she just needed some fresh air.'

'Hmm,' said Emily, in tones of one who had never known Sybil do anything so irrational as need fresh air, when there was plenty of the stuff whirling through the window panes once the wind came in with the storms from the sea. 'You don't have to do that, Miss.'

'Yes, I do,' returned Bea. 'I have a feeling you have enough to do as it is.'

Emily grinned. 'I'm sure there are worse places. At least I don't have a housekeeper or a butler ordering me around and telling me what to do and putting me in my place all the time…' Her hand shot to her mouth. 'Not meaning anything, Miss Tressillion.'

'I think I prefer things as they are here,' returned Bea, with a smile.

* * *

Gwen was a little brighter that evening. With Emily's help, Bea took the finished soup up to the little sitting room, where she and Olwen ate their meal with Gwen. Sybil had sent a message through Emily that she would not be reappearing that evening.

Bea was both thankful and apprehensive. There had been such venom in Sybil's voice. Why on earth had she bought the place, if she hated the Tressillions so much? Something was wrong here, she could feel it. The place was so vast, echoing with footsteps, with the creaking of boards and the hiss of wind through the attics, she had never felt easy here in the dark. But that had been childish imagination. The figure in the garden had been in broad daylight. And Sybil, with that hatred in her eyes, was in possession of the house and grounds.

Long after the others were asleep, and she heard Emily creak wearily up the stairs to her own bed, Bea could not settle. She could not even undress. She placed a chair against the door handle as quietly as she could. If anyone tried to get in, they would wake the house. She curled in the armchair by the fire, covering herself with the quilt as the embers died down.

Memories rushed in around her. Memories of Papa and the boys. She dozed now and then, waking to the sound of their voices. Of Mama's gently complaining tones downstairs with her friends. Of Papa scolding some unfortunate housemaid, his door slamming, the rush of footsteps up the winding servants' stairs at the back of the house, and sobbing in the attics.

She must have slept. When she woke again the embers had burnt themselves out, leaving only cooling ash in the fireplace. The air was chill. She pulled the quilt closer, drawing herself tighter into the chair, trying to make herself as small as possible. Invisible. Bea shook herself, and opened her eyes. The house was still. Oppressively still. The knowledge that hung about her dream, coming closer all the time, had left a taste of ash in her mouth.

She could not stay in that room a moment longer. Carefully releasing the chair, she took the remains of her candle and crept along the corridor to the empty bedroom at the end.

Did Sybil know, she wondered, as she pushed the half-open door, that this room, where Grandmama had spent her last years, was the place where the secrets had always been whispered? And where the answers must surely lie.

Chapter Thirty-Six

The room was just as she remembered it. Bea shivered slightly. One of the windows was open and her candle flame swayed, sending crazed beams of light into the corners. The curtains billowed and twisted as the wind got up. She could hear the crash of rollers on distant rocks. The gust stilled, leaving the room once more in silence. The bed was neatly made up, the dark old furniture polished. A vase of sweet peas had been placed on the dressing table next to the window, their rich, delicate fragrance banishing the scent of the sea. The room stood as if waiting for someone to return. Deep inside, she could feel her heart breaking.

She shouldn't be here. She turned to leave when a second gust, stronger than the first, caught the flame of her candle, nearly extinguishing it, and sent the curtains into an even wilder dance. Somewhere inside the house, a door banged. Emily must have forgotten to shut the window. Bea hesitated. She could feel the storm brewing, racing in from the sea on the in-coming tide.

Quickly, she placed her candle on the dressing table, out of reach of the curtains, and pulled the window shut. As she did so, a movement caught her eye below in the grounds. Nothing definite. A slow, stealthy movement in the darkness. A fox, she told herself firmly. Most probably a fox. She secured the latch, and retrieved her candle. Her hand paused as the flame swayed, catching the decoration on the hairbrush next to the mirror. It was her grandmother's brush, something she must have seen countless times. Bea picked it up. The embroidery of flowers was so familiar, and yet she had never noticed before that they were camellias, white camellias.

It could be a coincidence, of course. Grandmama Tressillion had never mentioned a tearoom. But then she had not spoken much of her life in London at all. It had been too painful, that loss of her independence and the home and the city she had loved. That had filled her life with meaning, Bea saw, remembering the coiled energy of the woman who had been brought here to join them in the prime of her life, but within a few years had grown frail and old. This room must have seemed a prison, permitting Papa to first rent out her beloved home in Twickenham then, as he grew more desperate, announcing it would be sold.

Against the closed window came a gentle tapping. Gentle, but insistent. Growing stronger and louder with every tap.

'What on earth are you doing here?' Sybil stood at the door, flashlight in hand, eyes blazing with fury. She caught sight of the hairbrush still in Bea's hand. 'Taken to stealing, have you?' She snatched the brush from her. 'I should have expected nothing less of a Tressillion. You never think twice about taking something that's not yours. I'll put you on the train back to London myself tomorrow morning.'

'I wasn't stealing!' Bea glared at her. 'And I'm not my family. I can't help that my father took money from so many people. Tressillion was sold to pay the creditors.'

'But not to return the mine,' retorted Sybil. 'There was never any mention of returning the mine.'

Bea stared at her. 'I know Papa took over the mine…'

Sybil snorted. 'If you mean ignoring it until there was a rumour gold had been found, and then claiming it was on Tressillion land… Using his money and connections to the local magistrates to deprive a family of all their hard work, and their livelihood… Then, yes, he did take it over.' She scowled at Bea.

'Is that why they sent you here, that precious family of yours? First I get threats, telling me I might have no rights to the mine, for all I bought the land it stands on, and then you appear. Do you really think I'm that easily bullied out of my own home? Do you think I don't know my rights, and have money to back them up? A bit too much like history trying to repeat itself, don't you think?'

'Someone really is trying to claim the mine?'

'So you did know.'

'It's nothing to do with me. My cousin said something, just before I left London. Believe it or not, I came to warn you.'

'And why would you do that?'

'I don't know. Because the Tressillions have caused enough harm? Because I didn't like the way Jon spoke of you, as if getting what he wanted would be easy, because you were a woman? But I don't see how. Jon could hardly claim the mine still belonged to him.'

'He could try and claim it had belonged to the Hargreaveses all along,' said Sybil slowly.

'Mr Hargreaves died, about the time Dad took over the mine.'

'Didn't it ever occur to you he might have a son?'

'I...' Bea blinked at her. 'I never asked,' she confessed in a small voice.

'Well, perhaps you should have done, then I might not have to pick up the pieces your wretched father left behind.'

The tapping on the window began again. Tap, tap, tap. Bea turned. Sybil moved too, her eyes fixed on the slight swelling of the curtains from the ill-fitting windowpane.

'It's the tree.' Bea frowned at her. 'You didn't chop it down.' Something fell into place. 'You knew.'

Sybil jumped. Her face, pale in the beam of her flashlight was drained and taut.

'You knew this was Leo's room,' said Bea, certain now. 'Before

Papa insisted Grandmama lived here. That's the way he got out. And it's the way he'd come in, if he ever returned.'

Sybil glared at her. 'Don't be ridiculous. The dead don't return, not even from an unquiet grave.'

'But you were looking in case he had, just as I was.'

'I'll take you to the first train tomorrow morning. Mr Lewis' nephew can take care of you until you get back to London.'

'I don't need taking care of,' retorted Bea. 'I didn't come here to look after Gwen. I came to find someone. Lillian Finch said I'd know her when I found her. I wasn't sure at first, but now I think I have.'

'Never heard of her…' Sybil came to a halt. 'Lillian sent you here? She couldn't. She never would. We haven't spoken in years.'

The branch tapped again, louder this time, leaves scratching against the windowpane. Sybil swung round, her face filled with anticipation mixed with fear. The wind subsided once more.

'How did you know about Leo?' demanded Bea.

Sybil took a step back. 'I'll put you on the train tomorrow, Miss Tressillion. Tell Lillian she's a meddling fool and to keep her nose out of my business. When I need your help, I'll ask for it.' She turned on her heel, fleeing headlong down the stairs.

Bea took a deep breath, blood rushing to her head. She wasn't going to leave it like that. She wasn't going to sit meekly and allow Sybil to get rid of her. Not with so many questions to be asked.

Grabbing the candle, she followed Sybil out into the night.

* * *

The storm was gathering pace. The candle went out the moment Bea stepped outside and threw the useless stump onto the gravel path. She knew the gardens like the back of her hand, and she had a good idea of where Sybil was headed. It was where she had always gone herself in times of trouble, when the need to escape Tressillion's shadows and secrets had become too much.

She found Sybil, where she had come to a halt with one hand on the metal gate. Sybil looked round at the crunch of footsteps on the path. 'You shouldn't be here.'

'I don't care what you think. How did you know Leo?'

'I didn't come here to be questioned.'

'But you knew him. You knew that's the tree he used to get away from Papa. And you knew that if he could, even in death, he would never completely abandon Tressillion.'

There was a moment's silence.

Finally, Sybil turned back. She couldn't escape. She should have known, the moment she had followed Roach, rather than turning the Chevrolet around and taking the first liner she could find back to New York, that this would always be waiting for her.

'Yes, I did know your brother, Bea. I met him when I was in America. I didn't know who he was, that he was a Tressillion, not at first, anyhow. He used another name. I suppose, like me, he didn't want to be found. He came into one of my hotels one day, looking for work photographing guests as a souvenir they could take home with them. It seemed a good idea, one I hadn't considered before, so I gave him a trial period. He was very good. He quickly became very popular. He was my employee and he was English, I didn't ask anything else about him for a long time, and I never mentioned my own past. I didn't use my own name. I knew he came from Cornwall. We used to talk sometimes about how we missed the Cornish coast, and how neither of us felt we could ever go back. That's all I knew until it was too late. Far, far too late.' Her eyes glinted dangerously in the dark. 'And then you wrote that letter.'

Bea started. 'The one begging him to come home?'

'You shouldn't have written, Bea.' She wanted to shake her. She could no longer be rational. She wanted to scream, shout, make Bea feel her agony. 'Everything would have been all right, if you hadn't tried to find him.'

'Do you think I don't feel that? That it hasn't tormented me every day since the accident? I have regretted writing that letter every day of my life, knowing that it led to his death.'

'You didn't kill your brother, Bea.' Sybil's voice was barely above a whisper. 'I did.'

* * *

She had to get away. Bea turned, breath short in her chest, stumbling over twisted roots.

'Stay there.' Sybil's voice was a hiss. She grasped Bea, pulling her back and down to the ground, placing a hand over her mouth. 'Shhh.' Sybil held her down with the weight of her body, terror making her ruthless. 'Stay still, Bea. If it's the last thing you do, don't move.'

Bea stopped struggling. The hand holding her down moved a little. In the starlight Bea caught the gleam of a pistol resting on the grass at her side. Its barrel was pointing not towards her, but along the path.

'Hide your eyes, they'll give you away.' Sybil lay as flat as she could make herself, still with her hand over Bea's mouth. Bea could hear her breath, short and ragged. Frightened. Sybil, who appeared fearless, was afraid. Bea saw her manoeuvre the pistol with her free hand, so its gleam was concealed beneath the folds of her skirt, still pointing towards the path. A flicker of pure terror shot through Bea's body.

Sybil held her breath. Bea held hers. A shadow passed over them, a faint starlight shadow, as the racing clouds parted. Footsteps padded soft on the grass, then stumbled with a low curse. Sybil's grasp tightened. The figure stopped. Bea could sense the man standing still, straining to listen. The footsteps moved one way, then another. The beam of a flashlight strafed the undergrowth, barely missing their heads.

The beam turned, this way and that, it seemed like forever, as they lay, scarcely daring to catch a breath.

'What are you bloody waiting for?' Bea bit her lips to stop herself calling out. She knew the voice coming out of the dark right only a few paces away. 'And shut off that light, will you, unless you want to rouse half the neighbourhood.' The man with the torch muttered something. His companion snorted. 'You're not afraid of the odd fox, are you? That comes of spending far too long in the city. Pull yourself together, man. The sooner we are out of here and back on the road to London the better. Come on.'

The torch vanished. Boots tramped beneath the arch and into the fields.

Sybil released Bea and they slowly rose. First to their knees, then they helped each other until they were standing upright.

'That was Jon,' whispered Bea.

'Jon?'

'Jonathan Tressillion. My cousin who sold you the house. What's he doing here?'

'Up to no good,' said Sybil, grimly. 'Did you recognise the other voice?'

'I think so. There was a man.' Bea hesitated. 'I thought I saw him, just after we arrived. He was in the gardens looking up at me. I thought at the time – but it couldn't be.'

'What couldn't?'

'That it was the same man who followed me in London once. That's how I found the White Camellia, trying to escape him. Then he was there, at Lillian's refuge.'

'What kind of man?' demanded Sybil.

'He looked like a man who lived on the streets, but he didn't talk like one. He said something about all that gold and not being able to spare anything. I'm sure I saw him later, talking to Jon near the house in London.'

Sybil cursed. 'Beatrice, why did you come here? He'd never harm me. I know he'd never harm me. But now he's seen you in the house, he'll think I've made a pact with the Tressillions.'

'It might not have been the same man.'

'Of course it was. Who else would it be? I knew Lillian still looked out for him. She always did. She could have been the toast of London society, if it hadn't been for that refuge. His grasp on reality never was strong, and now he thinks I've made a pact with your family. He'll never forgive me. Now none of us are safe.'

Bea swallowed. 'He took my scarf.'

'Be thankful that's all he took.'

'Whenever I saw him, he was still wearing it.'

'A red scarf, striped with different colours? A woollen one?'

'Yes. It was the way he wore it, as if it was some kind of talisman.'

'Hell.' Sybil swallowed. 'I need to get you out of here. Harri and Madoc can look after you tonight, and get you away tomorrow. Don't take it as flattery, Bea, but I think you've just become every Tressillion there ever was in Alexander Hargreaves' deluded mind. He once swore he'd destroy every last one of you. Your cousin might think they're going back to London, but I've no doubt Alex has other ideas.'

'No!' Bea grasped her arm.

Sybil shook her off. 'There isn't any time to argue.'

'No, Sybil. Look. Look at the house.'

Sybil turned and peered through the trees. Tressillion was etched against the starlit sky, its chimneys outlined, its windows dark. But above the house came a whirl of white smoke, and the faint smell of bonfires.

'That's what they were doing,' said Sybil, mesmerised by the flames licking the air. Deep in her heart, she had known that this was how it would end. That there would never be any other way.

'We can't leave it!' Sybil was jolted into life again as Bea set off running towards the house. 'Gwen and Olwen and your maid are still asleep in there. With this wind, if the fire takes hold, none of them will stand a chance. Come on!'

Chapter Thirty-Seven

Sybil raced after Bea in the darkness. As they reached the lawn in front of the house, a window in one of the empty bedrooms cracked, sending glass flying into the air, followed by the lick of flames.

'It's got hold already.' Sybil pushed at the door of the kitchen, which swung open, to just the faintest smell of smoke. 'At least it's not in this part of the house. That rain earlier should help. Come on. The sooner we all get them out the better.'

As they reached the hallway, smoke was billowing at the top of the stairs. They could hear coughing.

'Olwen?' Bea yelled at the top of her voice.

'We're here. We can't get across.' The landing was alight. As they reached the top of the stairs, flames were licking round the door of Bea's bedroom.

'It must have been started in there. That door will go any minute.' Sybil grabbed the large vase of flowers on the windowsill half way up the stairs, dowsing herself. She stepped through the smoke, reappearing seconds later with Olwen, supporting an unconscious Gwen between them.

Bea grasped Gwen as they reached her. Olwen leant against the wall, coughing, desperately attempting to catch her breath.

'Quickly. Downstairs.' Sybil looked up towards the attics, to where smoke was rising. 'Emily!' she shouted, with all the breath left in her. 'Emily!'

There was no reply.

'I'll go,' said Bea.

'No.' Sybil pulled her away from the stairs. 'You'll never make it. Once the door goes, nothing will stop it. We'll have to find a way from outside.' As she spoke, the door cracked, flames burst through, shooting along the corridor towards them. They raced downstairs, pulling Gwen between them, flames following behind. Paint was peeling, and an acrid stench filled the air. Already the curtains were alight, the wooden staircase smouldering, smoke rising as they passed.

'There's no time,' called Bea, as Olwen turned towards the front door. 'The bolts will take too long. This way.' She led the way through the kitchens, out into the cold air.

They stood, catching their breath. 'I'll get Emily,' said Sybil.

'Where are you going?' demanded Bea.

'The tree. Leo said there was a way onto the roof.'

'I'll do it.' Bea pulled off her boots, tucking her skirts up as high as she could get them. 'You'll never find it in the dark, Sybil. I've done it plenty of times with Leo when I was a child. I can do it with my eyes closed.'

'Bea…' Sybil clutched her shoulder.

'It'll be all right. Look, the fire hasn't reached the attics yet. It's not on this side of the house. I can see where I can find the way down to the kitchen roof.'

'Take this.' Sybil shoved a flashlight into the pocket of Bea's skirt. 'I'll go round to the other side and meet you. Make sure you get there, do you hear?'

Bea climbed through the branches of the tree, until she reached the windowsill of Leo's room on the second floor. She could hear the roar of the fire in the distance, but at least the wind was blowing the smoke away from her so she could breathe. The ledge beside the window was lit up in an orange glow. She pulled herself up, feeling her way with her toes. The muscles of her arms and her legs were burning, but she kept on, her feet finding by instinct the old familiar footholds between the tiles, her hands pulling her up, until she swung herself up over the guttering and onto a flat roof between the chimneys.

She could just make out the attic window, with its little stone balcony in front. She glanced down, glad there was no moon. As it was, she could only just about make out the figure of Sybil on the lawn looking up at her. It was an even longer way down than she remembered. A gust of wind caught her, nearly toppling her off balance. As a child she had raced up here fearlessly, unaware of the consequences of any slip. Now she felt her way on hands and feet, crouched down, steadying herself until she came to the attics.

'You need to be quick, the flames are moving up towards you,' Sybil shouted.

Bea peered in through the window, calling for Emily. The flashlight showed nothing, just the faintest trail of smoke. Bea pulled off her jacket, protecting her hands as she smashed the panes of the window. She found the catch, and climbed inside, stepping carefully over the broken shards.

The room was empty. She could see smoke billowing and swirling in the beam of the flashlight, catching at her throat, while heat and the crack of burning wood came from below. As she reached the door into the little corridor between the attic rooms, a crash set the entire building shaking.

'Well, at least that settles that. I know there's no way down the staircase,' she told herself grimly. In the corridor, smoke billowed, thicker and darker. Flames shot up from the hole where the staircase had been. In its flare she could make out a bundle of clothes hunched up on the floor. 'Emily!'

She reached her in an instant. Emily's eyes were closed, and she could not tell if she was breathing. The flames swept upwards again, right to the ceiling, catching the curtains at a small window.

There was no time to lose. It was becoming difficult to breathe and the heat was unbearable, while the cracking below was growing louder. She grasped Emily by the shoulders, pulling her as fast as she could along the corridor into the first room, shutting the door behind them.

'Wake up, Emily. Wake up!' In the rush of fresh air from the open window Emily stirred, coughing and drawing great breaths of air into her lungs.

'There was smoke,' she gasped. 'The others…'

'Sybil's safe and so are Gwen and Olwen.' Bea glanced back towards the door. It would not hold for long. Already smoke was following them, easing under the door and around the frame. The roar of the fire was deafening. As she watched, the paint began to peel, and the first flame flicked through the narrow gap at one side. 'We need to get out on to the roof. We can get across and down next to the kitchens. I know the way, but I need you to help me.'

'Yes,' said Emily. The door began to crack. 'Oh my lord. Once that goes…'

'Come on.' Bea half dragged, half supported her over the glass and out onto the balcony. 'No time,' she gasped, as Emily lent, retching against the stone. 'You need to put one foot on the ledge and then pull yourself over onto the roof.' She supported Emily as she made her way up, shoving her with all her strength onto the roof, and scrambling up behind. As Bea pulled herself over, there was an ear-splitting roar and a great sheet of flame shot from the window below, out into the night sky.

'It's right beneath us,' gasped Emily. 'The roof will collapse.'

'Not if we hurry. Just pray it doesn't reach the back of the house before we do.' Bea pulled her upright and led her through the maze of chimneys towards the kitchens.

* * *

Sybil watched until she was certain Bea and Emily were safely on their way, then raced to the outhouse behind the kitchen, pulling out the longest ladder she could find, manhandling it towards the wall.

As she positioned it as firmly as she was able, a figure ran towards her. 'Where's Bea?' demanded Harri, reaching out to help her with the ladder.

'On the roof, rescuing Emily,' replied Sybil. 'If we get up this way, we can help them to get down.'

'It's too well alight, and no fire engine is going to get down here,' exclaimed Madoc, arriving behind them.

'It doesn't matter about the house,' said Sybil. 'Just keep this part safe for as long as you can. This is the only way Bea and Emily are going to be able to get down, the other roofs are far too high for the ladder to reach. This is their only way.'

'We'll get them,' called Harri, already clambering up. 'We'll get them down before the fire can get near them.'

'That's not the only danger I'm afraid of,' muttered Sybil, hitching up her skirts and following him upwards, towards the flames.

* * *

The route between the chimneys was familiar, but twice Bea almost lost her way, once doubling back, until the crack of flames warned her. At last she reached the final chimney.

'There's a ladder,' she said, searching with the flashlight. 'It goes down onto the next roof. Then there's a ladder on the far side that will take us to the roof above the kitchens. Once we're there, we'll be safe.' Heaven knows what they would do then to get down from the kitchen roof, if Sybil hadn't found a way to reach them, but at least they would be nearer the ground and away from the flames.

The first ladder was still in place. Bea almost shook with relief as she peered down. Someone must have inspected the roofs recently: the ladder looked mended and reasonably firm. The next one down to the lower roof would be longer, but this meant it should be in place too.

Bea shuffled down as quickly as she could, reaching up to help Emily, who slid, feet barely touching the rungs, to collapse beside her. At least here the roof was not so steep, and their balance would be less precarious. Emily's breathing was laboured, her eyes closed. Bea swallowed. To have got so far – well, she wasn't giving up. Gritting her teeth, she grasped Emily by the shoulders and began pulling her unceremoniously to the ladder down to the kitchen roof, just visible at the far edge of the roof tiles.

Flames shot up from the roof they had just left. She shut her mind to what might have happened, had they been just a few minutes longer. She could see from the corner of her eye that she was nearing the edge. She pulled Emily closer, then swung the flashlight round to find the way down.

As she turned, a hand grabbed her arm. 'No, you don't.'

She knew the voice, even before she saw the ruined face, gaunt in the light of the flames, the tattered coat opening to reveal her scarf still around his neck.

'You might have persuaded Sybbie to join you. But you're not fooling me.'

'I haven't persuaded Sybil to do anything.' His eyes were a dark glint of flames, his grin not that of a man anywhere near sane. 'You know Sybil, Mr Hargreaves, no-one could fool her into doing anything.' From the corner of her eye, she could see the ladder quiver slightly. Someone was coming up. She swallowed. Whatever he might be, Jon was not a lunatic, and he would have no reason to harm Emily. She wasn't so sure about herself, but at least if she knew Emily was safe she could fight tooth and nail to save her own skin.

Bea pulled herself round slightly, so that the ladder was out of Alex's line of vision. 'The fire is going to be here soon. Let's get down to safety and sort this out with Sybil.'

He frowned at her, his eyes intent on her face. The movement of the ladder was strengthening. Whoever it was, was growing closer. She had to distract him. 'You know Sybil would never lie to you.'

'She let you in. She even put you in your old room. She was going to let you stay. She was planning to do that, all along.'

'Sybil didn't know I was in Cornwall. I was here with a friend who was ill. Sybil wouldn't throw a defenceless woman out into the night.' His eyes were still focussed on her, oblivious to all else. Bea raised her voice as loud as she could. 'Didn't you hear her telling me she'd let me stay tonight, but only tonight? She's putting me on the first train back to London.'

He took a step forward. 'She shouldn't let you out at all.'

'She's decided to let the law punish me,' improvised Bea, desperately. 'She's found a way. There's nothing I can do about it.'

He was beginning to pull her back towards the flames.

'It's the only reason she's letting me go. Don't you want to see the Tressillions pay for what they've done?'

He came to a halt. A gust caught them, sending them both staggering nearer to the side and the sheer drop down to the glass conservatory. Smoke swirled, extinguishing the rest of the roof. Bea watched him in despair. There were just the two of them, isolated in the small space between the encroaching flames and the drop below. She must have imagined the new arrival. Or he had given up, believing there was no-one there. Emily was still unconscious on the roof. 'Come on,' she said, doing her best to sound calm. 'Let's get down to safety.'

At that, he grinned. 'I don't care to be safe.' He pulled her behind him. Through the smoke, she could see they were right on the edge. The flames shot up again, glowing crimson on the glass below.

'Bea!' It was Harri. Somewhere on the roof, hidden by the smoke. Alex's eyes flicked towards the unexpected sound, his grip fractionally lessening. It was her only chance. Bea sank her teeth into his fingers, hauling herself free as he yelped, fleeing towards the sound of Harri's voice. Alex's curses were close behind.

Harri loomed out of the smoke, catching her in his arms. 'You don't lay a finger on her head,' he said, grimly, as Alex stumbled towards them, head bent, overcome with coughing.

He straightened. 'You're the lawyer,' he said. 'I've seen you at Lillian's.'

'I help the poor, not the rich,' returned Harri. 'I've no quarrel with you.'

Alex hesitated. He glanced from Harri to Bea, and back again. He looked up at the sound of someone else on the roof.

'Mr Lewis is right, Alex.' Sybil sounded calm but firm. 'There's no point in this. Come down. You are not in any trouble. There won't be any trace of the Tressillions left after tonight. The house is destroyed, just as you always planned. The Tressillion boys are all dead, there's no-one who can inherit. The women don't matter. They never did.'

'You opened the mine, Sybbie. You showed them where the gold was. You broke our agreement.'

'I did it for you, Alex. You, me and Lillian.' She met Bea's eyes briefly. 'So the Tressillions would have to watch us become rich, while they had lost everything. So that they'd know what it was like. And what we had done.'

'But we agreed.' He was frowning at her, as if trying to remember. 'The night we made the rock fall. The night we altered the maps when that lawyer said the Tressillions were right, and their land went as far as the mine, even though he knew it was a lie, and it was just because Tressillion had paid him. They all knew it was a lie. The night Dad died.'

'It was a very long time ago, Alex.' Sybil walked carefully towards him. 'The mine is just as rich as Dad thought it would be. Perhaps even more. There's enough to make us all wealthy forever. You don't want the Tressillions to get their hands on that, do you?'

'No.' He looked back towards the flames. 'He's a Tressillion too.'

'Who is, Alex?'

'The man who brought me here. He thought he could use me. He didn't know who you were, see. All I wanted was to have the mine. It was always mine. But he wanted everything. He wanted to frighten you. Make you think the village hated you. He said if the mine wasn't yours, and the house was damaged, then you'd leave. He said you'd soon be wanting to sell it back to him. And then we could be rich. Him and me. Except he didn't mean it. I could tell. He'd have blamed me for starting the fire, so I'd be out of the way, and he could have it all to himself. I knew what he was thinking. I didn't let on, but I knew.'

Sybil swallowed, fighting to keep her voice calm, not to startle him, not to break the spell. 'What have you done with Mr Jonathan, Alex?'

A crack like an earthquake shook the tiles. In the glow of the flames, one of the chimneys leant over drunkenly, and then fell. They heard the crash as it hit the ground.

'That's the main roof,' exclaimed Harri. 'Time to get out of here.'

Sybil didn't move. 'Alexander, what have you done with Mr Tressillion?'

'I was going to stop him.' Alex's voice was a child's plea. 'I wanted him to scare you, so you'd know what you'd done, but not to hurt you. I'd have shared the mine with you, Sybbie. Then

I saw her at the window. I saw you'd taken in a Tressillion. I was angry, Sybbie. I thought you'd betrayed us.'

'You know I'd never betray you, dearest Alex,' she replied, grasping one of his hands. 'Come on. We need to get off this roof. We can find Mr Tressillion afterwards.'

Their progress was painfully slow, with Sybil cajoling Alex every step of the way. As they reached the ladder, they found Emily pulling herself to a sitting position, retching, struggling to get to her feet.

'We're nearly there.' Harri gathered up Emily in his arms. Bea could hear voices below, coming towards them on the kitchen roof. 'She'll need help coming down, Will,' called Harri. Hands reached up to take Emily. 'Your turn.' Harri turned to Bea, relief in his voice. 'We'll be safe now.'

'There'll be coppers.' Alex halted.

'I expect there are, darling,' said Sybil. 'But they won't take any notice of us.'

'He'll blame me. That Mr Jonathan. I should have left him in the fire. He'll say it was all my idea and I did the fire, and they'll believe him.'

'No, they won't. Not if we explain.' Sybil grasped his wrist, feeling him squirm, his mind slipping away from her. 'Besides, we've got money now, Alex. We can buy the best lawyers. We can prove it was him.' He was tugging her back into the fire. Desperately, she tried again. 'We can get away, my darling. Get you out of here while it's dark. We can get on a ship tomorrow. I'll take you back to my hotels in America. You've been promising to come over for years and help me. I need your help, Alex. Come back with me. No-one need know who we are.'

There was a shout below, sending Sybil off balance. Alex pulled himself free. Instinctively, Bea caught Sybil's arm, holding her back as she tried to follow her brother fleeing across the roof towards the flames.

'Let me go!' cried Sybil, twisting, beating at Bea with her fists.

'We must get down,' said Harri, taking her free arm. 'The roof's giving way, Sybil. There's nothing more you can do for him now.'

* * *

Flames roared above them as they finally reached the ground. Miners and villagers, headed by Madoc, were making a line of buckets from the stream at one side of the grounds, keeping the flames from taking hold of the back of the house.

'Thank Heaven.' Sybil grasped Emily, who was shivering in a blanket, and hugged her tightly. 'I could never have forgiven myself if anything had happened to you.'

'Where's Gwen and Olwen?' demanded Bea.

'The landlord of the Fossick Arms has taken them in,' said Harri. 'We could all see the flames for miles around. The landlord is sending the wagon back for you and Emily.'

'I can still help…'

'No,' said Sybil, back instantly to her practical, non-nonsense self. 'You've done enough, Bea. You were incredibly brave, and thanks to you, Emily's alive. There's nothing more you can do for the house.' She headed off to take charge of one of the lines of water buckets.

Within minutes, Bea was wrapped in a blanket and lifted into the wagon. She held Emily tight as they rattled up to the village. They passed villagers on their way to help, or to simply stand and watch the spectacle.

Behind them, the chimneys glowed in the flames, the mullioned windows gleaming as if for a celebration. Then a second chimney, and a third, folded over and collapsed, this time taking the remainder of the roof crashing in a fiery avalanche to the ground below.

Bea heard the onlookers scream as the house finally folded in on itself. Then there was silence.

Chapter Thirty-Eight

'Your feet, Miss! They're bleeding.' The landlady of the Fossick Arms stared horrified.

Bea looked at her bare feet sticking out from under her skirt. 'Oh – I took my boots off,' she said vaguely.

'Let me see?' Olwen came down the stairs, having settled Gwen in a room above.

'I'll see if I can find you some slippers, Miss Bea,' said the landlady. She shook her head. 'What a business.'

By the time Harri and Madoc arrived with Sybil and the remainder of the villagers who had helped put out the fire, Olwen had checked the cuts on Bea's feet for any glass and cleaned and bandaged them.

'They'll be sore for a while,' she said. 'But it looks like there's no lasting damage. That was a mad thing to do, Bea.'

'I knew the way.'

'Well, you saved Emily's life,' said Sybil gruffly, joining them in the little sitting room at the back. 'No-one in the village will forget that.'

'Then perhaps a Tressillion has done some good, after all,' replied Bea. Sybil met her eyes then looked away again without replying. Bea bit her lip. 'Did you find…?'

'No,' replied Sybil.

She turned as Madoc appeared at the door, covered in soot. He shook his head. 'There's still no sign of either of them.' He cleared his throat. 'The embers are still too hot to search the building. The police are on the lookout in case, by a miracle, anyone managed to survive.'

'I see.' Sybil sat down heavily on a chair next to the fire. Her clothes and face were streaked with soot and her coat was peppered with holes from burning cinders. She put her head in her hands.

Madoc turned anxiously to Olwen. 'How is Gwen?'

'Asleep upstairs. She's breathing a little easier. The smoke has aggravated the damage to her lungs, but she'll recover. She can stay here tonight, and we'll see how things are in the morning.'

'Tea,' said the landlady, a little gingerly, as she arrived with a tray, as if afraid Sybil might bite her head off.

'Thank you.' Sybil took the tea as it was poured, warming her hands around the teacup.

The landlady coughed delicately. 'You're welcome to stay here as our guest, Miss Ravensdale. The rooms are all made up.'

'Thank you.' Sybil looked up. Beneath the soot her face was drawn and weary. 'Yes, I would like that, until I can see how much damage there is.'

'Surely you're not thinking of going back to Tressillion?' exclaimed Bea.

'The back of the house is relatively undamaged,' said Harri, returning from handing out beer to the firefighters. 'We'll be able to see the damage to the rest of the house once daylight comes.' He met Sybil's eyes. 'That was one fast-moving fire, even taking account of the wind.'

'Most probably an unattended lamp in one of the upstairs rooms,' said Sybil. 'The place was full of wood and those old curtains. It could easily have happened.'

Harri glanced at Bea. 'I expect that was it.'

Sybil turned her face to the fireplace. 'What's done is done. There's nothing to be achieved by pointing the finger of blame.'

* * *

The next morning, Bea limped painfully to the edge of Porth Levant. Someone had found her a pair of outsized boots, but her feet were sore and swollen.

Tressillion House stood, a blackened shadow of its former self, smoke still rising from the collapsed part of the house. She found Sybil perched on a fallen tree trunk, gazing down at the scene.

'Well, at least I shall be able to rebuild it exactly as I wish,' she remarked, as Bea joined her.

'It always was a bit of a monstrosity,' replied Bea. 'You'll stay then?'

'I don't know.' Sybil cleared her throat. 'I once swore I'd never come back to Cornwall. Strange how quickly a place can become home.'

'Yes.' There were so many questions Bea wanted to ask, she did not know where to begin. 'I hope your brother is found.'

'I'm not sure whether I do or not,' said Sybil. 'No, you are right. I would like to know. Either way, I would like to know. I'll probably murder your cousin Jon though, if I ever get hold of him.' She grimaced. 'If Alex hasn't done the job for me.'

'You are not responsible for their actions,' said Bea. 'No-one forced either of them. They are both grown men. Jon is just as much to blame. He might have wanted to frighten you, but he must have known the strength of the wind last night, and what it might do.'

Sybil gazed out over the remains of the house. 'Maybe. I'm not so sure about Alex, though. He always swore he'd ruin the Tressillions and wipe them, and the house, from the face of the earth.' She swallowed. 'For years I agreed with him. Alex was the baby of the family, he was still only a child when our father died. Lillian and I… It was hard, but we have both built our own lives. We might have gone our own ways, but we made lives of our own.

Alex never could forget losing our home and everything we owned. We were thrown out straight after Dad's funeral, as if we were bits of rubbish, as if we didn't count at all. The only place we could have gone was the workhouse.' Her eyes narrowed. 'I wasn't going to let that happen, whatever it took. But maybe for Alex it might have been better. At least he might have had something else to focus his resentment on, rather than the Tressillions.'

'No-one can know how things are going to turn out,' said Bea.

'No.' Sybil smiled faintly. 'And they can turn out in the strangest of ways.' She was silent for a few minutes. 'Believe me, I would give anything not to have persuaded Alex to help me create the rock fall and alter the map to the mine. I was so angry, and I felt so powerless.' She met Bea's eyes. 'And it was utterly unjust, what your father did to us. He used his wealth and connections to make sure we lost that land. We were powerless. That's what killed Dad in the end. It was hard enough after our mother died. He couldn't bear the fact that if he had continued to be a tin miner, at least he would have been able to scratch a living. His luck and hard work in finding that old mine ended up benefitting the Tressillions, who had more than any human being could possibly need. Because they were rich, and he was poor, he lost everything. I wasn't going to let them get away with it. So I did the only thing I could.'

'I truly didn't know, and I never thought to ask. I wish I had. I'm glad it didn't bring my father any happiness, but tormented him for the rest of his life. I can understand why you did it. In your place I'd probably have done the same.'

'No!' Sybil grasped Bea's hands. 'No, Bea. You'd have had more sense, and walked away and made your life a happy one, leaving the misery behind you. As you will do now, when you return to London.' Her eyes filled with tears. 'Don't you understand what I did? What I really did? Don't you see that the only real revenge I ever had, was on myself?'

'But surely…' Bea came to a halt. Shouts were coming from the grounds.

Sybil jumped to her feet. 'They've found something. Come on. I need to know.'

When they arrived at the house, a stretcher lay on the ground, covered by a sheet.

'Where was he found?' demanded Sybil.

'Over by the rocks, down by the sea,' said the constable. 'We've found a Rover abandoned on the lane down to the beach. A bit of a coincidence, don't you think, Miss Ravensdale?'

'Whatever the man's intentions, the fire could still have been an accident,' said Sybil. She looked down at the swathed figure. 'I'd like to see.'

'I'm not sure, Miss…'

'I'm a miner's daughter,' retorted Sybil fiercely. 'I've seen what fire and water can do. I'm not squeamish.'

'It wasn't either,' replied the constable, with a grudging respect. He removed the sheet from the top of the body.

Sybil stared down at the pallid features, set for eternity in a grimace of surprise. 'I don't know that man,' she said. She turned to Bea.

Jon looked strangely peaceful, despite his expression. Bea turned her head away.

Sybil pulled the sheet back over his face. 'How did he die?'

'Stabbed. Looks like one blow, probably went straight through the heart. He would have died almost instantly.' He glanced towards Bea. 'There was nothing on him that would identify him, but there were papers in the vehicle that belonged to a Mr Jonathan Tressillion.'

Bea nodded. 'Yes. That's my cousin.'

'Did you find the knife?' demanded Sybil.

'Not yet, Miss Ravensdale. But it will only be a matter of time.'

A look of despair came over Sybil's face. 'So it wasn't suicide?'

'Suicide?' The constable raised his eyebrows. 'Lord, no. No man could have inflicted that wound himself. The angle is all wrong. He must have tried to stop the ruffian who did this from escaping.'

'I expect he did,' murmured Sybil, placing a hand on Bea's arm.

'You can't allow them to think that!' exclaimed Bea, as Jon's body was taken away and the men returned to the beach to continue their search. 'They thought he was the perpetrator, until they knew who he was. Now they'll throw all the blame onto Alex.'

'It doesn't matter. Let them think what they want. The last thing your mother and sister need is for the Tressillion name to be in the papers, bringing up the story of the mine again.'

'Why should you care?'

Sybil was silent for a moment. 'Because Ravensdale was the name your brother used when I met him.'

'Leo?' Bea stared at her.

'Yes. Leo said it was the name of an old school friend, and that no-one would know who he was, not even you. I'd left the name of Hargreaves behind when I left England, so I had no name to be sentimental about and wish to keep.' Sybil turned her face away. 'He was a good man, your brother. The best man I ever knew.' Her voice shook, then steadied. 'He was the first man, the only man, I have ever truly loved. Even after I knew who he was, I still loved him, more than I can ever say. He was my friend, my soul mate, and I'd give all my riches, everything, to have him back again, if only for a moment. His name is all I have left of him now. It was the name we had decided to take once we were married.'

Bea took her hand. Sybil didn't return her grasp, but she did not pull herself free. 'Mama knew.'

Sybil nodded. 'Your mother knew Leo was settled and happy,

and about to be married. He didn't tell her anything about me, we both thought that might be too much of a shock,' she added. 'And not just because I was a Hargreaves. We were arranging for you and your mother and Ada to come over to New York for the wedding.'

'And not go back.'

'Leo thought your mother might return, and of course she would have taken Ada with her. There was nothing we could do about that. And we didn't know about your grandmother, and what your father had done. But Leo had talked to a photographic studio that would have been happy to take you on as an apprentice. He thought that you could join him in his business, and eventually set up your own studio.'

'And you agreed?'

'Yes, of course.' Sybil gave a faint smile. 'Leo was the only man I've ever met who didn't mind my being independent and opinionated, not to mention being his employer before he set up his own business. He told me he had a sister who knew her own mind and so had trained him well. I thought I might like to meet her. Even though she was a Tressillion.'

'And then I wrote that letter.'

'I swore I would never forgive you for that. But I was fooling myself. Leo would always have come back here, at some time, to see if he could make some kind of peace with your father.'

'But he might not have been here at the time of the accident.'

'No.' Sybil placed her face in her hands. 'But that wasn't your doing, Bea. I knew when Alex and I hid the real mine that we would send your father on a wild goose chase. He had no experience, and I doubt he'd have listened to anyone. I loved the idea that your family would ruin themselves. I didn't understand, until it was too late, that they would ruin so many other people as well, or that desperation would make them careless. That in killing them, I would kill Leo too.'

'You weren't to know,' said Bea, steering her round to face her. 'Sybil, they knew the dangers, and Leo would never have been able to live with himself if he hadn't at least tried to rescue them.'

Sybil did not answer, but her head lent forward, until it rested on Bea's shoulder. Bea held her tight.

Eventually Sybil stepped away, blowing her nose. 'The workmen are arriving,' she said. 'I need to see how much of this monstrosity can be saved. And, if you look round, you'll find there's a young man waiting for you.'

'What about Alex?'

'What will be, will be,' said Sybil, gloomily. 'I searched as much as I could before the police arrived. I've got other lives to think of.'

'She'll be all right,' said Harri, as Sybil launched into a discussion with the workmen from the village.

'She's not as tough as she makes herself out to be.'

He smiled. 'But most don't work that out, which I rather think is the point.' He drew her away from the house, back towards the village. 'They are searching the rocks down there.' He took her hand. 'I heard your cousin was found. I'm sorry.'

Bea shivered. 'I hate what he tried to do, but I hate to think of him lying there all night. That mine seems to cause nothing but madness.'

'Will you come back to London? Mrs Anselm is on her way here to fetch Olwen. She's hired a doctor and a nurse to look after Gwen, so Olwen can resume her training. Of course, if you'd prefer to stay…'

Bea shook her head. 'There's nothing for me here, and I need to get back to Mama.' She came to a halt. 'Harri, what will happen now? Jon's wealth will be inherited by another member of the family. Mama and Ada could already be out on the streets.'

'Then we'll just have to rescue them.'

'I don't want to drag you into this. When it was a matter of choice, that was different. But now…' She looked at him in despair. 'I don't want you to end up resenting me.'

'Oh, Bea.' Despite the men around the ruins, he caught her in his arms. 'How could I ever resent you? This is still our choice. We could never walk away and pretend your mother and Ada and Olwen don't exist. We talked about this rationally, remember?' He drew her closer. 'We'll just do as we had planned. We'll find a way between us of supporting those we love, until they no longer need us. One day we'll be together, Bea, just you and me in a home of our own. But until then, at least we will be together.' He kissed her, much to the delight of the children escaping from lessons to see last night's drama. 'This makes up our minds for us. No more waiting for the right time, and trying to get your mother used to the idea, or even waiting until we find the right house to rent. You are going to have to marry me immediately, whether you like it or not.'

Bea laughed, feeling warmth returning to her body at last. Ignoring the gathering crowd of children, she kissed him back. 'It looks as if I shall have to obey.' She disentangled herself, slipping her arm through his as they made their way towards the village. 'But I put you on warning that, whatever wedding vows I might have to speak, this is the last time.'

'I wouldn't expect anything else,' said Harri, holding her tight. 'Or I rather suspect I'll have the entirety of the White Camellia to answer to.'

* * *

Mrs Anselm arrived the following day. Bea was on her way to meet Harri when the Ford swept into the driveway of the guesthouse. As she strode inside to deal with the owner, Bea saw that she was not alone. Lillian stepped out stiffly from the passenger seat, and stood looking around her, as if in a dream. Her gaze focussed on Bea as her face grew even paler.

She pushed her hair away from her face. 'Have they found him?'

'No. I'm sorry. They are still looking. I thought he might have gone to you in London?'

Lillian shook her head. 'If Alex is in trouble, he always comes straight to me. But I know in my heart it's different this time.' She started walking towards the smoking remains of Tressillion House in the distance. Bea accompanied her. 'Sybil didn't say it had been destroyed.' Lillian pulled her coat closer about her. 'You were lucky to get out. Sybil isn't hurt, is she? She said she wasn't, when she telephoned Mrs Anselm, but Sybil never would say, not even if she was suffering from a mortal wound.'

'She's unharmed, apart from a few minor burns and singed hair.'

Lillian's shoulders relaxed a little. 'I never thought Alex would hurt Sybil. He wouldn't if he was in his right mind.' She paused. 'He has been so rarely in his right mind, these past years. It wasn't just the drink. All that hatred ate him up inside, leaving nothing left.'

'I'm sorry.'

'Alex and I both owe Sybil everything. She worked and fought to keep us safe. When she was able to earn enough, she helped me to finish my course at art school, and to start the refuge, even though she thought I was wasting my talents and my training. She set Alex up in so many businesses, and paid for him so many times when they failed, as they always did. She always looked out for us, and in the end, we broke her heart.'

'I'm sure not,' said Bea, gently. 'And you are here now. I have a feeling, whatever she might say, Sybil is going to need you.'

They had almost reached the house. Sybil was sitting on a wooden chair on the lawn, bending over a small table from the kitchen, pouring over plans, pencil poised. She looked up as they reached her.

'Lillian. There was no need for you to come. Who's looking after the refuge?'

'How could I stay in London, and leave you to deal with all this on your own?' replied Lillian. 'The refuge can survive without me for a few days. It is in safe hands.'

'Yes, of course.' Sybil relaxed a little. 'I forget, I can't order you around any more. I'm afraid I can't even play lady of the manor.'

'I'm sure you will, soon enough.' Lillian kissed her. 'If I know you, Sybbie, you're already planning a new house, exactly to your own specifications. I've seen the way you run your hotels, remember.'

Sybil gave a wry smile. 'I've a few ideas. I once swore I'd wipe Tressillion House off the map. This is not exactly the way I'd intended.'

She swung round as Harri hurried towards them from the beach, urgency in every step. Behind him, a group of men were carrying a stretcher covered in a cloth.

'Oh no,' breathed Sybil, rising to her feet. 'Oh my dear lord, no.'

Lillian swallowed. 'I think we both knew it was going to end this way, Sybbie. Alex would never have been able to face you. Why do you think I came to be with you?' She took her sister's arm. 'Come on. They'll want someone to identify him.'

'I can't,' said Sybil, wildly, her heart breaking open at last. 'Lily, I just can't.'

'Yes, you can, my dearest. You'll never rest unless you do. I know you.' Lillian's arms came around her, holding her tight, as the men and their burden drew closer. 'Come on. Alex was my brother too. For both good and ill, we made him.' Gently, she began to move them both towards the shrouded form. 'We'll do this together.'

Chapter Thirty-Nine

'You will always be welcome,' said Sybil, as they waited at the station for the train to draw in.

'Thank you,' said Bea, uncertainly. A short distance away Harri and Olwen were saying goodbye to Lillian and Mrs Anselm, who were both staying with Sybil until after Alex's funeral.

Over the last few days Sybil's energy had begun to return. Harri had found her a large house to rent on the outskirts of the village, where she could overlook the restoration of the house from her breakfast table. She and Emily were already filling the second parlour and spare bedroom with bits and pieces they had retrieved from the ruins and cleaned and polished. The kitchen section had survived more or less intact, apart from soot and the smell. At least it gave her something to do while her grief healed.

Sybil reached into her pocket. 'I thought you might like this.' She brought out the hairbrush with the entwined camellias. 'I found it a few days ago amongst the roses. It must have fallen out of my pocket when I ran away from you that night.' She looked down at the pattern. 'If we hadn't left the house when we did, we might not have known about the fire until it was too late. I suppose you could say it saved our lives.'

Bea took it in her hands. 'Grandmama would have liked that.'

'I think she would.'

Bea glanced at her curiously. 'You sound as if you knew her.'

'Another Tressillion I couldn't hate. Your grandmother was a volunteer at the White Camellia when I took Lillian and…' she hesitated, still unable to say his name, 'And our brother, to London to try and find work. We had nothing left when we got there. She found us begging by the station after she'd seen you off to Cornwall on the train, and she took us back to the White Camellia. There was a small refuge in one of the meeting rooms at the time, where they fed us and gave us room to stay.' Sybil smiled down at the etched pattern of white camellias in Bea's hands. 'It was your Grandmother Helen who taught me to cook, Bea. Proper cooking, not the stews and bacon bits I'd made after our mother died. She found me work, and cheap rooms to rent, so that the three of us could stay together, and she made sure we attended lectures and went to the lending library to continue our education.'

Bea looked down at the intertwined pattern winding their way around the back of the brush. 'I didn't know anything about Grandmama's life in London. I know she hated leaving it. I think it took her sense of purpose away.' She swallowed. 'Papa forced her to leave the house in London because he was planning to sell it to pay for the mine. And then he put her in Leo's room out of spite.' She fought back tears. 'This must have been one of the few things she had to remind her of London.' She met Sybil's eyes. 'My grandmother encouraged me to learn being a photographer from Leo, all the bits with the chemicals and the timing. She told me it was too late for her, but that I should make sure I could earn my living, so I was never dependent on a man. That I should always be an independent spirit. I owe her so much, too.' She held out the hairbrush. 'Keep it, Sybil. I think Grandmama would like you to have it. I'm sure she would have loved to see it take pride of place in the new Tressillion House.'

Sybil hesitated. Then she smiled. 'Very well.' She replaced the brush in the woven bag she wore slung over one shoulder. 'Thank you. But there is one thing I insist you accept.' She reached into the bag, bringing out a package muffled in cloth.

Bea unwrapped it. 'It's a camera!' She held in her hands, trying to hide the longing in her eyes. 'It's Leo's. It must be. Sybil, I can't accept this.'

'Yes, you can.' Sybil swallowed. It had been the hardest choice, giving away anything that she had seen so often in Leo's hands, but there was no doubt in her mind. 'It was Leo's, but he intended it for you. After your letter, he was determined to bring you back with him when he returned to America. You have to take it, Bea. I couldn't bear it not to be used.' Her eyes filled with tears. 'Don't ever blame yourself for asking him to return. Leo missed Cornwall every day of his life. I knew that he wanted to come back here one day. Why do you think he jumped at one last chance to make peace with your father? So that, one day, he and I could return to Cornwall. Maybe not to Porth Levant, but at least somewhere with the cliffs and the sea.'

'Thank you,' whispered Bea, wrapping up the camera and placing it into the singed carpetbag at her feet.

Sybil sniffed loudly. 'Besides, your photographs and your articles will be the best weapon there is against greed and stupidity and the cruelty of those who want to hang onto their privileges at all costs. If you ask me,' she added, 'that's the best kind of revenge. The kind that might lead to the rise of the downtrodden. Just you wait, I'll be visiting you at the White Camellia to make sure you are doing your duty. And I shall expect to see your articles in the national press.'

Bea kissed her. 'Dear Sybil. I know exactly why Leo loved you. I'll have to make sure I don't disappoint you,' she said.

* * *

Madoc was sitting on the wooden steps of the cottage by the sea one evening when Sybil arrived. He reached under the steps for the brandy bottle. Two glasses, she noted, were ready and waiting on the boards of the little porch.

'I hear the mine is progressing well.'

'Very well,' he replied, pouring a large dose into each glass and handing her one. 'It looks as if Porth Levant could be booming before long. Not champagne, I'm afraid.'

'I'm glad to hear it. Can't stand the stuff.' They drank in silence for a few minutes. 'I hear you are looking to buy this place with the money you have made from the mine,' she remarked at last. 'Don't be surprised that nothing is a secret in Porth Levant for very long.'

'It was kind of you to give Gwen a place to stay while she recovers, but I think that maybe it's time I made a home for her.' He sighed. 'I don't expect I can persuade her to stay, but at least I'll know I'll be able to look after her if she should get hurt again.'

'Oh, I don't know.' Sybil sipped her drink. 'I'm considering selling a couple of my hotels in America and investing here in Cornwall. What's the point of having wealth tied up unused? I shall rebuild Tressillion, of course, but I don't need a grand place to live. It doesn't suit me. I think I'd be better employed creating a school for young women in the grounds. A place where they can train in the skills I insist on in my hotels. And a number of other skills, too. I thought I might suggest to Gwen that she considers training young women to prepare them for skilled employment, as well as to fight for the right to vote. I was hoping it might keep her out of harm's way.'

'Such a plan might meet with disapproval once word gets out.'

'It might. At first. I've a mind to get myself voted onto the local school board, and the local council. I could do with a new challenge. Always fight the enemy from within.' She grinned. 'I shall enjoy being on the campaign trail, persuading men and women to vote for me. Besides, it will serve to point out just how ridiculous it is, that women can stand for and vote in local government, but can't get near the Houses of Parliament without being dragged off to be brutalised in jail.'

Madoc laughed. 'I've no doubt you will succeed. I'm sure you can do anything you set your mind to.'

She was silent. 'Not everything. There are always things that are outside anyone's control.'

'And some losses that can never heal.'

Sybil looked up at the house. 'I suppose that's why I came. And why, once here, I couldn't leave. I longed so deeply for Leo to return, it made me almost certain that he would. I would leave the window open to his old room, however hard the wind blew, hoping that one day, however briefly, I could hear his voice again, feel his touch, just one last time.'

Madoc's hand rested for a moment on hers. 'Each time I hear the wind in the sea, I still hear a woman's voice calling me, and feel the same.'

His touch, though brief, was warm. Sybil glanced at him. 'I thought you might return to Wales.'

'Me?'

'I know all about the call of *hiraeth*.'

'*Hiraeth*.' He took a thoughtful drink. 'Yes, I suppose I will always have a longing to see Pont-y-Derwen. But I can visit, take Gwen and Harri and Olwen back to see what remains of our family there. The railway makes all things possible.' He gave a faint smile. 'And you never know, I might even take on the trappings of a prosperous gentleman and acquire a motor car.' He met her eyes. 'But I can't live there, just as Gwen, and Harri and Olwen have made their own lives in London. This is my home now.'

They sat for a while, lost in thought. Sybil longed for it to stay that way, for the evening to end in this companionable silence, two people at ease in each other's company. But there were some things that had to be said, even if they were never to be referred to again. No more secrets, eating away at her, whatever it might cost. She would rather see coldness in his eyes than live a lie.

'It should have been me you found,' she said at last. 'You, or whoever else worked out that the Tressillions had been led a wild goose chase, and that the gold was in the old tunnels, after all.'

'Found? You mean, behind the rock fall?'

She nodded, cold despite the warm summer breeze. 'We didn't know what we were doing, Alex and I. We set the explosive off far too early. We only just made it back into the tunnel in time.'

'The lantern.'

'Yes. We didn't have time to go back for it. It was our only light, the last piece of candle in the house. We had to feel our way on hands and knees to get back to the entrance.' She looked up. 'That's why I had to be there when you opened it up, to make sure no-one recognised it. And that's why I had to go back that night. Alex had left his knife there as well. It had his initials on it, and even a fool could work out what 'AH' stood for. I'd hoped it would have rotted away before the cave was found, but I would never have been sure.'

'It was a long time ago,' said Madoc.

She shook her head. 'Not long enough. Memories run deep here. Someone would have known whose those initials were, and remembered the hatred between the Tressillions and the Hargreaves, and guessed what it meant. It was my idea, to change the maps and create the rock fall, but Alex would have been blamed. They'd never believe a girl had the wit or courage to carry out such a thing. I was afraid that, even after all this time, there might be a Tressillion eager for revenge, and with the money and influence to make sure Alex hanged. I couldn't risk that happening.' She sighed. 'Poor Alex. We destroyed him between us, my hatred and Tressillion greed. He never stood a chance.'

'Who could blame a child,' said Madoc. 'Who had no understanding of consequences, and where an act of revenge, done in the heat of the moment, might lead? I've found the hardest thing in the world is to find it in your heart to forgive yourself.'

'Thank you,' breathed Sybil. She made no attempt to stop the tear that crept down her face, splashing onto her skirt. He was silent, gazing over the sea, as if unaware that her frozen heart was beginning to uncurl at last, reaching out towards the warmth.

They finished their brandy. Madoc poured another dose, not quite so hefty this time. 'And yet life goes on,' he said, breaking the spell.

'So it does.' Sybil kept her eyes on her glass. 'And you never know, Mr Lewis, one day, I might shock you.'

She looked up to meet Madoc's smile. 'Then I hope that one day, Sybil, when you are ready, you might try me.'

* * *

In the White Camellia, the rush of the day was slowly drawing to a close.

'I'll see you at the Institute later,' said Olwen, as she finished her work on the newest edition of the magazine and grabbed her hat, heading for her next lecture. 'Save me a seat near the front if I'm late!'

'We will!' called Bea. A short time later Harri joined her, slipping in through the side door. 'Did she get there in time?'

'Just about,' he replied with a grin. He looked at her enquiringly.

'Mama still disapproves,' said Bea. 'But this time she admitted you were a "personable young man with reasonable prospects". I have a feeling she is beginning to realise that she might not see me married at all, unless I marry you. She keeps on mentioning my "notoriety" and hopes I won't bring any influence to bear on Ada. She paused. 'There is something odd, though.'

'Oh?'

'The house isn't being sold. Mama had a letter from Jon's nephew, the new heir, to say that Jon had left her the house and a small annuity for its upkeep.'

'That was generous of him,' said Harri.

'You don't believe that any more than I do! This is Sybil's doing. We can't possibly accept.'

'Oh, yes, you can. At least, your mother can.' He took her in his arms. 'Don't you see, darling, this way the Tressillions can maintain the story of Jon dying to save you and your friends from ruffians and burglars. However much Sybil paid to bribe them, I'm sure they consider it a cheap price to pay to avoid more scandal and preserve Jon's name as a hero.'

'It just doesn't seem fair, that's all.'

'Even though it gives you your freedom? That's what Leo wanted for you, wasn't it, when he planned to take you to America to be with him and Sybil? Let Sybil do this for you, Bea. I have a feeling this is her way of finding some peace.'

Bea smiled. 'I don't suppose it will hurt for Mama to believe that Jon chose to look after her. But I'm not leaving Ada to her tender mercies.'

'I never thought you would.' He kissed her. 'Come on, I need to return the Ford to Mrs Anselm before this evening's meeting. But there's time to have another look at that house we thought would be too small for all of us.'

'It would still be quite small for three of us.'

'That won't be for long. Olwen is so near qualifying, and then she'll soon be setting up a practice of her own. Now we don't need to use the basement, you will be able set up a darkroom.'

'Yes, that's true.' Bea gazed around at the photographs adorning the walls of the White Camellia. 'Mrs Pankhurst is holding another march in a few weeks' time,' she added.

Harri tucked her arm in his. 'Then perhaps it's as well we are still having the banns read, and we won't be able to afford a honeymoon for a year or so. At this rate, I can see you spending our wedding night in Holloway.'

'That,' said Bea firmly, 'is something I can promise I would never do.'

Arm in arm, they walked out into the busy streets, joining the men and women going in and out the White Camellia, in the calm summer air.

* * *

As the sun began to set, Sybil walked from Madoc's cottage, through the golden fields. When she reached Tressillion House, she paused, hand on the little metal gate. Work had already begun to demolish the burnt remains, and clear the space for the new buildings. In the flowerbeds, roses were blooming, their scent drifting through the summer evening.

'I knew you'd get me in the end,' she said aloud. 'Well, you old monstrosity, you are quite done for now. No more grandiose towers for you. You are going to be clean and new and just as I want, and you are going to have to work for your living. Whether you like it or not, you are going to be filled with life.'

There was a crackling in the undergrowth at her side.

'Leo?' Sybil swung round to meet the breeze that caught her, warm and soft, blowing her hair around her face with the tenderness of a kiss.

She breathed it in deep, holding on as long as she could to the scent of salt air and the richness of summer meadows. Then it was gone, in the whispering leaves high above, out into the clear blue sky, to where the first glimmer of stars hung over a gentle sea.

'You will always be a part of me,' she whispered. And, smiling, she made her way towards the deep peace that hung around Tressillion House, and in the richness of its grounds.

More from Honno

Short stories; Classics; Autobiography; Fiction

Founded in 1986 to publish the best of women's writing,
Honno publishes a wide range of titles from Welsh women.

The Seasoning *Manon Steffan Ros*
*On my eightieth birthday, Jonathan gave me a notebook: 'I want you to
write your story, Mam.'* Peggy's story is the story of her Snowdonia village
but not until everyone's story is told does Peggy's story unfold…as thick,
dark and sticky as treacle.

> *"…a charming, heartbreaking and captivating novel"*
> Liz Robinson, Lovereading
> ISBN 978909983250 – £8.99

In a Foreign Country *Hilary Shepherd*
Anne is in Ghana for the first time. Her father, Dick, has been working
up country for an NGO since his daughter was a small child. They no
longer really know each other. Anne is forced to confront her future
and her failings in the brutal glare of the African sun.

> *"intelligent, subtle and sensitive... a thought-provoking,
> absorbing and rewarding read"*
> Debbie Young
> ISBN: 9781906784621 – £8.99

Left and Leaving *Jo Verity*

Gil and Vivien have nothing in common but London and proximity, and responsibilities they don't want, but out of tragedy something unexpected grows.

"Humane and subtle, a keenly observed exploration of the way we live now…I am amazed that Verity's work is still such a secret. A great read"
Stephen May
ISBN: 9781906784980 – £8.99

Ghostbird *Carol Lovekin*

Nothing hurts like not knowing who you are… Nobody will tell Cadi anything about her long gone father and her sister. In a world of hauntings and magic, in a village where it rains throughout August, as Cadi starts her search for the truth, the secrets and ghosts begin to wake up.

"Charming, quirky, magical"
Joanne Harris (author of *Chocolat* and *Blackberry Wine*)
ISBN: 9781909983397 – £8.99

Someone Else's Conflict *Alison Layland*

Jay is haunted by the ghosts of war who threaten his life and his love. A compelling narrative of trust and betrayal, love, duty and honour from a talented debut novelist.

"A real page-turner about the need for love, and the search for redemption… If you like a fast-paced thriller but want more – then buy this book"
Martine Bailey, author of *An Appetite for Violets*
ISBN: 9781909983120 – £8.99

My Mother's House, *Lily Tobias*

A poignant story of belonging, nationhood and identity set in Wales, England and Palestine.

The twenty-fourth publication in the Welsh Women's Classics series, an imprint that brings out-of-print books in English by women writers from Wales to a new generation of readers.
ISBN: 9781909983212 – £12.99

All Honno titles can be ordered online at
www.honno.co.uk
twitter.com/honno
facebook.com/honnopress

ABOUT HONNO

Honno Welsh Women's Press was set up in 1986 by a group of women who felt strongly that women in Wales needed wider opportunities to see their writing in print and to become involved in the publishing process. Our aim is to develop the writing talents of women in Wales, give them new and exciting opportunities to see their work published and often to give them their first 'break' as a writer. Honno is registered as a community co-operative. Any profit that Honno makes is invested in the publishing programme. Women from Wales and around the world have expressed their support for Honno. Each supporter has a vote at the Annual General Meeting. For more information and to buy our publications, please write to Honno at the address below, or visit our website: www.honno.co.uk

Honno, 14 Creative Units, Aberystwyth Arts Centre Aberystwyth, Ceredigion SY23 3GL

Honno Friends

We are very grateful for the support of the Honno Friends: Annette Ecuyene, Audrey Jones, Gwyneth Tyson Roberts, Jenny Sabine, Beryl Thomas.

For more information on how you can become a Honno Friend, see: http://www.honno.co.uk/friends.php